KAYLON TRAN

Lives Intertwined

Book 2 of the Agent Orange Trilogy

First edition

Cover art by Miblart

This book was professionally typeset on Reedsy.
Find out more at reedsy.com

For All Those Affected by Agent Orange

Preface

Lives Intertwined is a work of historical fiction. All characters described or mentioned are fictitious and any similarities to real people was unintentional. Nevertheless, numerous places (e.g. Ben Hoa Hospital), historical figures (e.g. Martin Luther King, Jr), and historical events (e.g. the Tet Offensive) are quite real, but used fictitiously. In particular, the inadequacy of ARVN training and the history and presumptive effects of Agent Orange are accurate to the best of my knowledge. Information regarding methods associated with forensic genealogy are also accurate, although quite rudimentary in my description. Use of this method to capture the fictitious Green River Killer was inspired by genealogists that were essential to the capture of the the notorious Golden State Killer. Additionally, the reader should be aware that GEDMatch is a real company that aids in genealogy assessments while *DNAStory, MyDNA,* and *Au.DNA* are fictitious. If the reader is interested, more information on many of the topics touched on in *Lives Intertwined* can be found in the books and websites listed within the *Appendix*.

Characters, Historical Figures and Abbreviations

Major Characters: *Alpha by first name*
Ashley England, DNA analyst at CBF
Benjamin "Ben" Franklin, Intelligence analyst with CBI
Dennis Dordi, U.S. Special Forces
Kevin Vong, Son of Lucy and Loc Tin Vong
Loc Tin Vong, ARVN soldier, Vietnamese refugee
Lucy Vong, wife of Loc Tin
Tony Pham, adopted son of Anh and Lanh

Minor characters appearing in more than one chapter: *Alpha by first name unless last name is used primarily*
The Admiral (James "Jimbo" Higgins), Retired U.S. Navy, former Swift boat commander
Andrew, Minh's son and Emily's brother
Miss Anne, nurse at St. Bethlehem
Anh Pham, Emily's great aunt, Tony's adoptive mother
Bao, Loc Tin's brother
Billy, owns the Feed Mill
Binh, ARVN comrade of Loc Tin
Betsy Ingalls, daughter of Hazel Ingalls (St. Bethlehem)
Cai, Loc Tin's sister
Cam Nguyen (pronounced "when"), neighbor of Loc Tin and Lucy
Christina, co-worker of Ashley's

Dai Bay Chan, wealthy businessman (owner of the *California Dreamin'*)

Debbie, friend of the Old Man

Emily, friend of Ashley and Anh's niece

Eric, owns a construction company in California where Dordi sometimes works

Hazel Ingalls, mother of Betsy Ingalls (St. Bethlehem)

Heather Sinclair, TV journalist; Friend of Ben Franklin

Dr. Beverly Jansen, Ashley's former boss (also known as "Dr. J")

Jacobs, John, a victim of the Virginia Vigilante (killed in California)

James, Andrew, a Richmond Police Officer

Jamison, Fred, a victim of the Virginia Vigilante (killed in Virginia)

Jeffry, Minh's husband (Grandfather of Emily)

Jeremy Dordi, Dennis Dordi's son; friend of Vivian and Ashley

Jim, co-worker of Ashley's

Joe, owns cabins in the Blue Ridge Mountains of Virginia

Joseph, son of Tony and Rebecca

Johnathan, son of Tony and Rebecca

Kim, first wife of Loc Tin

Lam, son of Loc Tin and Kim

Lance Davis, Ashley's supervisor at CBF

Lanh, Anh's husband, adoptive father to Tony

Linh, wife of Dennis Dordi

Lisa, daughter of Anh and Lanh, sister to Tony

Maria Barlow, TV anchor

Monica, Joe's estranged wife

Rebecca, wife of Tony Pham

Radhika, wife of Kevin Vong

Rhonda, Co-worker of Ashley's; genealogy specialist

Samantha, daughter of Kevin and Radhika

Suong, daughter of Loc Tin and Kim

Ted, Co-worker of Ashley's

Timothy, son of Kevin and Radhika

Trinh Nguyen (pronounced "when"), neighbor of Loc Tin and Lucy

Twan, ARVN comrade of Loc Tin

Historical Figures

Ngo Dinh Diem, president of South Vietnam, 1955-1963, assassinated in 1963

Lyndon B. Johnson, U.S. President, 1963-1969

John F. Kennedy, U.S. President 1961-1963, assassinated in 1963

Martin Luther King, Jr civil rights leader, assassinated in 1968

Gia Long, Emperor of Vietnam, 1802-1820

Abbreviations:

CBF, California Bureau of Forensics

CBI, California Bureau of Investigation

CODIS, Combined DNA Index System

DA, district attorney

DNA, Deoxyribonucleic acid (hereditary genetic material)

MO, Modus Operandi (a specific method used)

NSW, New South Wales (a state on the east coast of Australia)

NVA, North Vietnamese Army

PCR, polymerase chain reaction (a method for copying DNA)

Post-doc, post-doctoral fellow (a training position after completing a PhD)

POW, prisoner of war

PTSD, Post-traumatic stress disorder

SFG, Special Forces Group (U.S.)

UCSD, University of California, San Diego

UCSF, University of California, San Francisco

US, United States

USS, United States Ship

VC, Viet Cong

WGS, whole genome sequencing (a method of DNA analysis)

Chapter 1

The old man sat in front of the sleek new laptop his son had given him a week ago. "Write your memoir, Dad," his son had suggested when he gave it to him. That was the same day his son had left him in this godforsaken hellhole. His son had insisted, "It isn't a retirement home. It's an assisted living facility. They're better equipped to help you now that you're in the wheelchair."

"Write my memoir," the old man said aloud, rubbing the stubble on his chin. He stared at the blank screen in front of him and contemplated his life. He knew his son was just trying to give him something constructive to do with his time. He had never been one to watch much TV. These days it probably seemed to his son that he preferred to be alone. He knew he had become unpleasant to be around.

After his wife died, he had reluctantly moved in with his son's family. His daughter-in-law was a lovely and kind young woman and was a wonderful mother to his grandchildren. Initially, he had very much enjoyed the lively chaos that young children brought to his son's home. But then the memories came flooding back to him. They had been unexpected and painful. On a daily basis they reminded him of how much he had lost. Once he could no longer compartmentalize the multiple facets of his life, he had begun the steady slide into becoming a grumpy and bitter old man. Then there was the accident. It was entirely his fault and completely avoidable. He had

1

gotten sloppy and had broken his own rules. His son was probably relieved that he now needed the wheelchair because it gave him an excuse to move him to this place.

He looked around at his tiny apartment. His daughter-in-law had tried to make it cheery and homey with family photos and the grandkid's artwork, but it was depressing nonetheless. The space had no real warmth, and the hospital bed that took up most of his bedroom added to the clinical feel. He knew he would die in this place.

"Write my memoir," he said again, turning the idea over in his head. Maybe it wasn't a terrible idea, though he was certain his son was unaware of the darkness that lay in his father's past. The old man closed the laptop that sat on the desk. He opened a drawer and pulled out the spiral-bound notebook he used to keep up with his expenses. Perhaps the world needed to know that the man who had come to be known as the Vigilante Virginian had not been born a killer; he had been made. The old man opened the notebook, flipped to a new page, and began to write.

Chapter 2

Tony Pham sat in bed with a book, but he was too distracted to read. He stared at his wife, Rebecca, as she got ready for bed. She was standing at the dresser mirror taking off her earrings. In the mirror, she saw him looking at her. She narrowed her eyes and turned to face him, "You have that look again."

Her voice startled him out of his reverie. "What?"

"You have that look again—the one where you stare a hole in something without actually seeing it. What are you thinking about?"

He sighed, "My mother and Mai. I mean, Mikayla."

She nodded, then sat beside him on the bed and said, "It's really amazing how they found each other after so many years."

Last month, for the first time in more than 20 years, Tony and Rebecca had spent Christmas apart. Tony had flown to the United States with his mother, Anh. She wanted to see Denver, Colorado, the place where her daughter Mikayla had grown up. Anh was also anxious to meet the woman who had raised her oldest child.

Mikayla had been born in Vietnam in April 1975 just two weeks before the fall of Saigon and the end of the war. When she was born, Anh had named her Mai Khai DiAngelo. Tony DiAngelo, an American serviceman, was Mai's father. He and Anh had been engaged to be married and she had planned to move to New York with him when his tour in Vietnam ended,

3

but he was killed a month before Mai was born. After he died, Anh had wanted to take Mai to the U.S. to find Tony's family, hoping they would be willing to help them. But a series of unfortunate and tragic events resulted in Mai being adopted by an American physician and his wife. The adoptive parents, John and Janine Thomas, changed the baby's name to Mikayla. Their own child, Sydney, had been born just two weeks before Mai's birth. Since Janine was half-Korean, they made the decision not to tell Mikayla that she had been born in Vietnam; instead, they told the girls they were fraternal twins. They made this decision out of love and kindness—they never wanted Mikayla to feel like an outsider in her family. But the women learned the truth last year after Sydney bought them both *DNAStory* kits.

After the shock and anger of being lied to dissipated, Mikayla decided to search for her birth mother. The DNA analysis ultimately allowed Mikayla to find a second cousin, Emily, and, eventually, her birth mother, Anh Linh Pham. Anh had immigrated to Australia after the war and was Tony's adoptive mother. Unlike Mikayla, he had always known he was adopted. He knew his biological mother was dead but had no idea what happened to his father. Anh had taken him in when he was three or four—no one knew for sure how old he was or even what his given name had been. Anh picked a birthdate for him and named him Tony, after her lost fiancé. He had few memories of his life before Anh, but ever since she found Mikayla, a desire to find his father had begun to build.

"He's probably dead," he said to his wife.

"Maybe. But that is worst-case scenario. What if he's not dead? What if you find him?"

"Well, that would be best-case scenario." He thought for a moment, "I guess it doesn't hurt to try."

Rebecca smiled at her husband and then stood. She walked over to the dresser and opened a drawer. She took out a small box and then returned to Tony's side. "I'm glad you want to look for him. I bought you this while you were in Denver but then wasn't sure you would want it."

He looked at the box as he took it from her. It was a DNA kit from an Australian company called *au.DNA*. It was surprisingly small and lightweight, given the magnitude of events a similar kit had set in motion for Mikayla and Anh. He turned the box over in his hands and wondered what it would bring him.

Chapter 3

Rural Vietnam, 1959-1963
  Loc Tin and Family

The Vongs lived on a moderate-sized rice farm in rural Vietnam. They also had a small vegetable garden, some chickens, and a few pigs. Every member of the family was needed to work the land and tend the animals that sustained them. The Vongs, like most Vietnamese at the time, were fiercely patriotic, and when the government drafted their eldest son in 1959, they proudly sent 20-year old Bao to join the Army of the Republic of South Vietnam (ARVN) to fight the communist threat from the North. Obligatory service at that time was only one year with a third of that time spent in training. One year in service to their country was a manageable sacrifice, and they rejoiced when Bao's obligation had been fulfilled and he returned home safe and heathy. Only a few weeks after Bao completed his service to the Army, the Vong's second son had to report for ARVN training. However, by late 1960, when Chinh was drafted, obligatory service had been extended to two years. Sadly, it did not matter as he was killed almost immediately after his training had ended.

Bao explained to his parents that the training he had received was mostly just an explanation of why communism was not right for Vietnam rather than teaching the men battlefield strategies or even how to load and fire a weapon. Bao had been fortunate because the Vongs owned a shotgun—one of the few personal weapons that the government allowed for private citizens. As a teenager, Bao had been curious about the weapon, and, much to his mother's dismay, Mr. Vong had taught his eldest how to use it and care for it. Although the shotgun was very different from the army-issue rifle, his limited experience with it had been far more training than his peers had received. The attitude of the ARVN commanders seemed to be that the men could learn about guns in the field. Unfortunately, this view resulted in a large number of men dying in their very first battle—never having fired a shot.

The Vong's third child, a daughter named Cai, would be spared the draft. But after Chinh's death and with no end to the war in sight, Bao took his youngest and now only brother aside. He taught him how to use the shotgun—how to aim and fire while on the move, over and over again until Loc Tin was used to the sound and the kick of the weapon. He made him take it apart and clean it. When he could do so with ease, he made him do it again while blindfolded. Then Bao drew a sketch of the M1 carbine that he had been issued by the army. He made Loc Tin learn the parts of the weapon and instructed him on how to load it and fire it. He stressed that he had to keep it clean. Perhaps even more important, Bao taught Loc Tin survival tactics: how to hide, how to "see" in the dark with his ears, how to move silently and evade capture. He taught him how to use the jungle as cover so that he was invisible to all but the keenest observer.

Finally, Bao told Loc Tin to learn English. "The Westerners will never learn Vietnamese, but they are your best chance of survival. Be their friend and they will be yours. They like to joke around. Laugh with them and don't be angry if they play tricks on you. They will be there for you when you need them." He gave Loc Tin an English-to-Vietnamese book that he had gotten from one of the American advisors. It had been a gift from the man's wife, but he had interpreters and never needed it. Recognizing that Bao was attempting to learn English, the officer had passed the book to him. Now Bao gave it to Loc Tin. At first, Loc Tin wasn't sure how helpful it would be. However, when he flipped it over, he realized it was also a Vietnamese-to-English book.

All of the time Loc Tin and Bao spent in training took time away from their chores on the farm, but the men's parents and sister never complained. They all knew it was only a matter of time before Loc Tin would be conscripted. Indeed, by 1963 the draft age had been lowered to 18, and so in February of that year Loc Tin began his two years of service.

.

Chapter 4

San Diego, California, January 2021
Emily and Ashley

Emily sat on Ashley's bed watching her friend pack. "I still can't believe you're quitting," she said.

Ashley shrugged. "Time to move on. I'm a little tired of Dr. Jansen. I am not and do not ever want to be a graduate student." She looked at her friend, "I thought you came to help me?" she chided. Mostly, it seemed to her, Emily was just trying to talk her out of moving.

"But you could get your PhD if you wanted to," Emily urged. Emily was one of several post-doctoral fellows working with Dr. Beverly Jansen at the University of California, San Diego (UCSD).

Ashley was Dr. Jansen's lead research assistant. Ashley had a master's degree in molecular biology and was a technical genius. She could make anything work. But although Dr. Jansen had encouraged her to go back to school and get her PhD, Ashley didn't want the responsibility of running her own lab and figuring out what all the data meant. She also didn't want the responsibility of convincing the government or some philanthropist that the work was worth funding.

Once Emily finished her post-doc, she would be expected to find a faculty position somewhere and fund her own lab. It wasn't an easy path, and Ashley didn't want that as her life. She wanted to work 9 to 5 with weekends off instead of the crazy hours Dr. Jansen had come to expect.

"You're smart enough to get your PhD," Emily said as she watched Ashley

9

load clothes into a large moving box.

"Yes. And I am also not stupid enough to actually do it." Ashley frowned and looked at her friend apologetically. "I'm sorry. That was rude. Look, I genuinely appreciate your enthusiasm, but academic research just isn't for me. I really want to just work a normal job at a place where funding isn't constantly in jeopardy."

Emily crossed her arms and responded, "So instead of helping millions of women with endometriosis by figuring out what causes it, you're going to help put people in jail."

Ashley smiled sweetly, "Or prove them innocent. DNA is objective." Ashley had accepted a job with California's Bureau of Forensic Services (CBF) in their DNA analysis division. They worked directly with the California Bureau of Investigation (CBI) to solve crimes. Ashley would be working in the laboratories at the Sacramento location. "I am hoping I get to work with the forensic genealogy team. They are the ones that caught the Green River Killer a few years ago by comparing DNA he had left at a crime scene to DNA in databases like *DNAStory*. They tracked him down because a second or third cousin had his DNA analyzed. How amazing would it be to be part of something like that?"

"Not as amazing as curing endometriosis," Emily retorted sharply, but then softened and added, "I know you are excited and I hope it is everything you think it will be. But I will miss you."

"Sacramento is not that far. Come visit me anytime." Ashley smiled. "Remember, I get weekends off from now on."

Emily nodded, but then grew concerned and said, "You're still coming to the wedding? You and Vivian are my only bridesmaids other than my sister and cousin." Emily, who was in the U.S. on a work visa, was getting married in September in Sydney, Australia.

"Yes, of course! I told the CBF about it when they offered me the job. They agreed to let me take those two weeks off. And I finally got my passport—so I am ready to go!" Ashley responded, clearly excited about her first international trip. Then she sat on the bed next to Emily and asked, "How is Kristy?" Emily's sister, Kristy, had recently undergone surgery for severe endometriosis. The gynecologic disease had brought her much pain over the years, but Emily was hopeful that Kristy's newest doctor would finally be able to help her. Even if he couldn't, Emily had been relieved that he had at least taken her sister's pain seriously.

"I'm not really sure. She is still recovering from the surgery, but she tried to sound cheery when I spoke to her."

Ashley asked, "Do you really think her disease was caused by your grandmother's exposure to Agent Orange during the war?"

Agent Orange was the name given to a powerful combination of herbicides used to destroy enemy food crops and ground cover during the American War in Vietnam. Unfortunately, use of the herbicide was now suspected to have caused numerous health consequences among not only the Western servicemen and Vietnamese population in-country at the time but also multiple generations that have followed. Emily's grandmother Minh and Minh's sister Anh had both been exposed to Agent Orange when they were children in Vietnam.

"Yes, I really believe it," Emily said emphatically. Then she sighed and added, "The hard part is proving it."

Chapter 5

Agent Orange
1941-1945

In 1941, E.J. Kraus, a botanist at the University of Chicago, began assessing various compounds that might have herbicidal activity. By 1945, two chemicals had been identified as the most effective agents for crop destruction. Eventually, the two chemicals would be mixed, creating the formulation that would later be known as "Agent Orange." Although the intent of Kraus' work was to identify herbicides that could be used against the Japanese, World War II ended before the compounds could be put into use.

Chapter 6

Memoir: First Kill

The first man I killed after I was drafted into the army was not an enemy soldier, but he still deserved to die. It was my first patrol and two of us had been tasked with interviewing civilians in a nearby village because an informant had said the locals were hiding guerrilla soldiers, known as Viet Cong or simply VC. They were also called by the derogatory name "Charlie," although that could refer to regular North Vietnamese Army (NVA) soldiers as well. As we cut through a rice field on the way to the village, I noticed a woman working alone in the field. She wore a cone-shaped straw hat to protect her face from the sun. As we approached her, she looked up from her work and smiled at us. She was quite pretty and younger than I expected. She reminded me of my sister, who was about the same age and had the same long dark hair. Today my sister was probably working on our farm doing the work I should have been doing. It made me angry and resentful.

When I reached the village and turned to my partner to plan our next move, he wasn't there. I backtracked to find him—concerned a VC might have snuck up behind us and taken him out without my knowledge. But I was wrong. Instead I found him in the field with the girl. She was naked, bloody, and dead. My partner didn't notice me—he was too busy buttoning his pants. Without thinking, I pulled my knife from its holster, crept up behind him like the VC I had feared, and slit his throat the way my father had taught me to slaughter pigs. Soundlessly, he fell to the ground in a heap.

13

I wiped my blade on his shirt and turned away, disgusted with myself as much as with him. I took no more than three steps before I turned and walked back to the dead man. Using my knife, I quickly removed the flag patch from his uniform. This man did not represent my country.

Chapter 7

Kangaroo Valley, NSW, Australia, February 2021
Tony and Rebecca

Tony and Rebecca were taking a long weekend to celebrate their 19th wedding anniversary. They had rented a cabin in the Kangaroo Valley and would spend the next three days exploring waterfalls and hiking trails…or maybe they would just stay inside and enjoy being alone together. Their twin sons were now 17 and had been left home unsupervised for the first time. The fridge was stocked and their grandparents were nearby, but Tony knew Rebecca would worry despite her promises not to. The trip had been his idea. He knew he had been sullen and distracted since returning home from his trip to the U.S. in December. It had been a great trip for his mother, but it made him wonder about his own family—the one before Anh. He knew it was irrational. He had a good life. But still, he wondered…and it had begun to eat away at him.

As always, Rebecca knew how to reach him, and she pulled him out of his funk by giving him the *au.DNA* kit. Even though he thought it was unlikely that he would find his father, the kit had given him hope and lifted his spirits. He loved Rebecca and wanted to make sure she never forgot how much she meant to him. Rebecca enjoyed the countryside and was always happy to get out of the city. She had been thrilled when he told her he had rented a cabin on the lake for just the two of them. It was a long drive, but Tony didn't mind because it gave him time to reflect. He glanced at his wife as he drove. As always, she was reading. Occasionally she would laugh and share a tidbit from her book with him, and then they would once again slip into a companionable silence.

Rebecca had been born in Queensland, Australia, the daughter of an English teacher mother and a handyman father. Her father had dropped out of school when he was 16, preferring to work alongside his own father who supervised a construction crew. He married Rebecca's mother when he was 21, and a little more than a year later they had a son. For a while, the small family was doing well. However, Rebecca's father unexpectedly lost his job when the construction company he and his father worked for declared bankruptcy and closed.

Rebecca's father moved the family to Sydney in hopes he would find another construction job, but nothing panned out. To support his wife and son, he joined the Australian Army and did two tours in Vietnam. Rebecca was born in 1973, two years after her father returned home. According to Rebecca's mother, her husband had always enjoyed the occasional beer, but she had never seen him drunk until after Vietnam. By the time Rebecca was 5, they rarely saw the man sober. He was not a mean drunk, but he was useless as both a provider for the family and as a father to his children. Her mother continued to teach, but she also had to take on numerous odd jobs to pay the bills. Rebecca's older brother mowed lawns and got a part-time job which helped keep food on the table. At 12, Rebecca started babysitting so she too could help support the family—including the man who was her father. It was not an easy life for any of them.

When Rebecca was 16, her father passed out with a lit cigarette in his mouth. The alarm of the smoke detector woke him up long enough for him to stumble outside, but he couldn't even muster enough brain function to call for help. No one else was home, so no one was hurt. But the family lost their house and everything in it. Although the fire had been devastating in many ways, it was also an important turning point in Rebecca's life. Very quickly after the fire, Rebecca's mother filed for divorce from her father. The divorce had been a relief to Rebecca, and a whole new world began to open up for her. Suddenly, without her mother having to support her father, Rebecca's money became her own. The teen's life was also more predictable, and she could safely have friends over without the embarrassment of finding her father passed out on the living room couch.

The fire and divorce were also turning points for Rebecca's father, because he was finally forced to recognize what the rest of the family already knew—that he was suffering from PTSD (post-traumatic stress disorder) due to his wartime service. The loss of his family woke him up, and he sought help from Anh Pham, a nurse practitioner specializing in trauma associated with the war. Her patients included both veterans and the Vietnamese civilians who had immigrated to Australia. She was also Tony's adoptive mother. Anh had been born in Vietnam before the war and, after being orphaned, had grown up in the Sisters of Mercy orphanage in Saigon. After his own mother died, Tony and his sister were found wandering the streets alone. The children had been picked up and brought to Sisters of Mercy orphanage. A day later, when the fall of Saigon was eminent, Anh took the two orphans and her own infant to the Embassy where she had hoped they would be evacuated. But in the chaos of that day, Tony's sister was killed and Anh was separated from her baby. Mai ended up in the U.S., while Anh and Tony were left behind in Vietnam.

Within a year of the fall of Saigon, the makeshift family of Anh and Tony joined the millions of Vietnamese civilians that fled the country in overcrowded boats. Eventually, they were able to immigrate to Sydney, sponsored by Anh's sister Minh, who had left Vietnam with her Australian boyfriend two years before. Anh's experiences in Vietnam, at the refugee camp in Malaysia, and in trying to acclimate to life in Australia led to her decision to become a psychiatric nurse practitioner. She felt she was in a unique position to help both soldiers and refugees transition to life after the war.

And so in the Spring of 1991, Tony and Rebecca first crossed paths in the lobby of Anh's clinic. Rebecca was just 18 and had not spoken to her father in two years. Nevertheless, Anh wanted to meet with the teen in an effort to better understand how to help the girl's father. Her brother, now in his mid-20s, had moved away. Tony, who was 20 at the time, had stopped by the clinic to talk to his mom and hoped to catch her between patients. While they both waited for Anh, Rebecca and Tony struck up a conversation and immediately hit it off. Although it would be more than ten years before they married, they were rarely apart after they met. Because of her difficult childhood, Rebecca had been reluctant to marry and was adamantly opposed to having children. But, eventually, Tony won her heart and they were finally married in 2002. Despite her earlier protestations against having children, Rebecca quickly became pregnant and their sons, Joseph and Jonathan, were born in 2003. Although Rebecca had been hesitant to become a mother, she was good at it. And Tony was determined to be the best father that he could be.

Although he had lost his biological father, Tony had been fortunate to grow up with a strong father figure. Anh had married Lanh, also a refugee, soon after moving to Australia. Lanh had embraced Tony as his own son from day one and he had been a major influence on the man Tony had become. Tony knew he was luckier than many, but lately he had not acted like it. He was determined to make it up to his wife. This weekend was all about making sure Rebecca knew she meant everything to him.

Two and half hours after leaving their home in Sydney, Tony pulled up in front of the rental cabin. It was a little more rustic than it had appeared online, but, as promised, it was right on the lake and was surrounded by lush greenery. The log cabin itself was small, but it had a wide, covered porch that wrapped around the entire structure. Multiple rocking chairs lined one side of the porch, and a large, green hammock was strung between two of the support beams. Inside they found one great room with a galley kitchen on one end, a bedroom area on the other, and a small sitting area with a fireplace in between. A tiny bathroom was tucked into the corner. They unloaded the groceries they had brought from home and prepared a light lunch. They opened the side door next to the kitchen and found a small table and two chairs where they could sit outside and eat.

"You should get your results soon," Rebecca said as she added cheese to a cracker and took a bite.

"*Au.DNA* said it could take up to six weeks. It's only been four since I sent the sample back."

Rebecca nodded. "I really do hope you find him."

"I know it's a longshot," Tony replied, frowning. "But maybe. Honestly, just to know what happened to him would be good. My mom thinks he was probably in the army and was captured at the end of the war. But he also could have escaped on a boat the way we did. He could be anywhere in the world—even Australia." The thought made him smile.

Rebecca had heard all this before but didn't stop Tony from telling her again. She knew he was just trying to convince himself that his father was alive and could be found. She thought of her own father and how much the war had damaged him. She had been so angry with him after the fire that she had never spoken to him again. He took his own life a few years later, and she had been devastated. She knew he was seeing Anh and thought he would get better. She assumed he would eventually show up on their doorstep and apologize—ask for forgiveness. She had wanted to make amends with him, but, childishly, she wanted him to initiate it. Too late, she realized that he needed her to make the first move. He was a broken man, and she had failed him. Thinking about her own dad made the tears threaten to start. She blinked them away and refocused on Tony.

"What would be your first question? If you found him?" She had asked him before, but it was an easy way to get her mind off of her own past.

"More than anything I want to know what happened. What is my given name? I don't even know how old I am. I would also really like to know about my sister and my mother. What were their names? What was my mother like? Were they happy?" Tony sighed heavily and looked at his watch, "Is it 5 o'clock yet?"

She smiled, knowing he was joking and just trying to lighten the mood. "What is it that the Yanks say? 'It's 5 o'clock somewhere.'"

He laughed. "Yes, well, I think they're referring to us when they say that. No one is further in the future than we are." Tony thought for a minute, "Though maybe it's 5 o'clock yesterday in California?"

Rebecca smiled again then stood and took his hand. "Let's walk down to the lake and see what the water is like. We can open a bottle of wine when we get back."

"Skinny-dipping?" Tony grinned.

She rolled her eyes at him and pulled him off the porch toward the lake. He kept smiling, thinking that she didn't *actually* say no.

Chapter 8

Rural Vietnam, 1963
  Loc Tin

In February of 1963, Loc Tin and 200 other young men reported to the induction center in DaNang. There they would fill out paperwork, and, if determined to be fit for service, they would be assigned to a battalion and sent on their way. He expected to be at the induction center for a week. From Bao's description, he knew they would first undergo mental and physical testing as well as medical evaluations. He had no doubt he would pass these tests; he was strong and in excellent health. However, the first three days the men were left with no instructions at all, and they simply wandered around the buildings trying to figure out what they were supposed to do. They slept on the floor because there was nowhere else to sleep. Food was in short supply. All the men grew restless, irritable, and anxious. Several of the conscripts simply left and never returned.

Finally, four days after arriving at the induction center, the previous group of conscripted men moved on making room for Loc Tin and his group. They were given forms to fill out with their biographical information. Loc Tin had brought with him his identification card and carefully listed his information as requested. However, he noted that a large number of others had "forgotten" their official I.D. and seemed to be making up the information that they listed on the forms. These men soon deserted and could not be found because the army didn't actually know their real names. Loc Tin realized that things were even worse than Bao had said. He began to wonder—if the induction center is this poorly run, how will we ever win the war? Indeed, a few weeks before, news had spread of a disastrous defeat of ARVN forces in Ap Bac, a village in the Mekong Delta southwest of Saigon. Although ARVN troops outnumbered the VC four-to-one, the South Vietnamese troops were decisively defeated. Even the significant technical and planning assistance of their U.S. advisors had not been enough to defeat the enemy. Loc Tin and the other draftees were understandably fearful of their fate.

A month after arriving at the induction center, Loc Tin and only about 50 of the draftees that arrived with him in February remained. Some had not passed the physical and mental exams, but many others had simply deserted. Loc Tin was appalled that so many of his fellow countrymen refused the call to service. However, he would soon understand why the ARVN troops performed so poorly in battle and why so many cheated to avoid being sent to participate in a war they were destined to lose.

A week after passing all of their tests, Loc Tin and the others were transferred to a nearby training facility. There they sat in classrooms for six hours a day while instructors read to them from American Army manuals that had been translated, often inaccurately, into Vietnamese. Other times they would be lectured on the evils of communism and why the North must be defeated. The lectures were mind-numbing and contained no information at all that seemed relevant to winning the war. They were occasionally promised demonstrations in which trained soldiers would undergo a mock battle or other field operation, but these never materialized.

One afternoon, the men were excited to be issued rifles and eagerly awaited their next class. However, instead of being shown how to load and fire the weapon, the instructor droned on and on about how many pounds of pressure it took for a bullet to be fired from a gun. He talked about the composition of the gunpowder and even the evolution of weapons over the course of history. He told them that the M1 and M2 carbines they had been assigned were the same guns used by the Americans during World War II. The bayonet at the end of the rifle was precisely 6.75 inches long and was made of stainless steel that had been blackened by a carbon coating.

Loc Tin leaned over to Binh, another recruit with whom he had become friendly, and said, "How is any of this going to help us defeat the communists?" Binh just shrugged; he had no answer. Loc Tin looked back at their instructor, who was now explaining why their boots had 12 eyes instead of 14. Loc Tin shook his head. We will be slaughtered, he thought. But an idea was forming in his head...

In their barracks that night, Loc Tin gathered the men around and started sharing the information that Bao had given him. Thanks to his brother, Loc Tin was quickly able to understand the M2 carbine he had been issued. It was better than the M1 which Binh had received. The M1 was a semi-automatic—only firing once with each pull of the trigger. But the M2 he knew from Bao had "selective fire" capability, meaning he could choose semi-automatic or full automatic. Full auto meant the gun would keep firing as long as he held the trigger down. He thought the latter might be useful under some circumstances and felt the men with the M1 would be at a disadvantage but said nothing about it. Once he himself was comfortable loading and unloading the gun, he taught the other members of his barracks. He explained how to carry the gun safely and the importance of keeping it clean. He also made sure all the men knew to keep the safety engaged when they were not in the field. Soon he was giving lectures on stealth movement and the battlefield strategies that Bao had taught him. The men were hungry for knowledge that would help them not just survive but also win the war. They were grateful for Loc Tin and soon looked at him as their leader.

By mid-May 1963, training was complete, and Loc Tin and his group learned which battalion would be theirs. Assignments were scribbled on white cards which seemed to be handed out at random since no names were listed. Loc Tin and Binh were disappointed to learn that they had been assigned to different divisions as the two men had become friends. Although the men were both 18, to Loc Tin, Binh seemed younger and less worldly than the other draftees. He had a childishness about him that made Loc Tin want to look out for him the way Bao had always watched out for him. Another conscript, Twan, was equally disappointed that he had been assigned to the 7th Infantry based in Duc Lap. He was hoping to get the 2nd Infantry, which was stationed at Quảng Ngāi only a few kilometers from his home. Loc Tin looked at Binh's assignment card and then Twan's. Loc Tin grabbed each card from their hands and handed them to the other.

Loc Tin looked at Binh, "Now you're with me. And Twan," he turned to the other man, "you are going home."

As the three men joined the others and continued to compare assignments, word spread of an incident that would come to be known as the "Buddhist Crisis." Under the orders of South Vietnam's President Ngo Dinh Diem, government representatives opened fire on a group of Buddhist protestors in the city of Hue. Eight people, including children, were killed. It was a shocking attack on civilians ordered by the president of the country to which these men had sworn allegiance. Morale, which was already low, sank even farther.

Chapter 9

For many years after Tony, Anh, and Lanh immigrated to Sydney, they would join Anh's sister, Minh, and her family for Sunday dinner. Over the years as their families grew because of marriage or the addition of children, these gatherings became more haphazard. Although Anh and Minh and their husbands, Lanh and Jeffry, rarely missed a Sunday evening together, their children and grandchildren were often elsewhere. However, tonight Minh and Jeffry's small house was filled to overflowing. In addition to the patriarchs and matriarchs of the family, several of the adult children were there with their spouses. Tony and Rebecca had missed several Sundays due to work and travel but were back for tonight's meal. Minh's son, Andrew, and his wife, Lai, were also in attendance.

Andrew had grown-up hearing about the orphans left behind in Vietnam—many fathered by Western soldiers—and had decided long ago he would adopt when he was ready to start a family. Lai, whose family had also immigrated from Vietnam, loved the idea of adopting children from her home country. Four years after marrying in 2001, Andrew and Lai traveled to Vietnam to begin the process of adoption. On a whim, Lisa, Tony's sister, had traveled with them. A year later Andrew and Lai adopted siblings who were two and four at the time. The girls were now grown and were attending a local college.

For Lisa, the trip had been transformative. She was shocked and dismayed at both the number of orphans and the unmet needs of the orphanages. Although the war had ended long before their trip, the problem of abandoned children in Vietnam continued to get worse due to extreme poverty in many areas of the country. Children from these families were often left at a church or temple in hopes that they would be taken to an orphanage, but many ended up homeless and lived life on the street. Even more tragic, the lingering contamination of the country with Agent Orange had led to thousands of children being born with severe, debilitating birth defects. Often their families were unable or unwilling to care for them, and so these children also filled the orphanages or died alone on the streets of Vietnam. Lisa had been appalled to learn that Vietnam had as many as 2 million orphans, and she had been motivated to "do something".

In the years since that first visit, Lisa had become a staunch ally and advocate of Vietnam's orphans. She helped to raise both awareness of the problem and money to help open more orphanages in order to get kids off the street. After college she went to law school and eventually became a lawyer that specialized in foreign adoptions. Tonight everyone was excited to see her since she just gotten back from a trip to Vietnam. Although she had been several times with another member of her law firm, the most recent trip was the first time she had gone alone.

"Tell us all about it," Anh said. The pride in her voice for her daughter was evident.

Lisa sat at the dinner table surrounded by her family. "It wasn't a big deal—just standard stuff. Our firm has two couples in the process of adopting children from one of the orphanages we work with. They asked me to accompany them for their first meeting with the children. They wanted me to check that the paperwork was all accurate and get the orphanage to agree to a date for the parents to return and take custody of the children."

Tony poured her a glass of wine and said, "Well, you need to come up with something more interesting than that or this lot will never leave you alone."

Lisa sighed and picked up her wine glass. "Well, I did meet someone interesting."

"A man??" Anh asked, anxious for her 34-year-old daughter to finally settle down.

Lisa cocked her head at her mother, "Well, yes, but it's nothing like that."

"Oh," said Anh, clearly disappointed. "Tell me anyway."

"His name is Jeremy...Jeremy...something with a D, I think? Dandy, maybe? I can't remember. Anyway, he is a doctor. He was volunteering with that organization—um..., Doctors Without Borders, I think."

"A doctor! Is he married?" Anh asked.

Lisa exchanged a look with her brother and resisted the urge to roll her eyes. "It isn't like that. He was at St. Mary's House of Hope orphanage the same day that I was there. He was giving the children vaccinations, I think."

"You didn't answer the question. Is he married?" her mother asked again.

"I didn't ask," Lisa said, hiding her annoyance. "But it turns out, his mother was a street child in Vietnam. She was homeless for nearly 20 years. She did odd jobs and begged on the street for food in order to survive. She also took care of another little boy that had been abandoned as a baby."

"How awful," the group murmured, all of them now listening attentively.

"Somehow—I didn't get the whole story—she left Vietnam and ended up in the U.S. She got married and had Jeremy. Now he is an advocate for Vietnam's orphans."

"Just like you are," Anh said, beaming with pride.

"Not exactly. I'm a lawyer. He's a doctor."

"But still—that could be a good match for you. You have the same passion."

"He lives in Los Angeles. Or maybe he said San Francisco. At any rate, a long, long way from Sydney," Lisa said, trying to dampen her mother's enthusiasm. She continued, "But the whole point of mentioning him is that he knows Emily. Well, not exactly. He knows Emily's friend Vivian. They have a grant together or something. Isn't that amazing?"

Anh shrugged, "Maybe you could ask Emily if he is single. Or better yet, get Emily to invite him to the wedding." This time Lisa did roll her eyes.

Chapter 10

Duc Lap, Vietnam, 1963
7th Infantry Division, 2nd Infantry Regiment
Loc Tin

A few days after receiving their assignments, Loc Tin, Binh, and the rest of the men assigned to the 7th Infantry Division climbed onto large, canvas-covered transport trucks and were taken to their division headquarters in Duc Lap. The small city was located in South Vietnam very near the Cambodian border and the infamous Ho Chi Minh Trail which was used by the VC and North Vietnamese to move troops and supplies. After several hours in the trucks, they arrived at a large, black metal gate suspended between two stone columns. The sign above the gate informed them that they had reached their destination—the home base of the 7th Infantry Division.

A uniformed man appeared at the side of one stone column and opened the gate to allow the trucks to pass. Although there was no fence surrounding the base, it was encompassed by thick jungle, which Loc Tin thought would provide some protection against attack. The area inside camp was devoid of anything green, save from the dozens of tents that lined the perimeter. In the middle of the camp were four or five large, long metal buildings. The men would soon learn that the buildings housed the officer quarters, latrine, and mess hall. Enlisted men slept in the tents.

A month after arriving at the base camp of the 7th Infantry, Binh was nervous. Because the 7th Infantry's base was located so close to the Ho Chi

Minh Trail, the unit was frequently sent on patrol to monitor NVA and VC movement in the area. The VC, of course, were aware that the 7th was located in Duc Lap and also knew about the patrols. Consequently, other than an assault on the base, patrol duty was considered the most hazardous. Today Binh was scheduled for his first patrol near the trail, and he was looking to Loc Tin for advice.

"Constantly scan the area around you. Keep your weapon at the ready," Loc Tin told him. He also reminded Binh that the number of men on patrol had recently been increased from two to six. Although that meant more patrol duty for each of them, it had also dramatically increased the likelihood of survival. Loc Tin tried to calm his friend's nerves, but, honestly, everyone feared patrolling the areas near the trail. Loc Tin always felt as though they were being watched—and they probably were.

Although Binh survived his first patrol, one member of his group did not return. No one knew what happened to him. They had been walking in a line, taking turns being the point man as well as the rear guard. Binh thought he heard something and turned back to ask Chinh—the man at the rear. He was gone. The patrol doubled back, fearing he had been killed, but they never found him. Binh was shaken, "It could have been me."

Loc Tin nodded, "Rumor is that he deserted."

"But what if he was captured or killed?" Binh asked.

"It's a possibility," Loc Tin agreed. The price of war.

A few weeks later, the men of the 7th woke to a loud whistling—the unmistakable sound of incoming rockets. Without hesitating, Loc Tin grabbed his rifle and dove under his bunk just as a rocket hit a few yards away. He crawled out from his bunk and, along with other members of the team, headed outside as the compound continued to be pounded with rockets and mortars. Many of the buildings had collapsed; wounded were everywhere. Loc Tin looked around. The darkness of the night was compounded by the smoky haze left by the rockets. It was impossible to tell which direction the rockets were coming from. But he knew if they didn't take out the enemy position, no one would survive the night.

He heard his brother's voice in his head, "Close your eyes and listen." Loc

Tin heeded the words of his brother and closed his eyes. He focused on the sound of the whistling as it grew louder and closer. He realized the rockets were coming from the northeast. He opened his eyes and followed the direction his ears had told him. A short distance from the perimeter of the camp, he saw several small trees had been recently cut down, creating a clearing. The sun had started to rise and he could just make out the half dozen VC, recognizable by the black "pajamas" they wore, manning a mortar gun. Two others had shoulder-mounted rocket launchers. They fired as rapidly as they could reload. A single guard stood at the rear of the group keeping watch from behind. Loc Tin would take him out first.

Loc Tin moved as stealthily as he could—perhaps unnecessary since the noise of the rockets and mortars would easily cover the sound of his movement. When he was no more than 6 feet away from the lookout, Loc Tin removed the bayonet from his rifle and felt the weight in his hand. Heavier than the one he used to throw at home, but he was confident in his ability. He watched the lookout carefully pace back and forth behind the group firing on his camp. When he turned his back to Loc Tin, in one fluid movement, he jumped up and threw the knife. It hit its mark and the lookout dropped silently to the ground. Loc Tin picked up his M2 and in one long burst of fire took out the entire enemy group. He let go of the trigger, and suddenly the only sound he could hear were the voices of the wounded calling for help.

Loc Tin walked cautiously to the men he had just killed—wanting to make sure they were indeed dead. First he went to the lookout—the most likely survivor. He also wanted to retrieve the bayonet. The man was smaller than he expected and, after pulling out the knife, turned him over to check for signs of life. Loc Tin was taken aback to realize the lookout had been a woman. Her eyes were open, but they saw nothing. She was dead. Although he knew there were many women in the ranks of the VC, he had never considered that he might have to kill one. It didn't feel right to him, but he tried to shake it off. She was the enemy. He did his job.

After confirming that the remaining VC were also dead, Loc Tin walked back to camp. Casualties were high and medical supplies were scarce. Two of the medics were among the wounded. He found his commanding officer and reported that the enemy had been taken out and they should be in the clear. The officer was visibly surprised at Loc Tin's quick thinking and bravery. He stared at Loc Tin for a brief moment then turned away and began barking orders. Soon the chaotic activity during the attack became more organized and purposeful.

Twelve men had been killed, including the two assigned to patrol the northeast perimeter. Their names were noted, and their bodies were removed. Dozens of men had been wounded, and while most were evacuated to a nearby field hospital, the more seriously injured were transferred to a fully equipped military hospital—the closest one being nearly 60 miles away. After the dead and wounded had been taken care of, the enlisted men turned their attention to putting the camp back together. Some of the tents had only collapsed and could easily be set up again, but others had caught on fire and were a total loss. By the time night fell again, the camp was as back to normal as it could be. Eventually, the camp would receive replacements for the lost tents, but it was anyone's guess when that would be.

That night as the men lay on their cots in the now even more crowded tent, Binh said to Loc Tin, "Remember how you thought having the thick jungle surrounding the camp would be as good as a fence?"

"Yeah," replied Loc Tin.

"You were wrong."

Chapter 11

Sacramento, California, February 2021
  Ashley

Ashley stood in her closet trying to decide what to wear. For the last five years she had worked in a research lab on a college campus. Jeans and T-shirts were the norm. Even Dr. Jansen dressed fairly casually unless she had a presentation or visitors. Ashley's interview for the new job had been via online video chat rather than in person. Since there had been no opportunity to visit the lab, she wasn't certain of the dress code. She had been to other government labs, and they were all just as casual as the one she had left. But she didn't want to show up in jeans on her first day, just in case. She decided on a "middle-of-the road" look—not too dressy and not too casual. Black slacks, a mint green, lightweight sweater, and closed-toed shoes, the latter being a requirement of any laboratory. She debated on wearing low heels, to add an extra inch to her diminutive frame but rejected the idea. Being 5'4 wasn't worth giving up her comfortable flats.

She looked in the mirror, satisfied that no matter what everyone else was wearing, at worse, she would only be slightly over or underdressed. She ran a comb through her hair one last time. She had recently gotten it cut and was just starting to get used to having short hair. It was certainly easier to manage now than when it was long. Her chestnut hair had been just long enough to donate to a charity that made hair prostheses for children who had lost their hair due to disease or injury. When she was in high school, the organization helped a friend of hers who had been severely burned in a fire. Ashley decided then and there she would donate if her hair ever got long enough. It had taken ten years, but, finally, it had.

"Time to go," Ashley told herself, though, truthfully, she would probably be early. She wasn't sure of the traffic, and having never been there, she could not rule out the possibility of getting lost. However, using the GPS on her phone, Ashley found the Sacramento location of California's Bureau of Forensic Services (CBF) without too much difficulty. She parked in the employee section, grabbed her purse, and headed to the entrance. The building was huge—at least ten stories—and looked to have been built recently. The steel building was a sleek blue-gray with huge windows on all sides. She couldn't help but smile. Maybe her new lab had a window. That would be a nice change. Inside she was greeted by a security guard, and after having her bag inspected, she walked through a metal detector and made her way to the front desk. Without looking up, a woman dressed in a security guard uniform asked for her name, ID, and the purpose of her visit.

"Ashley England. I'm a new employee. I'm supposed to meet with Dr. Lance Davis." Dr. Davis was the senior analyst and would be her boss, even though he wasn't the one who hired her or even interviewed her, which she thought was odd. But Dr. Jansen had told her things in the government sector worked differently, and, as usual, she was right.

The woman looked up at her, "England? Like the country?"

"Yes, exactly," Ashley responded to the familiar question.

"That's funny. You don't sound English," the woman chuckled.

Ashley just smiled. It was not the first time someone had made that joke, and it probably wouldn't be the last.

The woman pointed to a bank of chairs that lined the wall, "Have a seat and I'll let Dr. Davis know you're here."

"Thank you." Ashley picked up her purse and headed toward the chairs, but before she had a chance to sit down, the woman called to her.

"Ms. England, that's Dr. Davis coming in now." She pointed to a man walking through the doors Ashley had entered a few moments before.

Ashley smiled at her, "Thank you." She turned to wait for Dr. Davis. He was younger than she expected, maybe 40. His dark hair had just a touch of gray. Although he was slightly overweight, his tall frame carried it well. He was dressed casually, wearing wrinkled khakis and a navy blue polo shirt. She breathed a sigh of relief—slightly overdressed was just fine with her. As Dr. Davis made his way through security, she noticed he had a slight limp and wondered if he had injured his knee. He said something to the security guard, and the man laughed, clapping him on the back. Ashley was nervous, and that small gesture made her relax a bit.

As Dr. Davis headed for the front desk, she intercepted him. "Dr. Davis? I'm Ashley England. We spoke on the phone."

He stopped and looked at her, "Yes. Good. You're the new research assistant. Please call me Lance. You're a bit early. I haven't had my coffee yet."

"Oh, I'm so sorry. I can wait in the lobby until you're ready." Ashley felt her face flush, and she heard Emily's voice in her head, "Don't apologize so much for things that are irrelevant."

He shook his head, "Not a big deal. We will just start the tour in the cafeteria." Lance started walking and Ashley had to hustle to keep up with his long legs, which moved quickly despite the limp. As they walked, he pointed out various offices. "That's where you'll get your CBF identification badge. Over there—they can help you with forms to get your insurance and stuff. They can also let you know if there's any online training you have to complete. You can take care of all that after we get coffee."

The cafeteria was exactly as she expected. On one end there was a large open area with various stations offering the usual: pizza, burgers, salad bar. Adjacent to the food stations, an even larger area held dozens of tables and chairs, many of them occupied with people working at laptop computers. Lance pointed, "This is the hot meal station. It has options that change daily. It's pretty good and beats packing lunch every day. It's also cheaper than restaurants in the area and a lot faster." He pointed again, "They also have microwaves if you want to bring your own lunch. Lots of people do." In the corner of the room, Lance led her to the coffee bar. It was designed to look like a little bistro, complete with a green awning over the bar. A sprinkling of tall tables without chairs were set up close by. Lance spoke to the woman behind the counter, "Morning, Julie."

"Hi, Lance. The usual?" He nodded. She looked at Ashley, "Who's your friend?"

"This is Ashley. She's just joined the DNA lab." Then he turned to Ashley, "Do you want a coffee or latte or anything? My treat."

Ashley hesitated but then said, "Yes, thank you." To Julie she said, "Vanilla latte, please."

"You got it. And welcome to CBF," Julie smiled at her and then busied herself with their orders.

Coffee in hand, Lance and Ashley made their way toward the tables with chairs and found an empty one near the windows.

"I love how there are windows everywhere. Does the lab have a window?"

Lance shook his head as he sipped his coffee. "Not our lab. The windows run all along the four outside walls of the building, as does the hallway. The labs and offices are all in the center of the building with another hallway running down the middle. Rooms next to the outside hallway have transom windows that let in light, though they are too high to see out. Can't even see what the weather is, but it's still better than the interior rooms—like our lab—they don't get any natural light at all."

Ashley shrugged, "Oh, well. Maybe someday." She sipped her coffee and looked around, optimistic that she had made a good decision to change jobs.

Chapter 12

Two weeks after the VC attack, Loc Tin and Binh were eating breakfast in the mess hall when a U.S. Army Jeep and two trucks pulled up in front of the officers building. One man jumped out of the Jeep and went into the captain's office. A few of the remaining men started unloading the trucks. Curious, Loc Tin and Binh wandered outside.

"Hello," Loc Tin said to a man wearing fatigues and leaning against the Jeep, smoking. Using an English phrase that Bao had taught him, he added, "What's up?"

"You speak English?" The soldier was surprised.

Loc Tin smiled, "Learning."

"And I am trying to learn Vietnamese, but it isn't going so well." The man laughed and held out his hand, "Dennis Dordi, 5th Special Forces Group. My friends call me Dordi."

Loc Tin shook the man's hand. He understood enough of the words to respond, "Are we friends?"

"Well," the man laughed again and said, "we are fighting on the same side, so I hope so."

Loc Tin thought for a moment, taking in the man's uniform. "Special Forces? Green Berets?"

"That's right." Dordi smiled again.

"I've heard of you guys. You guys are crazy."

36

Dordi laughed, "Right again."

The men continued to talk—mostly English. But Dordi spoke more Vietnamese than any other American Loc Tin had ever met, and using bits and pieces of both languages, they were able to communicate. The 5th Special Forces Group was also based in Duc Lap just a few kilometers from the home of the 7th ARVN Infantry. The 5th SFG had brought tents to replace those that had been destroyed during the VC attack. They also brought wire and posts. They intended to fortify the base.

"You need a damn fence around this place," Dordi told him, looking around.

"A fence would not have prevented the rockets from hitting us," Loc Tin pointed out.

"No," Dordi agreed, "but it keeps out the riffraff."

"Riffraff?" Loc Tin had no idea what that meant.

Over the next two weeks, the men of the 7th ARVN and the 5th SFG cleared 10 feet of jungle around the entire base and then built a perimeter fence. They also set up the new tents and helped dig a dozen bunkers along the perimeter of the base, which they fortified with sandbags. At night, before heading back to their own camp, the men would sit around smoking, drinking, and telling stories. Some of the men had been in-country for nearly a year and would be headed home soon. Dordi, however, was only halfway through his tour in Vietnam.

Loc Tin learned that these men, who had spent days and days fortifying his unit, had conducted dozens of covert missions into Cambodia to spy on the North Vietnamese or VC units that had base camps in the region. They would also ambush North Vietnamese troops moving supplies along the Ho Chi Minh Trail. On more than one occasion, members of the 5th SFG had parachuted into North Vietnam to rescue a downed American or South Vietnamese pilot. Loc Tin was also intrigued to learn that a cadre of South Vietnamese Special Forces was attached to the 5th SFG.

Not long after the 5th SFG had fortified the 7th Infantry's base, they were attacked again. This time the attack was not carried out by a small group of VC but by an entire NVA regiment. The siege on the base lasted more than a week. Reinforcements were called in, and the 5th SFG, along with another regiment of ARVN forces, arrived. Finally the North Vietnamese were beaten back. Although it was a military victory for the South, no one felt like celebrating. The base of the 7th Infantry was heavily damaged, casualties were high with more than 100 men killed. They also learned that on November 2, 1963, while they were fighting the NVA, Ngo Dinh Diem, the president of South Vietnam, had been assassinated by his own men. Although Diem was not well regarded by the men of the 7th Infantry, many expressed concern that the South Vietnam government would be destabilized. However, for better or worse, his death had no apparent effect on the war, and life at the camp remained unchanged.

Day or night, the perimeter of the 7th was patrolled by eight-man teams, two on each side. Every member of the regiment took their turn on the fence. Tonight Loc Tin and Binh made up a quarter of the team, despite both having been wounded in the recent NVA attack. Loc Tin had been shot in the left arm, but, fortunately, he was right-handed, and the bullet had missed any major arteries. Although it hurt like hell even after a week, he could still use it, and that's all he cared about. Binh had it worse. A grenade had landed in their bunker. Without hesitation, Dordi had picked it up and thrown it back out. It exploded just outside the bunker nearest Binh. He and Dordi both caught some shrapnel, though not enough to keep Binh out of perimeter duty.

Binh and Loc Tin checked their equipment and tested their walkie-talkies. Right at midnight, they relieved the men walking the westernmost perimeter—the side facing Cambodia. There were no lights outside the perimeter, and the men stared into darkness as they trekked back and forth along the fence. There was no talking, only listening. The next six hours passed slowly. Loc Tin found his mind wandering. He thought of his family and hoped they were okay. He thought of Twan, his friend from training, and wondered if he was still alive. In his mind, Loc Tin relived the moment just a week ago when the grenade landed in their bunker. He had been certain he would die. Then he watched in astonishment as Dordi had picked up the live grenade and tossed it like a ball. Thinking of his American friend made Loc Tin realize he had stopped listening. He refocused his energy and attention to the job at hand. Not paying attention could get them killed. At last in the distance, Loc Tin began to see the sun peeking above the horizon. Shortly thereafter, the next group of men with perimeter duty arrived and relieved them. Exhausted from the mental strain far more than the physical effort, the men went to their bunks and collapsed.

A few hours later Loc Tin, who Dordi had taken to calling LT, was awoken when his American friend filled his hand with shaving lotion, then tickled his face with a feather. Dordi and Binh thought it was hilarious when a sleepy Loc Tin covered his face in shave cream as he attempted to brush away the feather. At first Loc Tin was annoyed. But as he wiped the mess from his face with a towel, he remembered his brother's advice. "Don't be angry if the Americans play tricks on you. They will be there when you need them." Indeed, Dordi had already saved his life at least twice. He hid his annoyance and laughed with the others at his own expense. It was the first of many stupid pranks that Dordi would pull. That morning he had come by to see if Loc Tin and Binh wanted to join a training mission he was leading with some of the other ARVN troops. Loc Tin readily agreed, but Binh shook his head. If it wasn't a requirement, he wasn't doing it.

Loc Tin learned much from his time with Dordi, and he also taught the Green Beret a few things. For one, the art of knife throwing. One night when they were passing the time playing poker—another skill Dordi had taught him—Loc Tin noticed a rat making his way around the barrack looking for food. He watched the rat disappear under Binh's bunk. He looked back at his cards, contemplating his move. The rat reappeared, and Loc Tin nonchalantly reached down, grabbed the knife he had started keeping in a holster on his ankle, and threw it at the rat who was now scurrying up the wall. The knife hit the animal squarely in the head, killing it instantly. Its limp body dangled on the wall.

"Holy shit, man!" Dordi exclaimed jumping up and knocking his chair over. "You've *got* to teach me that!"

After that, Dordi had become Loc Tin's student. Quickly they also became good friends, and they saw each other at their best and worst moments. The amiable but tough-as-nails Green Beret had broken down in tears upon learning that the beloved U.S. President, John F. Kennedy, had been shot and killed. His assassination hit all the Americans hard, and Loc Tin wondered if they would abandon South Vietnam. However, over the next few months under the leadership of Lyndon B. Johnson, the new U.S. President, American involvement in Vietnam actually increased.

Days passed slowly. The intense boredom broken only by moments of sheer terror. When he didn't have perimeter duty or patrol duty, Loc Tin often went to the 5th SFG base to hang with Dordi. Some days he would get to train with the Vietnamese Special Forces, while other days he would go with Dordi and the others on some project to help civilians in the area. It seemed the Americans were constantly rebuilding things after VC attacked civilians. Sometimes they rebuilt after an accidental bombing by the Americans. More than once, Loc Tin had joined Dordi and the others rebuilding a school or church that had been destroyed. Occasionally, if one of the soldiers got a package from home, they would go to the nearest village and hand out candy to the kids.

"What does it take to join the Special Forces?" Loc Tin asked Dordi one day when they were alone.

"Well, first and foremost, you must be crazy," Dordi said, laughing. Then, realizing his friend was serious, he added, "You thinking about becoming one of us?"

"Maybe. It just seems more effective. Small, targeted raids rather than these huge battles for a hill or base. Win a hill only to lose it a month later. Lots of people die. For what? If we want to get the communists out, we have to be smarter. We aren't going to win as long as the North doesn't care how many people die."

Dordi nodded, "I can't argue with that."

Eventually Dordi's tour in Vietnam ended, and it was time for him to rotate out. Before heading to the Ton Son Nhut airport in Saigon, he came by the 7th base camp to say goodbye to his friend. "LT, my man, if you ever get to the States, you gotta look me up."

Loc Tin nodded, "And where would I find you?"

Dordi shrugged, "I have family in the middle-of-nowhere Virginia. But I'm going to head out to California. Man, it's beautiful there. Right on the ocean—always sunny and warm, but not too warm. And girls in bikinis everywhere. A buddy of mine from high school runs some kind of factory out there now. He said if I came back in one piece, he'd give me a job." He smiled and then added, "I'm sure the skills I have carefully honed here chasing Charlie will be valuable back in the world."

"Especially if you have a rat problem," Loc Tin replied.

"Damn straight," Dordi grinned. They clapped each other on the shoulder and parted as brothers. Loc Tin was happy for him but also sad to see his friend and compatriot leave. Dennis Dordi was about the only thing that made life in camp tolerable, and he knew he would be dead by now if not for him. Later that night after another six-hour stint walking the perimeter, Loc Tin gratefully collapsed onto his bunk. The mattress immediately fell to the floor. Someone had removed the supporting slats. Loc Tin yelled, "Dordi, you damn asshole!!" But even as he said it, he was laughing.

Finally, Loc Tin's own service requirement was up and he too was going home. Loc Tin, Binh, and several others who had also been released from service climbed onto the same canvas-covered trucks that had brought them to Duc Lap two years before. They didn't talk much, just settled in for the long drive back to the training camp. There some would be met by family, while others would try to catch another ride that would take them home. However, less than an hour into the trip, their convoy was ambushed by VC. Loc Tin survived the attack, but Binh and many others did not. It was February 1965.

In March of that same year, U.S. Marines landed on beaches near DaNang. Although U.S. Special Forces had been in-country "advising and training" since 1961, the Marines who landed on the beach that day were considered the first American combat troops to enter the country. In response, the Soviet government increased their support of North Vietnam. The war was escalating.

Chapter 13

It was Friday, the end of Ashley's first week at her new job, but she was still learning her way around. She knew everyone in her lab—Lance, of course, though she didn't see much of him. He didn't do bench work anymore and was usually in his office, which was a small room in the corner of the lab.

Aside from Lance and herself, there were three people in her lab. Jim, the lab manager, had a PhD in molecular biology and had worked with the CBF for six years. He seemed okay. He didn't say much but still managed to keep the lab running smoothly.

Christina was a research assistant just out of college. Lance said she was "really green, but also really smart." She planned to go back to school for her PhD but wanted to get some work experience first.

Ted was a Research Assistant III, same as Ashley. He was nice enough but talked all the time. Predictably, Ted was the one, who upon being introduced to her asked, "England? Like the country?" But at least he refrained from adding the joke about her southern accent. She thought he would run out of things to talk about after a few days, but he never did. She found the constant chatter distracting. She took Christina's advice and started wearing headphones to discourage conversation. She wasn't actually listening to anything, but Ted didn't have to know that.

She liked the way the lab was set up. She had her own bench and some of her own equipment, but she quickly realized the work was very routine.

At UCSD, every day was different—sometimes frustratingly so. Priorities were constantly shifting, and at the time she found it upsetting. She could never plan her day, and it was hard to even plan a day off. Some experiments would take days and would require her to come in over the weekend, which she came to resent. Whenever Dr. Jansen was working on a new grant, everyone would drop whatever they were working on to get some critical piece of data she needed before submission. The work was important, but she wanted a life too. She thought working in a forensics lab would be just as important but more interesting—exciting even. But now that she was here, she felt a different kind of frustration. Every day was the same—sequence this sample, amplify that sample. She began to understand why Ted was so chatty.

Finally it was lunchtime, and she and Christina took the elevator down to the first floor and walked to the cafeteria. Christina had brought her lunch and headed toward the microwaves. Ashley went to check out the day's hot meal selection. As Christina walked away, Ashley called out, "Find us a table?"

"Sure thing—probably near a window."

Ashley made her selection—roast chicken and veggies. She thought about bread but decided against it. She grabbed a bottle of water, paid, and found Christina.

They ate and made small talk. Christina told her as much as she could about the other labs and technicians, although she herself had only been at CBF for about six months.

Halfway through their lunch, Ashley noticed someone she had not seen before. "Who is that?" she asked Christina, pointing as surreptitiously as she could.

Christina looked in the direction Ashley indicated and smiled, "Oh, that's Ben. He's a Criminal Intelligence Analyst." The questioning look from Ashley prompted her to continue, "As best I understand, he uses logic to analyze data from a crime scene to figure out stuff."

"Like a profiler?" Ashley asked.

"Not exactly. He can explain it better. He works a lot with Rhonda in the genealogy lab. Want me to introduce you?"

"Well, yeah. He's cute. Is he single?" Ashley asked, taking a bite of her lunch.

"Umm…I think so. He was dating someone last year, but I'm pretty sure they broke up."

Ashley nodded and continued watching Ben. He looked to be around her age—late twenties or maybe early thirties; medium height and muscular, but not overly so. His hair was dark and very short—almost military-like. He was getting coffee and making small talk with Julie while she prepared his order. She laughed at something he said.

Christina took a bite of her sandwich just as Ben turned in their direction. She waved him over. Ashley looked at her anxiously, "Don't embarrass me."

Christina smiled, "No worries. Just introducing the new kid to the old guard."

Ben reached their table, pulled out a chair and joined them, "Hey, Chrissy." He turned to Ashley, "Hi. I'm Ben. Ben Franklin."

"Ben Franklin? Like Benjamin Franklin?" Ashley couldn't believe she just said that. It's as bad as, "Funny—you don't sound English." She wanted to crawl under the table.

Ben sighed. "Yes, exactly like that."

"I'm Ashley. Ashley England. Like the country." What is wrong with me!? Ashley thought. I sound like a moron.

"Well, Ashley like the country, it is nice to meet you. What brings you to the CBF?"

They chatted a few minutes discussing the usual things, where were you previously and where did you go to school. Christina finished her lunch and made an excuse to leave. She said to Ashley, "I'll see you back in the lab." She turned to go but then turned back and said, "Don't forget—Lance likes us to have happy hour together first Friday of the month. Tonight's the night. 5:00 P.M. at Rita's across the street." She looked at Ben, "Ash is interested in genealogy and that logic stuff that you do. Maybe you and Rhonda should join us."

Ashley suppressed a groan. Subtle, Christina. Real subtle. But Ben just smiled, "I think Rhonda has something with her kids tonight. But I'm in. Thanks."

Right at 5:00, Lance, Ashley, the rest of their lab, and Ben gathered at Rita's for happy hour. It was fun—a good group of people made even better by a bit of alcohol. Even Ted was less annoying when she wasn't trying to work. Around 7:00, people started to drift out.

Ashley got up to leave, but Ben stopped her, "Hey, you haven't finished your wine." He motioned to his nearly full beer, "I'll keep you company."

Ashley smiled, unsure. Everyone else was leaving. But he *was* cute. And he seemed nice. She sat back down. With everyone else gone, she suddenly felt nervous and was trying to think of something clever to say. Instead she blurted out what she had been thinking all night, "I can't believe your mother named you Benjamin Franklin."

Ben paused and looked down at his beer. "Actually, she didn't. I was Benjamin Perez. But then my parents died in a car accident when I was two and I went into foster care. I was adopted when I was three. My adoptive parents were Franklin," he shrugged, "so I became Benjamin Franklin." Ben took a sip of his beer without making eye contact.

"Oh," Ashley responded, "I'm so sorry."

He shook his head setting the bottle on the table. "No, it's okay." He hesitated a moment, but then continued without looking at her, "Actually, it was much worse for my sister....Aretha."

Ashley stared at him blankly, searching for the appropriate response. But then Ben laughed. She realized he was joking, and she laughed as well.

"Sorry. People ask me about the name all the time. So I tend to make jokes about it." He looked away from her and started picking at the label on his beer. After a long pause he continued, "I really was adopted, but I don't have a sister. I just say that sometimes—probably to deflect from the whole dead parents/foster kid story."

"I *totally* get it." Ashley smiled but inside she was mortified. Totally? Who am I? Valley girl? She screamed at herself in her head.

But Ben didn't seem to notice. They continued talking and eventually ordered dinner. Over the course of the meal, Ashley learned Ben had joined the National Guard after high school as a way to pay for college. After college, he enlisted in the Marine Corps and became a human intelligence analyst.

"What does that mean exactly?" She asked.

"Well, I had a variety of responsibilities. Basically, I analyzed all kinds of data. I would study and interpret surveillance video or other photographic evidence. I took part in debriefings, and on occasion I was involved in interrogating prisoners. When I was in Afghanistan, one of the most important things was to take a variety of different data—sometimes conflicting—and try to make sense of it, what was real, what was accurate." He shrugged, "Not so different than what I do for the CBI."

"You were in Afghanistan?" she asked, surprised.

Ben nodded, "Four years. 3rd Battalion, 5th Marine Regiment. We were stationed in the left Helmand Province. I got out in 2018."

"Thank you for your service," Ashley said softly. Although she meant it, she always felt the sentiment was inadequate, never quite conveying how grateful she truly was for men and women that willingly put their lives on the line for the rest of the nation. The two were silent for a few minutes, each lost in their own thoughts. Finally Ashley asked the question on her mind, "The oil fires and burn pits—were you exposed?" Oil fires were common in both Iraq and Afghanistan—some of them intentionally set. Burn pits had been used by the military in both countries to destroy waste—any kind of waste, including paint, computers, medical waste, and even unexploded ammunition. The smoke produced by the burn pits was filled with toxicants and created very unhealthy air for the soldiers.

Ben nodded, "Yeah, some. Hard to completely avoid in-country. Fortunately, I was usually able to stay upwind. I never had to stand watch over the pits the way some guys did." He sipped his beer, "That's an odd question. Most civilians ask me if I shot anyone or if I was hurt."

She pondered this for a moment and then responded, "In a way I am asking if you were hurt. A lot of veterans are suffering the effects of exposure to toxic fumes from the oil fires and burn pits. The oil fires couldn't be helped, I suppose, but the burn pits...those are a really bad idea." She shook her head.

"How do you know about burn pits?" he asked, genuinely surprised.

Ashley sat up and leaned forward, "Because of my research. Well, the research I used to do." She became animated—gesturing with her hands as she talked. "The burn pits produce hundreds, if not thousands, of toxicants, including dioxin—the same chemical present in Agent Orange that's been linked to a whole bunch of diseases in Vietnam veterans. I spent five years studying the effects of dioxin with Dr. Beverly Jansen at UCSD." She paused, took a sip of wine, and then continued, "It just makes me sick. You think we would have learned *something* from Vietnam. But noooo." She gestured wildly, glass in hand, "A whole 'nother generation of veterans—and very likely their children—will suffer because of it. It's like Agent Orange 2.0."

Ben wasn't sure how to respond, so he changed the subject. "I think it might be time to cut you off. Your Mississippi is showing."

"My what?" She looked at him confused for a moment before realizing what he meant. "Oh, the accent? Yeah, it really comes out when I drink. I should probably stop." She set her glass down and looked at it, making an exaggerated sad face.

He laughed, set his beer aside, and then ordered them both coffee. They talked a while longer, and then Ben walked Ashley to her car.

"Well," Ashley said, awkwardly, "good night. See you Monday."

Ben nodded, "See you Monday."

Ashley got in her car and watched Ben in her rearview mirror as he watched her drive away. She liked him and wanted to get to know him better. She wondered if he felt the same way.

Chapter 14

Rural Vietnam, 1965-1968
  Loc Tin

Although Loc Tin survived the attack on the convoy, the injuries he
sustained significantly delayed his return home. But finally in April of
1965, he arrived at the family farm in rural Vietnam northwest of DaNang.
In his absence Bao had married and his sister Cai had been killed. She had
started working at the parochial school in the village and was attacked and
murdered on her way home the year before. Everyone suspected VC, but
no one knew for sure who had killed her or why. Loc Tin's mother had
been completely grief-stricken. However, two months ago, Bao and his
wife had a baby, and the joy of becoming a grandmother helped to distract
her from the pain of losing her daughter.

In 1967, 22-year-old Loc Tin married 20-year-old Kim Anh Tran who
was from a village farther south. The marriage had been arranged by Loc
Tin and Kim's mothers, as was common in Vietnam at that time. After the
wedding, Kim moved to the Vong family farm, and the young couple hoped
to start a family of their own.

Unfortunately, the war was going badly for South Vietnam, despite
the ever-increasing contingent of Western forces that provided soldiers,
equipment, and other support. The South Vietnamese government, upon
recommendations from their American advisors, decreed that more men
were needed to fight against the communists and VC forces. Shortly
thereafter in 1968, the government of South Vietnam announced that all

men between the ages of 18 and 33 were eligible for conscription. Older men with needed medical or technical expertise would also be drafted. Finally, all veterans up to age 45 were to immediately report for military service. And so, after less than three years with their family intact, the Vongs and many other families watched helplessly as the majority of their sons and husbands were forced into military service for an unspecified period of time. Loc Tin and Bao were grateful that their father, who was still strong and in good health, was too old to be drafted. He and his shotgun would be the only defense the family had if the VC decided to attack. On January 15, 1968, Loc Tin and Bao left their family with heavy hearts.

Unlike the last time the brothers had been conscripted, there would be no three months of training this time. Bao was sent South to Nha Trang to join the infantry division stationed there. Loc Tin was headed to the 1st Infantry Division, which was based in Hue, in the northernmost part of South Vietnam. It was just 100 kilometers from the demilitarized zone that divided North and South Vietnam along the 17th parallel. Hue was known for being home to the Imperial City, a walled complex built in the early 1800s for the self-proclaimed Emperor of Vietnam, Gia Long. To Loc Tin's surprise, the trucks carrying the veteran conscripts entered the citadel, the fortified part of Hue that contained the Imperial Palace. They drove past the famous site without stopping and quickly reached their destination. The base camp of the 1st Infantry was far different from that of the 7th. Where the 7th was surrounded by jungle, the 1st was surrounded by multiple waterways as well as a *wall*. Loc Tin learned that Hue was also home to U.S. Navy supply boats and that Highway 1, which ran through the city, was a supply line for both American and ARVN forces. Loc Tin felt that Hue must be one of the safest cities in the country. Unfortunately, Loc Tin would soon find out Hue was not impenetrable despite the wall and waterways that surrounded it.

The major holiday, Tet, which celebrated the Lunar New Year, was fast approaching and many members of the 1st Division had been granted leave. However, whether based on intelligence or just a gut feeling, the commander of the 1st began recalling his soldiers, fearing the NVA would take advantage of the holiday. Indeed, on January 31, 1968, the North Vietnamese army and their Viet Cong guerrilla forces led a country-wide coordinated attack on more than 100 cities across Vietnam. Hue was one of the first cities to come under attack. Thousands of NVA soldiers and VC guerrillas descended upon Hue and quickly occupied much of the city. Multiple ARVN divisions as well as American Marines and U.S. and Vietnamese Special Forces were called in to defend the city and regain control. It would take nearly a month of fighting, often going house-to-house, before the communist forces were driven back.

Once the fighting had ceased, in the city of Hue alone thousands of civilians were injured or killed and the military casualties were staggering. Much of the city had been destroyed, and the citadel was also heavily damaged. Across South Vietnam the story was the same—the loss of life and destruction of property was astounding, but in the end the NVA and VC had been defeated militarily by the joint efforts of Western forces and ARVN troops. Nevertheless, the communists had won an important and significant emotional victory that took a toll on the South Vietnamese soldiers as well as their Western allies. News of the Tet Offensive quickly reached the U.S. and contributed to the growing anti-war sentiment in that country.

Loc Tin's training and past experiences served him well during the Battle of Hue. He not only survived the siege but also distinguished himself for both his bravery and his cunning. At the height of the fighting, Loc Tin and a few other men from the 1st Division were attempting to take out a sniper that was firing from the roof of a multistory building. The sniper was keeping the ARVN from advancing, but the man could not be reached because the building was booby-trapped, a common tactic of the VC. Several soldiers had already been mortally wounded trying to reach the sniper from inside of the building.

Loc Tin stood back and surveyed the building carefully and then developed a plan. Behind the building that held the sniper was a large two-story warehouse with a flat roof. They found a long rope and would attempt to secure it to the railing of a balcony on the building with the sniper. Once on the balcony, Loc Tin felt confident he could climb up to the roof, although it would require climbing from one balcony to another on the next-higher floor. It was a dangerous plan but the only one that seemed feasible.

Loc Tin and two men who would provide cover if anyone started shooting at him set the plan in motion. They tied a hook to the rope to help it catch the railing, and the men took turns trying to land the rope just right. Loc Tin tried twice and failed both times. But the second man, a rancher from the central highlands of Vietnam, hooked the railing on his first attempt. They quickly tied the rope off, and Loc Tin began to shinny across it to the balcony. It was a span of about 30 feet, two stories up. If he fell, he would probably survive with only a dozen or more broken bones. Loc Tin assumed the VC had not bothered to booby trap the outside of the building, but he would soon find out if he was wrong. In his head, he heard Dennis Dordi say, "Dude, you are *crazy*."

He made it to the balcony and easily pulled himself over the rail. He sighed with relief that there were no explosions—no booby traps. As planned, he took the rope and swung it toward the balcony above him. He hooked the rail without difficult and climbed up. He repeated the process until he was on the 6th floor. One floor to go. But on the next attempt, on the last balcony, the hook hit the railing and bounced off. As it fell, Loc Tin lost his grip on the rope and watched helplessly as it sailed past him. He leaned over the railing and looked at the rope far below him. "Damn," he said. He looked up at the last balcony and said, "Damn," again.

But he had to find a way to keep going. The rail was thin—too thin to balance on to try to jump. He looked around for anything he could use. There was a sturdy little table that held a potted plant with bright red flowers. He tossed the plant aside and set the table near the railing. It was not as high as the railing, but he thought if he stood on the table he could step on the rail and launch himself toward the balcony that was above and to the side of where he now stood. He didn't think very long—lest he think about the consequences of failure. He climbed onto the table, rubbed his hands together, and focused on the spot he needed to reach. He took a deep breath and then stepped onto the rail. With all of his strength, he launched himself toward the balcony. His left hand missed but his right hand caught hold at the bottom of the corner rail. He flailed for a minute, bloodying his nose as his body swung around and his face hit the concrete floor of the balcony. He ignored the pain and grabbed another rail with his left hand. With strength and flexibility that he did not know he possessed, he swung his legs upward, hooking his left leg over the top of the rail. From there, he was easily able to pull himself over and onto the floor of the balcony. Exhausted from the effort, he took a moment to breathe.

The sound of the sniper fire motivated him to move again—he had to complete his mission. The 7th floor balcony had no covering since there was not a balcony above it. All he had to do now was get to the roof. Without the rope and hook, he needed a new plan. He opened the window that looked out over the balcony—realizing a moment too late that it could have been booby-trapped. Clearly it wasn't or he would be dead. With the window open, he put one foot on the window ledge and one on the railing. The added height the maneuver gave him made it possible to grab the sloped edge of the roof. Now, he thought to himself, it is just a simple pull-up. Easy. He would have no time to think when he landed on the roof, so he thought through his plan now. Based on the sound, the sniper should be just in front of him and to the right. All he had to do was land on the roof and take him out. Simple. Would there be a lookout behind him? They had not seen one from the warehouse and no one had noticed him climbing up, so probably not. Anyway, he was about to find out.

He took a deep breath and using nothing but strength and determination he pulled himself up. The instant he landed on the roof, he grabbed the knife from its ankle holster and threw it. With a thud, it landed squarely in the man's back. The sniper dropped his gun and fell to the ground. Loc Tin ran to him and put a bullet in his head just to be sure he was dead.

He holstered the pistol and looked around. With the sniper taken out, Loc Tin realized he had two choices. Dodge booby traps in the stairway or go back down the way he came. Neither option held any appeal. As he tried to think of a third option, he pulled his knife from the sniper's back and wiped it on the dead man's clothes. Just then, the door to the roof swung open. Instinctively, Loc Tin jumped up, ready to throw the knife—but to his great relief, the three men who entered were American. U.S. Special Forces. Loc Tin surmised that they had been dispatched to disarm the booby traps.

"How the hell did you get up here, LT?" a confused, but familiar voice asked.

Loc Tin smiled and shook his head, "Well, Dordi, I was just wondering what the hell took you so long?"

After the siege and the city of Hue was once again secured, Loc Tin made his way to the nearby American base where Dordi and his team were temporarily housed. They had been sent to Hue during the siege but would soon return to DaNang. In the meantime, Dordi had promised him a beer. The Americans, he thought, they always had beer and cigarettes. And they were always willing to share.

He met Dordi in his barracks, which the Americans referred to as a hooch. Everyone was gathered around the radio listening to "Hanoi Hannah."

Loc Tin didn't understand why they listened to her. Everyone knew it was mostly just propaganda from the North. But the men listened. They often yelled at her or threw cans at the radio when she told them to desert or to kill their captain. However, they liked it when she played music, even if it was music in protest of the war. And when she read the news from the States, the room got quiet. This, the men said, was the main reason they listened to her.

After Hanoi Hannah had finished reading the latest news about war protests in America, Dordi grabbed two beers and the men sat on an empty bunk away from the others. Without preamble, Loc Tin asked the question he had been thinking ever since seeing Dordi burst onto the roof. "Why did you come back? You were home. No fighting."

"Well…," Dordi rubbed his chin and responded, "I was home, but I can't say there was no fighting. Man…the States…they're just different now. I went to California. Looked up my friend. He said he didn't have anything for me. But I could tell by the way he looked at me, he didn't *want* to give me a job. Nobody wants to hire a vet." He sipped his beer. "Maybe I don't blame them. The whole country is pissed off. The hippies hate the war. The old guys hate the hippies. A lot of clashes. You know, I got spit on a couple of times? Even without the uniform, the hair gave me away as a vet." He took another long pull of his beer, "Maaannn, I could not *wait* to get home. And then after a couple of months of being there, all I wanted was to come back. Finally, I did. As fucked up as this war is, at least I fit in." He finished his beer and grabbed another.

Loc Tin had no idea what to say to his friend. He didn't understand America. Why would they treat their soldiers so poorly? Why send so many men to die in Vietnam if the people didn't support the war? Finally, Loc Tin said truthfully, "Well, for what it's worth, I was damn glad to see you on that roof." He took a sip of his beer, "And I will get you back for the mattress prank." Both men laughed.

Chapter 15

Agent Orange
1948-1960

A state of emergency was declared in the British colony of Malaya (now Malaysia) in June of 1948 when the Chinese-backed Malayan Communist Party began attacking rubber plantations, mines, and police stations. They also derailed trains and burned the homes of civilians. The British responded by sending in troops and by using the chemical herbicides identified during World War II to destroy both the insurgents food crops and the jungle where they hid. The use of deforestation agents by the British in Malaya set a critical precedent that would later be used by the American Defense Department as justification for the use of similar chemical weapons in Vietnam.

Chapter 16

Memoir: The beginning

I killed many men during the war. No doubt, some did not deserve their fate. We were all doing the bidding of our governments and fighting for a cause we hoped was just. Loss of life was the cost of war. After the war ended—although does it ever really end in the minds of those who survived it?—I vowed my killing days were over. But it wasn't long before I broke that vow.

My first civilian kill was not planned. I had been out late, and it was nearing midnight when I headed home. Hungry, I stopped at one of those convenience stores that sells premade sandwiches. I was the only patron. I spoke to the young man working. He could not have been more than 18. He had red hair with a lot of freckles. He smiled and waved to me when I spoke and asked if I needed any help. When I said no, he nodded and returned his attention to the comic book he was reading as he sat behind the counter. I remember thinking he was lucky. When I was his age, I was slogging through the jungle carrying a rifle and trying not to die. But I held no resentment. I was glad the country was at peace and he had no fear of being drafted.

I quickly headed to the back of the store where the deli case was located. As I picked out the freshest-looking sandwich I could find—turkey and cheese on wheat with lettuce that was only slightly wilted—I heard the bell indicate the entrance of another customer. I am not a tall man and could not see over the shelves that lined the small store. But I heard the new arrival clearly. A man's gruff voice said, "Open the register! Hand over the money or I shoot!" I heard the register open, but almost immediately a shot rang out. I raced to the front of the store. The thief had set his gun down and was leaning over the counter pulling money out of the register. The boy was not visible. I came up quietly behind the man, grabbed his head, and hit it hard against the unyielding, metal register, knocking him out. I jumped over the counter and found the boy dead. He had been shot point-blank in the head. Blood oozed from the wound and pooled over the cartoon characters in his book. Being careful not to leave fingerprints, I dialed 911. I didn't respond when the operator answered, just dropped the phone with the line open next to the boy. I turned my attention back to the thief. I was enraged. The boy should not have died. Without making a conscious decision, I picked up the man's head in both my hands and twisted hard, snapping his neck. I jumped over the counter and left, sirens wailing in the distance as I drove away.

I heard the story on the news the next day. The boy—named Toby—had just graduated from high school and had been working to save money so he could attend the local community college in a couple of years. According to his mother, a Vietnam war widow, he had hoped to own his own business someday. The police were confused by the scene. The young man had died instantly, yet apparently killed his attacker and dialed 911. Obviously, there was another individual in the store—but who was it? And why take off? But the police had no leads, and the case eventually went cold. Soon I heard no more about it. Honestly, it felt good knowing the bastard that had taken Toby's life was now rotting in hell instead of on the loose to hurt someone else. It wasn't long after that that I started planning other death sentences. I would carry out justice when the system could not or would not. The army had made me a killing machine. I would just continue the work they had trained me to do.

Chapter 17

Agent Orange
1961

The widespread use of chemical defoliants in Vietnam began in 1961. The military campaign was originally dubbed, "Operation Hades" but was ultimately changed to "Operation Ranch Hand." Although "hades" was more accurate, it was determined to be too inflammatory for a call sign.

The various combinations of defoliants used were shipped in 55-gallon drums and were given nicknames based on the color of the stripe on the black barrels—Agent Green, Agent Blue, Agent Pink, Agent Purple, Agent White, Agent Orange. Of these, Agent Orange was the most toxic to plants and animals, including humans.

Chapter 18

Loc Tin was decidedly anti-communist, but he resented being conscripted a second time. He felt it unlikely that he and his brother Bao would both survive what looked to be an unending war. However, there was a ray of hope that things would finally start to turn around. After the Tet Offensive, the South Vietnamese government finally acknowledged that ARVN soldiers were not receiving adequate training and "combined operations" were implemented. Instead of Americans simply advising the South Vietnamese Army commanders, starting in 1968, ARVN soldiers began conducting training and other activities alongside the U.S. forces. Of course, Dordi had been training Loc Tin for a long time, but now it was official. After Tet, at Loc Tin's request, he began the rigorous training required to join the ARVN Special Forces. His new unit was attached to the U.S. 5th Special Forces Group—Dordi's unit—which was currently based in DaNang.

He reported to his new unit in April of 1968 only to find the Americans abnormally somber. A man Loc Tin had never heard of—Martin Luther King, Jr—had been assassinated in a place called Memphis. Loc Tin learned that he was a civil rights leader pushing for racial equality.

"What does that mean?" Loc Tin asked Dordi.

"You know how the Vietnamese believe in racial purity?" Dordi asked.

Loc Tin nodded. Loc Tin knew well the importance his society placed on being Vietnamese. Mixed-race children fathered by Westerners were not allowed to attend school or hold a job. Many were abandoned by their families and lived on the street. Even the Montagnards, an indigenous population of the country, were much maligned by most Vietnamese who considered them second-class citizens.

Dordi continued, "Well, it isn't that bad in the States, but Blacks don't always get fair treatment. In a lot of places the schools are still segregated—one school for whites and another—usually not as good—for Blacks. King was one of the leaders that was trying to change that. And the country was making progress." Dordi shook his head, "His being killed—it's bad. Really bad. The Black soldiers—suddenly they don't trust the rest of us. I haven't changed, but things aren't the same now."

"Do they know who killed him?" Loc Tin asked.

"I don't think so—not yet anyway. I wish I knew who did it, though. I'd take him out myself." He said, drawing his finger across his neck. Then he sighed heavily and shook his head again. He looked at his friend, "This is just really bad, LT."

Loc Tin nodded as though he understood, but he really didn't. He had lived and worked with the Americans for years now. It didn't seem to him that they cared about race. Black and white soldiers ate together, slept in the same barracks, and protected each other in the field. Some of the Special Forces were even working with the Montagnards and training them to be soldiers. The Americans he knew loved the Vietnamese children—and especially went out of their way to help the mixed-race kids living on the streets. And he had yet to meet an American soldier who didn't think Vietnamese women were beautiful. From his perspective, race didn't seem to matter to them. Once again, he was confused by America. Was the country so different from Dordi and the other men he had met?

A month after transferring to the Special Forces, Loc Tin received devastating news from his family. He learned that his father had been killed during the Tet Offensive. Shortly thereafter, Bao's baby had fallen ill and also died. The three women, all grieving, were left alone to fend for themselves. Like so many other soldiers, Loc Tin decided to bring his family to the base. He knew that they would be far too vulnerable in the countryside with his father gone and all the young men from their village in the army. When he was finally granted leave in June of 1968, he borrowed a Jeep and left for home. He found only his mother and wife at what was left of his family farm. Bao had returned for his wife earlier and had offered to take all of the women with him. However, Kim steadfastly refused to leave, knowing that Loc Tin would come for her. Naturally, his mother refused to leave Kim alone. Although the women had been able to keep up much of the garden, most of the animals had been stolen or slaughtered by bandits. Only a few chickens remained. They packed up what they could, including the chickens, and Loc Tin drove them to DaNang.

When they arrived in DaNang, his mother was saddened to see how different the city looked from her days there as a child. Located along the South China Sea, the city had always had a coastline lush with vegetation. But that was all gone now. Loc Tin explained to her that the U.S. Air Force routinely sprayed the coastline with Agent Orange to kill the vegetation and keep the area clear. He told her that by preventing the growth of forest and other plants, it made it hard for the VC to ambush the supply ships when they docked for unloading. His mother asked no more questions, but the sadness in her eyes was evident.

When they reached the civilian camp outside the ARVN base, Loc Tin was surprised to see that it had nearly doubled in size in the week he had been gone. The tent city, which had always been attached to the base, was now nearly as large as the base itself. Civilian tent cities located near ARVN bases were common in South Vietnam and were a constant hub of activity. When on base, many soldiers would spend their down time in the civilian camp, even if they did not have family of their own. The single men could pay other men's families to cook and do their laundry. The married men would typically spend nights with their wives, and Loc Tin was no exception. When any of the soldiers were away from camp on missions, those remaining on the base kept watch over all the families. Loc Tin trusted these men, and now with Kim and his mother safely inside the civilian camp, he turned his attention back to his training. He was determined to live up to the Special Forces reputation.

Chapter 19

"Hi, Ashley!" Her mom had picked up the phone after the first ring. "I'm so glad you called! How is the new job?"

Ashley sighed, "It's okay. People are nice enough." Ashley had just left her lab and was driving home, careful to use her hands-free device so she wasn't pulled over and ticketed.

"Well, you don't sound very enthusiastic."

"No, it's okay. I just feel like I do the same thing all day, every day."

"You're not getting to put criminals in jail?"

Ashley smiled, "I'm not a lawyer." But she knew what her mother meant. "I just analyze DNA. I am not really connected to the cases. I thought I would be. I just do PCR and WGS all day."

"You know those letters don't mean anything to me," her mother admonished.

"I know," Ashley paused while she changed lanes. "PCR is just amplifying DNA. Like making copies. If you don't have enough to analyze, you just keep copying it until you do. It is a really powerful technique. Back in the nineties, someone won a Nobel Prize for developing it. But once you know how to do it, which I do, it isn't all that difficult."

"And what's that other thing?"

"WGS. Whole genome sequencing. That's just where you read someone's DNA. Well, not exactly. More like transcribing. Basically I use an expensive

63

piece of equipment to identify a person's DNA sequence. Everyone's is unique—except for identical twins, although they can have some minor variations. Anyway, the sequence gets handed over to someone else who does the analysis. I guess that just makes me the middleman. It isn't very interesting."

"Well," her mother said, "you have only been there a couple of months. Once they get to know you, maybe more opportunities will open up."

"Maybe. I hope so." The two women continued to chat for most of Ashley's 45-minute commute. Ashley purposely avoided mentioning Ben. That probably wasn't going anywhere anyway. Just before hanging up, she promised her mom she would call again soon.

Chapter 20

Cam Ranh Bay, Vietnam, 1969
 Dennis Dordi and Linh

Dordi had been given four days of R&R and he fully intended to use it. He had sex and alcohol on his mind, and he knew Cam Ranh Bay was the place to get both. He parked his Jeep in front of the first bar he came to—a place called the "Yankee's Dream." He walked into the dingy, poorly lit bar and scanned the room. Even though it was early afternoon, the place was full. Mostly American soldiers on R&R like he was, but a few Vietnamese—whether they were ARVN or NVA, he couldn't be sure. No one wore a uniform. There were also civilian men, both Western and Vietnamese. You could pick out the civilians because they were softer and the look in the eyes was different. They had not seen the same things the soldiers had seen, and the eyes gave it away.

Dordi spotted an open seat at the bar and quickly made his way to claim it. He ordered a beer and continued his survey of the room. A couple of Vietnamese women, obviously prostitutes, worked the room looking for their next trick. They were scantily dressed and attractive, but for reasons he could not explain, they did nothing for Dordi. Disappointed, he sipped his beer and debated whether to make small talk with the bartender. He waved to the man behind the bar to get his attention. He looked in Dordi's direction and began yelling in Vietnamese, *"Ra! Ra!"*

Dordi was confused for a moment. Why was the bartender ordering him out? Then he realized the man's attention was behind him. He turned and saw a small boy—maybe six years old—dirty and barefoot standing nearby. The bartender was yelling at him. The boy held out his hand, clearly pleading for something. The bartender yelled again, *"Ra! Ra!"* and threw an empty bottle at the boy. It struck him in the head and knocked him down. Dordi jumped up, went to the child, and helped him up. Now the bartender yelled at him, "Don't waste your energy on him. He needs to leave."

Dordi didn't understand the man's aggressive behavior, "He's just a child."

"He is a beggar. We don't want him here. He needs to get out." He looked at the boy and snarled, *"Ra!"*

Dejected, the child turned and left the bar.

Dordi looked back at the bartender, "He's starving."

"Not my problem. He is the child of some soldier. His problem, not mine. Mixed breeds are not welcome here." Then the man's demeanor completely changed. He smiled at Dordi, "Get you another beer? Something to eat?" He winked, "Maybe a lady friend?"

Disgusted, Dordi shook his head. He threw some money on the counter next to his half-finished beer. Outside, he saw the little boy again and followed him. He went into the alley between the bar and a restaurant. Behind the restaurant, the child started picking through the garbage, clearly looking for something to eat. Dordi walked toward him, intending to buy him a meal when the back door of the restaurant opened and a man started yelling at the boy, *"Ra! Ra!"* The boy held out his hand and said something. In response, the man jumped off the small porch and punched the boy in the jaw. The small child fell to the ground, unconscious. Without thinking, Dordi ran to the man and kicked him in the gut. He then grabbed the man's head and twisted, snapping his neck. He picked up the boy and started walking, although he didn't know where he was going.

When he was a couple of blocks away from the restaurant, Dordi became aware that he was being watched. He stopped and looked around but saw no one. Cam Ranh Bay was off-limits as far as the war was concerned—at least that was the rumor. There was no North versus South in Cam Ranh Bay. Both sides enjoyed R&R here and both sides wanted to keep it that way. So who was following him? He walked a few more yards and then whipped around quickly—there! He saw someone dart out of view a moment too late.

"I know you are there! Show yourself," he said in rudimentary Vietnamese.

A few moments passed with nothing happening. Then a teenage girl appeared from the bushes along the alleyway.

Dordi took in the girl. "Why are you following me?" he asked, struggling with the Vietnamese words.

She looked defiantly at him. She held her head high and stood up straight. Dordi thought she was trying to make herself look taller. "Where are you taking my brother?" she asked in a mix of English and Vietnamese.

Dordi had almost forgotten about the boy he carried—he weighed almost nothing. "He's hurt and hungry. I wanted to get him away from...from...," he looked back in the direction he had come from as he searched for the right words, "...people that wanted to hurt him."

She stepped toward him, holding out her arms. "I will take him."

Now that she was closer, he realized how thin she was. Like the boy, she was also dirty and barefoot.

"Where do you live?" Dordi asked.

She shrugged, "Around."

"Show me."

"Why?"

"Let me buy you and your brother something to eat."

She shook her head and stepped back, "I am not for sale!" she said in perfect English—clearly a phrase she had used many times.

"No, that's not what I meant." Dordi was appalled. She was little more than a child. "No I wanted to buy the boy something to eat. He was kicked out of the bar I was in, and then I saw him going through the garbage. A man punched him, and I...I...dealt with him."

"You! You killed Hung?" She stepped toward him again, smiling as she pulled the boy from Dordi's arms. He was now conscious and confused. He wrapped his arms around his sister's neck. "I saw his dead body. Good riddance to him. A terrible man." She gently pried the boy's arms from her neck and set him down. He hid behind her, clinging to her skirt.

"Let me buy you and your brother something to eat. Any restaurant you want."

She shook her head, "No restaurant will serve us."

"Even if you're with me? I have money."

She could tell he didn't understand so she explained, "No. We are not welcome anywhere because we are not pure Vietnamese." She pointed to the boy, "His father was an American soldier. I don't know who my father was, but he was definitely *not* Vietnamese."

He looked at the girl again. Her hair was long and dark and her eyes almond shaped, but her skin was different. Not white, not black, not yellow. It was golden—like she had a permanent tan. He thought she was beautiful—exotic even. But that wouldn't matter. He looked at her a moment longer and then turned to the little boy. He had not noticed before, but his father was clearly Black. He would never be able to hide the fact that he was mixed. Finally, he looked back at the girl and said, "Show me where you live. I will buy you food and bring it to you."

She looked at him—defiant again. "No—I am not a prostitute."

"Please, Linh. I am so hungry," the little boy whimpered.

Dordi shook his head again, "I want nothing from you. I promise."

"Please, Linh," the little boy was now crying.

Linh looked at the malnourished child that clung to her and then back at Dordi. "No sex?"

He shook his head. "No sex."

Linh took a deep breath and nodded. Dordi could tell she didn't quite trust him—and he couldn't blame her. Nevertheless, she led the way to a small farmer's market where Dordi bought fruit, vegetables and dried fish for her and her little brother—though he learned they were not actually related. The boy had been abandoned when he was only a few months old. Linh had found him in the woods in a basket. She "adopted" him, though she herself had no real home and no means. She lived in a makeshift camp with a dozen other mixed-race children, and they survived any way that they could.

Linh was 15 the day Dordi met her. She told him that most of the girls her age had turned to prostitution to survive, but she had avoided that so far. "I know it is in my future, though," she told him sadly. "There are no other options for me."

Dordi didn't know what to say, but he knew she was right. Of all the unintended consequences of this damn war, the fatherless children had to be one of the most tragic.

Dordi spent his four days of R&R with Linh and the little boy named Teo. He bought them food and clothes and managed to procure a tent from a nearby U.S. Army base whose supply depot had been left inadequately attended.

A few months later, Dordi was again granted a few days of R&R and he returned to Cam Ranh Bay. He drove directly to the homeless camp where he found Teo but not Linh. The little boy told Dordi where to find her. "Linh is at the Yankee's Dream. She works there now."

Indeed, he saw her as soon as he walked into the bar. She was scantily dressed and laughing at something the soldier on whose lap she was sitting had said. When she saw Dordi in the doorway, her smile disappeared and she turned away.

Chapter 21

Memoir: Family Man

My family means everything to me. My wife, my children. It is my job to keep them safe—to protect them at all costs. Despite all my effort, I failed. I know what it is like to lose a child. The pain is unimaginable, and, without hesitation, I would give my own life in exchange for theirs. Isn't this the way a parent should feel? To love their child more than themselves? But then I read in the paper about this man named Addison. He was a husband and father to two beautiful little girls, but he killed them and his wife just so he could be with another woman. As many as I have killed, I could not comprehend what this man had done. The evidence against him was solid. But his attorney claimed Addison was mentally unfit to be tried and that he should be transferred to a mental hospital for evaluation. Unbelievably, the judge agreed. The entire state of Virginia—no—the country was outraged. Everyone was afraid the man would feign being confused or unstable and would ultimately be allowed to live out his days in the relative comfort of the mental hospital. But I would not let that happen.

The day came when he was to be transferred from the local jail to the mental hospital. They loaded him into the van, along with four others that would be taken to the medium security prison that was en route to the hospital. The van stopped at the prison, and the two police officers who traveled with them escorted the four convicted criminals inside. The murderous family man remained alone in the back of the van, the driver oblivious to my existence. The officers returned, climbed in beside the driver, and proceeded to the next stop. When the van reached the hospital, the two officers walked around to retrieve their prisoner. When they opened the doors, they found the man slumped on the floor, dead. His throat had been slit.

Since this was the third civilian I had killed in less than two years, they said I was a serial killer. The media needed a moniker, and so they gave me one. The Vigilante Virginian.

Chapter 22

Vietnam, 1970
  Loc Tin and Dordi

By the summer of 1970, Loc Tin had been with the Vietnamese Special Forces for nearly two years. He had carried out multiple search and destroy missions, he had parachuted into North Vietnam, and he had frequently conducted special reconnaissance missions behind enemy lines. Many times Dennis Dordi had been by his side. Together the two men seemed invincible. Tonight Loc Tin and Dordi would embark on yet another dangerous mission. They would enter Cambodia to retrieve a pilot who was being held captive. Although Cambodia was supposed to be neutral territory, it was well known that the enemy used that country for planning and staging operations and that numerous NVA and VC camps were located just inside its border. For these reasons, in March of 1969, the U.S. began a clandestine bombing campaign against communist force encampments in the region. Recently a secret recon mission had determined that an American pilot who had been shot down several months before was alive and being held by the NVA in an encampment located deep inside the Cambodian jungle that bordered Vietnam's central highlands.

This mission was especially dangerous because the U.S. and ARVN leadership would deny knowing about it if it failed. The men carried no ID and no dogtags. Loc Tin and Dordi would both wear uniforms devoid of any embellishments—no patches, no rank, no names. They had nothing on them that would indicate who they really were. If they were captured, there would be no rescue attempt. Traveling through enemy territory, Loc Tin could easily pass for NVA; however, anything more than a cursory look at Dordi would reveal his allegiance. His hair was dark, but he was taller than most Vietnamese and his round, blue eyes could not be disguised. Their goal was to not be seen. If they were, their orders were to kill before they were killed.

Their weapons, including the knives they carried, were Swedish made and could not be traced to the U.S. or other Western forces. Dordi also carried a bow and six arrows that he obtained from a Montagnard soldier who he had trained in Western combat tactics. Back in the States, Dordi had enjoyed bow hunting deer as a teenager. In Vietnam, the weapon had proven useful on more than one covert mission. Although not the typical weapon of choice of U.S. Special Forces, Dordi was anything but typical.

The only thing the men carried that could be problematic was the AN/PVS-2 starlight night vision scope. Undoubtedly U.S. Army-issue, but without it the men had no chance of successfully navigating the jungle at night. Although it made a high-pitched whining sound when in use, the jungle was alive with sounds of wildlife day and night which would aid in disguising the noise of the scope.

The mission, although dangerous, was straightforward. Under the cover of darkness, the helicopter would drop them into the jungle just a few kilometers into Cambodia. From there, the two men would be on their own to cover the remaining 20 kilometers—roughly 12 miles—before daybreak. When they reached their destination—a clandestine NVA camp—they were to find Captain Blizzard and rescue him. The three men would then make their way back to the original location just inside the Cambodian border. They had to be in and out in 12 hours. They had no radio. If they were not at the rendezvous point by 1200 hours, they would be on their own to make it back to friendly territory. In the event they were captured, both men had cyanide capsules—suicide pills. The NVA would not be kind if they were discovered. Although suicide pills were no longer commonly given out by the U.S. military, they could be obtained if you knew the wrong kind of people—and the Green Berets most definitely did.

As planned, just after midnight the helicopter flew the men a short distance into Cambodia. The men jumped from the craft as it hovered 10 feet above the ground. As soon as they were away, the chopper turned and was gone. The two men were now alone in the blackness of the jungle. Although they traveled light and without packs, the trek would not be easy. The jungle was nearly impenetrable, and they would have to wade through a small tributary in the darkness. But the men were determined. By 2:00 A.M., they were at the halfway point. They had seen no one and had not had to perform any evasive maneuvers. However, they were now at the bank of the "small tributary." The night vision scope revealed the breadth of the water to be far larger than anticipated. The water was also moving swiftly and its depth was impossible to determine. They would need to proceed cautiously.

Loc Tin pulled a 30-foot vine off the side of a banana tree near the riverbank. They managed to tie it to the base of a smaller tree and used it to prevent being swept downstream. Nevertheless, making it to the other side was difficult, and it took nearly an hour before both men were safely across. Anticipating that Captain Blizzard was likely not in peak condition, they tied the vine to another tree on the opposite side. With the vine anchored on either side, crossing the river would be infinitely easier. Whether or not the vine would still be there when they returned or whether they would find this exact spot on the return trip was anyone's guess.

They now had only two hours before daybreak. They pushed on, trying to make up time. The terrain was more rocky on this side of the river and the jungle no less dense. Loc Tin felt as though the trees were clawing at him in an effort to hold him back. He was not superstitious, but he still had the feeling that the jungle was telling him not to continue. But he did. The incessant, sometimes deafening, chirping of the crickets was both annoying and comforting. Silence in the jungle indicated the presence of a predator. Both men kept their pistols at the ready, less concerned about Charlie than being ambushed by one of the many tigers that roamed the area at night.

Finally, at 4:35 A.M., they had reached the outskirts of the NVA base camp. The jungle thinned ever so slightly, and there was the tell-tell sign of broken tree branches a few feet above the ground—indicating the movement of men who were not concerned about leaving a trail. They turned off the night vision scope to avoid it being heard by the guards patrolling the camp. Now the camp disappeared into the inky blackness that was Southeast Asia at night. Loc Tin and Dordi sat in silence and waited.

Just after 5:00 A.M., the sun began to cast a sliver of light across the horizon. It was enough to make out buildings, concertina wire, the patrolling guards, and punji sticks. Punji sticks were sharpened sticks with points that had been dipped in human excrement. They were driven into the ground at an angle and would rip into a man's skin above his boot. Painful, yes, but the greater concern was that without treatment a man would die slowly of sepsis.

According to the recon info that Loc Tin and Dordi had been given, Blizzard was in the third building from the back of the camp. It was the smallest and also the most heavily guarded. Guards were relieved at six-hour intervals. The sky grew lighter by the second. Time was of the essence. Loc Tin and Dordi silently made their way to the treeline closest to their target. Two guards were visible, suggesting a total of eight—two per side. If the data they had been given was accurate, the men guarding Blizzard would be relieved in 45 minutes. No time to waste.

Dordi pulled out his bow and shot the first man in the heart. Before the second man could fully comprehend what had happened, he too fell to the ground, dead. Without a word, Loc Tin and Dordi cut a hole in the concertina wire and cleared a small path through the punji sticks. Then they rushed to the building, each taking a side and tasked with killing three men each—if their assumption was correct that there would be six men left guarding the building. However, Loc Tin encountered no one on the South side of the building. Cautiously, he peered around the corner to check the back. One man stood with his back to the door of the building, Loc Tin to his right. No way to throw the knife. He would have to get closer. He watched and waited for an opportunity to strike, listening for any movement behind him. The man shifted on his feet and adjusted the weight of the rifle he had slung over his shoulder. It was just enough of a distraction for Loc Tin to strike. Two long strides and the knife Loc Tin carried slashed the man's throat. As the guard fell to the ground, he saw Dordi peek around the corner. The men exchanged the all-clear sign. The door to the building was locked, but Dordi quickly found the key on the guard Loc Tin had just killed.

Blizzard was alone in the center of the room. He was tied to a post, standing, with his hands above his head. He had been beaten, perhaps tortured, and was half-starved, but he was alive. He saw Loc Tin first, who pressed his fingers to his lips, indicating that Blizzard was not to speak. The captain shifted his gaze to Dordi. In an instant he took in the unadorned unform and the blue eyes. The confusion on his face cleared, and he understood he was being rescued. Dordi whispered, "Can you walk?" The man nodded. "Good. Let's go."

They cut the ropes, and Blizzard nearly collapsed but caught himself. He was very weak, and Dordi had to hold him upright. Loc Tin opened the door and looked out. All clear. Loc Tin and Dordi each grabbed an arm of the captain, and the three ran awkwardly but quickly to the treeline using the path they had cut moments ago. Without slowing down, Loc Tin glanced back. No activity behind them. His watch read 5:32 A.M. They might have until 6:00 A.M. before anyone noticed. They needed to be as far away as possible.

Even at noon, the jungle was dark, the thickness of the vegetation allowing little of the sun's light to penetrate completely. Nevertheless, the small amount of light that came with the beginning sunrise made a huge difference compared to the night, and even with having to half carry the captain, progress was faster than it had been before. They estimated they were less than 2 kilometers from the river when they heard shouting behind them. No doubt the dead men and missing pilot had been discovered. They had no choice but to keep moving. They found the spot in the river that they had crossed earlier—the vine was exactly where they left it. With their improved visibility, Loc Tin could see that the river narrowed significantly a short distance upstream. It was the narrowing of the river that caused the strong current just below—at the point they had crossed over during the night. Now they made their way to the wider part of the river before it narrowed. Although the distance was greater, the flow of the water was far more gentle and crossing it took very little time. They quickly continued on to the rendezvous point.

Less than an hour later, at 10:00 A.M., the three men were at the designated pick-up location. Two hours before the chopper would arrive. NVA behind them, Vietnam six klicks ahead. Continuing on meant crossing the highway known as the Ho Chi Minh Trail, which was extremely risky. Staying put was even more risky. The three men quickly agreed that they would keep going. Eventually they heard the sound of large trucks and other vehicles, indicating that they had reached the highway and were very close to Vietnam. They stayed hidden in the thick brush and vegetation and watched the road. A convoy of NVA trucks filled with supplies plodded along the highway with a few Jeeps and motorcycles keeping watch. Finally the last vehicle disappeared from sight, and the three men crossed as quickly as they could. Just as they made it to the cover of the treeline, they heard a helicopter pass overhead—no doubt headed to the rendezvous point. The men trudged on. Although they were increasingly confident that they were now in Vietnam, they were not out of danger. VC could be anywhere, and dressed as they were, there was also the possibility that Loc Tin or Dordi would be shot by friendlies.

Dordi offered a plan. "The chopper won't hang around long at the rendezvous. We need to signal it when it flies back over us."

Loc Tin was skeptical, but Blizzard thought it might work. "They will be looking for us. They know your mission?"

"Yes. If we got caught, they would deny knowing anything, but, yeah, the chopper crew knows the deal," Dordi replied.

Loc Tin tore off his shirt and tied it to the largest stick he could find. The three men found a small clearing in what they estimated would be in the helicopter's flight path. They stayed out of sight, waiting. When they heard the unmistakable sound of the rotors, they emerged from the woods. Dordi and the captain waved their arms and Loc Tin waved the makeshift flag. The chopper flew past, but quickly circled back. The clearing was not large enough for it to land, but a rope ladder was thrown out to them. Neither Loc Tin nor Dordi thought the captain was strong enough to climb the ladder. The decision was made that the captain would go last. With Dordi and Loc Tin on the chopper, Blizzard would only have to hang on; the other two men would pull him up. The plan worked; however, rifle fire from the treeline began just as Dordi and Loc Tin began to pull on the rope ladder. The chopper picked up speed and height as Blizzard dangled a dozen feet below clinging to the rope. The sound of rifle fire receded into the distance as Dordi and Loc Tin pulled the rescued pilot onto the floor of the Huey. Exhausted but still filled with adrenaline, the men just sat on the floor of the chopper breathing hard and not speaking. The co-pilot handed Blizzard a canteen, and they passed the water around. Another moment of silence passed, and then the captain finally spoke.

"I've been a P.O.W. for months. I've been beaten, burned, and starved. But I held out. I knew you guys would come. I fantasized continuously about being rescued." He shook his head, "But I can assure you that in not a single one of my imagined rescue scenarios was I getting shot at while clinging to a damn rope on a moving helicopter!" The man leaned against the wall of the aircraft and then added, "Not that I'm complaining."

Chapter 23

Agent Orange
  1964

Scientists at Dow Chemical, one of the manufacturers of Agent Orange, realized that dioxin, known to cause cancer and severe birth defects, was an unintended by-product of the manufacturing process. This resulted in the defoliants used in Agent Orange being contaminated with the deadly chemical. Although the scientists were able to develop a process that would drastically reduce the presence of dioxin in Agent Orange, these practices were not widely adopted due to the resulting increase in production time and expense.

Chapter 24

Saigon, Vietnam, April 1971
  Dennis Dordi

At Ton Son Nhut airport in Saigon, Dennis Dordi waited with two dozen other men that had survived their year in Vietnam. They milled about outside the terminal and listened for their number to be called. Then they would board a plane that would take them home to the States. Charlie knew they were there—at the airport—waiting to leave. Sometimes, probably for that very reason, he would rain rockets down—killing men that had served their time. It had happened more than once, and everyone knew it. They had laid down their weapons. Their fight was done. But Charlie's war raged on. He was still out there, watching and waiting. And as long as you were in-country, you could still become a casualty of war. The men knew it. And they were nervous. Today even the non-smokers were chain-smoking.

The loudspeaker crackled and a woman's voice called out a few numbers, but not Dordi's. A few men stood and Dordi watched them walk into the terminal. A minute later, the loudspeaker crackled again, and this time it was his turn. He dropped his cigarette in the dirt and ground it out with his boot, still feeling nervous. He wanted to leave, wanted out of this place, but it didn't feel right. He was leaving people behind. People that depended on him. People he cared about. He thought of Loc Tin, the men of the 5Th Special Forces, and, especially, Linh.

He and Linh had grown close in the two years since he first met her—he gave her food and money when he could and never asked for anything in exchange. There were thousands of orphans in Vietnam. Why was he so attached to this one? But he knew the answer. She was a survivor, just like he was. Before he left, he offered to take her with him to the States. But she said no. She had told him she had managed 15 years without him; she could could do it again. But, inexplicably, he still felt as though he was deserting her. He rubbed his face and tried to clear his head.

Inside the terminal, he and the other men whose numbers had been called stood in a line near the gate waiting to board. Before they could take their seats on the plane, the arriving passengers had to be unloaded. The new arrivals in their clean and pressed uniforms walked off the plane and filed past the veterans. It was a surreal moment for Dordi. Is that how he looked when he was a cherry? These men looked so young, though most were only a few years younger than he was. But a day in 'Nam aged you far more than what the calendar said. Dordi watched the new draftees and looked each man in the eye as they walked past. He knew more than one would not be standing in his place a year from now. The cherries knew it too. You could see it in their eyes. No one spoke. There was nothing to say.

He took his seat on the plane and looked out the window. Once again, his emotions were mixed. He had served his time, done his duty. He told himself that he had every right to leave. Why did he feel so guilty? He knew it was his time to go, but he could not shake the feeling of letting his men down. He had always had their back. Who would have it now? He thought of the newbies that had just left the plane he was now sitting on. They would be worthless for a while. No amount of stateside training could compare to the experience you got from actual combat. Dordi—and the men he was surrounded by on the plane—were incredibly well-trained and effective soldiers. But they were leaving—replaced by a bunch of cherries who might get killed—or get someone else killed—before they understood how things worked in Vietnam. What a stupid way to run a war.

The plane taxied down the runway and took to the air. Finally he was out of Charlie's reach. His third tour in Vietnam had ended. Would he do another? Maybe. He was a soldier now and always would be. He had been trained to kill. But as he learned the first time he left, that was not a skill set that translated well to the real world. He looked out the window and thought of Linh again.

"What the hell do I do now?" he asked aloud. He sat back in his seat and closed his eyes. It was a good question, but he had no answer.

Chapter 25

Once again it was Sunday night, and Tony and Rebecca were on their way to his Aunt Minh's house for family dinner. Tony had finally gotten his DNA results back and he was anxious to tell Anh that he had decided to try and find his father or anyone else that he might be related to.

"How do you feel?" Rebecca asked as they drove.

"I don't know. I don't want to hurt my mom and dad. I don't want them to think I am not grateful for everything they did."

"They won't be hurt. After Anh found Mikayla—I think she would want you to try to find your dad."

He nodded but said nothing. A few minutes later Tony parked in front of Minh and Jeffry's house, and he and Rebecca went inside without knocking.

"Tony!" his mother exclaimed and gave him a big hug. She always acted as though it had been months since they had seen each other, even if it had only been a few hours. He didn't mind. The genuine enthusiasm she had always expressed for him had gotten him through some dark times in his youth. After dinner, Tony and Anh sat on the couch in the living room.

"So, Mom, I have been thinking," he started but then he hesitated. She waited for him to continue, so he did. "Ever since you found Mai...I mean, Mikayla..."

Anh smiled broadly and interrupted him, "Are you looking for your father?"

He was surprised by her enthusiasm. "Yes, I..."

Before he could continue, Anh interrupted again. "Did you have your DNA analyzed?"

Tony nodded. "Yes. Do you mind? Will Dad be upset?"

She shook her head, "Of course not! He loves you no matter what. Let's go tell him." She pulled Tony off the couch and went in search of Lanh, who was probably making coffee, his preferred after-dinner drink.

Sure enough, they found Lanh in the kitchen. He and Minh were both waiting for the coffee pot to stop.

"Guess what?" Anh said.

Her husband and sister turned to look at her. "Tony had his DNA tested. He wants to find his biological father."

Lanh looked at Tony, "That's good. I hope you do. Did you get your results back yet?"

Relieved that neither of his parents seemed upset, he happily shared his information. "Yes, I am 85% Vietnamese and 15% Chinese. Not very interesting, I know. But maybe it will be enough to find him."

Lanh frowned, "I'm not sure how DNA works, but I'm guessing most 'full-blooded' Vietnamese have a dose of Chinese. But I really do hope you find him."

Chapter 26

By late March of 1975, everyone knew it would not be long before South Vietnam was completely taken over by communist forces from the North. Except for a few Americans, mostly Marines, Western forces had pulled out two years before, leaving the ARVN forces to defend the country on its own. They had fought hard, and millions of Vietnamese, both soldiers and civilians, had died. For what? They had failed. Now Loc Tin and most other soldiers were just trying to get their families somewhere safe. He knew they needed to leave Vietnam. He hoped if they could make it to Saigon that the Americans who were left would be willing and able to help. He thought of Dordi and all of the other Americans he had fought alongside. Many had died trying to save his country. But now the NVA were steadily marching South—leaving death and destruction in their wake. In early March, Buon Me Thout, a city in the Central Highlands of Vietnam, was the first to fall. Now Hue was under attack. Loc Tin knew it would not be long before the NVA came to take over DaNang, and he made the hard decision to desert his position. In the end, he did it to save his family.

His mother had died not long after he had moved her and Kim to the civilian tent city next to his base in DaNang. There was nothing wrong with her that he could see. He suspected she died of grief over the loss of her husband, two of her children, and then her first grandchild. But his wife, Kim, was remarkably resilient and made the best of life at the civilian camp. The woman managed to stay happy and optimistic no matter the circumstance. Although she grieved with the widows of fallen soldiers, she also helped them to be strong and to face an uncertain future. In 1971, Loc Tin and Kim welcomed a son, Lam, and barely a year later, a daughter they named Suong. The kids kept her busy, but she loved it. He knew life in the camp wasn't easy, but she never complained. However, now they must leave the only home his children had ever known, and he truly had no idea what lay ahead.

He tried to sound strong and confident when he described the plan. "We will go to Saigon. The Americans are evacuating their allies." In truth, he was not sure they would make it to Saigon. Even if they did, how could the Americans possibly evacuate everyone who needed to get out? But Loc Tin felt it was his family's best chance. Dordi had shown him how to hotwire a car, and he managed to get one of the Jeeps running that the Americans had abandoned. In white paint, someone had carefully written "*California Dreamin'*" on its side. He smiled. He had heard that song. He thought it was by a band called the Mamas and the Papas but couldn't be sure. He remembered Hanoi Hannah liked to play it, and she would tell the American servicemen that the girls were waiting for them in California. Thinking of California made him think of Dordi—and he smiled again. Loc Tin sincerely hoped his friend had made it home.

Loc Tin looked at the Jeep and wondered if it was really possible to drive it all the way to Saigon. There were at least two major problems. Gas was in short supply and NVA and VC were rounding up ARVN soldiers. Depending on the captor, ARVN soldiers would either be executed on the spot or taken to a P.O.W. camp. Obviously, he preferred to avoid either scenario, but he feared for his wife and daughter far more than for himself. They would have to stay hidden at all costs.

Kim didn't argue with him. She just packed as much food as she could. She grabbed a few other essentials and then put everything in the Jeep. She put the kids in the footwell of the Jeep's backseat. Loc Tin could not bear to part with his ARVN Special Forces rucksack and uniform. It was stupid and sentimental he knew, but it had been such a significant part of his life. He would carry the Special Forces moniker with pride until his dying day. He shoved the rucksack under his seat and slipped his M-14 between the driver and passenger seat, just in case. Finally, Kim laid down on the backseat, and Loc Tin covered her and the children with an old army tarp he had found. Civilians frequently made money by reselling items left behind by the Westerners. That was his story if anyone asked. For good measure, he threw random items on top of the tarp to further the illusion that he was hauling things he had procured from the base. He tried to make himself look older by adding a bit of gray to his hair with the camouflage greasepaint he and Dordi had sometimes used. He also wore civilian clothing he got from one of the older men at the camp near the base. The disguise would be enough as long as no one looked at him too closely—or searched the Jeep. They left DaNang on March 25, 1975. Three days later, the NVA invaded the city and overtook the base. Loc Tin and his family had gotten out just in time.

Under the best of circumstances, Saigon was a full day's drive from DaNang. Of course, these were not the best of circumstances. The highway between the cities was heavily trafficked and after decades of war was in poor condition. By nightfall, they were on the outskirts of Pleiku, barely a third of the distance they needed to go. The Jeep had been on empty for several miles, and he knew it would soon stop running. He pulled off the highway when he saw what looked to be an abandoned hamlet. The grass huts had long ago been heavily damaged. Many had been burned to the ground. Most likely the residents had either been killed or had moved on. Using the Jeep and the grass roof from a destroyed home, he fashioned a lean-to and he and Kim made the kids as comfortable as possible. He wanted to let them run around and stretch, but they were not out of danger yet. He reminded them to be very quiet. While Kim fed Lam and Suong, Loc Tin tried to sleep. Tomorrow would be another long day.

At first light Loc Tin was ready to get moving again, but the Jeep refused to start. He looked at his wife and two small children. Walking nearly 600 km—375 miles—was not an option. He kissed his wife and made her and the children promise to stay in the lean-to. It was imperative that they stay out of sight. He left his wife his pistol because it would be easier for her to use if she needed it. He left with only his knife since he could not risk being seen carrying a rifle. He needed to find gas or some other means of transportation. He promised them he would return as soon as possible.

Loc Tin was gone nearly two full days. He returned to the makeshift campsite empty-handed, but he knew he had already been away too long. He found the Jeep where he had left it, still hidden by the grass roof—but his family was nowhere to be seen. All of their belongings, including his rucksack, were gone. Panic was beginning to set in when he noticed a cross scratched into the "D" in *California Dreamin'*. He was certain that had not been there before. He walked around the deserted hamlet, eventually finding the remnants of a small church. It was made of wood. What was left of the white paint was peeling. The front steps were gone, but the bell tower was intact, albeit missing the bell. Although he had never had much use for religion, Kim was a devout Catholic. He could not help but smile. Leave it to her to find a church. The front door would be difficult to access without the steps, so he walked around to the back. All the windows were broken and several were low enough to the ground to crawl inside.

Inside, Loc Tin was astonished to see Kim and an old priest sitting at a table drinking tea. His children sat on the floor rolling a ball between them. When Kim looked up and saw him, she rushed to his side. "Thank you, Lord!" she exclaimed. Then she flung her arms around him and said, "I have been praying non-stop since you left."

The old priest nodded, "She speaks the truth."

When Kim finally let go of him, Loc Tin took in the scene before him. He had noticed from outside that the church was small but quite tall. Now he realized that the basement served as the priest's living quarters. The room in which he stood was dimly lit and very dusty. He asked the priest, "What happened to the hamlet?"

The old man got up and walked to where Loc Tin stood. "Two years—" he scratched his head—"maybe three— an army helicopter crashed nearby. Several of the villagers ran to try and help the crew. Most died in the crash, but a couple of them survived. They were brought back here. The VC didn't like that—destroyed the village. Killed everyone but me. They let me live so I could warn other South Vietnamese not to help the Americans." The old priest's eyes filled with tears at the memory.

Loc Tin started to speak, but Kim asked him, "Were you able to find gas? Or another vehicle?"

Dejected, Loc Tin responded, "No. Nothing. I am afraid we have no choice but to walk."

"Well…," the priest motioned Loc Tin to follow him, "your wife told me your predicament. I may be able to help."

The priest climbed out the window that Loc Tin had entered moments before and walked around to the other side of the church where a horse grazed in the tall grass. "I also have a wagon. I used to use the horse and wagon to pick up the older parishioners before church services. I'm afraid the horse has gotten fat and lazy, but she has a good temperament."

The family spent several days with the priest. The wagon needed repair and Loc Tin needed a decent night's sleep before they continued on. Before they left, he showed the priest how to start the Jeep in the event he was able to get gas. The priest gave him a straw, cone-shaped hat to protect his head from the sun. Loc Tin gladly accepted it as it would add to his disguise.

Once again, Loc Tin hid his family before they set out. They lay in the back of the wagon and he covered them with a tarp. He admonished the children to be very quiet, no matter what. They must stay hidden. Additional items were piled on top of them. Loc Tin thanked the priest for his help and they left. Progress was slow but steady. A few times, the wagon was passed by NVA trucks, but none stopped to question him. The third day of the trip, a small group of NVA soldiers walking along the road flagged him down. Loc Tin had no choice but to stop. Several of the men jumped in the back of the wagon and another man sat beside Loc Tin. He ordered Loc Tin to drive them to Boun Me Thout, the first South Vietnam city to fall to the North Vietnamese. The soldiers talked loudly and sometimes argued, but they took no interest in him or his cargo. Several hours later they reached their destination, and without a word, the men jumped off the wagon and walked away. Finally Loc Tin was able to breathe again.

Day by day the roads became more and more congested. Everyone was headed South, toward Saigon. Several times men attempted to steal the wagon from him. But those attempts failed. He was not the frail old man that he appeared to be, as they each quickly learned. After more than two weeks in the wagon, they reached Ben Hoa, a city on the outskirts of Saigon. The road was crowded with desperate people trying to stay ahead of the approaching army. But there were also bands of NVA soldiers looking for ARVN deserters. Soon traffic slowed to a crawl and then stopped altogether. Finally he saw why. NVA soldiers had set up a checkpoint. All vehicles were being searched. He was contemplating his options, which seemed extremely limited. Suddenly a young man, still clad in his ARVN uniform, attempted to knock Loc Tin out of the wagon. Loc Tin was stronger and had far more training in hand-to-hand combat than the other man and he easily dispatched his attacker. Unfortunately, the altercation drew the attention of several NVA soldiers who began approaching. He climbed out of the wagon to head them off—hoping to keep them from searching it. Just then two more men cut the ropes holding the horse. They jumped on her back and attempted to ride away. The soldiers easily shot them in the back as they fled. The horse galloped off—riderless and no doubt terrified.

Anxious, desperate, and highly agitated people behind Loc Tin started trying to push the wagon off the road—it was blocking the path. To try and stop them, he grabbed the M-14 and fired into the air. But it was too late. The wagon tipped over and rolled down a hill and out of sight. "Kim!!" Loc Tin screamed and ran down the hill.

But the soldiers were on him. They took his rifle and grabbed his arms. He tried to fight, but there were three of them holding him down. They tied his hands behind his back and hauled him back up the hill. They threw him into the back of a canvas-covered truck—the same kind that had first taken him to the 7th Infantry base at Duc Lap a decade before. Inside the truck were a dozen other men. No doubt, former ARVN. His heart ached for his children and his wife. Were they alive? What would happen to them? He tried to think. He had to get back to them. He was about to jump off the truck when two NVA soldiers climbed in, rifles at the ready. The truck began to move. Loc Tin collapsed onto the floor of the truck bed. His head hung low, he realized his family—if they were even alive—were on their own. His heart was broken.

Chapter 27

Agent Orange
1969-1971

A paper was released to the public in 1969 detailing studies in mice that demonstrated Agent Orange's toxicity. The paper concluded Agent Orange would likely be hazardous to humans. But the wheels of government turn slowly, and another two years would pass before the use of all deforestation chemicals in Southeast Asia was finally halted. By the time Operation Ranch Hand ended, it was estimated that 20 million gallons of herbicides were sprayed in South Vietnam, Cambodia, and Laos, the majority of which was Agent Orange.

Chapter 28

Richmond, Virginia
The St. Bethlehem Home, 1935-1975

The mission of the St. Bethlehem Home for unwed mothers had always been to provide young, pregnant women shelter and support during their pregnancies. In 1935, Hazel Ingalls had been 16 when she found herself pregnant and alone. Her parents had been furious and embarrassed at her indiscretion. They had always been rather cold to her. She knew that her father had wanted a son and was disappointed that his only child was a girl. "And a homely one at that," he would often add. Her mother had married her father for his money and cared little about the child to whom she had given birth. She was happy to pay for a nanny and spent her time enjoying the luxuries her husband's money provided her.

When Hazel became pregnant, her parents kicked her out of their home. They seemed to be happy to have an excuse to be rid of her. Hazel was devastated. But her nanny, a kind soul whom Hazel loved dearly, told her about St. Bethlehem and arranged for the young girl to be taken there.

At St. Bethlehem, Hazel found the love and kindness that she had longed for from her parents but had never gotten. Although she was expected to leave within two months of her daughter's birth, she convinced the headmistress to let her and her baby, Betsy, stay on. In exchange for room and board, Hazel did any odd job that was needed. She cooked and cleaned and learned to sew. Because she was a new mother herself, she taught the mothers-to-be about breastfeeding and changing of diapers. Hazel was the happiest she had ever been, and everyone doted on her baby.

When Betsy was a small child, all the women loved her and showered her with attention. However, Betsy was always big for her age, and the women and girls residing at St. Bethlehem began to lose interest in her as she grew older and quickly lost her childish looks. As a teenager, where her mother had been tall and willowy, Betsy was very tall, broad, and big-boned. There was nothing dainty about Betsy. Hazel tried to reassure her daughter and told her she was smart and unique. But Betsy knew the women who worked at St. Bethlehem called her "Betsy the Bull" behind her back because of her size and lack of grace. Over time, she became angry and sullen and she resented the pretty young pregnant girls that she was expected to help. To avoid them, Betsy spent more and more time in the garden where she was alone and where her size and strength were assets. She cleared small trees and expanded the garden's footprint. She planted a variety of vegetables, and when the garden produced more than the residents of St. Bethlehem could eat, she sold the rest at a local farmer's market. Betsy's mother allowed her to keep the money she earned, although she felt Betsy spent it foolishly.

Over the years, Hazel took on more and more responsibilities within St. Bethlehem, eventually working closely with the headmistress. It was no surprise to anyone that in 1948 when Hazel was just 29 years old, she was asked to take over as the headmistress of St. Bethlehem. Hazel gladly took on the responsibilities of overseeing the home for wayward girls. She could readily relate to the young women, most of whom had been brought by their own parents who were ashamed of their daughters for becoming pregnant outside of marriage. The vast majority of these women chose—often coerced by their parents—to put their child up for adoption, and Hazel began to facilitate this process by allowing prospective parents to meet the girls prior to the baby's birth—a practice that was quite uncommon at the time. St. Bethlehem was a not-for-profit organization, and so the money that the adoption services brought in was used to provide support to the women living in the home. Adoptive parents were often well-off and frequently gave generously to St. Bethlehem for years after their adoption was finalized. The system worked well for a long time.

However, by the early seventies, the rules of society had begun to change. Being a single mother started to become more acceptable. Hazel realized the mission of St. Bethlehem needed to expand. She initiated the development of numerous classes that would help the women and girls who chose to keep their babies. The goal was for the women to become independent and productive members of society despite the difficulties of raising a child alone. Frequently, women in these classes would band together to rent a home and share expenses and childcare duties after their children were born. Although adoption services continued to be available for those who chose that path, by 1975 the primary goal of St. Bethlehem was to give the women the tools they needed to be successful as single parents. Of course, fewer adoptions and more services strained the budget of St. Bethlehem, and they began to rely more heavily on donations, which were also fewer because there were fewer grateful parents of adoptees.

Soon St. Bethlehem's financial strain forced Hazel to keep the money Betsy made from selling her produce at the farmer's market. Her daughter did not accept this turn of events graciously. Betsy felt she did enough for St. Bethlehem without also forfeiting her profits from the garden. Hazel reminded Betsy that in addition to a modest salary, she also received free room and board in exchange for her work. Nevertheless, when Betsy could no longer afford her little luxuries, her dislike for the women and girls of St. Bethlehem quickly intensified.

Hazel Ingalls died unexpectedly in 1975 when she fell down a small ravine on the property of St. Bethlehem. She and her daughter Betsy had been together in the garden when Hazel stumbled. She fell 15 feet and smashed her head on a rock. She was 56 years old. Her daughter, Betsy, who had just turned 40, immediately stepped in to oversee the running of St. Bethlehem.

Chapter 29

Saigon, Vietnam, April 1975
  Loc Tin

Loc Tin sat on the floor of the truck as it lumbered farther and farther away from his family. His heartache turned to anger, and he forced himself to think. He needed a plan. There were only two guards in the back of the truck with 15 other ARVN deserters. Like him, their hands were tied behind their backs. No one had searched him and his knife was still in his ankle holster. If he could get to it, he would have a chance. He slid to the side of the truck and managed to squeeze between two other men for a place on one of the benches that lined the walls of the truck. The two guards talked between themselves ignoring their captives. He worked the ropes that tied his hands together. Slowly he made progress. The minutes ticked by. He wondered how far they had traveled and how much farther they would go. He had to get back to his family. Just as he set his hands free, the truck came to a stop.

The two guards jumped out and barked at the men, "Everyone out!"

Loc Tin grabbed the ropes he had just slipped out of and wrapped them around his wrists. He followed the other men as they jumped from the truck. He looked around. They were in a large fenced-in area with a number of tents and a few wooden buildings. The fence was topped with concertina wire. NVA with automatic rifles yelled at the large cadre of former ARVN. Like them, he was now a prisoner of war. Loc Tin quickly surmised that there were hundreds of prisoners and relatively few guards. They seemed uncertain and disorganized. Perhaps he could start an uprising? He stood in one place looking around a little too long and a guard prodded him with the muzzle of his rifle, "Get moving!" The men were being herded toward one of the wooden buildings.

Loc Tin looked at the men around him. He needed a distraction. He caught the attention of one of the other prisoners. He looked directly at the man, then glanced toward the knife at his ankle and then back to the single guard. The man nodded. Did he really understand? Loc Tin was surprised because he didn't really have a plan. Just hoping to create some kind of a distraction so he could take the guard out.

Suddenly, the prisoner that Loc Tin had exchanged glances with stopped and turned to the guard, "Where are you taking us? What is this place?"

The guard was both surprised and irritated. He leveled his rifle at the outspoken prisoner. Clearly, he had no qualms about killing the man in front of him. But he never got the chance. Loc Tin plunged the knife deep into the side of the man's neck. He dropped to the ground, dead. Quickly, Loc Tin severed the ropes of the dozen or so men around him. Predictably, they all ran in different directions. Loc Tin frowned. They will likely all be shot, but he could not be concerned. He had a mission to complete. He ran to the side of the wooden building that had been their destination, attempting to keep out of sight. He heard gunshots—two in rapid succession and then a third and fourth. After that, shouting and then nothing. Carefully, staying between the tents and the fence, he made his way back toward the gate where they had unloaded from the truck. Another group of prisoners had just been brought in. Most wore ARVN uniforms. The prisonors were accompanied by two more guards. Loc Tin stayed out of sight and let them pass the tent that he was hiding behind.

The truck was just a few yards away. Would the cab be empty? Could he steal it? It was risky, but what other choice did he have? Just then a small faded yellow pick-up truck pulled up next to the army truck. An older woman wearing khaki trousers and a man's oversized shirt as a jacket got out of the passenger side and a barefoot teenage boy in shorts climbed out of the driver's side. They both walked to the back of the truck and began unloading baskets filled with vegetables. They were bringing food to the prison. Loc Tin did not hesitate, he ran to the truck and jumped inside. Despite squeezing himself into the footwell, he was not well-hidden. Anyone glancing into the truck would see him, but it seemed clear to him that the woman and boy were known to the prison guards. They had been expected and would not be suspected of subterfuge. He hoped they brought food under duress or threat and were not willingly collaborating with the enemy.

Thirty minutes passed with Loc Tin crammed into the footwell before he heard the door to the cab open. The woman was startled upon seeing the man hiding in the small space but recovered quickly.

Loc Tin held the knife in front of him, "Act normally. Get in. I won't hurt you." The woman turned to the boy and said something Loc Tin couldn't understand. The driver's door opened, and the visibly shaken teenager climbed in without looking at him. Loc Tin's voice softened, "Try to act normally. I won't hurt you. I just need to find my family."

Wordlessly, the woman pulled off the oversized shirt she wore, revealing an equally large T-shirt with the faded logo of an American rock band. She covered Loc Tin with the shirt and propped her feet on his curled-up legs. Loc Tin breathed a sigh of relief. They were his allies and were not working with the NVA by choice. She told the boy to drive. They stopped briefly and Loc Tin heard the teen speak to one of the guards, but then the truck began to move again and they left the camp without incident.

The woman pulled the shirt away from Loc Tin, "We are away from the prison. You need to leave us now."

"Please, can you take me to Ben Hoa? I need to find my family."

The woman shook her head, "Saigon is being overrun with NVA. We cannot be seen with you. You must go." He felt the truck come to a stop, and the woman got out so he could do the same. He knew he could overpower the two of them and just steal the truck. But he didn't.

He looked at the woman and asked, "Can you tell me where we are?"

It was the boy who answered, "Just North of Saigon. If you want to get to Ben Hoa, head west. Not far. Maybe 20 kilometers." Twenty kilometers was a little over 12 miles.

Loc Tin nodded a thank you, and then the truck drove off. He looked around. He was on a dirt path surrounded by trees. He looked to the sky and found the sun, which would soon drop below the horizon. He began walking as quickly as possible. Two hours later he had not yet arrived at his destination, but the darkness forced him to stop. He slept on the ground as best he could and was up and moving again as soon as the sun began to rise.

He found Ben Hoa Hospital, which was bustling with activity. He debated on stopping. If his wife or children had been hurt, they might have been taken there. But he felt he needed to continue. Once again, the main road was crowded. More and more people were trying to get to Saigon. Most were in a vehicle of some kind. Cars and motorcycles were most common, but he saw a few mini-buses and a number of bicycles. Dozens of people were on foot as he was. But he was the only one headed away from the city.

Finally by mid-morning on April 30, 1975, he reached the ravine the wagon had tumbled down the day before. He found Kim's body next to the wagon, her head had been smashed. He guessed that she had been thrown from the wagon as it rolled and hit her head on the bloody rock next to her when she landed. Frantically, he searched the wooded area next to the ravine for his children, but they were nowhere to be found. He called to them but got no answer. He climbed up a tree and looked around again, hoping to see them hiding somewhere, but he did not. He climbed a different tree and looked again. He spotted something white in the leaves. Too small to be one of his children, but it clearly didn't belong there. He jumped from the tree and rushed to the spot he had seen from his perch. He bent down and picked up the doll his wife had made for Suong. He brushed the leaves and grass from the doll's hair and clutched it to his chest. He could no longer hold back his grief.

He returned to his wife's side and knelt beside her. He recited a prayer memorized during his childhood long ago because he thought it would please Kim. He wanted to cover her body and went to the wagon to retrieve the tarp, but it was gone. Anything of value or usefulness seemed to be gone. He walked around again and again, looking for any sign that might tell him the fate of his children. He found a few small items that had been thrown from the wagon. Remarkably, he also found his rucksack, which had been lodged between two trees 10 feet above the ground. The green bag was nearly invisible in the foliage of the tree. He retrieved it and threw it over one shoulder. Finally, dejected, he decided to return to the hospital in Ben Hoa.

An hour later he arrived at the civilian hospital. It was busy but unexpectedly quiet. Something was different. He asked around and quickly learned that Saigon had fallen. A few hours before, the South Vietnamese government had surrendered. All ARVN forces were ordered to lay down their weapons. The war was over—and the South was now under the control of the communist regime.

Chapter 30

After filling the first notebook, the old man had asked his son to bring him more. Surprisingly, he found it cathartic to write it all down. He was surprised how much he remembered, but it all was coming back to him. He was also surprised that he had few regrets. He picked up a new notebook just as there was a knock on his door. He looked toward the sound but made no move toward it. "Yes?" he said loudly.

The door opened just slightly, and the orderly that had brought him his breakfast earlier in the day poked his head in. "Sorry to bother you, but there's a new volunteer for you to meet. May we come in?"

In the months that he had been there, the facility had sent several volunteers to him. They would stay for a little while but never came back. At least, they never came back to his room. He knew he was unpleasant to be around. He guessed that's why his son rarely came to see him. The volunteers were all college students trying to beef up their resumes before applying to medical school or something. Like him, many of the residents had few visitors, and these young college kids, regardless of their motivation, were genuinely trying to do a good deed. But he didn't want to be someone's "good deed." He preferred to be alone. At least that was what he told himself. But Ms. Jones, the lady in charge of the volunteers, kept trying to find someone that would put up with him, though that wasn't the way she put it. The old man sighed and wheeled toward the door with little enthusiasm.

Maybe he should try harder. Otherwise, he would keep having to suffer through these first visits which were excruciating. The kids came in eager to be his friend but typically left feeling defeated. He really didn't mean to depress them, but he always did. He told himself he would do better today and told the orderly as pleasantly as he could, "Come on in."

The orderly introduced them and quickly left. The girl's name was Debbie, and she looked like all the others. Young, perky, with a big smile. She had long blonde hair pulled back in a ponytail, which made her look even younger than she probably was. He invited her in and motioned for her to sit in the chair opposite the TV. He wheeled his chair so that they were facing each other and attempted small talk, which he had never been good at, "So, Debbie, I assume you're in college?"

"Oh, no, I'm not really the college type. I design websites."

The old man was genuinely surprised, "Uh...what?"

"I design websites. You know. If you have a business and people want to look you up before they buy from you or use your services, they will check you out on the web. You have to have a good website to be successful these days."

The old man nodded. He knew what a website was. How old did she think he was? But he reminded himself that he was not going to be unpleasant and simply said, "No. I meant, I am just surprised. If you are working, you don't need to volunteer here."

She looked directly at him, frowning as though she were confused. "I volunteer because I want to. My grandparents died a year or so ago. I miss them. I never knew my dad or his family, and since my mom was a single parent and worked all the time, I grew up spending a lot of time with her parents. They were retired. My MeMe taught me how to cook and PaPa taught me to play chess, and, when I got older, they bought me a car. PaPa taught me to drive and how to take care of it—oil change, replace a flat, things like that. As they got older, they were less active, but I would still visit them a few times a week. We would just sit around and talk. They had the best stories!" She laughed, but then the smiled faded, and she looked down at her hands. "They died within a few months of each other, and I just miss them so much. I guess that's not the right motivation to volunteer. I am supposed to be here for you, not for me."

The old man was completely taken aback. All the other kids made him feel like they were doing him a favor. This girl actually *wanted* to be here. He smiled and said, "Well, if you like stories…I have a few I could share."

Debbie's eyes lit up, "Really?"

He nodded, thinking he would tell her about his family and childhood—not the stories he was writing in the notebooks. He had a lot of happy memories, despite his "other" activities. Debbie was so young and seemed very naïve—the world would take that away from her soon enough, but it would not be him.

That first visit lasted more than two hours. When she saw he was getting tired, she got up to leave. "Thank you for the stories today. Would you mind if I visit you again next week?"

"Not at all. Actually, Debbie, I think I would like that very much."

Chapter 31

Vietnam, April-July 1975
  Loc Tin and Dai

At the hospital, Loc Tin found a nurse who looked friendly. He asked, "I'm looking for my children...we were separated yesterday. They may be hurt."

The nurse responded, "I am so sorry. If they are here, they will be in the children's ward." She pointed to a doorway to her left. He thanked her and hurried off.

He found a large room filled with beds and cribs. All were full, most held more than one child. Many were crying. He walked up to a nurse changing a bandage on a small girl. "I'm looking for my children, a little boy and little girl. They might have been brought in yesterday."

The woman looked at him sympathetically. "You are welcome to look for them. They will be in this room or out in the hallway if they are here. We don't have a list of names."

He thanked her and slowly began walking the narrow aisle that passed between the beds. Many children appeared to have broken bones; others were covered in bandages. Burned, he wondered. He saw a little girl with a large patch over one eye. In the bed next to her was a young boy, maybe ten, who was missing both his legs. A toddler was curled up next to him in the same bed, sucking his thumb. He was horrified at these youngest victims of the war. He moved on looking at each injured child. He was both relieved and disappointed to not find his own. He reached the last bed and turned to search the hallway that the nurse had indicated and was surprised to see a young nun approaching him.

She spoke softly, "You are looking for your children?" He nodded sadly, and she continued, "A boy and girl? Around three or four years old?"

Loc Tin was suddenly hopeful, "Yes! Are they here?"

She shook her head, "No. I am sorry. But late last night I found two children walking alone on the road just outside Ben Hoa. I asked their names, but they would not speak. The little girl had on a blue dress."

"Yes! That must be them. Were they hurt? Where are they?"

"The little girl had a gash on her head, but it wasn't serious. They were both just very tired and scared. I took them to Sisters of Mercy. The orphanage near here—it's just outside Saigon near the old American base. I am so sorry, but the nuns were preparing the children to be evacuated."

An emotional Loc Tin responded, "Evacuated? To where?"

"America. They promised to take all the orphans. I am sorry—I didn't know they had family when I took them to the orphanage."

Loc Tin just stared at her and tried to comprehend what she was telling him. He couldn't speak. He felt as though his knees might give way. Finally he mumbled, "Thank you," and then quickly departed. He knew exactly where the American Army base had been and thought he could walk there in just a couple of hours. Outside, however, he spotted a young man with a cyclo, a three-wheeled bicycle with a front compartment for a passenger. He rummaged through his rucksack looking for anything of value that he could offer him in exchange for a ride. He had very little he thought the kid would care about until he found the *Playboy* magazine Dordi had given him as a joke trying to embarrass him. He offered the magazine to the teen, who turned red in the face but agreed to the exchange. A short while later, the cyclo stopped in front of a large, rambling old warehouse built of whitewashed concrete. One wall had completely crumbled, and the rusted metal roof lay on the ground.

"I guess it was damaged in the rocket attacks," the cylco driver said. "It wasn't like this before. I hope the children are okay." Loc Tin, once again his heart broken, slowly climbed out of the cyclo. The teen spoke again, "Do you want me to take you somewhere else?"

Loc Tin shook his head. He walked carefully around the rubble until he found a way inside. He ventured carefully throughout the building, but there was no sign of anyone. Although it was clear that the place had been occupied very recently, everyone was gone now. Were his children here during the attack? Once again, he feared for their lives. He held onto the hope that if they survived, the nuns would have taken care of them. Back outside, he looked up to the sky wondering if his little boy and girl were on a plane even now headed to America. Convinced the orphanage had been abandoned, he left and did not return.

Loc Tin wandered aimlessly for several hours before pulling himself together. If Lam and Suong were on their way to the U.S., then he needed a plan to get there. Within a few days of leaving the orphanage, the president of the newly unified Vietnam began insisting that former ARVN soldiers register with the government. As soon as they did, these men were rounded up and sent to reeducation camps and, at least so far, had not been seen since. Loc Tin did not feel safe staying in the city and made his way North, staying in the countryside as much as possible. He was young and strong and would do just about any odd job he could do in exchange for food or lodging. When he realized he had reached Cam Ranh Bay, he decided to walk down to the beach and see it for himself.

The small city of Cam Ranh was located several hours drive North of Saigon on an inlet of the South China Sea called Cam Ranh Bay. Loc Tin had heard about the city on the bay during the war. Many of the Americans would come here on R&R and they all spoke of how beautiful it was. Dordi had told him that rumor had it there was an agreement between the NVA and the ARVN forces that the city was off limits as far as the war was concerned. It was said that even the VC would come to relax in Cam Ranh Bay. Upon arriving, Loc Tin was not disappointed. Cam Ranh Bay was everything he had been told and more. The white sand and clear blue water were simply spectacular.

Without making a conscious decision, he sat on the beach at the edge of the water. He slipped off his shoes and stretched out, letting the gentle waves caress his feet. Before long, the sound and feel of the water began to relax him. He laid back on the sand and enjoyed the sensation of the water. He tried to clear his mind of everything that had happened over the last few days. His mind drifted back to when each of his children were born, and he wondered if he would ever see them again. He pictured the dutiful, sweet Kim—who he thought would grow old beside him but now she was gone. Eventually, the sadness and exhaustion overcame him and he slept. He was abruptly woken by a man pulling him out of the water.

"What??" Loc Tin mumbled, confused. Slowly he stood. He was soaking wet. Why was he wet? Why was he on the beach? Gradually, it all started to come back to him.

The man was talking to him. "Are you okay? My kids told me there was a dead body on the beach. I came running down—afraid of what I would find. I pulled you out because the tide was starting to come in. I thought you might drown."

"Thank you. I am sorry if I frightened your children. I...I...the water just felt nice. Something good for a change." Loc Tin started to walk away.

"Hey—are you hungry? My wife is making *pho*. You are welcome to join us."

Pho was the Vietnamese noodle soup that was a staple of every restaurant and household in the country. He had not had *pho* in a very long time and was sorely tempted, but he said, "Thank you, but I am soaking wet—not a presentable guest."

"Nonsense! We can eat outside and enjoy the view. My name is Dai Bay Chan. I own the little house at the top of the hill over there." He pointed to a long, wide house with huge windows all along the front. A large patio looked over the water. Loc Tin would never have described it as little.

"I don't want charity, but I am strong. Perhaps I can work in exchange for a meal?"

The man smiled, "I'm sure we can work something out." He led him toward the house, adding, "I might have some clothes you can wear." Loc Tin thought he might be joking but wasn't certain. Dai was a head shorter than Loc Tin and at least twice as wide. Not many men grew fat in wartime Vietnam, and he realized that Dai must be quite wealthy.

Dai motioned for Loc Tin to sit in a chair on the patio, and the portly man disappeared inside. He saw three children sneaking glances at him through one of the windows. When he smiled and waved, they ducked out of view.

Before long, Dai was back. He held a pair of cotton, khaki trousers and a brightly colored shirt. Surprisingly, they looked like they would fit him. Seeing the confusion on Loc Tin's face, Dai explained, "My brother-in-law is more your size. He comes here whenever he gets a chance." Then the man frowned, "Well, he used to. He was drafted in '68."

Loc Tin nodded, "Pretty much every man was." He had lost all modesty and shyness in the army and gratefully changed into the dry clothes after checking to make sure the kids had not taken up at the window again.

Dai turned away from him as he changed but continued talking. "Duc was killed in '69. His wife and daughter are here with us. I was lucky. Considered unfit for service."

Just then, two women and an older girl who had not been at the window began bringing food to the table on the patio. Dai introduced them as his wife, his sister, and his niece. The three women went back inside and returned with more food as well as the three younger children. The youngest was a little boy who looked to be the same age as Lam. Loc Tin watched him for a few minutes, but then he had to look away.

During the course of the meal, Loc Tin learned more about the man and his family. But they were both cautious, not knowing the other man's politics. Over the next few weeks, Loc Tin helped Dai with a number of odd jobs, and the two men came to trust each other. Eventually, they became confident that they were of like minds—both were mistrustful of the new government and both wanted to leave the country.

Dai was a businessman and entrepreneur. He had been very prosperous in his efforts, but he knew his fortune would not last under the new communist government. Many businesses had been permanently closed while others were taken over by the government. The government had taken over everything. There was no longer a free market where people could buy and trade for goods and services. Instead, the government promised to take care of everyone. Quickly, food and gas had to be rationed. Even electricity was rationed by being turned off for periods of time. Loc Tin shared his own story and his fears. After the ARVN surrendered to the North, the NVA began rounding up anyone who had been associated with the South Vietnamese government or military. Even some civilians had been sent to reeducation camps if their views did not align with the new regime.

Like everyone with strong ties to South Vietnam, Dai was making plans to leave. Leaving, however, was illegal. Loc Tin too hoped to escape. Loc Tin told Dai of his friend Dordi and how he had made plans to go to California after the war. He told him about the Jeep with the paint on the side. "Now I am California Dreamin'." Both men laughed, but then grew quiet, each lost in their own thoughts.

Finally, Dai broke the silence. "California can't be as beautiful as this," he said, looking out to the water.

Loc Tin said, "Perhaps not. But at least we will be free men again." The other man nodded.

Sometime in July of 1975, Dai trusted Loc Tin enough to tell him of his plan. He had traded his family home in Saigon, now called Ho Chi Minh City, for a boat sight unseen. He had planned for his family to live at their small vacation home in Cam Ranh Bay for a few days until they could set sail. Dai said that both Malaysia and the Philippines had set up refugee camps for those fleeing Vietnam. However, when he and his family first arrived in Cam Ranh Bay, he found the boat was not seaworthy. Much of the wood was rotten, and it was also smaller than he had been promised. The pilot he had secured for his boat quickly found someone else who needed him to navigate, leaving Dai with a broken-down boat and little else.

"The only good thing is that the boat had been pulled out of the water and set up on blocks, otherwise it would likely have been at the bottom of the bay." Dai frowned, "I have been very successful in business, but I have no idea how to make the boat seaworthy again."

"How bad is it? Can it be repaired?" Loc Tin asked.

Dai shrugged. "Perhaps, but I am afraid to go to the city and try to hire someone. Too many spies."

"I may be able to help. Can I see it?"

The two men walked down to the beach. A crumbling wooden boathouse jutted out over the water but wasn't visible from a distance because it was hidden behind large trees and bamboo growing wild. Dai walked past the boathouse and into the tall weeds that grew behind it. He walked around the boat, removing the boulders that held down several large, heavy-duty, green tarps. Loc Tin went to the opposite side and did the same. Finally, together, the two men removed the tarps, revealing a boat. It looked as though it had not been in the water for many years. It was not a large vessel. Loc Tin estimated that it was only 10 feet wide and maybe 30 feet long. At the back was a wheelhouse, presumably for the engine and pilot. The front narrowed so that at its tip the boat was only 4 feet wide. Loc Tin walked around it. He felt along the side, occasionally knocking on different planks to test their integrity. He stood on a wooden box and peered inside. He thought it might hold 18 people comfortably. Perhaps 25 if they were desperate. And weren't they all?

"Well, what do you think?" Dai asked, anxiously.

"I can repair it. Do you have tools? I need wood as well." Then he frowned, "But I don't know much about engines. Do you know if the engine is working?"

"Yes. One of the men who works for me—he is a mechanic. He tested it."

"How many people have you promised passage?" Loc Tin asked. Then added, "We need space for supplies, as well as people. We can't overload it."

Dai thought aloud, "My family—we are seven. There is a family down the beach," He pointed to a house not far from where they stood. He hesitated before continuing, "They, uh…, they have connections. They know who to bribe when we sail so government lackeys turn the other way."

"And how large is that family?" Loc Tin pushed him for details.

"Eight, I think. And then there is the mechanic and his family. That's another 6. With you, that makes a total of 22. I still need someone who can navigate. Depending on his family, that could be another four or more."

Loc Tin rubbed his face, concerned. "Try to find a bachelor."

Chapter 32

Sacramento, California, March 2021
Ashley

Ashley had been at CBF for nearly three months but rarely saw Lance, her boss, outside weekly lab meetings and monthly happy hours. By chance, one day Ashley ran into him in the cafeteria when both were in line at the hot food station.

"I was going to try and find a table outside if you want to join me," Lance said.

"There are tables outside? Why didn't I know that?" Ashley exclaimed, both delighted and annoyed.

"You can't see them from inside, and there aren't that many, but we've missed the rush so we might get lucky and find one open."

Ashley followed Lance out a side door and, sure enough, a dozen four-top tables were scattered across a patio surrounded by greenery. Flowers were starting to bloom in some of the large pots that served as a barrier to people wanting to use the patio as a cut through. They found only one vacant table, which held the tray and refuse of the previous diner. Ashley moved the trash aside, and she and Lance sat down.

"So you seem to be settling in. Your sequencing is really top-notch. Really clean data," Lance told her.

"Thanks. I have a lot of experience with PCR and WGS. I guess that's why they hired me."

"But it's probably a little on the mundane side," Lance asked as he dug into his lunch.

"Well…," she hesitated, but she knew her poker face was abysmal, so there was no sense lying about it. "Yes, it does feel like I am just a middleman. I thought I would be more involved with the crime-solving. I guess that seems silly."

"Not at all. I blame all those crime dramas on TV. Complex murder cases solved in less than an hour by pretty people in stylish clothes. In no way do they show the reality of what we do. But never doubt that you are a critical part of the process." Ashley nodded without responding, so he changed subjects. "What were you doing in your old lab? I believe you were at UCSD?"

"Yes. I was the lead research assistant in Dr. Beverly Jansen's lab. She was one of the first people to suggest dioxin exposure may be linked to endometriosis in humans."

"Really? My sister has endometriosis. Actually, she has a lot of medical issues. She hasn't been able to work in years." He thought for a moment, "Dioxin? Wasn't that in Agent Orange?"

"Yes. Used in the Vietnam War as an herbicide to destroy enemy crops as well as the jungle."

Lance frowned. "I know all about Agent Orange. My dad served two tours in Vietnam, from 1968-1970. He was Air Force, and we know he was exposed to it. He died of cancer that the VA said was due to his exposure."

"That's good that they acknowledge it. The list of diseases that the VA recognizes are linked to a veteran's Agent Orange exposure is completely inadequate. I'm glad they took responsibility for your dad's cancer. They don't always." She took a bite of food before continuing, "It's even worse for the children of veterans. They more readily accept that a woman's exposure can affect her children but seem reluctant to accept that the dad's exposure also matters. Except spina bifida. The data is overwhelming for that. Even the VA can't pretend otherwise."

Lance looked at her in stunned silence. He put down his fork which was loaded with food and had been headed to his mouth. He scratched his head and said, "I was born with spina bifida. I also was born without my left lower leg. I have a prosthetic." He knocked on the leg with his fist making a loud, hollow sound. "That's why I have a bit of a limp. Was I born without my leg because of my dad's service in Vietnam? Is that why my sister is so sick?"

Ashley couldn't tell if the man was angry or upset. Maybe both. "Obviously, I can't say for sure, but, yes, I believe it's likely."

Lance pushed his tray away, having lost his appetite. Ashley felt awful and didn't know what to say, so she just sat there—watching him.

Lance finally spoke. "I have a brother. He was born before my dad went to Vietnam. Even though he is older, he is in perfect health."

Ashley nodded, "That's good circumstantial data right there." But she regretted the words as soon as she said them. She sounded insensitive, which she wasn't.

Lance didn't seem to take offense and continued talking. "I am doing okay. The spina bifida was surgically corrected right after I was born, and I have my fake leg. But my sister—would she be eligible for disability from the VA? It would help out a lot if she was. She has dad's pension, but it isn't much." He looked at Ashley and shook his head. "I help her out as much as I can, but...but...I have a family—I can't do that much for her.

"Maybe. There's a process, but I don't know much about it. I could ask my friend Vivian. She is a post-doc in Dr. Jansen's lab and has a collaboration with a guy at the San Francisco VA. She could probably find out who you should talk to."

"Yes, please ask her, if you don't mind." He got up to go, "If it's okay with you, I'm going to head back to my office. I really appreciate the info." He stood there for a minute without moving and then looked at Ashley and said, "Christina mentioned that you were interested in forensic genealogy."

"Yes. I would love to learn more about that process."

Lance nodded, "I'll see what I can do."

"Thanks," said Ashley, but Lance was clearly lost in thought, and she wasn't sure he heard her.

A few days later, Ashley knocked on the door to Lance's office, which was open. Lance looked up from something he was studying on his desk and waved her in. "Hey, Ash. What's up?"

She held up a slip of paper. "I have a name and email address for you. Vivian's friend said this is the person to start with to see if your sister has a case with the VA. She relayed the info you gave me, and the woman said it was definitely worth trying. She said she may qualify for additional benefits for her own illnesses, not just your dad's death."

Lance stood up and took the paper from her. "Thank you. Thank you very much."

"I hope it helps your sister," she said sincerely.

Chapter 33

Cam Ranh Bay, Vietnam, July-October 1975
 Loc Tin and Lucy

Loc Tin worked on repairing the boat—ultimately using wood from the boathouse to replace the rotting wood of the vessel. Meanwhile, Dai set about finding them a pilot. By late September, the boat was ready to be put in the water and tested. With Dai's permission, Loc Tin christened the boat *"California Dreamin.'"* But to avoid drawing attention to the boat and raising suspicion that it was anything other than a fishing vessel, he painted the name on the inside.

A few days after Loc Tin finished the repairs, he and Dai walked down to the boathouse after dinner. It had become a ritual. As the realities of life under communist rule became more evident, the number of people attempting to flee grew. They had become concerned that their boat would be stolen by others wanting to leave or would be found and confiscated by the government. When they got to what was left of the boathouse—much of its wood was now part of the boat—they were relieved to see the *California Dreamin'* exactly where she should be. Loc Tin walked around the boat for the hundredth time, caressing its hull. He was clearly pleased with his work.

"I've found a pilot," Dai announced.

Loc Tin was animated, "That's really good news. I was starting to worry. When do I get to meet him? He should be here when we test the boat."

Dai hesitated, "Well…about that. There's something you should know first." Loc Tin just looked at him waiting for him to continue. Dai turned away from him but said, "You know we have to be cautious. I can't just advertise that we need a boat pilot. I had to ask only people I really trusted."

"Yes…but you found someone? Someone with experience navigating—not just experience driving a boat?"

"I did…but…," Dai thought about what he was saying and decided to start with the good news. "Our pilot has been navigating a fishing boat much like this one for nearly five years. Grew up in DaNang. The father was a fisherman and taught his four children to fish, but only the youngest—our pilot—had a knack for navigation."

"Five years is not that long. What about the father?"

"Drafted in '68. Killed a couple of years later. Two of the sons were killed as well. One son survived but lost most of his right arm and an eye. He will be a passenger, as will be the mother—she hopes to get her son to the U.S. and get him fitted for a prosthetic."

"Then our pilot is the remaining son." Loc Tin didn't understand Dai's hesitancy.

"Not exactly. The youngest child is a girl. A woman, really. She's 28."

Loc Tin looked at Dai, incredulous, "A woman?"

"Yes. Trust me. She's good. Kept her dad's business going after all the men were drafted. She has taken care of her mother and brother for years. She had a crew of men who worked the fishing nets and apparently they did pretty well, despite the war."

Loc Tin was very uncertain. He asked, "If she has her father's boat, why does she need ours?"

"She doesn't—we need her. But her boat is smaller. It was overcrowded with her crew and their families, but she didn't want to leave anyone behind. Now she is piloting our boat. She gave hers to the first mate. With Lucy and her family on our boat, it is better for everyone," Dai explained.

Loc Tin nodded. He still had his doubts about a woman pilot, but Dai was in charge, so he didn't argue. And Loc Tin was anxious to get going. Now that the boat was finished, he had too much time on his hands. If a lady pilot was his ticket out, then so be it.

A week later, Dai introduced Loc Tin to their pilot, Lucy, and her mother, Tho. Tho was a short, middle-age woman dressed in the traditional Vietnamese *Ao Dai*, a long tunic with split sides over wide trousers. In contrast, Lucy was tall and wore Western-style clothing, dark slacks with a fitted white shirt. Loc Tin thought Lucy, although not beautiful, was quite striking. He watched her walk around the boat much as he had—hand out to feel the wood and shape of the vessel. She found the same wooden box that Loc Tin had used and stepped up to peer inside. She looked quizzically at Loc Tin, *"California Dreamin'"*? The words were written in English, and he was surprised that she could read it.

"It's a long story," Loc Tin replied. "But I am hoping to get to America—get to California."

She nodded but turned back to the boat. Suddenly, Loc Tin was nervous that the vessel didn't meet her expectations. He realized he wanted her to like it.

Trying to sound casual, Loc tin said, "What do you think?"

"It's smaller than I expected but looks sturdy. Have you put it in the water yet? Dai said when he bought it much of the bottom was rotted. You've done a good job repairing it, but the water is the real test." She was still standing on the box, leaning on the boat and looking at him.

He could not take his eyes off her. He realized she was waiting for him to say something, but his mind had gone blank. He finally said, "Lucy. That's an unusual name."

She nodded. My given name is Lue Sien, but I had an American boyfriend for a while. He couldn't get it right and called me Lucy. I liked the nickname, so I kept it, even after I broke it off with him."

"He would have taken you to America!" her mother chimed in, clearly disappointed for her daughter.

She looked at Tho, "Not everyone wants to go to America, Mother. If he loved me as much as he said, he could have stayed here."

She turned back to Loc Tin, "He was a mechanic. Took care of helicopters. Didn't spend much time shooting at NVA. He was as safe as any of us. He could have stayed."

At this, her mother shook her head. "No man is going to want you. You are too headstrong and independent."

Lucy was nonplussed, "Then it's a good thing I don't need a man." She stepped off the box and looked at Loc Tin. "Can we put Miss California in the water now?"

They lowered the boat into the water, and Loc Tin and Dai climbed onboard. Loc Tin turned to offer his hand to help Lucy in, but she was already onboard walking to the wheelhouse. The men followed Lucy, leaving her mother to watch from the boathouse. Inside the wheelhouse, Lucy looked around, tested the wheel, and then examined the controls. Satisfied, she turned the ignition. It started on the first try, and the three motored around the bay for half an hour. The two men walked around the boat, watching for any sign of leaks—fortunately, they found none. Lucy then expertly maneuvered the craft into what was left of the boathouse and cut the engine.

"Well, what do you think?" Loc Tin asked, anxious for her approval.

Lucy, her hands still on the wheel, nodded. "It's a good solid boat. Very responsive. But we need to make a couple of improvements before we leave."

The men looked at each other, "Like what?" they said in unison.

"Well, first of all. There is no bathroom. What is your plan for that?"

Loc Tin thought that was obvious but said, "Just go over the side."

Lucy shook her head, "Maybe for you men, but not the women and children." She took a deep breath, "I'll think of something." She then turned to the boat, thinking. "We will be out in the elements 24 hours a day for who knows how many days. We need some part of the boat covered—otherwise we will all die of heatstroke."

Loc Tin was glad he had already thought of that. "We have several tarps we use to protect the boat. We will use the largest for sun protection. I will attach it to the wheelhouse and add a couple of poles to the front of the boat to hold up that end."

She nodded her approval and then said, "I'll need a co-pilot. I will steer at night and most of the day, but I need someone that can give me a break so I can sleep. If they can use a compass, I can teach them how to stay on course for a few hours. But I am in charge. They must be willing to listen to me."

Loc Tin immediately agreed to be the co-pilot. "I've driven a boat before, though I don't know how to navigate on open water."

Lucy smiled. "Leave that to me."

At that moment, Loc Tin changed his mind. Lucy *was* beautiful.

Over the next two weeks, the tarp went up, Lucy gave Loc Tin lessons in navigation, and she also solved the bathroom dilemma. Women and children would use a bucket, discreetly placed behind a curtain in the corner of the wheelhouse. Men were on the Loc Tin plan. Over those same two weeks, Loc Tin learned more and more about the mysterious Lucy. She spoke her mind. If you didn't want her opinion, don't ask. She didn't sugarcoat anything, unlike most of the women he had known. Her American boyfriend had given her a pistol—a Colt 1911—and taught her how to use it. Although it was illegal for him to give her the weapon and just as illegal for her to have it, he wanted her to be able to defend herself. The VC frequently ambushed both military and civilian watercraft in the area she and her crew fished. Loc Tin asked her if she had ever had to use it.

"No, luckily. Right after he gave it to me, the Americans sprayed the area around DaNang with that chemical—Agent Orange? It destroyed all of the jungle along the shoreline and pretty much eliminated the VC's ability to ambush anyone." Then she sighed heavily and added, "But it really changed the look of the waterfront. It will be beautiful again, eventually, I suppose. Hopefully, someday I can come back and see it."

Once again, Loc Tin realized she was leaving Vietnam only because of her mother and brother. She wanted to stay and help rebuild the country. More than once, she had said to him, "Vietnam needs us now more than ever. I sometimes feel like a deserter."

It pained him hearing her say that. He really was a deserter—though he didn't think she meant to hurt him. Although he sometimes wondered if she thought less of him because he tried—and failed—to save his family. She said she understood his desire to go to the U.S. and try to find his children.

But did she also see him as a traitor to Vietnam?

Finally, at the end of October 1975, they were ready to set sail. Twenty-five people, along with food and water for six days, were crammed onto the boat. As Lucy took the helm and started the engine, Loc Tin tried to remember if they were headed to Malaysia or the Philippines. But it didn't really matter. He just knew he could not stay in Vietnam. He stood in the wheelhouse next to Lucy and wondered what life would bring next.

Chapter 34

Sacramento, California, April 2021
Ashley and Rhonda

As promised, Lance had made arrangements for Ashley to spend some time with Rhonda, the lead analyst conducting investigative genetic genealogy (IGG), which she had recently learned was the proper name for forensic genealogy. The IGG division was responsible for analyzing the DNA sequences that she and others in her division provided from samples obtained at a crime scene.

Rhonda walked Ashley around the large room, which to her looked more like a business office than a research laboratory. There were at least a dozen desks neatly arranged in three rows. Each desk held a desktop computer with two screens. Most computers were occupied, and all the desks were piled high with reams of paper and books, although some desks were neater than others. Off to the side were three small offices with large windows that served as walls.

Rhonda told Ashley, "The first thing that happens after you get the DNA sequence of a possible criminal is that the information is put into CODIS."

"The Combined DNA Index System," Ashley responded, anxious to show Rhonda she wasn't a complete newbie to the process.

"Exactly. Anyone convicted of a crime is legally required to provide a DNA sample, which is put into the CODIS system. Let's say Joe Schmo killed a girl several years ago and left DNA at the crime scene. The DNA would go into CODIS, but it wouldn't link to anyone unless Joe was already in the system. A couple of years later, let's say he is *convicted* of killing his girlfriend. The conviction means he is now required to give a DNA sample. That goes into the system and then—BAM!—we get him for the first girl too. The FBI started CODIS in 1998, and we now have over 20 million DNA profiles in the system."

"But that's not what y'all do here? CODIS, I mean," Ashley responded.

Rhonda smiled, "I just LOVE your accent. Where are you from again? Alabama?"

"Mississippi," Ashley responded, suppressing her irritation. She had been in California for nearly five years—why were these people so obsessed with her accent? She asked Rhonda again, "But you don't use the CODIS system here?" With effort, Ashley forced herself to say "you" instead of "y'all."

"Right. If they get a hit in CODIS, then law enforcement agencies don't need us." Rhonda walked over to a huge chart taking up most of one wall and motioned for Ashley to follow her. "If there is no match in CODIS, then we might be asked to try to identify a potential suspect."

"So how exactly do you do that?" Ashley was trying not to show her frustration—Rhonda wasn't telling her anything she didn't already know. She said she was willing to introduce her to the process of IGG, but maybe she only agreed to do it because Lance was also her boss. Ashley wasn't sure she liked Rhonda. She wondered if she was one of those people who liked to protect her own turf, so she would act like she was being helpful but not actually share important information. Ashley sighed. At least it got her out of her windowless lab for a while.

Ashley joined Rhonda in front of the chart. It looked a lot like a periodic table of the elements, but clearly it wasn't. "What is this?" she asked.

"For our purposes, we need to know how much DNA is shared between two or more samples. The more DNA people share, the more closely they are related. Siblings and parent-child relationships are easy, but it can get tricky with less closely related people. Like third and fourth cousins. We compare the crime scene DNA with DNA available in national databases accumulated from people who submitted their samples willingly to companies to see what their heritage is. This chart," Rhonda pointed, "gives the potential relationship between two people based on shared bits of DNA. The amount is cut in half with each generation. If you go back far enough, you will find a common ancestor between any two people. If the first common ancestor that two people have is six or more generations back, then they are not considered to be related, but it's still helpful for our purpose."

"I am not following you. How does that help you? Say you have DNA from a crime scene and no matches in CODIS, how does knowing how much DNA a criminal has in common with some random person help you catch the bad guy?"

"You try to build a family tree based on relatives that have had their DNA analyzed. If you fill in the tree enough, the suspect will be somewhere in the lineage." She looked at Ashley and satisfied that she was following what she was saying, she continued, "There are several databases that we can use. GEDMatch, for example. You have heard of companies like *DNAStory* and *MyDNA*?" Rhonda looked at her again and waited.

Ashley nodded. "Yes. My whole family had our DNA analyzed using kits from *DNAStory*. Results were pretty boring. We are all just white people from Northern Europe. My dad was really disappointed. He was sure he was part Cherokee, but he isn't." Ashley felt her face flush. She should have just said yes to the question and not gone into her family genealogy. It was irrelevant information that no doubt highlighted her accent.

But Rhonda didn't seem annoyed at all. Just nodded and continued, "Although most companies ask users to opt-in to law enforcement access to DNA, most people don't read the fine print. If they don't check the opt-in box, then they are automatically opted out. But what is great about GEDMatch is that...," Rhonda stopped in mid-sentence because she decided an example would be a better explanation. She continued. "You said your family used *DNAStory*?" Ashley nodded and Rhonda continued, "So because most people don't choose to opt-in, they are opted out by default. That means law enforcement can't access your DNA information. However, let's say you wanted to find relatives that might still be in Europe. *DNAStory* is a U.S.-based company, and so its database will contain mostly Americans or people who have been here awhile. You probably wouldn't find a relative who was still in Europe. Or let's say you have a long-lost cousin but they used *MyDNA* instead of *DNAStory*. You wouldn't find each other because the companies don't share information. However, you can *choose* to have your DNA uploaded to GEDMatch—more than a million people have. That allows your DNA to be compared to DNA analyzed by many other companies—and companies from all over the world. Important to us is that users of GEDMatch are *automatically opted in* for use by law enforcement. They can opt out, but most don't."

"So you can compare DNA found at a crime scene to DNA in GEDmatch," Ashley said, beginning to understand.

"Exactly. If we find just one person who he or she is related to, we can build a family tree using standard genealogy techniques, not necessarily DNA. We use public records—marriages, births, etc.—and add people to the tree even if they didn't submit a sample to any company. We typically will trace back five or six generations and multiple family lines—like cousins and second cousins. We trace the lineages of both the crime scene DNA and the person or persons that they are related to until we find an ancestor common to both people—typically a great-great grandparent. Then we build out all the trees emanating from those individuals until we reach an individual that is most likely the person that left DNA at the crime scene. We do that by looking at things like where someone was living at the time of the crime. Oftentimes it is easier to rule people out. Say a person was a toddler when the crime happened or someone else died before the crime was committed or maybe a person was overseas at the time—clearly all of them could be ruled out as the suspect."

"And you can easily eliminate anyone that is the wrong sex," Ashley interjected.

"Exactly. The DNA tells us if the person who left it was a man or a woman. Once we eliminate all that we can, whoever is left is likely the criminal. That's how we did it with the Green River Killer."

"Then what happens? The cops show up and arrest someone based on a family tree!?" Ashley was mortified.

"No," Rhonda sighed. "But that is a common misperception. All we can do is identify the likely suspect. For an arrest to be made, there has to be independent confirmation. A direct DNA sample acquired from the accused must be obtained and compared to the DNA found at the crime scene."

Ashley raised an eyebrow, "They give that to you willingly?"

Rhonda smiled, "If they are guilty? Rarely. But there are other ways. That's why the cops like to give a guy brought in for interrogation a bottle of water. We can easily get DNA from it if he drinks. That's where you come in, of course." Ashley smiled and Rhonda sat down at an empty computer station. She tapped a few keys and the screen changed. She looked at Ashley. "Want to see an example?"

Ashley nodded eagerly, "Yes, ma'am," and took the seat next to Rhonda.

Rhonda laughed and repeated, "Yes, ma'am. You Southerners are so polite." But Rhonda was smiling and Ashley no longer felt as though the woman was making fun of her. She decided she did like Rhonda after all.

Chapter 35

As Lucy guided the boat across Cam Ranh Bay toward the open sea, Loc Tin, Dai, and the other men acted as though they were preparing to fish—they pretended to the check the integrity of the fishing nets and lines procured from Lucy's boat. They kept a careful watch for any approaching patrol boats that might want to stop them for questioning. Until they reached the relative safety of the South China Sea, female passengers and children were instructed to lay on the deck to keep from being seen. Lucy was in the wheelhouse and thus was not visible from the outside.

Although they saw two NVA boats patrolling the bay, neither approached their vessel and the *California Dreamin'* was soon sailing on the open water. Either the bribes or the pretense of fishing satisfied the men on patrol. Once they reached international waters, everyone relaxed. Loc Tin joined Lucy in the wheelhouse.

"Dai said you are aiming for the Philippines," he said to Lucy, just as an excuse to talk to her.

She looked at him quizzically. "Yes. We discussed the plan during our navigation lessons."

He frowned and then remembered. "Oh, right. The Philippines are closer than Malaysia, and you thought navigation would easier."

"Yes, almost due east. Just a little toward the south. Can't miss it."

"Maybe as long as you're at the wheel," Loc Tin joked, and Lucy smiled.

If they stayed on course and had no problems, Lucy estimated that they could travel the 965 kilometers—about 600 miles—in five days. They had left at the end of the monsoon season, but heavy rains were still possible. Nevertheless, everyone agreed it was riskier to postpone. The first two days of the trip were relatively uneventful. Although many people had been seasick the first day, most seemed to have adjusted. The children were restless but had invented several games that sometimes kept them occupied. One of Dai's children had brought a ball, but it was quickly lost over the side of the boat. Weather the first day had been clear, although very hot and humid. The second night, the boat had been buffeted by high waves. Lucy skillfully maintained control of the boat, but even she experienced a bout of seasickness during the worst of it.

When the storms quieted, Lucy had Loc Tin and Dai conduct a headcount, just in case anyone had been thrown overboard. All were accounted for and although some of the food had been lost, the group remained in good spirits. Dai joked, "I could stand to lose a few pounds anyway." Everyone laughed and agreed with his assessment. They were becoming giddy as they drew closer and closer to the Philippines and the promise of a new life.

On the third day, Lucy spotted something in the water and pointed it out to Loc Tin.

"Another boat?" he asked.

She shook her head. "Much too small. It is also moving very erratically." They both watched cautiously as they approached the unknown object bobbing in the water. Finally, they were close enough to see exactly what lay before them. It was an overturned boat. Four people clung to its hull. "Get the fishing nets!" Lucy commanded Loc Tin. "I will get as close as I can. Throw them the nets and let's get them onboard."

Loc Tin was concerned, "We will be overloaded." Lucy said nothing, but the withering look she gave him told him all he needed to know. "Uh...we'll get the nets." He promptly left the wheelhouse, and she reduced power to the engines. She approached the stranded people slowly to avoid causing waves that would push the overturned craft away. When she was as close as she dared, she cut the engine.

An hour later, the three men and one woman were onboard the *California Dreamin'*. They were sunburned and dehydrated, but otherwise okay. They told a harrowing story of first being attacked by pirates, who stole money and food. Two women had been raped in front of their children. Several of the men, including the pilot of their ship, had tried to stop the pirates and had been killed for their efforts. When the storm came later in the night, no one knew what to do and the boat capsized. As far as the four people who had been rescued knew, they were the only survivors of the original 82 passengers. Hearing the stories that these refugees told had a sobering effect on the passengers of *California Dreamin'*. The boat took on a somber air that it had not had previously. Even the children seemed to understand that something had changed.

On the fourth day at sea, Loc Tin was at the helm when he clearly saw a ship in the distance. He woke Lucy and suggested she get Dai. She quickly left the wheelhouse and returned with him a moment later. By then the ship was close enough for Lucy to recognize. She said simply and without emotion, "Thai pirates."

Lucy took the wheel. She did not change course, nor did she attempt to flee. The engine on the *California Dreamin'* was not powerful enough to outrun the Thai vessel. Even before picking up the refugees the day before, they had planned for the possibility of pirates. Although personal guns were illegal in both Vietnam and Thailand, Dai's money enabled him to buy a pump action shotgun off the black market. Lucy still had the Colt given to her by the American soldier. It was likely that the pirates had knives but nothing more. The plan was simple. Shoot a hole in the hull of the pirate ship, which would almost certainly be made of wood, before their own ship could be boarded.

Dai stood nervously on the deck; his gun hidden from view. He carefully watched the pirate ship inch ever closer to the *California Dreamin'*. A dozen Thai fisherman turned pirates by war and desperation stood on the deck waiting to attack. Dai whispered information to Loc Tin, who was crouched next to him and hidden from the view of the other ship. He held the shotgun at the ready. By pre-arranged plan, Loc Tin and Dai would both aim for a spot just at the waterline nearest the stern. As the boat drew nearer, Dai began a countdown, "One," and flicked off the safety on his weapon, "Two," weapon cocked, finger on the trigger, "THREE!" In unison, Dai raised the Colt and Loc Tin sprang from the deck. Both men fired. Loc Tin quickly put five rounds in the ship's hull exactly where he intended. Dai's first shot missed the boat entirely and hit one of the pirates in the knee. Dai's second shot hit the hull of the vessel which was already taking on water. The shotgun had left a large gash in the side of the boat, and it was starting to list to one side. The injured pirate collapsed on the deck screaming. His comrades ignored him, far more concerned about their boat. The refugees were forgotten. Lucy increased her speed, and the pirate ship faded into the distance.

Later that night the *California Dreamin'* was rocked by yet another violent storm. Although Lucy again managed to bring their craft through it, she was concerned that they had been knocked off course.

By day six their food stores were completely exhausted and water was in short supply. Dai's youngest, a little boy of four, became feverish and began vomiting uncontrollably. His mother tried in vain to bring his temperature down by drenching him in sea water. She gave him both her and Dai's remaining drinking water, but he could not keep it down. By the late afternoon, the child was dead. A day later, Lucy's brother also passed. The poor nutrition that they were all suffering from had caused him to develop severe skin ulcers, which quickly became infected. There was little anyone could do other than to try and keep him comfortable. He was already in poor health and, ultimately, he was unable to fend off the infection. Lucy's mother, who had been trying to console Dai's wife, was now herself inconsolable. Both had watched in anguish as their children had been lowered into the water for their final resting place.

As the sun rose on day seven, Loc Tin and Lucy were the only ones awake. In the distance, they could see storm clouds gathering. They watched as the black clouds grew closer and more dense. "We can't afford to be blown off course again. We are nearly out of fuel as it is," Lucy said, her eyes on the sky.

"Not to mention the lack of food and water," Loc Tin added, staring at the sky.

They watched in silence, helpless as the rain began to fall and the wind picked up. By midmorning the sun was blocked by clouds and the sky held little light. This was by far the strongest storm they had yet encountered, and for more than two hours the small boat was violently rocked. It took both Loc Tin and Lucy to hold the wheel and try to steer the boat into the waves at the best angle to prevent capsizing. At 10:45 A.M., the engine ceased to function—either due to lack of fuel or excess water. Regardless, they could no longer control the ship. The boat continued to take a beating and eventually began to break apart. There were no life jackets.

Realizing the inevitable, Loc Tin convinced Lucy to jump from the sinking boat to the large raft that moments before had been the roof of the wheelhouse. Loc Tin easily made the jump, but Lucy missed, plunging into the ocean. The instant she resurfaced gasping for air, Loc Tin grabbed the collar of her shirt and pulled her onto the raft. They clung to the wooden structure, praying it would hold together. Loc Tin laid on top of Lucy to protect her from the ship's debris being tossed around them and to keep her from being thrown off the raft as it was bucketed by the waves. After what seemed like hours but probably wasn't, the rain became a drizzle and the wind began to subside. They sat up on the raft as they clung to each other and looked around. They were completely alone, drifting somewhere in the South China Sea.

They both knew their situation was very grim. They kept watch for any sign of land or another boat, but several hours passed with nothing but water and sky everywhere they looked. When the sun began to dip below the horizon and the temperature began to fall, Loc Tin and Lucy wrapped their arms around each other for warmth. Lucy closed her eyes against his chest and prayed her mother had somehow survived and that they would all be rescued. She willed herself to stay calm. Soon all light had left the sky and they were surrounded fully in darkness. Loc Tin was exhausted but was afraid if he fell asleep they would both fall off the raft. To stay awake, he tried to make small talk with Lucy.

"When did you learn to read English?"

"When I was quite young. My parochial school had a teacher who spoke English. It was the beginning of the American War, and the school thought it would be a good idea to learn their language. I can't read it very well but can usually sound things out. I had seen the word 'California' before." Lucy's voice was quiet, and Loc Tin could tell she was shivering.

Loc Tin held her tighter and said, "My brother taught me a few words. Then I had an American friend who was trying to learn Vietnamese. We helped each other."

This made Lucy sit up. He imagined her looking at him, though it was too dark to see her face. "An American who wanted to learn Vietnamese? I'm impressed."

Loc Tin laughed, "He couldn't get the tones right. I often had to guess what he meant, but he really tried." They fell silent again. Her head returned to his chest.

"Tell me about your life before now," Lucy asked him. "Tell me about your children."

And so he did. He told her of being drafted at 18 and then again at 23. He told her about his arranged marriage with Kim, their two children, and his attempt to get them all out of Vietnam. She already knew Kim was dead and that he was separated from their children, but now he told her how it happened. At some point he realized she was asleep, but he kept talking to keep himself awake. He thought he was dreaming when he saw what looked like a flashlight playing across the water. He watched the dancing light for a while before realizing he was awake and that it was real.

"Lucy!! Lucy!!" He shook her until she spoke.

"I'm awake—I'm awake. What is it?" But then she saw it, "It's a ship!! A real ship!"

Soon the light scanning the water passed over their raft—the blazing light blinding their eyes for just a moment and then it was gone. But quickly the light was back and held them in its grasp. They waved and waved. As the ship drew near, the lights on the ship illuminated everything around them and Lucy began to laugh. She pointed to the side of the ship and read the words aloud, "USS Blue Ridge." Although Lucy and Loc Tin had no way of knowing it was the lead ship of the US Navy's 7th fleet, they did know that they were saved.

A small, rubber Navy raft was lowered from the USS Blue Ridge into the water two dozen yards from where Lucy and Loc Tin clung to the remnants of their small boat. Soon they left the last vestige of the *California Dreamin'* and were hoisted onto the USS Blue Ridge. On the ship they were reunited with three other people who had left Vietnam with them, though Lucy's mother was not among them. The five refugees were given dry clothes, food, and water before being taken to the ship's living quarters. Nearly 1,000 other refugees were already on the ship. Families were kept together while single women and children were segregated from the men.

When a sailor with a clipboard came by and asked Loc Tin and Lucy if they were family, without hesitation Lucy answered, "Yes."

She looked at Loc Tin, who immediately put an arm around her, "My wife, Lucy. I am Loc Tin Vong."

The sailor nodded and repeated the names as he wrote them down. "Loc Tin and Lucy Vong." Then he looked up at the couple and smiled, "Welcome to the USS Blue Ridge." He started to move to the next person in line, but then he came back to Loc Tin and asked, "Did you have an ARVN rucksack?"

A surprised Loc Tin answered, "Yes. You found it?"

The sailor nodded, "One of the other passengers from your boat saw it in the water and grabbed it. I remember seeing your name on it. We'll be sure to get it back to you."

"Thank you. Thank you very much." Loc Tin said, surprised how much getting that bag back meant to him.

Over the next few hours, Loc Tin, Lucy, and the others from the *California Dreamin'* learned that the Naval ship would continue patrolling the South China Sea picking up stranded Vietnamese until it was at capacity. The refugees would be taken to Guam, a U.S. territory, to be screened and processed for potential transfer to the mainland U.S.

After more than a month at sea, Loc Tin and Lucy spent seven months living in a tent city at Andersen Air Force Base in Guam prior to being sent to a refugee center in Fort Chaffee, Arkansas. When they were told that they had been approved for transfer to Fort Chaffee, Loc Tin asked, "Where is Arkansas? Is that near California?"

The airman smiled and said, "Well, it's a damn sight closer than you are right now."

Loc Tin and Lucy eventually found a priest, also a refugee, who was willing to perform a marriage ceremony. The newly married Vongs then spent another five months in Arkansas before getting the news that a church in Richmond, Virginia, had agreed to sponsor six refugees. The Vongs, along with the Nguyens, a family of four, would be provided food and temporary housing by the Holy Family Catholic Church. Members of the church would also assist both families in finding work. Loc Tin and Lucy arrived in Richmond in early November of 1976, just over a year after leaving Vietnam.

Chapter 36

San Francisco, California, March 1976
  Dennis Dordi

Dennis Dordi looked at his sleeping wife. He had met her in 1969 during his second tour in Vietnam when he had gone to Cam Ranh Bay on R&R. He went looking for sex, but that wasn't what he found. Linh was just 15 at the time. She had been abandoned as a baby and had grown up on the street. By the time she was 16, she had turned to prostitution just to survive. His heart had broken for her, but at the time, he knew it was her only real choice. During his second tour—and then third—they became friends, but never lovers. She was ten years younger than he was and, despite her profession, was still a child to him. He helped her when he could and tried not to get too attached. He told himself they were just friends, but he knew he was lying to himself. Ultimately she was the reason he had signed up for his fourth tour.

His friends and family thought he was crazy. His mother accused him of having a death wish. But they didn't understand. He had to go back for Linh. She was special. He loved her. He was amazed by her grit and determination and her hunger for life despite all she had been through. After he came home in 1971, he could not stop thinking about her—worrying about her. He had to go back.

He was finally able to get back to Vietnam in 1972. This time, she readily agreed to leave with him. He told her he just had to survive one more tour and then they would leave together. He moved her to a nearby ARVN base—to the civilian camp that was attached to it. Then he got lucky. Only three months after he arrived in-country, President Nixon signed the Peace Accord that ended U.S. involvement in Vietnam. The Americans were leaving, and his tour was cut in half. When he told Linh his division was being sent home—six months early for him—she told him she was ready. She was already packed.

At the time he honestly didn't know if she loved him or just hated her life in Vietnam. But he knew how he felt about her and hoped she would be happy with him. They had married soon after they got to the States. She had been ecstatic to learn she was pregnant. Their daughter, Lily, was born in 1975. However, the tiny baby had been born with a serious heart defect and died just after her first birthday. Dordi's mother, Michelle, had flown to California to comfort the devastated Linh. A few months later, Linh learned she was pregnant again. She was happy but also scared—would her next baby die too? Dordi was at a loss as to what he should do for her, so he called Michelle.

"She needs her mother."

"She's an orphan. You know that," Dennis said, slightly annoyed with her.

"She has me. Why don't you move back here? Let me take care of Linh," his mother had immediately responded, and he knew it was the best thing for his wife.

Dordi's parents lived about ten miles outside of Charlottesville, Virginia. Both were retired but still had rental property that brought them a pretty good income. Dordi and Linh had settled in a small town in California, about 30 miles from San Francisco. They loved it but really didn't have any strong ties to the area. He was working with a construction company building an apartment complex, but the job would finish in the next few months and he wasn't guaranteed another.

His mother was still talking, "Y'all could live in one of the rentals and you can help your dad. He's not as young as he used to be, you know. Those college kids are pretty rough on the houses, and he can't always get good workers. And I can help Linh with the baby when he's born."

They talked a while longer. Dordi only promised his mother that he would talk to Linh, but the more he thought about it, the better he liked the idea. Linh had never had a family, but he had a good one. He needed to share it with her.

After discussing it with Linh, Dennis Dordi resigned from his job more than a month before the apartment complex was complete. They moved into one of his parent's rentals—a quaint two-bedroom house near the university in Charlottesville. Dordi worked with his father and Linh spent most of her time with his mother preparing for the baby. Michelle had been a godsend for Linh and was able to help her both physically and emotionally. Lucas Thomas Dordi, who his dad sometimes called LT, was born in July of 1977. Much to his parents and grandparents' great relief, his heart was perfect.

Chapter 37

Memoir: California

Between 1994 and 1996, 15 women living within 30 miles of Richmond were murdered. These were ordinary, hard-working women that rode the bus home late at night. Not the same bus, but eventually the police focused in on one guy. John Michael Jacobs. He was a daytime driver of one of the bus lines—not one that any of the dead women had used, but because he was an employee of Metro Transit, he could ride any bus for free. Apparently, after he got off work, he would ride random buses until he found a potential victim. Then he would follow her home and wait outside—presumably making sure she lived alone. Evidence at the crime scene of the first two women he raped and murdered suggested he didn't stay long. However, the more women he killed, the more brazen he became—making himself at home by watching TV or raiding their refrigerators after they were dead. Since every crime scene was a little bit different, it took a while for the detectives to see the pattern, but eventually they did.

In the mid-1990s, when Jacobs was committing his crimes, the use of DNA as evidence was very new. Few investigators had been properly trained in the collection and preservation of biological samples. Nevertheless, the men and women charged with investigating the serial killer terrorizing the women of Richmond were highly motivated, and they were determined to perfect their skills. Ultimately, samples were adequately collected from three of the victims and the analysts at the VBI were successfully able to amplify male DNA that was presumed to be from the rapist. All three samples were a match to Jacobs, whose DNA had been obtained from the cigarette butts he left in the ashtray when he was brought in for questioning.

The police were confident that Jacobs was responsible for the deaths of all 15 women because they had good circumstantial evidence linking him to the victims. However, they felt their strongest cases were those with DNA evidence, and it was decided that they would only try Jacobs for those three murders. Unfortunately, the judge presiding over the case was not convinced that the DNA had value. He ruled the genetic evidence to be inadmissible, and the case fell apart.

Jacobs smirked as he left the courtroom—flipping off the prosecution after he was found not guilty. We all knew he would continue to kill. I would not let that happen. I knew where he lived, and the Vigilante Virginian would end Jacobs' reign of terror. However, the night I came to kill him, I found his apartment abandoned and filthy. There were dozens of empty pizza boxes, a pile of dirty dishes in the sink, multiple bags of trash, and a scattering of papers on the floor. Clearly, the man had moved and, based on the condition he left the apartment, was not the least bit concerned about getting his security deposit back. I walked around the apartment, thinking. I opened one of the trash bags and my nostrils were assaulted by the stench of days old pizza and beer. The next bag, filled with paper, was more promising. Although it contained mostly bills and old newspapers, it also held an apartment guidebook from Chico, California. I knew the man had a stepsister—or maybe she was a half sister—that was a professor at the University in Chico. Would he have gone there? I didn't remember if she had been at his trial, but maybe.

It took me six months to track him down and then plan the trip that would stop him. I told my family I wanted to spend the weekend fishing, but I was lying to them. In May of 1998, 15 hours after kissing my wife goodbye and nearly seven months after Jacobs walked out of the courtroom a free man, I was hidden in his grungy apartment, waiting. It was Saturday night and he had gone out drinking with his low-life friends. He stumbled in at 1:00 A.M., fell onto his bed without undressing, and immediately began to snore. I slipped out of my hiding place and looked at him. He was lying spread-eagle on his chest. It would be awkward to slit his throat. No easy way to slide the knife across his jugular veins. I stood there for a minute, contemplating my next move. Although he was bigger than I was, he was soft and looked weak. I was strong. And sober. I grabbed a discarded piece of clothing from the floor and tickled his face with it. Without opening his eyes, the man turned over to get away from the nuisance, but I kept tickling his face. When he brought his hand up to wipe away the offending cloth, I grabbed his arm and yanked him to the side of the bed so his head hung off the edge. I quickly pinned his head between my legs and slit his throat before he was even aware of what was happening.

But I was too fast—not careful—because I also slit the back of my knee. I was wearing cloth gloves, the same gloves I wore when pulling weeds from my wife's flower garden. Instinctively, my hand went to the cut on my leg. It wasn't serious, just a nick, really, but it would bleed for a while because of the clean cut my razor-sharp knife had left. I held the glove to the wound to keep from dripping blood everywhere.

How ironic, I thought, if I were convicted of killing Jacobs because of DNA evidence when he walked because the judge didn't trust it. But even if I left a little blood and the police found it, they would have nothing to compare it to. Nevertheless, I was careful. Once the bleeding stopped, I removed the glove and shoved it into my pocket for safekeeping. I wiped my knife on the man's bedding and quietly slipped out of the apartment the way I had entered. I opened the window using only the gloved hand so no fingerprints would be left behind. As I raced down the fire escape, I checked my pocket for the bloody glove—still there. Good. But when I went to change out of my clothes a short time later, it was gone. I retraced my steps to my car, scanning the area. No glove. I checked everywhere inside the car. No glove. I contemplated going back to Jacobs' apartment, but it would be light soon and people in the complex would begin to stir. No, I decided, it was not worth the risk of being seen. Even if the police found the glove, it had to be outside Jacobs' apartment. The glove could have come from any of the two dozen tenants that lived in the complex. It would not be a problem, I decided. By Sunday evening, I was home with my family. My wife had made a pot roast, and I opened a bottle of Cabernet. It was delicious.

Chapter 38

Sacramento, California, July 2021
Ashley and Ben

It was the end of the day on Thursday, and Ashley was the last one in her lab. She had an experiment she wanted to finish before taking off. She was just loading her samples into the thermocycler, the instrument used to amplify DNA, when she heard the door to the lab open. She looked up to see Ben.

"What brings you to my windowless world?" she asked as she pushed the start button on the machine.

He smiled at her, "I was thinking about trying that new steak place off West Elm. *The Tipsy Cow.* Any interest in joining me?"

Ashley hesitated. Was he asking her out? Or was everyone else gone and he just didn't want to eat by himself? She deflected by pointing to thermocycler in front of her. "I will be here another 30 minutes."

He shrugged, "I can wait. Meet you downstairs in 30?" She nodded, and then he was gone.

She stood, hands on her hips, looking at the door Ben had just left through. "So...," she said aloud, "...is this a date or what?" She realized that she hoped it was.

An hour later they were seated in the dimly lit but stylishly appointed new restaurant sipping wine and enjoying their salads. They spent the first 30 minutes talking about Ashley and how she was enjoying the new job. Ashley didn't have much to say on the subject, so she asked, "Tell me more about what it is you do exactly. I know you work with Rhonda a lot."

"Technically, I work for the California Bureau of Investigation and am just a consultant to CBF. Although I work with Rhonda some, it is not as much as it may seem. Her lab had an empty office, and they let me use it when I'm at the CBF. That's why you see me there so much." He took a bite of salad and looked like he was thinking for a minute. Then he continued, "My official title is 'criminal intelligence analyst.' I look at all the data that is available with a crime—crime scene photos, interrogation footage, witness or suspect testimony, DNA evidence—all of it. I try to identify any patterns in criminal behavior or between similar crimes. What type of person committed the crime? Were two or more crimes committed by the same person? Was it a crime of passion or one of convenience? The goal is twofold—aid law enforcement in identifying potential suspects and try to prevent a similar crime in the future."

She nodded as though she understood but wasn't completely sure she did. "And you enjoy it?"

He frowned, "I like the mental challenge of it. But studying crime scenes and trying to get into the heads of evil people—sometimes that gets to me a little." He sat back and shook his head. "There are some seriously deranged people out there. I don't understand how they can do the things they do. But I seem to be pretty good at the analysis, and we have put quite a few criminals in jail—and I am happy about that."

Ashley sipped her wine and looked at Ben carefully as he spoke. He looked like such a tough guy but was admitting that the work could bother him. She didn't expect that. She turned away from him, thinking that she was really starting to like this guy—but was this a date or not? She realized Ben was talking to her and turned back to him.

"Explain something to me," Ben said, leaning forward. Ashley wasn't sure what he was about to ask her, so she set her fork down and gave him her full attention. He continued, "I don't get why you study dioxin. I mean, what's the point? We know it's bad. But what are you going to discover that makes a difference?"

Ashley nodded, "I get why you might think that, but there is a lot to learn that can be helpful. For example, my old lab—Dr. Jansen's lab—they are focused on endometriosis, an incredibly painful and life-altering disease that women can get. If we can gather enough evidence to show that it can be caused by dioxin, maybe the VA will recognize it as being associated with Agent Orange. That could help daughters of Vietnam veterans. Secondly, if we understand exactly how dioxin works, which a number of labs are working on, we may be able to *prevent* its effects. Think about all the burn pits the military uses or all the forest fires we have in California—they produce not just dioxin but other toxicants that bind the same receptor." Ben wrinkled his brow and looked confused. Sometimes Ashely forgot he wasn't a scientist. She tried to explain, "It's like a lock and key. The dioxin is the key. For the key to do anything, it must have the right lock—that's the receptor. If we can figure out how to block access to the lock, then it won't matter if you have the key."

"Would that help the Vietnam veterans? Or the Iraq and Afghanistan veterans? They have already been exposed," Ben asked.

She shook her head, "Probably not. Although it is possible that we could identify better therapies for anyone with a past exposure, it is more likely to help future veterans. It could also help firefighters. Think about their exposure to smoke and toxic fumes over a lifetime. Most exciting, it may be possible to intervene so that the children of veterans or firefighters don't also suffer the consequences of their parent's exposure." She said emphatically, "Imagine the impact on future generations of Vietnamese children. That country has already suffered so much. We have to try to help them."

Ben mulled her answers over for a moment before asking, "Do you seriously believe you can do that? Prevent disease and birth defects in children of veterans?"

"Absolutely! We just need to know more about how dioxin and similar compounds work. Then we can block or reverse its effects." She leaned back in her chair and sighed, "Of course, that was my *old* lab. I'm not doing anything like that now." She frowned and sipped her wine, "Sometimes I wonder if taking this job was a mistake. I don't feel like I am doing anything important anymore."

"I disagree. We are helping to take criminals off the street."

She shook her head, "No...that's what you do. I just sequence DNA all day."

"You are a critical part of the process. We need you doing exactly what you are doing." He picked up his wine glass and continued, "Besides, if you were still in your old lab, you wouldn't have met me." He grinned at her.

She smiled back but said, "Well, the jury is still out on whether meeting you was a good thing or not—but we'll see."

Chapter 39

As promised, the Holy Family Catholic Church fully embraced the Vongs and the Nguyens. One of its members owned a large apartment complex and would allow the newcomers to live rent free for one year. The church would pay their utilities. It was expected that both families would be self-sufficient by the year's end. Neither Cam Nguyen or his wife, Trinh, spoke very much English, so they and their children were soon enrolled in classes to help them master the language. To earn money, Trinh began taking in laundry for some of the neighbors. Cam had few options but was constantly looking for odd jobs or anything he could do to earn money. Loc Tin and Lucy, however, quickly found employment. Loc Tin would work nighttime security at a clothing manufacturer while Lucy joined the staff at a local nail salon. Although it was hard for them—Lucy worked days and Loc Tin worked nights—they were both determined to make the best of it. For the first year of their life in the U.S., breakfast was the only meal they shared.

Each morning they told the other about their day or, in Loc Tin's case, his night. One morning, Lucy said, "I was able to get Trinh a job at the salon. It doesn't really matter that her English isn't very good yet. We just paint rich women's fingernails while they gossip and drink fancy coffee." Lucy hated her job but knew it was just a stepping-stone. She hoped to go back to school, maybe get a business degree and start her own business. Although she had no idea what the business might be, she was certain she wanted to

145

be her own boss.

Loc Tin nodded at her news, "That's good. Cam is anxious for them to get on their feet and not depend on the church so much, but he can't find anything at all. They say it's the economy, but I'm not so sure. We really need another night guard and I recommended Cam. With me there, he doesn't have to speak fluent English, but the owners said no."

"Well, you're a hard worker—and dependable. If you keep recommending him, maybe they will change their mind," Lucy suggested.

Loc Tin nodded, "Maybe. We really do need a third guy. Mac and I can't cover that whole building effectively by ourselves at night. They don't even have decent lighting outside. Last shift leaves at 11:00 P.M. and then they shut off most of the lights. Mac and I just walk around with flashlights. If someone tried to break in...," he sighed. Lucy had heard it before and knew he was frustrated. But it was a good job and paid well, even if he did work 10:00 P.M. to 6:00 A.M. They finished breakfast and began clearing the dishes just as Trinh knocked on their door.

Lucy said, "She is riding the bus with me today. First day on the job and she's nervous. But I told her to just smile and fuss over the housewives, and it will be fine."

"Then you should go on. I can take care of the dishes," Loc Tin kissed his wife goodbye.

After putting the breakfast dishes away, Loc Tin sat at the kitchen table next to their phone. He opened the notebook and stared at the list in front of him. When Loc Tin and Lucy first arrived in Virginia, he spoke to one of the women at the church who had been so helpful and asked if she knew what happened to the orphans who came to America after the war. She didn't but promised she would ask around and see if she could find someone who could help. A week later Loc Tin received a phone call from a woman who worked with the Pearl S. Buck Foundation, one of several groups that had flown orphans out of Vietnam in April of 1975. Operation Babylift, as it was called, rescued more than 7,000 infants and children from the war-torn country. Although many children came to the U.S., others ended up in Canada, Australia, and Europe. The children were placed with adoptive families. She asked him a number of questions, most of which he could not answer. He knew their names, of course, but had no idea who would have been with them or even what day they would have left. He wasn't even sure that they were evacuated.

"The last day I was with them was April 28th," he told her. "We were near Saigon. A nun told me she took two children to Sisters of Mercy Orphanage and that they were evacuating children."

"Do you know the nun's name?" He did not and she asked another question, "Did the children know their own names?"

"Yes, but the nun said they wouldn't say anything. That's my fault. I told them they had to stay quiet and not make a sound until I told them it was okay. I...I...was trying to protect them."

The woman was very sympathetic and tried to be helpful, but Loc Tin realized there was little hope of finding Lam and Suong. They could be anywhere—and probably their names had been changed.

Sensing his desperation, the lady on the phone gave him a list of other agencies he could call. He thanked her and hung up. Now he looked at the list he had slowly been working through. Every morning after Lucy left for work, he would try a different agency. There was only one name left. He dialed the number and a woman answered. Her name was Sophia, and she was also very sympathetic but had no information for him. Once again, he hung up the phone filled with despair. He got up and went to bed, but sleep eluded him.

Chapter 40

The Dordis had been back in Virginia for several years and things were going well. Linh had grown very close to Dordi's parents, especially his mom, Michelle, who had taught her to cook more traditional American dishes. At Christmas, Dordi's two brothers and their families would come to town, and Linh seemed to thrive in the chaos that the holidays would bring. Last year, with Linh and Dordi's permission, his younger brother had given Lucas a puppy. Linh had never had a pet before and was even more excited than three-year-old Lucas to have the small, black, mixed-breed dog join the family. Lucas named him Pepper, and the two were nearly inseparable. Life was good, but Michelle was concerned about Lucas.

"He isn't like my boys when they were little," she told Linh one day. "He is so quiet. I don't think I have ever heard the child laugh. And I have never known a three-year-old to do anything for more than five minutes." Lucas was obsessed with Legos and would spend hours building elaborate structures.

Linh nodded, "I know. He isn't like the little boys I knew growing up, either." She sighed, "But we didn't have Legos or a TV, so it is hard for me to compare."

"Loud noises bother him so much. I've never seen anything like it. Well, not in a child. Dennis' older brother, Phillip, did two tours in Vietnam. He has been so jumpy ever since. Every little thing sets him

148

off. Fireworks—even gunfire on TV—can send him into a full panic. That's what Lucas is like. It doesn't seem normal for a little boy."

Linh nodded again, "I know. I just don't know what to do for him."

Indeed, at Lucas' next well-child checkup, his pediatrician recommended Linh take him to be evaluated at the University of Virginia in Charlottesville. "It may be nothing," he said. "But he has some signs of autism—mild ones—but if he is and can be diagnosed early, there are interventions that can make a huge difference in his life."

The physicians at the University of Virginia agreed with Lucas' pediatrician, though they said autism was difficult to diagnose in children as young as he was. They gave Linh an information booklet and told her the signs she should watch for. They told her to bring him back when he was five or six if she was still concerned.

Chapter 41

Richmond, Virginia, 1978-1980
  Loc Tin and Lucy

Loc Tin's next shift at the Western Mountain Clothing Company started like all the others. Loc Tin and Mac clocked in right at 10:00 P.M. and made their usual rounds around the building. Promptly at 11:00 P.M., they met at the entrance of the parking lot to make sure the workers—mostly women—made it to their cars safely. Typically by 11:20 P.M., the place was deserted except for Mac and Loc Tin. Tonight however, Jenny, one of the women who worked in quality control, was just heading to her car as Loc Tin was locking the door.

"I am so sorry! I had to leave earlier for a doctor's appointment and then needed to stay late to finish," she said to Loc Tin apologetically.

"No problem. I will walk you to your car." Loc Tin unlocked the door and held it open for the pretty, young woman.

"Oh, no need to do that. I'll be fine," she told him, but he insisted.

They walked in an awkward silence to her car, which was parked in the farthest corner of the huge lot near some overgrown bushes. She apologized again, "Because I had to leave, there were no good spots left when I got back."

"It's really no trouble," Loc Tin said, eyes scanning the area out of a long-ago acquired habit.

They said nothing else as they walked, but as they neared her car his sixth sense told him something was amiss. He used his walkie-talkie to radio

Mac, but he didn't answer.

Jenny, anxious to get home, had stepped up her pace as they neared her car and was now just ahead of him.

"Wait," Loc Tin said, the tone of his voice unusual—more commanding rather than the friendly voice she was used to.

She stopped and looked back at him, "Why? What's wrong?"

He shook his head, "I'm not sure. Just a bad feeling. Is your car locked?"

"Why would it be locked? It's a rundown '57 Oldsmobile I inherited from my grandmother. Who would want to steal it?"

"It's not the car I am concerned about." He put a hand on her shoulder directing her to stay where she was, and he put his finger to his lips indicating she should be quiet. Slowly he pulled his gun from its holster and approached her car—the only one left in the lot. He yanked open the door to the back seat as he raised his weapon. But no one was there. He frowned, not convinced he was wrong, and checked the front seat. Nothing. He had Jenny open the trunk—again, nothing. Finally, he holstered his weapon and told her it was safe for her leave. Jenny wondered if the macho act was supposed to impress her. She knew he was married, but that didn't seem to mean anything these days. She got in her car and left Loc Tin without another word. Still uneasy, he walked around the lot but saw nothing of concern. He went back inside the factory and found Mac, who had left his walkie-talkie in the bathroom again. Loc Tin finally decided his imagination was playing tricks on him.

Outside in the bushes not 10 feet from where Jenny's car had been parked, a frustrated man dressed in all black stood up. He had been watching the factory for weeks and had waited for one of the single women to be alone as she left the factory late at night. He had planned to go home with her and play some games she probably wouldn't enjoy and definitely wouldn't survive. Tonight it almost happened. But that two-bit security guard had ruined his plans. He would make him pay for that.

At 2:00 A.M. the few lights that stayed on all night at the Western Mountain Clothing Company went out. Loc Tin was on one side of the building and Mac was on the other. Loc Tin clicked the button on his walkie, "Hey, Mac. You there?"

"Hey, buddy, I'm here. Dark as it can be and my dang flashlight is dead."

"Mine is okay. Where are you? I'll come get you and then we need to check the breakers."

Loc Tin headed to the South side of the building where Mac said he was. Just as he was rounding the last corner, he heard what sounded like someone throwing a fist and making contact with something soft. He heard an, "Oomph," then another punch and the sound of metal clattering to the floor. Loc Tin ran toward the sounds and shined his light in that direction. Mac and a man who had been fired a few months back were on the ground—the latter looking around for the knife he had dropped. With the aid of Loc Tin's light, he quickly found it and was ready to plunge it into Mac's side when Loc Tin pounced on him, easily knocking the knife away. Now two on one, Mac and Loc Tin dragged the man upright and tied his hands behind his back.

Mac shook his head, "Damn, Johnny. Were you really going to stick me with that knife?"

Johnny, clearly agitated, said nothing.

"We better call it in," Loc Tin said. Then he asked Johnny, "Nothing here worth stealing. What were you thinking?"

Loc Tin and Mac both knew Johnny had been let go for harassing some of the women at the factory, but despite their complaints, most people thought he was harmless. He was finally fired when he took a liking to the boss's daughter.

Loc Tin called the police to report the incident. Officers arrived a short time later and took Johnny back to the police station. After questioning him, the police became suspicious and obtained a warrant to search his apartment. They found evidence that linked him to two unsolved murders of young women in the Richmond area. Loc Tin testified at the man's trial and through that process became friends with some of the Richmond police officers. Within a year, Johnny was serving a life sentence in the state prison, though he would be eligible for parole in 15 years. For a short while, Mac and Loc Tin were local heroes. Loc Tin developed a good working relationship with several of the Richmond officers. He was told, "We are always looking for good men." However, as much as Loc Tin would have liked to join the police force, it wasn't an option until he became a U.S. citizen.

Shortly after Loc Tin and Mac helped capture Johnny, the Western Mountain Clothing Company promoted them to the first shift—6:00 A.M. to 2:00 P.M.—and added a third security guard to the overnight shift. Finally, on Loc Tin's recommendation, the new security guard was Cam. Occasionally after work, Loc Tin would join Mac or his new police buddies at a local bar, but mostly he preferred to be home with Lucy. Before long she announced that she was pregnant.

Six months later, Lucy was at her obstetrician's office for a routine checkup. However, her physician was concerned that she was developing a condition called preeclampsia. In order to protect both Lucy and the baby, the child would need to be delivered right away. It was a month before her due date, but if Lucy's conditioned worsened, the baby might not survive. Lucy called Loc Tin and told him she was being admitted to the hospital. He had just gotten home from work but quickly changed out of his uniform and arrived at the hospital soon after she called.

Later that day Kevin Bao Vong was welcomed to the world by his adoring parents. It would be a few days before Lucy was allowed to come home and perhaps a full two weeks before little Kevin would leave the hospital. Loc Tin stayed by his wife's side as long as she would let him. Finally, she told him to go home and rest. She also asked for him to bring her the bag she had packed for the hospital a couple of weeks previously. She had packed it thinking it would be easy to "grab and go" when she went into labor. Now it would be easy for Loc Tin.

He reluctantly left the hospital and promised to return as soon as he could. He easily found the bag she had packed—it was in the corner on the floor of the closet. But when he picked up his wife's bag, he noticed his old army rucksack. He picked it up and sat on the bed. Slowly he pulled out the contents. His uniform with the Special Forces patch he had been so proud to get was on top. The patch made him think of his old friend,

153

Dennis Dordi, and he wondered for the hundredth time where he was. He hoped he was okay. The uniform was worn in places, but he was grateful it had survived the war and their escape to America. Next he pulled out the knife that had served him so well and so long. He had a newer one now that he sometimes used because this one belonged with his first life. He found the doll that Kim had made for Soung and held it for a long moment, remembering the day she had given it to their daughter.

He set the doll aside and returned to the rucksack. He found the lighter that Dordi had given him, a small metal box with a "U.S. Army" logo embossed on its lid, and finally an old photograph. The edges were ragged and the colors were almost gone, but he could still make out the four people that made up his family long ago. Kim was wearing a blue *Ao Dai* and holding Suong, who was sucking her thumb. Loc Tin's younger self looked back at him as he held the hand of his son Lam, who smiled and waved at the camera. He looked at the photo for a long moment. Then he carefully placed everything back in his rucksack. He stood on a chair and placed the bag on the highest shelf in the closet. That life was over. His attention must be focused on Kevin and Lucy. A tear escaped his eye as he closed the closet door. He stood staring at the door for just a minute. Then he picked up Lucy's bag and headed back to the hospital.

Chapter 42

Richmond, Virginia
The St. Bethlehem Home, 1975-1984

Betsy Ingalls had run the St. Bethlehem Home for unwed mothers for nearly ten years, taking over its operation from her own mother following the woman's untimely and, some might say, suspicious death. Almost immediately, the focus of St. Bethlehem moved away from helping the women and girls successfully transition to motherhood to actively encouraging adoption. Growing up in the home, and later working side by side with her mother, Betsy realized that the adoption of the babies was far more lucrative than providing educational services to unwed mothers. Unfortunately, Betsy did not possess the altruistic nature of her mother—she wanted the money to enrich her own life. She had found a lawyer who asked few questions and preferred to be paid in cash. They worked out an arrangement for adoption services that was profitable for both of them, although the legality of the system was questionable. Since so little of the money Betsy received from the transactions was used for support services at St. Bethlehem, the increasingly tight budget led her to dismiss most of the staff. For this reason, Betsy decided that the pregnant residents should do all of the cooking, cleaning, and even the grounds upkeep.

One of the few remaining paid employees was Miss Anne, who had provided prenatal care for the girls since before Betsy had taken over as headmistress. She begged Betsy to reinstate the staff arguing that the girls

155

needed love and support rather than to be used as free labor. But Betsy was steadfast. She said the work was good for them, and it would teach them to make better choices in the future. To accomplish her goal of more women and girls opting for adoption, she first simply adjusted the classroom curriculum to focus on the difficulties the women would face trying to be single parents. The young, impressionable girls were easily convinced that keeping their baby was selfish and would destine both mother and child to a hard life of poverty. However, some girls stubbornly refused to place their babies up for adoption, frustrating Betsy. She wanted *all* the babies to be adopted. She needed a new strategy.

When Betsy's mother, Hazel, was headmistress, she tried to maintain the longstanding policy that if a mother opted to keep her baby, she must have a place to go within two months of the child's birth. St. Bethlehem was a home for pregnant women, and they had little room to accommodate babies. However, perhaps due to her own experience as a young mother, Hazel had frequently bent this rule. She had allowed more than one new mother to stay well past the two-month mark. Hazel felt they had already been abandoned by one family; she did not want to abandon them as well.

However, when Betsy took over as headmistress, she began rigorously enforcing the two-month rule. Now to encourage more adoptions, she made the rule even more restrictive. Once a woman went to the hospital to have her baby, she was not to return other than to collect her personal items, which would be packed up by the other tenants while she was away. There would be no exceptions. As expected, more women were forced into giving their babies up.

But Betsy still wasn't satisfied. She wanted all babies to be adopted. How could she coerce women into that decision? In 1981 an idea occurred to her when a young woman named Lidia was nearing the end of her pregnancy but had yet to find work or a place to live. Lidia had no family and had grown very desperate as the time for her baby's birth became imminent. She very much wanted to keep her child.

Betsy went out of her way to spend time with Lidia and made her feel like they were friends. One day Betsy approached the young woman, "Come to my office later. I have a secret to share." Betsy winked and tried to sound light and girlish.

"Of course, Miss Betsy! I will come by after I finish my chores," Lidia responded, smiling.

Two hours later, Lidia knocked on Betsy's door. She entered when prompted and asked, "You wanted to see me?"

"Oh, yes. Shut the door and come sit down." Lidia did as she was told, and Betsy came around her desk and sat in the chair next to her. She tried to sound casual, but, in truth, she was quite excited about her idea. She reached over and squeezed Lidia's hand. "I know you have been worried about finding a place to live."

Lidia sighed heavily, "Yes, ma'am. I don't know what to do. I need a job before anyone will rent to me, but no one will hire me because I'm pregnant." She was on the verge of tears. "I really want to keep my baby." She looked despairingly at Betsy.

"I know, I know." Betsy patted her hand. "I've gotten very fond of you, and I have worried about you too. But I have an idea that will help. For a while now I have been considering converting two or three rooms of St. Bethlehem into small apartments to accommodate new mothers who, like you, have had trouble finding a place to go."

Lidia's face lit up with excitement. "Really?! That would be amazing!"

"Well, don't get too excited. I'm not sure how it will work, but I was thinking you could be the test case."

Lidia jumped up and threw her arms around Betsy. Betsy was appalled but tried hard not to show it. She pulled the girl off of her. "I will let you stay in the small bedroom next door to my apartment, but you won't be able to leave your room. I will bring you whatever you need. The nurse will look in on the baby. However, you must understand, this is only a test, you cannot tell the other girls. I don't want anyone to get the wrong idea and think they can stay too."

"I won't! I promise I won't!" The young girl left happier than she had been in weeks.

Betsy let out a huge sigh of relief. She had been expecting the girl to ask all kind of questions that would be difficult to answer. She thought she would ask, "How will I look for a job and place to live if I can't leave my room?" But Lidia didn't ask any questions at all. She was young, naive, and desperate. And that was perfect for Betsy's plan.

Unfortunately for Betsy, despite Lidia's promises to the contrary, the girl did tell her secret to Miss Anne. Miss Anne had been terribly worried about the expectant mother who had become more and more despondent as the end of her pregnancy drew near. Miss Anne was surprised and delighted when Lidia arrived in the clinic for her weekly prenatal checkup smiling and happy.

"You found a place to live?" Miss Anne asked, guessing the reason the girl was so happy.

But Lidia shook her head. Lidia could not hide her elation and was never good at lying, so she told the nurse her secret—that Miss Betsy would let her stay. She added, "I guess it really isn't breaking my promise to Miss Betsy if I tell you. She must have told you since you'll be checking in on me and the baby. Did I tell you I picked a name?"

The girl went on chattering excitedly, but the nurse was not really listening. She was relieved that Betsy would allow Lidia to stay on at St. Bethlehem but was also surprised. Betsy had never been known for being the least bit tenderhearted. And, importantly, Betsy had never mentioned to her that she would be checking in on Lidia and her baby.

The day came for Lidia to have her baby, and Miss Anne drove her to the hospital. She assured the young girl that she was in good hands and that she would see here again soon. However, more than a week went by without the girl returning. Finally, Miss Anne asked Betsy when Lidia would return.

"What?" Betsy asked in surprise, then quickly regained her wits. "Oh, yes, Lidia. She was coming back, but her parents came to see her in the hospital. They took pity on her and the baby. So they took her home." Betsy turned away abruptly and hurried down the hall before Miss Anne could even respond.

The nurse watched the heavy-set Betsy scurry off faster than she would have thought possible. The news about Lidia was wonderful, but quite unexpected. From what the girl had told her, she didn't think her parents even knew she was pregnant. Lidia had not spoken to them in several years. The nurse had no choice but to accept Betsy's explanation, but she couldn't shake her feeling of unease. When Betsy disappeared from view, the nurse finally turned away and headed back to her clinic.

What Miss Anne did not know was that Lidia was dead. Shortly after her baby was born, Betsy had offered to drive her back to St. Bethlehem. When the baby was safely in the car, Betsy walked around to the trunk and pretended to help Lidia put her suitcase away. As the young girl leaned into the trunk, Betsy hit her in the head with a crowbar, killing her. She stuffed the girl's body in the trunk and immediately drove to her lawyer's office. Lidia's baby girl was adopted by a lovely couple from just outside Washington, DC. Later that night, Betsy buried the dead girl's body in the garden behind St. Bethlehem.

Over the next four years, three more women confided in Miss Anne that Betsy would allow them to stay even after their babies were born. However, none had ever returned after leaving for the hospital. Suspicious, Miss Anne decided she could be silent no longer and went to the police. By then there were four young women buried in the garden and a dozen others whose bodies had been dumped in the James River.

Chapter 43

Mac, Loc Tin's friend and co-worker at the factory, had rented a cabin in the Blue Ridge Mountains just north of Richmond. Mac had invited Loc Tin to join him, his two brothers, and his brother-in-law for a boys' weekend. Loc Tin had never had a "boys' weekend" and had not been sure what to expect. Mostly they drank and fished and told highly embellished stories of past adventures. The group quickly nicknamed him LT, which made him smile broadly. He explained that it had been the nickname given to him by Dennis Dordi, his Green Beret buddy from the war. Two other men in the group had also been in Vietnam, but they seemed to hold no ill will against him. They did have a lot of negative things to say about the war and how it was mishandled by both governments. Loc Tin tried to stay neutral whenever they talked about the politics of the war, but he gladly shared his stories from that time. The men especially enjoyed hearing about the tricks Dordi had played on him.

Then Loc Tin explained how he had finally gotten one on Dordi. "It was late one night. I had talked to a couple of the guys Dordi bunked with, so they were in on it. They had gotten me a couple of flash bang grenades." Loc Tin looked at the men that had not been soldiers and explained, "Flash bangs are used for training. They sound like a grenade, but there's no actual explosion and no shrapnel. Anyway, I got to his hooch and poured an excessive amount of medicinal alcohol that one of the medics had given me all around his bed." Loc Tin started laughing as he remembered the scene and had to pause to catch his breath. Finally he continued, "One of the guys set off the flash bangs just as I lit the alcohol. Dordi woke up, surrounded by flames thinking they were under attack and that the hooch was on fire. He jumped up and ran through the flames butt naked carrying his M-16. All of us just stood around watching and laughing. Once Dordi's heart rate settled down, he was laughing too."

"So where's Dordi now? Do you keep up with each other?" Mac asked Loc Tin.

He shook his head, "He said he had family in Virginia, but I don't know how to find him. He may have gone to California."

"Have you tried the phone book? It's an unusual name. Can't be a hellava lot of Dordis around here," one of Mac's brothers suggested.

Loc Tin nodded, "Yeah. I found a couple of listings in the Richmond book. One had never heard of Dennis; the other number was disconnected."

"You said he was Special Forces? Maybe try one of the Vietnam veterans groups."

Loc Tin nodded again, "That's a good idea. I will do that."

The following week, he contacted the Richmond Vietnam veterans group and learned that Dennis Dordi was indeed a member. However, the only info that the man he spoke with had was that Dordi had moved to California. There was no forwarding address or phone number. "I know his family is in Virginia. Do you have any idea where they might be?" Loc Tin asked. The man did not but promised he would ask around and call him back if he was able to find out anything. However, no call ever came.

Chapter 44

Sydney, Australia, June 2021
Tony

By early June, Tony was frustrated. He had gotten his DNA results back over a month before, but *Au.DNA* had not linked him to anyone else. Rebecca told him to be patient. "It probably takes time for the computer to sift through all the data," she told him. Though, truthfully, she had no idea. Then another thought occurred to her. "Why is that kit called '*Au.DNA?*'"

Tony shrugged, "I don't know. I guess because it's an Australian company?"

"Exactly! What if they only have samples from people in Australia? Remember Anh asked Emily to do a DNA test when she got to the States?"

Tony was nodding his head, "You may be right. If my father survived the war, he could be anywhere, the U.S., Canada, Australia, the U.K. He might still be in Vietnam."

They discussed the possibility a bit more, but before long Tony had made up his mind, "I think you are right. I will call the company tomorrow and ask."

The lady Tony spoke with at *Au.DNA* confirmed Rebecca's suspicion. Tony asked her, "What can I do then? There's a good chance my father isn't in Australia."

"Well," the service rep suggested, "you might consider having your DNA results uploaded into GEDMatch." She quickly explained what GEDMatch was and even gave him the contact information. Then she said, "Good luck, I hope you find your dad."

"Thank you," replied Tony as he hung up. He immediately contacted the other company and started the enrollment process. He hung up the phone feeling hopeful again.

Chapter 45

Loc Tin had very much enjoyed the boys' weekend with Mac and the other men. He had forgotten how much he loved being in the woods and had been especially fond of the nearby lake. He thought Lucy would also love it and felt it would be good to get Kevin out of the city. He decided he would rent a cabin and bring them to the Blue Ridge Mountains as soon as he could.

The first time they went to the lake, three-year-old Kevin ran and jumped in the water as soon as Loc Tin stopped the car. Fortunately, Lucy had insisted Kevin learn to swim before they came. He had been a natural and loved being in the water. After the success of the first trip with Lucy and Kevin, Loc Tin was anxious to find time to bring them back. Finally, he had a long weekend off at the same time a cabin was available. They drove up early on a Friday morning and arrived at The Woodland Feedmill, the little market near the cabins that Mac had taken him to previously. It was a small grocery/bait/camping store with an eclectic mix of things one might find useful in the woods. Loc Tin and Kevin picked out some live fishing bait while Lucy went in search of fresh produce. Although she had packed grapes and peaches, now Kevin wanted bananas.

The little family met back up at the register where Kevin immediately saw they had ice cream by the scoop. His father quickly relented to his son's request despite Lucy's objections. "He won't eat his lunch now," Lucy scolded.

After getting Kevin his ice cream, the family waited in line to pay. A man with a scraggly beard that Loc Tin had not seen before was in front of them. As the man turned to leave, he noticed little Kevin. He smiled at him and tousled his hair. He looked up and nodded to Loc Tin and then his gaze fell to Lucy. He stared at her for so long, Loc Tin finally stepped between the man and his wife. "May I help you?" Loc Tin asked him pointedly.

At Loc Tin's words, the tall man looked away and seemed to shrink a little. He glanced once again at Lucy and then looked at Loc Tin apologetically. The man said nothing. Just turned and walked out of the store.

Loc Tin and Lucy exchanged glances. Then Loc Tin looked at Billy, the man behind the counter, "Who was that?" he demanded.

"Oh, that's just Joe. He's actually the owner of all the rental cabins. Lives in the one at the top of the big hill. His dad built all of them years ago. Joe inherited them when his dad died. He keeps them in good shape and rents them out."

"I thought you owned the cabins," Loc Tin asked, surprised.

The man shook his head, "Nah. I just handle the communication for him. He's a bit antisocial. He was over there. Vietnam. Ain't been the same since."

"He gives me the creeps," said Lucy, shuddering.

"He don't mean you no harm, ma'am. He probably just ain't seen a pretty woman in a while. He and his wife—they split up. She lives in the city, and he stays up here. He offered to divorce her, but she's Catholic and won't hear of it. I think they get along okay. He sends her money. I know because he gives it to me to send to her. He ain't a bad guy. Just messed up because of the war." Suddenly the man was embarrassed, remembering that Loc Tin and Lucy were Vietnamese. "I don't mean no offense."

"None taken," Lucy said, sincerely, picking up Kevin before continuing. "The war affected all of us in different ways."

The man nodded but didn't say anything more. Loc Tin took Lucy by the hand and the small family left.

Out in his truck, Joe thought about the woman he had just seen. She looked so much like Tam, his girlfriend in Vietnam. Well, no, he admitted. Not his girlfriend. She was a prostitute. Just trying to survive the war any way she could. But whenever he could get R&R, he would find his way to Hue and, for a ridiculously cheap amount of money, he would buy her time for the duration of his stay. Sure, they had sex, but she meant more to him than just that. She had been beautiful and funny. He helped her with her English. She had big dreams for after the war. They had a real bond, he thought. He had a girl back home, but he and Monica weren't married yet. He didn't expect to survive his year in Vietnam, and so he never felt guilty about Tam.

But less than 24 hours into what would be his last R&R, he had woken up in the night. He was thirsty. He was always thirsty in Vietnam. He was disoriented and stumbled around in the dark. He had forgotten where he was. Tam had come up behind him and put her arms around his waist. In his mind's eye she was VC—out to kill him. Maybe slash his throat. He reacted without thinking. He whipped around and snapped her neck, killing her instantly. As Tam fell to the floor, his eyes adjusted to the darkness and he realized what he had done. He dropped to the floor beside her and wept. He held her head in his hands, the grief threatening to overwhelm him. She was the only good thing he had found in this damn country—and he had killed her.

He had no idea how long he sat there holding her, but eventually he picked her up and gently placed her in her bed. He brushed the hair from her face and kissed her cheek. Finally, he left. He wandered around the city for two days, returning to his base a full day before his R&R was scheduled to end. No one questioned him. They all had their own demons—no time to worry about his. He had killed many men in-country and even a few women, but all had been enemy soldiers or VC, and he had no remorse. He was not convinced the war was just, but he recognized that he had a job to do and he had done it. He never thought about the soldiers that he killed. But Tam. He thought about her often, and he would never forgive himself. He came back to the States and married his high school sweetheart because he had promised her that he would. They had a couple of kids and tried to make it work. But he didn't argue when Monica asked him to move out. He was a different person than he was before the war, and he knew he was hard to live with.

He heard the door to the store open, and suddenly Joe was back in the present. He watched the Vietnamese family leave the store and let his eyes linger on the woman. Finally he looked away, put his truck in gear, and left.

Chapter 46

Agent Orange
   1984

On January 8, 1979, a class action lawsuit was brought against the major manufacturers of Agent Orange used during Operation Ranch Hand. In the lawsuit, the aggrieved party was defined as "any individual in current or future generations at risk from their own exposure, or a parent's exposure, to Agent Orange." The class action case was settled out of court in 1984 for $180 million and was used to create "The Agent Orange Settlement Fund." The money was to be used by Vietnam veterans and their families as compensation for injuries that allegedly incurred as a result of exposures during the war.

Chapter 47

Blue Ridge Mountains, November 1984
  Dennis Dordi and Family

Dordi loved his parents and was grateful that they had embraced Linh so completely, but sometimes it was good to get away with just his wife and son. Whenever he could, he would rent a cabin in the Blue Ridge Mountains, just like his dad had done years ago. When he was growing up, Mr. Dordi would often bring his three boys here—giving his mom a much-needed weekend alone. It was in the Blue Ridge Mountains that young Dennis had been happiest. Running wild with his brothers, climbing trees, fishing, swimming, and playing the very best games of hide-and-seek. As a boy, living here was his dream, and even as an adult Dordi never really lost that desire. Somehow breathing was easier out here. But at least for the foreseeable future the occasional weekend was the best he could do. Dordi and Linh sat on the porch of the cabin they had rented watching Lucas play with Pepper.

Dordi took a deep breath. "The air smells different out here," he said.

She smiled, "Yes, and it is good for Lucas to run and play. He's more like a typical little boy out here." They watched the eight-year-old chase the dog through the woods.

Dordi nodded. Lucas loved that dog. He looked at his wife and asked, "I know the woods are not as dense, but does it ever remind you of Vietnam?"

She looked at him sharply, "I try very hard not to think of Vietnam. You know that." She turned away from him, her head held high. "My life is here.

I am an American."

In his mind's eye, that gesture reminded him of the first time they met. When she was a 15-year-old girl trying to make herself look taller. The memory made him smile—but then reminded him of so much more. He hated that she hated her past.

She changed the subject, "Did you call Eric?"

Eric was his old boss at the construction company Dordi had worked for in San Francisco. He nodded, "Yes. He said they have a new job starting in January. He'll bring me on if we decide to go back."

"If?" Linh said, without looking at him. The Autism Institute in San Francisco had invited Lucas to participate in a study for adolescents on the autism spectrum. Lucas had been officially diagnosed when he was six and had been going to the University of Virginia for treatment. They now felt he would benefit from the study that the Autism Institute was conducting that was supposed to improve social skills and enhance cognitive ability. Linh very much wanted to take advantage of the opportunity, even though they would have to leave Virginia. The study would last nearly two years. "We have to do everything we can to give him a good life."

Dordi was not as confident in the Autism Institute as Linh. He thought Lucas was doing well and wasn't convinced moving was the best idea. "My mom will be really upset with me if I move you away. You're the daughter she never had."

Linh nodded, "And your wife will be really upset with you if you don't."

Dordi sighed. He knew there was no point in arguing with her. She had him wrapped around her little finger and they both knew it.

Chapter 48

Betsy Ingalls was livid. That nosy nurse would not leave well enough alone, and now the police were onto her. She needed to disappear. She packed her bags, emptied the St. Bethlehem bank account, and headed north. Using a fake name, she had rented a cabin on the lake and would lay low until she figured out a plan. Less than a week after she arrived at her cabin, she ventured out to the local grocery store—the Woodland Feed Mill. There were no cars in the parking lot, and she hoped the place was empty of patrons. She knew her photo had been plastered across the news. Before going in, she donned a hat and large, dark sunglasses that obscured most of her face. Inside the store, she grabbed a small, hand-held basket and quickly scanned the aisles for both people to avoid and food to buy.

Seeing a man in the canned food aisle, Betsy ducked down the aisle farthest away from him. She wanted to avoid any unnecessary interactions. She grabbed the essentials as quickly as she could and was on her way to the register when she noticed a small wine and liquor section. Yes. That is what she really needed. She picked out two bottles of cheap white wine and carefully balanced them in her already-full basket. She was still looking at the wine as she began walking toward the register. Her inattention led her to collide with the canned food patron. She and her basket—including the wine bottles—crashed to the ground. Her hat and sunglasses were knocked off her head. Betsy looked around, frantic to get her disguise. The canned food guy was suddenly by her side, "I guess I wasn't paying attention. Let me help you up." He grabbed Betsy's arm and tried to help the heavyset woman back on her feet.

Betsy tried to act nonplussed. She was anything but. With tremendous effort, she said calmly, "Oh, it's just some wine and broken glass. It will be fine."

The man picked up Betsy's hat, which had been crushed in the melee, and tried to reshape it, but the woman snatched it from him and shoved it back on her head. The man offered to pay for her groceries and replace the wine, but Betsy shook her head, "I think I'm just going to go."

Without another word, the woman turned and left, leaving the canned food guy standing alone in the mess left behind. Billy, the store's owner, brought out a broom and began cleaning up. The two men spoke briefly, and then only the owner remained in the store.

Two weeks later, Betsy's dead body was found in her cabin. Her throat had been slit.

Chapter 49

Sacramento, California, June 2021
Ashley and Lance

One afternoon in mid-June, Lance found Ashley working at her lab bench. "When you get a minute, stop by my office. I might have something for you."

Thirty minutes later, Ashley knocked on his open door. "You wanted to see me?" she asked.

He looked up from his computer and waved her in. "I have a case you can get a little more involved in. Still DNA sequencing, but if you can get the data, I'll let you take a lead on the genealogy. You'd work with Rhonda on that, of course, but you can really get involved and be part of the process."

"Really? That's awesome. Thank you," she replied and sat in the chair opposite him without being asked. "What's the case?"

"Guy named Jacobs," he said as he handed her a file. "The details are in here and also in your box on the secure server. But the short story is that this guy, Jacobs, was tried for three murders in Virginia. Prosecutors believed he was responsible for as many as 15 but they only had DNA from three. However the judge didn't trust the DNA data—this was back in the mid-nineties—and deemed it inadmissible. The guy got off and he moved to California. Several months later he was found dead with his throat slit. No good evidence at the crime scene, but a few days later a bloody glove was found."

"A few days later? Kind of sloppy investigation," Ashley interjected.

"Well, it wasn't found at the crime scene exactly. Murder was at an apartment complex. The glove was found in the building's parking lot." Ashley nodded but didn't say anything so he continued, "The glove may or may not have anything to do with the crime."

Ashley nodded again, "I see why you're letting me take a shot at it. A crime that is not a high priority to solve, because we all know the dead guy was a terrible human being and because any DNA on the glove may have degraded, and even if I can sequence it, it may have no value."

Lance nodded, "That pretty much sums it up."

"Where's the glove?" she asked.

"Evidence room. Cold storage. Instructions on how to get it released to you are in there," he said, pointing to the file.

Ashley picked up the file and stood up, "Thanks for the opportunity."

He shrugged, "I know it isn't much, but it's a start."

"I really do appreciate it."

A week later, Ashley knocked on his office door again. When Lanced waved her in, she sat in the same chair as before and said, "Well, good news and bad news on the bloody glove."

"You were able to get DNA?" he asked, surprised.

"Yep. But it's a mixture—clearly contaminated. At least six different people. White, Black, Asian, male, female—it's all there. Even something that isn't human. Pretty sure it's a dog. At any rate, not useful as far as using it for forensic genealogy."

Lance leaned back in his chair and put his hands behind his head, "Dog DNA?"

"Well, I'm not certain, but that's my best guess. How could that happen? I could see a mix of two—victim and killer. But six? Plus a dog?"

"Remember, the glove was found outside. I didn't get details on that, but my guess is that it was found by the dog. Then maybe the owners of the dog took it away, realized what it was, and then gave it to the police. They probably weren't wearing gloves either." He shrugged. "Back then, use of DNA was very new. We weren't as careful handling specimens at that time."

Ashley nodded, "I suppose. Still a bummer." She started to walk out, but then she turned and added, "Again, I appreciate your giving me a chance."

"No problem. We'll find you something else that's more promising."

"Thanks," she said as she walked back into the lab.

Chapter 50

Lucy was standing at the kitchen table folding clothes and talking to her husband. "You want to buy a cabin from Creepy Joe?"

"Yes! It's one of the bigger ones—the one with the porch that overlooks the lake. It's the one you like so much," Loc Tin was trying hard to convince his wife, but she was skeptical.

"But it has taken us so long to save that money. That was supposed to be for our trip to Vietnam someday," she said, purposefully focusing on the clothes and not looking at him.

"I know. And I WILL take you back to Vietnam. I will pick up extra shifts if I have to! We could even rent the cabin and make extra money that way. Then we can save even more. I promise I will make the money back. But this is a unique offer. Joe is really making us a great deal on the cabin...we will actually save money because now it won't cost us every time to rent it."

Now Lucy turned to face him. With her hands on her hips she said, "But there's still the upkeep. And the taxes. And why is he selling it anyway? Especially if it is the best cabin."

"Well...um...he has had trouble renting it lately," Loc Tin did not like the way this discussion was going. She was asking too many questions.

"Okay. Why? Why is he having trouble renting it?" She was annoyed that she even had to ask the question. He should explain without being asked. She knew he was hiding something.

"Well...," Loc Tin hesitated.

"Out with it," she demanded.

He sighed, knowing he would have to tell her eventually. "Remember a year or so ago—that woman that was on the run from the police for killing women and taking their babies?"

Lucy shuddered and turned back to the clothes. "I remember. She was murdered, wasn't she? By that vigilante guy...," her voice trailed off as she realized why he had been so evasive. She whipped around and pointed a finger at him, "You are NOT buying the cabin where that woman was murdered!!" She lowered her voice, "And what if it was Joe?" She looked around as though she were concerned that Joe might be able to hear her, and then she continued, "What if HE is the one that killed her? What if he is the vigilante?" She had another thought, and her hand flew to her mouth. She whispered again, "What if he comes back and kills us?"

Loc Tin smiled at his wife. "I don't think Joe is the Vigilante Virginian. Even if he was, why would he kill us? He only kills evil people. You don't have an evil bone in your body. Besides, you will never be there without me." He put his hands on her shoulders reassuringly.

"I don't like it," she said. "I don't like it AT ALL."

Loc Tin pulled Lucy close and wrapped his arms around her. "You know I will always protect you. And it's good for Kevin to get out of the city. He loves going to the lake." She sighed heavily, and he thought he was making progress convincing her. But it took two more weeks of discussion before he was finally able to get her to agree. Nevertheless, it would be a long time before she was willing to return to the cabin.

Chapter 51

Memoir: Regret

Since leaving the army, I have killed many men and one woman that the justice system failed to punish. Save for the first one, my method was always the same. Of all those I have killed, I have only one regret—a man who had done terrible things in his past but had turned his life around and was finally trying to do the right thing. But it was a difficult time in my own life. I was filled with rage and wanted to take it out on someone. Other than the convenience store killing long ago, the crime I committed that day was the only one that had not been carefully planned. It was just a chance encounter when I was out running errands early on a Saturday morning.

I saw him get out of his car and recognized him immediately. His 40-year sentence had been cut in half for good behavior. It was an atrocity. The man headed for the door of the big home improvement store, but it would not open for another 15 minutes. I sat in my car and watched him walk to the door. He pulled the handle, but the door was locked. He instinctively checked his watch and then checked the sign on the door. He stood there for a moment. Likely debating whether to wait there for 15 minutes or trudge back to his car. He made the wrong choice. While he walked, he looked at his phone completely oblivious to his surroundings. I retrieved my knife and gloves from the glovebox of my own car, quietly jimmied his locked vehicle, slipped into the back seat, and locked myself in.

Still with his attention solely on his phone, the man unlocked his car and climbed inside. I slit his throat and within seconds was back in my own car driving away. The man's death was the lead story on the nightly news. I watched with satisfaction as the reporter detailed the man's past sins. But then she discussed how he had found Jesus in prison and began trying to make amends. He started a dog training service within the prison—helping not only the people who would get the service dogs but also giving the prisoners work that gave them purpose. After serving 20 years for his crimes, he had gotten out, moved back in with his parents, and worked to get his high school diploma. When his father developed Parkinson's disease, the son was there to help. After his father died, the man had gotten a job in a local assisted-living facility and used what he had learned taking care of his father to take care of the patients there. Everyone spoke very highly of the man who had turned his life around and was finally headed in a good direction.

Listening to the news, I felt a twinge of guilt knowing that I had killed a man who had already paid his debt to society and had apparently left his criminal past behind. But the twinge I felt grew to overwhelming regret when the reporter showed a clip of the man's devastated mother. She had only recently lost her husband and now her only child was also dead. Despite his past, she had loved him. But I had taken him away from her forever. For the first time in a long time, I felt remorse.

Once again, I vowed I would never kill again. But, once again, I was lying to myself. My rage would grow exponentially in the months after this man's death, and I would take it out on those I deemed guilty.

Chapter 52

Blue Ridge Mountains, September 1988
  Dordi and Loc Tin

Lucy had suggested Loc Tin go to the cabin for the weekend. Kevin was having a sleepover party with six of his friends, and Lucy knew it would be too much for her husband. He loved his family but wasn't as tolerant of a house full of wild boys as Lucy was. It was a spur-of-the-moment decision, and he had packed light—a little too light—and he stopped at the Feed Mill to pick up a few supplies before heading to the cabin.

"Hey, Billy," Loc Tin spoke in the direction of the TV.

"Hey, yourself," Billy replied without taking his eyes off the screen.

Loc Tin gathered a few groceries and set them on the counter. Billy heaved himself out of his chair but continued watching the TV. After a few minutes, a commercial started and Billy turned his attention to his customer.

"How's it going, Billy?" Loc Tin asked.

"I guess it's all right. Not many people here this weekend. Though there's a guy rentin' the cabin nearest the lake."

"Just one guy?" Loc Tin asked. "Sometimes Joe rents to a bunch of college kids. They don't always clean up when they leave."

"Nah. No kids. Just the one guy. Another veteran. He usually rents a big cabin on the other side of the lake when his family is with him but rents from Joe when it's just him. I've talked to him a few times. He seems okay. Name is David. Or Dennis. Or maybe David Dennis? Two Ds anyway."

Loc Tin paid for his items and had turned to go when Billy added, "He can toss a knife nearly as good as you can."

Loc Tin stopped and turned back to Billy. "Dennis Dordi?"

Billy slammed his hand on the counter, "Yes! That's it. That's him. You know him?"

Loc Tin smiled, "I'm the one who taught him to throw a knife."

"Well, I'll be damned. Ain't it a small world?"

"So I have heard." Loc Tin was still smiling. He set his purchases down again and walked over to the store's limited selection of booze and wine. He grabbed a bottle of Jack Daniels and threw some money on the counter. "Keep the change, Billy," he said as he walked out the door.

A few minutes later Loc Tin parked his Jeep next to a beat-up, red pickup truck with a "Keep on truckin'" bumper sticker. He climbed out of the Jeep and took the steps to the small porch two at a time. Dordi had obviously heard the car pull up because he opened the door, shotgun at the ready, before Loc Tin had a chance to knock. The two men had not seen each other since 1971, but it didn't matter. Dordi set the gun down and said, "You look like hell, LT."

"But still better than you, Dordi," retorted Loc Tin.

The old soldiers embraced briefly, and then Dordi stepped away from the door, wordlessly inviting his old friend in.

Dordi got two glasses, and Loc Tin opened the whiskey. They took their drinks and the bottle out to the porch and sat in a couple of old rocking chairs that had come with the cabin.

Loc Tin asked, "How long have you been in Virginia?"

"Most of the last ten years, though we went back to California for a while. That's where my wife and I settled in '73 when I got out of the Army. We lived in the Bay area for a few years before moving back here when Linh got pregnant again." Dordi paused for a moment and sipped his drink. Then he told LT about Lily.

"I'm really sorry, Dordi." Loc Tin knew firsthand how painful it was to lose a child. He refilled their glasses and told Dordi how his life had unfolded after the war. He told him about losing Kim and his family. He told him about Lucy and the *California Dreamin'*, marriage, and Kevin, his work, and Lucy's business. "I try not to think about my life in Vietnam and just focus on Lucy and Kevin. When I do that, I can't complain. The States have been good to me."

"You mean other than the death and destruction we wreaked on your homeland with napalm and Agent Orange?"

"Yeah—other than that."

They talked long into the night. Mostly reminiscing but also adding details of their lives since they last met. The good and the bad. Many of the stories started with, "Remember that time..." They laughed a lot and, at least for a while, felt like young men again.

They drank in silence for a long moment, each lost in thought. Then one of them said, "I love the darkness of these woods at night. No city lights. Almost as dark as the jungle."

"Almost. Quieter, though. The sounds are different."

The other man nodded and added, "And no tigers."

"No tigers," his friend replied, smiling. But then the smile faded and he added, "Maybe a ghost or two."

"So I've heard," the other man agreed, sipping his whiskey and wondering if his friend meant the murdered woman.

They grew quiet again. They emptied the last of the Jack Daniels into their glasses.

"We left a lot of ghosts in Vietnam," one of the men spoke at last. "Some of them deserved to die."

His friend stared into his drink. "I might know something about the ghost around here."

The other man considered the statement carefully and then said simply, "She deserved her fate."

His friend nodded, "That she did." He held up his glass and the other man did the same. Wordlessly, they toasted their friendship and the many secrets that they shared.

Chapter 53

Sacramento, California, July 2021
Ashley and Colleagues

It was the first Friday of the month, and after work Ashley's lab members gathered at Rita's for happy hour. Although Ben was not previously a regular with the group, he hadn't missed a gathering since Ashley joined the CBF. Tonight Rhonda's kids were with her mother, so she was able to join as well. They were discussing a case that they had recently been given.

In 2017, Fred Jamison was convicted of a horrific killing spree that had occurred in Virginia the previous year. During his trial, it was alleged that Jamison had gone to his ex-wife's home to get a gun that technically belonged to him. After using it to kill his ex-wife, he went to the Virginia elementary school where his ex-wife's new boyfriend was a teacher. He opened fire in his classroom, killing the boyfriend, several students, and a student teacher. Because he was given the death penalty, his case received an automatic appeal.

Jamison had hired a new defense attorney who had successfully petitioned for having the strongest piece of evidence against him thrown out—DNA obtained from blood left at the scene of his ex-wife's murder. Since her home had also previously been his home, the attorney had argued that it was possible, even likely, that the blood was left when he lived there rather than during the commission of a crime. The defense also argued that although the gun was registered to Mr. Jamison, it could have been stolen without the former Mrs. Jamison realizing it.

The attorney even had a reason for Jamison, who had no children, to be at the school that day. Jamison's sister testified that she was considering buying a new house in the area. The sister swore under oath that she had asked her brother to check out the school that his niece would attend. While the defense admitted that Jamison was at the school when the carnage occurred, no adult could identify him as the killer. It was a flimsy excuse, but the sister appeared to be a credible witness. Once the DNA evidence was thrown out, the prosecution was afraid the man's conviction would be overturned. However, a few months later while waiting for the appeal to be decided, Jamison was found murdered in his jail cell. Most believed that he was murdered by another convict, but others thought he might have been a victim of the Vigilante Virginian. It was the latter theory that had pulled the CBF into the case.

Ever since the CBF had found the Green River Killer using investigative genetic genealogy, requests for their services had come in from all over the country. This time the request was from Virginia's new district attorney. She had ordered the Virginia Bureau of Investigation to find the Vigilante Virginian and put him in jail or else she would "clean house." Everyone's job was on the line, and the VBI had asked the CBF for help.

The investigators in Virginia had found three gray hairs at the scene of the Jamison murder. Although they had easily been able to get DNA, there were no matches in CODIS, which meant that either the killer wasn't another convict or that the hairs were not left by the killer. Since the Jamison murder was the first potential vigilante crime in which any DNA had been obtained, the VBI had asked the CBF to conduct a genealogical assessment on the DNA.

The California DA had assured the Virginia DA that the CBF was making progress on the case. They were not. Rhonda had yet to find a single person even distantly related to the owner of the gray hairs. Ben had asked and had received photos from all of the crime scenes attributed to the Vigilante Virginian, but they weren't very helpful. The team was under a lot of pressure to get a lead in the case, and it was on everyone's mind. It was not a very happy "Happy Hour."

After the waiter took their orders, a frustrated Rhonda asked, "What's the rush to catch the vigilante guy anyway? Sounds like he is doing a good job ridding the world of some real scumbags."

Ashley shook her head emphatically, "Vigilante justice isn't justice. This isn't the Wild West. And what about the guy that had already paid his debt to society and had turned his life around? You can't justify killing him."

Rhonda nodded and shrugged, "Still, most people think the guy is doing the world a favor."

"We don't even know if the DNA we have is from the Vigilante or not. The hairs could have been left by anyone," Ted chimed in.

Ben shook his head, "They still had the root attached. Hairs don't just fall out with the root; they were pulled out. That suggests some kind of a struggle between Jamison and the gray-haired guy. Although it doesn't mean the gray-haired guy is the killer, it certainly suggests that the man just wasn't casually walking by Jamison's cell."

"Any chance I can help? Or at least watch y'all work? I would really like to learn more about the process of IGG," Ashley interjected. She looked at Lance for his approval.

Lance nodded and said, "You are fully vetted by the CBF. No harm in letting you get involved."

Rhonda screwed up her face, thinking. "You mind doing a bit of computer sleuthing?" she asked Ashley.

"Anything. I just want to help," Ashley replied.

"Well," Rhonda began, "the VBI has identified 12 Vigilante murders in Virginia. I am wondering if there are others outside the state. It would be good to look at all the knife deaths in the surrounding states for the last few years, though that could be a huge number."

"We don't need to look at all of them. Just the murders of 'people that deserved to die,'" Ashley said, using her fingers to make air quotes.

"I don't think there is a computer algorithm for that," Ben said, but looked like he was thinking about it. "It would simplify things if we could narrow it down somehow."

The waiter came by with their food and drinks and everyone stopped talking. After he left, Rhonda suggested, "Maybe just go back one year at a time. We only need one hit."

Ashley asked, "What are we looking for exactly?"

Ben responded, "We really need DNA. If there is another crime scene that wasn't previously attributed to the Vigilante and had DNA..."

Ashley interrupted, "Then Rhonda might have something to work with."

"Yes," Ben agreed, "assuming the gray hairs are not from the Vigilante and that another sample would have a match in CODIS. But we need to know either way. If we found another DNA sample and they matched the hairs from the Jamison case, then that supports the theory that the Vigilante Virginian killed Jamison."

"It would also tell us that our vigilante has gray hair, which is something, isn't it?" Ashley asked, hopefully.

"Or at least some gray hair." Ben tapped his pencil on the table, thinking. "Even without DNA, if we can identify a few more cases, we may learn something about him that we don't already know, something that may help narrow down who he might be. Maybe all the crimes occurred at the same time of day or always in a wooded area. Anything that might help identify him."

Ashley frowned, "Well, so far the only common thread I have seen is a knife to the throat of a really bad person." Suddenly Ashley sat up straight realizing something, "The Jacobs case! The Jacobs case fits the MO." She looked at Lance.

"Yes, but that murder was in California," Lance reminded her.

"But wasn't *his* crime committed in Virginia?" Ashley asked.

Lance thought about it for a minute, but shook his head. "I still think it's a long shot to be the Vigilante—at least the one we are looking for."

Ashley leaned back, disappointed. She disagreed with Lance but didn't feel comfortable voicing that opinion. Instead, she just said, "Okay. I will do a computer search and see if I can find anything else, but," she looked at Ben, "I guess it will be up to you to figure out if the data is useful."

Ben smiled, "Well, that's why the CBI sends me a paycheck occasionally." Then more seriously, "I should show you the crime scene photos, though there isn't much to see from the cases we have so far." He thought for a moment and then turned to Lance, "Any reason why I couldn't show Ash photos from closed cases? Explain to her what it is that I do? Then she will have a better idea what to look for as she goes through the old cases—though I will look at them too of course."

Lance nodded again, "No problem using closed cases, but they still need to be treated with the same professionalism. And on your own time. You can teach Ashley if you want to but not during the workday."

"Understood," Ben responded. He then looked at Ashley. "You interested in learning some analytical techniques?"

"Absolutely!" Ashley replied a little too eagerly. She hoped she just sounded enthusiastic about the training rather than about spending more time with Ben.

"Great. It'll take me a week or two to pull some files together, but let's plan to meet...," he looked at the calendar on his phone, "...Sunday, August 15th?"

Ashley shrugged, "Sure. That should work. In the meantime, I will start looking for other potential Vigilante Virginian deaths."

Lance nodded his approval, and the conversation shifted to less serious topics.

Chapter 54

Richmond, Virginia, 1988
  Loc Tin and Dordi

In 1988, after Lucas completed the study at the Autism Institute, the Dordi's moved back to Virginia. Dordi easily found a job with a construction company in Richmond, and, with the help of his parents, he and Linh bought a small house. That same year, six months after Loc Tin and Lucy had become naturalized citizens of the United States, Loc Tin was finally able to join the Richmond Police Department. He had become friends with many of the officers during his years working security at the clothing company and felt it was the right move for him. As with all new officers, Loc Tin had to spend the first couple of years as a beat cop walking one of the local neighborhoods. Over time he got to know many of the business owners and people who lived in the area. Most people seemed to like him, and he enjoyed being a part of the neighborhood. He thought he fit in well with the Richmond Police Department and got along with most of the other cops. Like him, many were also former military. However, despite the camaraderie he felt with most of the other officers, Andrew James was clearly not his friend. The first day after Loc Tin's training was complete, the captain partnered Loc Tin with James, a three-year veteran of the department.

After the assignments were made, Loc Tin went to the locker room to grab his gear and get ready for his shift. He overheard James complaining to another officer, "Damn. Why'd capt'n stick me with Charlie? Spent two years in 'Nam trying to rid the world of those commie thugs. Now I'm supposed to work with one? *Trust* one? How do I know he ain't gonna stab me in the back?"

"Pretty sure Vong was ARVN—fought with us, not against us," the other officer responded.

"Whatever. They are all the same to me. Damn commie." Officer James slammed the door to his own locker. "I ain't teachin' him a damn thing. He just better stay outta my way," he said, as he stomped off to his patrol car.

The other officer said nothing but nearly walked into Loc Tin as he turned to leave, "Uh...I guess you heard that?"

Loc Tin nodded and shrugged. "I have dealt with his kind before. I'm here to do a job—not to make friends." The officer nodded and hoped Loc Tin was as thick-skinned as he appeared to be.

Loc Tin was proud to be a cop, but working with James grated on him. He told Lucy one night, "I don't see why he has to be an ass. Just do the job. He calls me 'Charlie.' He knows my name."

Lucy kissed his cheek. "He does it to get under your skin. Don't let him see it bothers you."

"No, I don't let him see. I don't care if calls me 'Charlie' or 'Commie'—or 'Chinaman'—that's the new one. I don't care about that. He's an ass. Fine. Whatever. But I have to be able to trust him. If something happens, I need to know he has my back. Right now I think I am more likely to be shot by him than anyone else."

"You could ask the captain to assign you to work with someone else," Lucy suggested.

Loc Tin shook his head. "I wouldn't give him the satisfaction," he replied, cutting up the vegetables for their salad a little too aggressively.

Lucy put a hand on his and gently pried the knife from his hand. "Maybe you should set the table. I don't think you need a knife when you talk about James."

Two weeks later, Loc Tin invited Dordi to join him and a half dozen other cops at a local sports bar to watch the Colts play. Late in the second quarter, the game was interrupted by a breaking news alert.

"Good evening, Richmond. I'm Maria Barlow with Channel 5 Action News. Tonight we have breaking news. Michael Samuelson has escaped from the Appalachian State Maximum Security Prison and may be in the Richmond area. As you may recall, Samuelson was convicted of killing two families who were camping in the Shenandoah Valley back in 1979. If you see Samuelson, do not approach him. Please call 911. He should be considered armed and very dangerous." The camera angle changed, and Ms. Barlow turned to follow it. She dropped the serious demeanor and flashed a big smile toward the audience, "Now we return you to the Colts game already in progress."

The police officers watched the news with great interest. James pointed his beer at the TV and said a little too loudly, "Better watch yourself in Richmond, prison boy. That Vigilante dude will smoke your ass." Then he laughed and burped loudly.

Another officer shook his head, "We need to catch the Vigilante. We don't need someone doing our job outside the law."

James disagreed, "What are you talking about? The Vigilante Virginian is a damn hero. HE-RO! I hope he crosses paths with that Samuelson dude and takes him out! Save us hardworking taxpayers a lot of money."

Nearly everyone at the bar had an opinion—hero or criminal—but no consensus was reached. Loc Tin and Dordi sipped their drinks and kept their opinions to themselves.

Two days later, Maria Barlow was back, "Good evening, Richmond. I'm Maria Barlow with Channel 5 Action News. Tonight we have breaking news. Michael Samuelson is dead. His body was found on the grounds of the Appalachian State Maximum Security Prison. His throat had been slit."

Chapter 55

Agent Orange
  2001

In 2001, the U. S. Environmental Protection Agency initiated a bi-national partnership to clean up Agent Orange/dioxin hot spots throughout Vietnam. Among the projects, the USAID awarded CDM Smith, a U.S. construction and engineering company, $19.7 million for the environmental remediation of dioxin at the site of the U.S. Air Force base in DaNang.

Chapter 56

Richmond, Virginia, 1990-1998
The Vong and Dordi Families

In 1990, Loc Tin and Lucy bought a fixer-upper in an up-and-coming suburb of Richmond. Dordi and Loc Tin worked hard to make repairs and improve the home's functionality, resulting in their wives and sons spending a large amount of time together. The women quickly became friends.

At the police station, Loc Tin had been promoted more than once and was optimistic he would eventually become a detective. When Dordi mentioned he was getting tired of working construction, Loc Tin tried to talk him into joining the police force. Dordi just laughed and shook his head, "I am not cut out for that bureaucratic law and order kind of justice." Then he looked at LT, "To be honest, I'm surprised it has been such a good fit for you. In 'Nam, you got pretty good at instant justice."

Loc Tin nodded, "But that was war—the rules were different."

Dordi shrugged, "Maybe."

Over the years, Lucy and Linh grew to be very close. Neither had ever had a sister, and they relished their friendship. Although Lucas had always had trouble socializing with kids his own age, he did well with Kevin, who was slightly younger. They both loved Legos and could spend hours and hours together building complex designs. Ten-year-old Kevin was the star of his middle school soccer team and was teaching Lucas to play.

Linh told Lucy one day, "Kevin has been really good for Lucas. I can see such a positive change in him. He's more outgoing now."

Lucy smiled, "Kevin likes Lucas a lot. He always wanted a brother, and he likes being able to help him and show him things."

"The Autism Institute helped Lucas a lot, but not nearly as much as being with Kevin," Linh observed.

Lucy smiled. "Maybe it's Kevin or maybe it's just everything finally coming together for Lucas. Anyway, I am just happy that he's doing so well."

Lucy frequently talked of returning to Vietnam, but Linh had no interest in it. She would just smile at her friend and say, "My life is here."

But Lucy was anxious to return to her home country. She and Loc Tin were frugal and saved as much money as they could in hopes of making the trip a reality; however, other priorities always seemed to eat away at their nest egg. In 1992, when Kevin was 12, the family splurged on a vacation to Disney World. They invited the Dordis to join them, but Linh thought it would be too much for Lucas, and by then their family included three-year-old Jeremy.

Before they left for Florida, Dordi pulled Loc Tin aside, "Don't worry about anything here, LT. I have it under control."

Lucy overheard the comment and asked Loc Tin later, "What did Dordi mean when he said, 'I have it under control'?"

Loc Tin looked at his wife for a second before responding. "Oh, that. He just meant he would keep an eye on the house for us."

Lucy nodded but still thought it was an odd thing to say.

The Disney World trip had been wonderful and Lucy had no regrets, but the adventure took nearly all of their Vietnam savings. For many years after that, the only vacation they took was to the cabin. It had taken a long time for Lucy to get past her initial feelings of disgust due to the woman having been murdered there, but once she did, she enjoyed the quiet of the wooded mountains almost as much as her husband and son. Sometimes Loc Tin and Dordi would take Kevin and Lucas for a boys weekend. Occasionally Loc Tin would go by himself. He told Lucy he really loved being away from the city and enjoyed the solitude of the cabin. As promised, he sometimes rented it to others, but mostly they kept it for themselves and the Dordis.

By 1995, although Lucy was still at the nail shop, she no longer filed nails and painted other women's toes—she was the co-owner. She had taken several business classes at the local community college, and her hard work had helped the salon grow and prosper. Lucy had suggested and then implemented several changes to the salon. First, it was just to make it neater, cleaner, and more inviting. Later, at Lucy's suggestion, the salon began offering more services. In addition to manicures and pedicures, they began offering facials, added a sauna, a masseuse, and other luxuries for local women—including a glass of wine with the "Pamper Yourself" package. The name of the salon was changed to "The Pampered Lady Day Spa" and business was booming. When Lucy mentioned that the salon was looking for more help, Linh quickly volunteered. Linh continued to homeschool Lucas but also found time to work a few hours a week at the Pampered Lady. Although Lucy became Linh's employer, it had no negative effect on their friendship, and the two women grew nearly as close as Loc Tin and Dordi.

In 1998, the year Kevin started college, Loc Tin was finally promoted to detective. It was a job he seemed to be born for, and he quickly earned the respect and confidence of his colleagues. He still ran into James occasionally, but he no longer called him "Charlie" or "Chinaman"—at least not to his face.

Chapter 57

Agent Orange
2004-2005

In 2004, in a New York City courtroom, a class-action lawsuit was brought against more than two dozen manufacturers of the chemical components that made up Agent Orange. The suit was filed on behalf of a group of Vietnamese citizens and alleged that use of the chemical weapon violated international law. The group sought billions of dollars in compensation for the Vietnamese people who were suffering due to the adverse health effects of Agent Orange. In 2005, a federal judge dismissed the lawsuit filed by the concerned citizens of Vietnam. The judgment was appealed, but that petition also failed.

Chapter 58

San Francisco, California, 1998-2016
  Dennis Dordi and Family

Lucas, the Dordi's oldest son, turned 20 in 1998. Despite being autistic, he was something of a computer genius. He had been offered a job in Silicon Valley that he wanted to take, but his mother worried about him being on his own in California.

"He's never lived by himself before," Linh said to her husband the night Lucas first told them about the job.

"He has made a lot of progress in the last few years. Most people don't even realize he's autistic. They just think he's awkward. This is a great opportunity for him—a chance at a normal life," Dordi argued.

"Don't you miss California?" she asked him, putting her arms around him. "Call your old company. Eric is always happy to have you back."

He sighed. He never could say no to her. Soon Dordi and his family were back in San Francisco. Before he left, Dordi made LT promise he'd come visit. "We've got cabins in the mountains out there too, you know." It was a promise that would be kept, although infrequently.

Lucas was quite successful at the new tech start-up that had hired him. It seemed he wasn't the only member of the team on the autism spectrum, and perhaps for the first time in his life he felt he fit in. Within a few years of moving to the Silicon Valley company, he met Eden. She was painfully shy but also gifted in her own way. They were good for each other and good together. They married in 2006, and before long they had a family of

196

their own.

Dordi and Linh's youngest son, Jeremy, was only 11 when they left Virginia. Although he had been upset to leave his friends, he quickly made new ones. In 2005, he graduated high school a year early and went to a small local college on a full scholarship. After college, he was accepted into medical school at the University of California, San Diego. Dordi and Linh had been overwhelmed with pride. When Jeremy was a little boy, he had told his parents he wanted to be a baby doctor so he could prevent birth defects like the ones his sister and brother had. Many years later, it wasn't a surprise when he chose to specialize in obstetrics and gynecology, although by then he knew preventing birth defects wasn't really something he could do as a physician. However, during his residency at UCSD, he met Dr. Beverly Jansen. Her research studying dioxin resonated with him, and he knew he had found his calling.

For a long time, life for Dordi and Linh was good. After the boys were grown and doing well, they were enjoying being empty nesters. But then in 2015, Dordi's father died, and he and Linh moved back to Virginia to be close to his mother. A year later Linh was diagnosed with advanced breast cancer. Jeremy had always been convinced that Lily's heart condition and Lucas' autism were connected to Agent Orange. Now, he wondered whether his mother's cancer was linked as well. He also wondered why he had been spared. Why was he healthy? As a son and brother, he felt guilty. But as a physician and scientist, he was also confused. If Agent Orange had caused Lily and Lucas' problems, why not him? Was there something in his genes that made him resistant? He wanted to know why, but answers were few.

Chapter 59

During Kevin's junior year of college, he met Radhika Patel, a freshman, when they both took Introduction to Biology. They began dating and quickly became inseparable.

Kevin was majoring in business and hoped to be his own boss someday like his mother though he had no interest in running a nail salon. Radhika was pre-law, majoring in history. After learning that Kevin's father had been in ARVN during the Vietnam War—known in Vietnam as the American War—she had delved deeply into studying that conflict, eventually writing her senior thesis on the subject. When Kevin graduated, Radhika still had two years left of her undergraduate degree, which weighed heavily on his decision to stay at the same school and pursue his MBA. After Kevin finished his master's degree in 2003, he found a job as a marketing manager for a large retail chain store. Radhika graduated college the same year. After the graduation celebrations had ended, Kevin proposed. He was surprised and hurt when she said no. She told him she wasn't ready to settle down—she wanted to travel.

Radhika was also tired of school and decided she wanted more free time to live her life than what being a lawyer would allow. She and her best friend from high school spent a year backpacking across the country, and Kevin thought he would never see her again. But, unexpectedly, they met in a law office in 2008. She had become a paralegal and was assisting with a case involving his company. Kevin and Radhika began dating again and were married in 2009. Before long, they welcomed a son, Timothy, and then a daughter, Samantha. Life was good and they were happy.

Loc Tin turned 65 in 2010 but was in excellent health and had no intention of retiring. He loved his job and felt he was contributing to society. Lucy, who was now the sole owner of the Pampered Lady, was ready to slow down and spend less time at the salon. She hired a manager to run the business day-to-day and enjoyed helping Kevin and Radhika with her grandkids. Life was busy but very, very good. Lucy felt they could finally afford the trip to Vietnam.

"You know," Lucy said to Loc Tin one morning as he was getting ready for work, "It's our 35th anniversary this year. We could visit Vietnam as an anniversary trip."

Loc Tin sighed. They had had this conversation many times. "I promise—when I retire, we will go back. If we go…"

"WHEN we go," Lucy corrected.

Loc Tin nodded, "Yes, of course. When we go. We need to plan to stay at least a month. It's too far and too expensive to go for just a week. I can't take off work so long right now. And, honestly, would you feel comfortable leaving the Pampered Lady for a month?"

Now Lucy sighed. She knew he was right, but still—time was passing. She wanted to be young enough to be able to walk around and really enjoy it. "Vietnam has changed so much. I want to see everything. Promise me we will go soon."

Loc Tin kissed his wife, "I promise."

Chapter 60

Sacramento, California, August 15, 2021
 Ashley and Ben

It was Sunday morning and Ashley was at Ben's apartment looking over old crime scene photos. He was teaching her to use her analytical skills to draw inferences on what had happened and who might be the perpetrator. He hoped studying old crime scenes would help her understand what she was looking for in trying to find more victims of the Vigilante Virginian.

"This is a case we solved last year. I picked it because it didn't get much press, and I am hoping you didn't see anything about it on the news," Ben told her as he laid out the images. A Hispanic man in work clothes, obviously dead, was laying in a beautifully landscaped flower garden.

Ashley studied the four photos of the crime scene taken at different angles. Then she looked at the autopsy report.

"Single shot to the back of the head from close range. Clearly he was busy working when someone came up behind him. An execution." She looked at Ben, but he said nothing. "But he either didn't hear whoever came up behind him or was unconcerned—someone he knew."

"Exactly. Our first thought was a gangland execution, but the guy was clean. Legal immigrant, working hard. No arrests—not even a traffic ticket. He was the senior landscaper working for a wealthy banker, guy name John Morris. The gardener lived on the property in a small house behind the Morris home."

"How long did he work there?"

Ben smiled, "Almost ten years."

"I assume the banker was married. What did she do?"

"Very little. Only one child—she was away at boarding school."

Ashley looked at him, slightly annoyed, "You could make this a little more challenging."

"Tell me your theory. It may not be what you think." He smiled knowing she was headed down the wrong path, but the same one he had taken at first.

"Gardener was having an affair with the banker's wife. Banker kills the gardener."

He nodded, "Exactly what we all thought at first, but the banker was out of town with his wife at the time of the murder. No evidence of an affair."

"Hired hit?"

"Think about what you said earlier."

"He knew his attacker." She thought for a minute. "Then I don't know."

"We were stymied too. Then the gardener's 16-year-old daughter broke down. She was dating some 20-year-old thug and wanted to get married. The dad, of course, forbid it. She and the thug went to talk to him, and he wouldn't even acknowledge them—just kept working. The boyfriend pulled out a gun and shot him. He took off and the daughter called 911. She initially said she had found him shot but fell apart under questioning."

Ashley looked back at the photos, "You can't get all that from these photos."

"No. But that's the point. We all have pieces of the puzzle. Just pieces. Don't get locked into one theory. You have to keep digging and keep asking questions—even when the answer seems obvious."

Ashley wasn't sure what to make of Ben's "lesson," although it was interesting. They looked at crime scene photos all morning, but by 1:00 P.M., they realized they were hungry and walked to a nearby sports bar.

While they ate, Ashley told him the details of her cold case and why she thought it could be the work of the Vigilante Virginian.

"It does sound like the same guy. Have you found any other cases outside Virginia? That would add strength to your theory."

"Not yet but still looking." She bit her lip, "I think Lance gave me the

Jacobs case because nobody really cares if the guy who killed him gets caught or not. He was definitely a bad seed. Anyway, Lance asked me to try and get a DNA profile. Well, I did, but it was crazy. At least six different people had handled that glove—white, Black, Asian, male, female, even something that isn't human. I am pretty sure it's a dog. When I told Lance about the sample being contaminated, he said, 'Oh, that may be because a couple walking their dog found it and turned it in.' He guessed that two or three people handled it after the couple that found it. At any rate, it's pretty worthless from our perspective. But at least I know my DNA. Picked out all of them."

Ben nodded and then asked, "What kind of dog?"

She had just taken a bite of pizza and didn't want to speak with food in her mouth, so she just looked at him quizzically and mumbled, "Hmm?"

"What kind of dog? Beagle? Cocker Spaniel? I mean, if you are as good as you say..."

She swallowed her pizza. "You're funny—real funny," she said, wiping the grease off her hands with a napkin.

Just then and within a few seconds of each other both Ashley and Ben's phones received a news alert that made Ben ask the bartender to turn one of the many TVs to a news channel.

The noisy bar grew quiet as more and more people noticed the chaotic scenes on the TV. After more than 20 years of the U.S. and other Western forces fighting against the Taliban, the capital of Afghanistan, Kabul, fell to the enemy. The long war was over. And we had lost.

A new Taliban-led government would be brutal and deadly. For that reason, the U.S. government had promised to evacuate all Americans in the country along with any U.S. allies. Not surprisingly, the airport in Kabul was being overrun with desperate people trying to leave the country. It was anticipated that the new Taliban-led government would kill anyone with ties to the U.S.

Ben and Ashley sat at the bar, helplessly watching the events taking place half a world away. Ben had been there. Fought there. Had friends die there trying to make a difference. This wasn't how things were supposed to end.

Not knowing what else to do, Ashley put a hand on his shoulder and tried to be comforting.

Chapter 61

The Old Man sat at his table watching the news. His dinner was in front of him, but he no longer felt like eating. He had not watched the news in over a week—which was unusual for him. He had been busy. Debbie had come by a couple of times and taken him outside since the weather had been surprisingly mild for August. He had also made progress on his memoir—finally deciding to include more of his happy memories in addition to the ugly ones. He hated to admit it, but Debbie had been good for him. He had not realized just how depressed he had become, and she had somehow pulled him out of it. She made him focus on the present. "You may be old, but you aren't dead yet," she had told him once. Surprisingly, the candid comment had made him laugh. It also made him appreciate a little more what he did have.

But now—the news. As he watched the horrific scenes unfold in Kabul, Afghanistan, images from Vietnam filled his head and long-suppressed emotions resurfaced. He felt the same anger, disappointment, and sheer frustration over what was happening in Kabul as he had in Vietnam. He was impotent to do anything—just like he had been in 1975. Everyone was frantic to get out, afraid of what the communists would do to Americans or their sympathizers left behind. At least for the civilians left behind in Vietnam, it had not been as bad as had been predicted. No mass executions, no torturing, as far as he knew. Nevertheless, the years immediately after the war had been difficult for many, especially the orphans. And there were so many orphans. He shook his head remembering it all. Finally, he turned his attention back to the TV. The people of Afghanistan would suffer a far worse fate than the Vietnamese who had been abandoned. The Taliban would have no mercy for anyone, not even the children.

Chapter 62

Anh felt as though she were back in Vietnam. She watched the TV and saw frantic women throwing their babies over the fence in Kabul. She had seen it before. In Saigon in 1975. When South Vietnam fell to the communists, everyone wanted out. She remembered how the U.S. Marines had tried to get as many people out as they could. Americans and their families had priority. In response, eighteen-year-old soldiers were claiming 60-year-old Vietnamese citizens were their brother or sister just to make them eligible for evacuation. But there were too many people and time was running out.

Anh had been on the roof of the American Embassy in Saigon—she was supposed to get on a helicopter. She had given Mai, her infant daughter, to John. He was an American doctor pretending to be her husband and Mai's father so that they could be evacuated.

When Tony and his sister were found and brought to the orphanage, John's "family" expanded to five. At the embassy, Anh held Tony's hand and tried to hold on to John. But the crush of the crowd—she could feel it now, as she watched the crisis unfold in Afghanistan—it pushed her down and ripped her away from him. He got to the helicopter, still holding Mai. But she and Tony couldn't reach it. She watched helplessly as the helicopter carrying her baby rose into the air. Now, in front of her eyes, Afghani mothers were just as desperate to escape with their daughters as she had been. She felt their panic—she had lived it. Her pain from so long ago coalesced with the anguish of the women in Kabul. She couldn't breathe. She looked at the TV in disbelief. How could this happen again?

Chapter 63

Blue Ridge Mountains, 2015
Joe

"Hey, Billy. How's it going?" Joe spoke to the man who had owned the Woodland Feed Mill for as long as he could remember.

Billy sat on a stool behind the register watching a small black and white TV set off to the side. Hearing his name, he looked up. "Hey, Joe. Haven't seen you around lately."

Joe smiled—something Billy didn't think he had ever seen before. "I've been in Richmond. I'm a grandad! Can you believe it? My wife called me a few days ago and invited me to come down. Got to see both my kids AND my new grandbaby. A beautiful little girl." Joe was beaming.

"That's great, Joe. I'm real happy for ya," Billy said. "That's really great."

"I'm heading back down there soon. Might be gone for a while. It was really good to see Monica. And she seemed to like having me around for a change. Her house needed some repairs, and I was able to take care of a few things for her. I came back for my tools so I can do a bit more. It's a good solid building, just getting old and rundown."

"Yeah, I know the feeling. I ain't as young as I used to be either."

"Ain't that the truth," Joe agreed and both men laughed.

The men continued to talk. Mostly Joe just wanted to let Billy know he would probably not be around as much and to give him a call if any of the renters needed anything. Billy had never before known Joe to be so chatty.

Billy asked, "How many cabins you got these days? I know you sold most of 'em."

"Just mine and the two closest to me. It just got too hard on me taking care of 15 cabins. That Vietnamese guy with the pretty wife still has his, but some of the others have already been resold. I hate it. Not everyone is particular about who they rent to."

Billy nodded, deciding not to mention that Joe had rented a cabin to the woman who the police had been after for murdering young mothers. Instead he said, "No problem, Joe. You enjoy your family for a while. I'll keep an eye on things here."

"Thanks, Billy. I'll come by as soon as I get back in town." Joe, still smiling, walked back toward the door. Then he stopped and turned back, "Maybe let me know if that Vietnamese guy comes back with his wife. She's real pretty."

"What about Monica?" Billy asked.

Joe shrugged, "No harm in looking."

Chapter 64

Richmond, Virginia, 2015-2018
  Loc Tin and Lucy

In May of 2015, Lucy began having troublesome symptoms. At first it was night sweats, and she assumed it was menopause rearing its ugly head again. She had just turned 68 and thought she was done with that, but what else could it be? By June, Loc Tin noticed she had lost a lot of weight. Lucy had always been slight, but now, she was shockingly thin and frail. Finally in July when she caught a cold and couldn't get over it, he convinced her to see a doctor. He ran a few tests, and a week later he asked Mr. and Mrs. Vong to meet him in his office.

"I'm afraid I have some bad news, Mrs. Vong," the doctor said with little preamble. He was seated at his desk and looked sympathetically at the old couple across from him.

"What is it?" Loc Tin asked, his anxiety evident. Lucy put a hand on his shoulder to comfort him.

The doctor looked at Loc Tin and then Lucy. "I'm afraid you have cancer. Non-Hodgkins lymphoma."

"What is that? Can it be treated? We will do anything," said Loc Tin.

"We can do chemotherapy, but her disease is rather advanced. I'm not sure how well she will respond," the doctor continued.

"How serious is this? Some cancers you can treat by cutting out the affected organ," Loc Tin suggested.

The doctor shook his head, "This is a cancer of the lymphatic system. You can't remove it. Unfortunately," he looked at Lucy, "this disease will very likely take your life. Although not today."

Now Lucy asked, "How long do you think I have?"

"Two, maybe three years. Longer if your cancer responds to the chemo. It is difficult to say with certainty. I am very sorry." The doctor stood, "I will give you a few minutes alone." He left his office, and Loc Tin and Lucy sat hand in hand without moving.

Finally Loc Tin spoke, "We just have to fight it. The doctors here are the best. I'm not ready to lose you."

Lucy smiled, "I'm not ready to leave, but when the Lord calls me home, I must go."

Loc Tin immediately put in for retirement and, being well past 65, was quickly approved. Over the next two years, Loc Tin cared for his wife without complaint. Lucy underwent several rounds of chemotherapy with little benefit. Radiation was next and the cancer seemed to respond, at least initially, but then it quickly returned. He took her to endless appointments and did everything he could to make her comfortable. Her hair fell out and she lost more weight than Loc Tin thought was possible. By April of 2018, Lucy was tired and wanted no more visits to the hospital. Loc Tin took her home and doted on her. She died on July 11, 2018. She was 71 years old.

Loc Tin wandered around the house aimlessly in the days after Lucy died. They had been together for more than 40 years, and he could not remember what life had been like before she was part of it. He had her cremated because he could not bear the thought of her being buried in the ground—it didn't seem right to him. Kevin bought a beautiful blue urn with a subtle design of flowers and a rising moon to hold her ashes. He told his dad, "When I saw it, I thought it was something Mom would like."

Loc Tin nodded, holding the urn in his hands and turning it to feel its smooth surface. "Yes, she would like the design. Thank you, Son."

But in his heart, he knew that she would not stay in the urn forever. He needed to return her to Vietnam—the country she had longed for for so long.

Chapter 65

Northern Virginia, 2018
  Dennis and Jeremy Dordi

Dennis Dordi stood over the freshly filled grave of the woman he had loved for nearly 50 years. They'd had a good life, despite everything. He had no idea how he would go on without her. He wasn't sure he wanted to.

"Dad, it's time to go," Jeremy touched his father on the shoulder.

The man reached up and touched his son's hand with his own. "I know. I just...I just don't want to leave her."

Jeremy nodded and patiently waited a little longer. The ceremony had been a small private affair with only a few people in attendance. Loc Tin had, of course, been there, but he was still mourning the loss of his own wife and Kevin and Radhika took him home as quickly as he would let them. Lucas and Eden, who had small children, had left as well. Now only Jeremy and his dad remained. They had buried Linh beside Jeremy's grandparents. They had been the mom and dad she never had, and she had loved them dearly. Someday Jeremy knew his father would be buried alongside them as well. He just hoped that it would not be soon. His father was in good health, but Linh's illness and now her death were taking an unimaginable toll on him. As a doctor, Jeremy had seen death many times. He had known his mother was very sick and that the cancer would take her life. He thought he was prepared, but her death hit him harder than he had thought possible. It was even harder on his dad, who always assumed the much younger Linh would outlive him. Jeremy stood next to his father at his mother's grave for a long time. When it started to rain, Dennis finally allowed Jeremy to lead him away.

Chapter 66

"I'm worried about your dad," Radhika told Kevin yet again. "Ever since Lucy died, he just isn't the same. He drinks too much. And I don't think he needs to spend so much time with his old police buddies. They just get him more agitated talking about criminals and such."

Kevin sighed, "I don't know what you expect me to do. He's a grown man."

"He's your father! Talk to him. He should spend more time here, with his grandchildren. Better than being in his house all by himself."

"I invited him to dinner this weekend, but he's going to the cabin."

"Well, maybe you could go with him. Take Timothy. A boys' weekend," Radhika suggested.

"I can't. I have that big meeting on Monday, and I need to spend the weekend getting ready. Besides, I think he prefers going by himself or with Dordi and they..."

"Drink too much!" Radhika interjected.

Kevin nodded, "They commiserate. They understand each other."

"I suppose," Radhika agreed. Still, she worried. Loc Tin and Kevin had always been so close, but now—since Lucy died—their relationship seemed strained. Radhika frowned, thinking. Finally, she said something that had been on her mind for a few weeks, "Maybe he should move in with us. At least for a while. Just until he adjusts to life without Lucy," Radhika suggested. Kevin looked at her like she was crazy. "I'm serious. You could move your home office to the basement, and we could convert the other room to a bedroom." She took her husband's hand, "He can't go on like this. You know it."

Finally Kevin nodded, "I'll talk to him. But I don't know if he'll agree."

Chapter 67

Agent Orange
 2009

In Tennessee, U.S. Veteran James Cripps won his lawsuit against the U.S. Veterans Administration for his exposure to Agent Orange that occurred *inside* the continental United States. He was exposed to the deadly combination of chemicals from 1967 through 1969 when he worked as a game warden at Fort Gordon, Georgia. It was his job to spray Agent Orange in the lakes around the fort to kill weeds. He developed chloracne and other health problems now known to be associated with dioxin exposure.

Chapter 68

Sacramento, California, August 2021
   The Vigilante Team

Ashley, Ben, Lance, and Rhonda sat around the conference table surrounded by the original case files, as well as the new ones Ashley had identified over the last few weeks that she thought might be connected to the Vigilante Virginian.

"Going back five years, I found four murders in the states surrounding Virginia that fit the profile," Ashley explained. Two in Philadelphia—although it was the same crime scene—one in West Virginia and one in North Carolina. What is interesting is that ALL of these murders, plus Jamison and two others in Richmond that we already knew about, were committed in 2019. That's seven murders in less than a year." She let that sink in before she continued. "Other than Jamison, none had any DNA evidence, or any kind of biological sample, processed or not. So then I thought, what if I go way back, before DNA was a thing? Maybe he left DNA evidence before he knew better."

"That's a great idea. Did you find anything?" Ben asked, sitting up and looking at her expectantly.

"Well, great idea or not, I still came up empty. The earliest vigilante-type killing that I could find was back in 1978—though I only went back as far as 1975." She told them about the guy at the convenience store whose neck had been broken after shooting the red-haired kid. "There were no fingerprints, no DNA, and no real leads. To this day, the case remains

217

unsolved. It wasn't a knife attack, so initially I dismissed it. But it was in the heart of Richmond—our guy's primary killing ground. What's interesting to me is that this killing wasn't planned. How could it have been? So I keep thinking maybe this was the first one. He saw the kid get murdered, and he killed the murderer. Instant justice."

Ben sees where she is going. "He gets off on it. Or maybe it just makes him feel good. Adrenaline rush or something. So he does it again and again." He nods, "It's a decent theory."

"But what I can't figure is how does he know about these other people? The guy at the big box store—okay, he'd been all over the news. A lot of people were upset when he got paroled. But how would the Vigilante know that he would be at that store? Did he follow him around and take him out when the opportunity presented itself? Same with some of the other victims—how would he know who they were or have access to them? The two in Philadelphia were killed in a bathroom *in a courthouse*. How is that even possible?"

"Is he a cop?" Rhonda suggested.

"Maybe. But even a cop wouldn't know that Betsy Ingalls was living in a cabin in the woods under a fake name. How did he find her?" Ashley shook her head, continuing to sift through the papers in front of her. Finally she told them about Jacobs, the cold case Lance had given her. The DNA is crap, but his throat was slit, just like the other knife attacks attributed to our vigilante. Interestingly, Jacobs had gotten off on murder charges in Virginia. So," She looked at Lance, "at least to me it seems reasonable that it could be our vigilante guy. On the other hand, almost immediately after he was found not guilty, Jacobs moved to California. How would the Vigilante Virginian know where he had gone? I don't know." She looked around the room, but no one else had any ideas either, so she continued. "Anyway, I compared the mixed DNA sample from the Jacobs case to the DNA from the Jamison case. I can't be sure, but there are some similarities. It is *theoretically* possible that the same person who left the gray hairs found at Jamison's murder scene is also one of the people who contributed DNA to the bloody glove from the Jacobs murder." She frowned, "But I don't know if that person is the killer or just one of the many people that handled it."

"Which could be a cop," Ben said.

"Yes, but a cop in California," Lance spoke this time.

Ashley sighed, "So we are nowhere?"

Lance frowned, "Sounds like it."

Chapter 69

Burn Pits
2009

On May 14, 2009, the Military Personnel War Zone Toxic Exposure Prevention Act (HR 2419) was introduced into the U.S House of Representatives. The bill would require the Secretary of Defense to establish a medical surveillance system to identify members of the armed forces who had been exposed to chemical hazards arising from the use of burn pits in Iraq and Afghanistan. Furthermore, it would prohibit the continued use of such burn pits by the U.S. Armed Forces.

Chapter 70

Joe walked into the Woodland Feed Mill and, as usual, found Billy watching TV behind the counter.

"Hey, Billy. I just sold the last of the rental cabins. I only got mine now."

Joe's wife, Monica had been in a serious car accident caused by a drunk driver. Although her health insurance helped, it wasn't enough. Joe had decided to sell the remaining cabins to help pay Monica's expenses.

Billy nodded, not sure how Joe would pay his own bills without the rental income, but it wasn't his business. "I'm sorry about Monica."

Joe nodded but didn't respond. He sighed heavily and then said, "I'm not sure when I'll be back. I closed up my cabin, and it should be fine. I sold the one closest to the lake to a young doctor from California. Jeremy Dordi. He came and looked at it with his dad. They used to rent from me a while back, but they moved away a few years ago. Anyway, the dad is back in Virginia and is going to live there full-time. You'll probably see him around sometime. Name's Dennis Dordi."

Billy nodded, "I remember him. He and that Vietnamese guy were friends in 'Nam or something. Okay, Joe. Don't worry about anything here. I'll keep an eye on your cabin and let you know if anything comes up."

"Thanks, Billy. I'll see ya later."

Chapter 71

Burn Pits
2013-2014

On January 10, 2013, Public Law 112-260 was enacted requiring the U.S. Veterans Administration to establish The Burn Pit Registry. The registry became a reality in 2014, and veterans exposed to burn pits were encouraged to add their name to the list in order to determine whether any diseases or conditions were related to exposure to the toxic fumes.

Chapter 72

Arlington, Virginia, April 2019
The Admiral

Retired Navy Admiral James "Jimbo" Higgins sat on his patio, cigar in one hand, bourbon in the other. It was 10:15 P.M and the Admiral was enjoying the surprisingly mild weather. He had lived in the condo for six years and hated the close proximity to the neighbors at first, but eventually he had settled into a routine and the neighbors were nice enough. And quiet. His patio backed up to a park, which was generally deserted after dark. It had become his habit to sit outside and enjoy the fresh air once the joggers and mothers with children had gone home. But after dark was also when the crazies and criminals came out. So his .380 pistol was tucked in his waistband, just in case.

It had not been a good day for the Admiral. He had been experiencing shoulder pain for months, which he initially ignored. He assumed he had injured it somehow and simply tried to not use it, but the pain only intensified. Finally he went to see his physician, a general practitioner at the VA in Arlington. The doctor said it was just a sprain, prescribed a muscle relaxant, and sent him home. But the pain continued to worsen. It became so intense he could no longer use his left arm. He found another doctor who ordered an MRI. Today he got the news. Pancreatic cancer. His doctor said he might live a year or two, but he couldn't be sure. He recommended he get his affairs in order. He also recommended he stop smoking and cut back on the alcohol. The Admiral had actually laughed out loud when the doctor said that. The Admiral told his physician, "I have a box of fine Cuban cigars and an unopened bottle of Pappy Van Winkle. I'll be damned if I let my ex-wife and her husband get their hands on those."

Now he sat on his patio defying his doctor's orders and thinking about his life. His father had been a fisherman trawling the coast of Maine. Jimbo, as he had been known back then, had grown up on his father's boat and learned the ways of the water. He loved being on the open ocean but had no desire to spend his life fishing. He went to college by joining the ROTC and married as soon as he graduated. He joined the Navy as an ensign and steadily climbed the ranks. Eventually the war in Vietnam started, and because of that he was made admiral long before he otherwise would have been. They gave him a fleet of Swift Boats to command, and he and his men patrolled the waters around the jungles of Vietnam.

Back then, Agent Orange had been a godsend, or so he thought. He asked for the defoliant to be sprayed along the banks in order to eliminate the thick foliage that allowed the VC to hide and attack his boats. The Air Force obliged him, and suddenly the surprise attacks from the shoreline were no more. But now, like so many others, he was dying because he had eaten, breathed, and drank those "harmless" chemicals. Agent Orange may have saved his life in Vietnam, but it was killing him now. The Admiral sipped his bourbon and wondered how long he had. He was 84 years old, but he wasn't yet ready to die.

Chapter 73

On November 7, 2018, the former U.S. airbase in DaNang, Vietnam, was determined to have been successfully cleared of dioxin/Agent Orange and was formally handed over to the Vietnamese people for expansion of the city's international airport.

Chapter 74

Vietnam, June 2019
  Loc Tin and Kevin

"Flight attendants, prepare for landing," the pilot announced on the overhead speaker.

Loc Tin had the window seat and watched as the landscape of Vietnam passed below him. The plane was on its last leg of its long journey and would soon land in what was now called Ho Chi Minh City—although it would always be Saigon to Loc Tin. As was typical, his thoughts were on Lucy. His heart ached for her. She should be with him now—not just her ashes. Lucy had always wanted to return to her birthplace, and he promised her over and over again that they would. He had failed her.

The guide that Kevin had hired met them at the airport. As he drove them to their hotel, he explained that the 50 years since the fall of Saigon had in many ways been good for Vietnam. The country had become a major tourist destination with vibrant cities, despite the communist takeover. Like China, the government of Vietnam recognized that economic development was dependent upon capitalism—people tend to work harder when they could reap the rewards of their own labor—a fact which also translated to money for the government.

Loc Tin and Kevin spent several days in Saigon. First they simply needed time to adjust to the time change and recover from the jet lag. After that, they enjoyed wandering around the city and seeing the sights. Despite the rosy picture that the guide had painted, Loc Tin and Kevin quickly saw that

Vietnam was a dichotomy. Soaring, modern skyscrapers surrounded by rows and rows of shanties, unscrupulous cab drivers, and street vendors hawking cheap goods to tourists. Chickens roamed the sidewalks, crossing the streets at random, and seemingly oblivious to the endless and chaotic stream of cars, motorbikes, and cyclos.

The guide returned four days after first leaving them at their hotel in Saigon. Now the threesome began the long drive to DaNang where Loc Tin would spread Lucy's ashes. They would spend only two weeks in Vietnam, despite Loc Tin telling Lucy they should go for at least a month. Although Loc Tin and Kevin could have flown directly to DaNang, Loc Tin wanted to see Saigon and he wanted Kevin to see the countryside. He wanted to visit Hue, where he had spent so much time during the war. He was also excited to see the newly opened DaNang airport as well as the city's coast where Lucy had once piloted a fishing boat. That was where he would leave her.

As the guide drove out of Saigon, they passed the site of the old U.S. Army barracks, and Loc Tin sat up realizing the Sisters of Mercy Orphanage would have been nearby. But the old warehouse, seriously damaged by a rocket attack at the end of the war, had been replaced by an apartment building. He watched as the new building faded into the distance behind him and then finally turned away.

As they moved away from the city and into the country, the landscape of Vietnam seemed almost untouched by the years. The rolling hills filled with rice paddies were very familiar to Loc Tin. The mountains and dense, lush jungle and meandering rivers mingled together to create amazing panoramic scenes.

Kevin was awestruck. "I had no idea Vietnam was so beautiful."

Loc Tin looked at him quizzically, "But you found all those Vietnam videos for your mom. Didn't you watch them?"

Kevin nodded. "Yeah. But they don't do it justice. Just like looking at the Grand Canyon in a photo isn't anything like standing on the edge looking into it."

Loc Tin smiled. He knew exactly what Kevin meant and was pleased that his son was here and getting to see where he and Lucy had grown up. But then his smiled faded and the guilt over not bringing Lucy returned and weighed heavily on him.

When they reached DaNang, the first stop would be one of the beaches so that Loc Tin could spread Lucy's ashes into the South China Sea. The beach that the guide took them to was nestled between two mountains. The water was a crystal-clear blue and the sand was the whitest Kevin had ever seen. The guide helped them find a rental canoe and then left them alone. "I can meet you back at the car in an hour," he said.

Without a word, Loc Tin and Kevin took off their shoes and placed them in the canoe. After rolling up their pants, they waded into the water, pulling the canoe with them. Carefully, they both climbed in and they paddled—Loc Tin in front guiding the boat. When Loc Tin was ready, he pulled in his paddle and picked up Lucy's urn. He held the small blue urn to his chest for a moment before removing the lid. He spoke to her, though Kevin could not make out the words. He held the urn over the water and started to spill the ashes, but then hesitated and pulled it back. He looked at the urn in his hands and then carefully spilled some of her ashes into his open palm which he then held over the side of the canoe and unhurriedly released them into the water. He watched as the ashes trailed behind the canoe, eventually disappearing into the clear, blue water. He repeated the steps several times until all the ashes were lost to the South China Sea. He looked at his hand, stained gray by the ashes. Slowly, he dipped his hand in the water until the last of Lucy was washed away. Tears in his eyes, he said his final goodbye. He and Kevin picked up their oars and paddled back to the beach.

They found their guide leaning against the car, smoking. He carefully put out the half-burned cigarette and saved it in his breast pocket. The three men climbed into the car, and the guide drove them to Ba Na Hills Resort which was nestled in the Truong Son Mountains. "You can't come to DaNang and not visit the Golden Bridge," the guide had insisted. "It opened last year and is amazing. And the view—you can't beat it."

Kevin had just said goodbye to his mother, and the finality of her death had hit him all over again. He wasn't in the mood to be a tourist and didn't think his dad would be either, but Loc Tin surprised him by saying, "Your mother would want you to enjoy this visit. She is home now and she is happy." Kevin looked at his father, who for the first time in a long time was smiling.

Just as the guide had promised, the pedestrian bridge which belonged to the resort was a sight to see. It had been built nearly a mile above sea level and stretched between Marseille Station and the Tiantai Gardens at Le Jardin d'Amour. The bridge got its name due to its golden color, but perhaps the most remarkable feature was that it seemed to be held up by two enormous stone hands. Loc Tin, Kevin, and the guide walked along the bridge, taking in the incredible view. Kevin was completely in awe and peppered the guide with questions. He learned that because the area had been heavily sprayed with Agent Orange, it had taken years after the war for the vegetation to return.

"But it is beautiful now," Kevin responded, looking out to the sea.

"Yes, but also different. It has been said that the chemicals really changed the soil. We have a lot more bamboo now. Other things that once grew here, well...they never came back," the guide told them.

"Lucy said the Agent Orange really helped," Loc Tin interjected. He pointed, "She guided her boat along these waters. And after the Americans sprayed the chemical, the VC ambushes stopped." The guide nodded but didn't respond. He had seen firsthand the damage Agent Orange had done to Vietnam, but he was not about to argue with a paying customer.

At Loc Tin's request, after leaving the bridge the guide took them to visit an orphanage in DaNang. Because Lam and Suong had spent time in an orphanage, he wanted to see what one looked like. He wanted to imagine what their life might have been. Who had cared for them? What were they like? His children must have been so afraid. Did they think he and Kim had abandoned them? He had no idea if they had escaped to the U.S. or if they had lived out their childhood in an orphanage. He had suppressed these thoughts for so long, but now as they drove to the orphanage, his heart broke all over again for the children he once held in his arms. They would visit St. Mary's House of Hope. Unlike most other orphanages, St. Mary's accepted older children as well as children with special needs. The guide who Kevin hired knew one of the nuns who lived and worked at the orphanage, and she had agreed to the visit.

St. Mary's House of Hope was a long way from the beautiful resort on the coast. However, it wasn't a distance measured in miles but in emotion. The guide drove them through neglected parts of DaNang to areas of the city that most tourists never saw. He parked beside a two-story white brick building with large windows. They entered through an oversized, windowless door and found themselves in a small office area. An older woman dressed in a traditional nun's habit looked up from the desk when she heard the door open. She smiled when she saw her old friend. "Ah—I have been expecting you." The woman stood and held out her hand to Loc Tin, "You must be Mr. Vong. I am Sister Sun. You want to tour the orphanage?"

Loc Tin nodded and took the woman's hand, "Yes, please. I hope we are not disturbing you."

"Not at all. The children always get excited when we have visitors. I hope you don't mind if some of them tag along."

"Of course not," Kevin responded, holding up a large box. "We were told you can always use extra supplies. We brought these for you—to show our appreciation for letting us visit."

The woman's face lit up, "Yes! Thank you. We operate on donations, and there never seems to be enough." She eagerly took the box and set it beside her desk.

Sister Sun walked them all around the orphanage. As promised, many of the children wanted to see the visitors. Only one or two children ventured close enough for Kevin or Loc Tin to speak to them. Instead, most would just giggle happily and follow them around from a distance. The orphanage was large, clean, and seemed to be well equipped with toys and books. Sister Sun showed them an art room where several of the older children painted. A little girl of about eight was playing the piano. For a moment, Loc Tin imagined that the little girl was Suong and tried to determine if she was happy. But then he realized Sister Sun had moved on and he hurried to catch up.

Occasionally, they saw a child with a missing or oddly shaped arm or leg, but most of the children seemed healthy enough. He was surprised at how many children there were. He thought by now, 50 years after the war, there would be fewer orphans.

Sister Sun explained, "Vietnam is still recovering. Not everyone can afford to raise a child, so they end up here. We try to keep them off the street, though that still happens."

Finally Sister Sun approached a closed door at the end of the hallway. "You may not want to visit this room, but I will show it to you if you want."

Kevin asked, "What is it?"

Sister Sun sighed, "This is where we keep the severely disabled children that cannot care for themselves. Few will ever be adopted and will live out their lives here, though most don't survive beyond their early twenties. I must warn you, the birth defects can be quite horrific and very disturbing if you have never seen firsthand what Agent Orange can do to a child."

"I don't understand," Loc Tin said. The guide had told him that the cancer that had taken Lucy was quite common in DaNang and that many believed it was caused by exposure to Agent Orange. When the guide had said it, it seemed unlikely to Loc Tin. Lucy's exposure had been so long ago. But the children here would not have been exposed to Agent Orange at all. "How could Agent Orange still be causing problems? The U.S. stopped using it in 1970 or maybe '71. These children weren't born yet."

"The chemicals never really go away. The U.S. has hired several companies to try and remove it, but that isn't easy. Some of the poorest Vietnamese still live in contaminated areas. Their children pay a steep price for it. Come, I will show you." She opened the door and they followed her into a large room with row upon row of cribs and low beds. "You saw several children earlier missing an arm or a leg. They are the lucky ones. These children," she sighed again, "have no chance at anything like a normal life. We just make sure they are clean and fed. There is little else we can do. Sister Minh sings and talks to them. Some are responsive, but most are not."

Loc Tin and Kevin walked around the room. Several children were born without eyes or even eye sockets. Others had severely misshapen heads

231

or bodies. Many were confined to their crib because they were unable to move. It was like a scene from a horror movie—but it was real. These children were alive and destined for a life filled with pain and sadness. In a corner of the room were the older victims of Agent Orange. They were perhaps in their late teens or early twenties with birth defects that could never be corrected. They spent their days—years—confined to oversized cribs. There was no laughter in this room, though it was not quiet. Crying could be heard and occasionally an awful guttural moaning sound.

Kevin excused himself from the room and began to vomit. The sound reached Loc Tin's ears, and his own stomach threatened to respond similarly. He willed it to settle and turned to Sister Sun, "Are the children—are they aware? Can they communicate at all?"

"In this room? No. We try to identify the children with mental function as early as possible and include them with the other children. But those that are both severely mentally and physically handicapped are kept here. We do what we can for them."

"And this is because of Agent Orange? I...I still don't understand," Loc Tin said—not wanting to believe his adoptive country—the country that had taken him in and given him so much—could be responsible for the horrific scene in front of him.

"Well, there is a lot of disagreement among the governments and politicians, but I have only seen these severe defects in children whose parents and grandparents live in the areas with the heaviest contamination," Sister Sun replied.

Loc Tin nodded, thinking he wanted to read much more about this chemical. Lucy—his amazing, wonderful wife—did she die because of Agent Orange? Kevin, thank God, was healthy. But the children in front of him, they weren't so lucky. He looked at Sister Sun, "Thank you. I think I have seen enough."

She nodded and led the way back to the front office. As they were leaving she said, "Thank you for the supplies. We really appreciate the donation."

Kevin, still looking quite green, just nodded and left the building with the guide. Loc Tin pulled out his wallet and handed the Sister all of the cash he had. "For the children," he said.

She thanked him and said goodbye.

Chapter 75

Burn Pits
  April 2019

Despite the introduction of legislation designed to eliminate the use of burn pits by the U.S. military in 2009, an April 2019 Department of Defense report to Congress admitted that nine burn pits were still in operation because "no good alternative exists." The report, written by the Undersecretary for Acquisition and Sustainment, stated that the remaining U.S.-sanctioned burn pits were located in Syria, Afghanistan, and Egypt.

Chapter 76

It was late on Saturday night, but Ashley could not stop thinking about the vigilante case. She sat on her couch with her feet up and laptop open, reviewing her notes. The team desperately needed DNA evidence, but she was convinced she had found all of the vigilante-type murders in the Virginia area. None had usable DNA. The earliest vigilante death she could find in Virginia was the broken neck guy in 1978, while the earliest vigilante *knife* killing was in 1980. As far as she could tell, the Vigilante Virginian didn't kill anyone between 1993 and 2004. That was a long time for someone to be on good behavior. "Either he was in jail or he wasn't in Virginia," Ashley thought. She looked at her notes. Jacobs was killed in 1998 in California. Despite what Lance said, she was convinced that the Vigilante Virginian had killed him. What if the Vigilante was living in California during the Virginia gap? She decided to look for vigilante knife killings in California between 1994 and 2003. Tapping into the CBI secure website which linked to databases all over the country, she found three murders in addition to Jacobs, that fit the Vigilante Virginian's MO perfectly.

The first, a nurse who had been convicted of euthanizing elderly dementia patients, had been murdered in 1995 after receiving what many called an inappropriately lenient sentence. Next, in 1997 a drunk driver had lost control of his car and careened into a soccer field filled with young athletes.

The drunkard had killed a coach and four of the players who had been on the field with him. The man's guilt was never in question, but he was considered mentally unfit and ordered to undergo therapy for his alcoholism. He never made it to the first session. A year later, in 1998, Jacobs was killed.

In 2000, a presumed arsonist was killed at home in his sleep by a knife to the throat. He was out on bail while awaiting his trial. He had been accused of purposefully setting the San Joaquin fire in 1998 that killed an entire boy scout troop that had been camping in the area along with two firefighters.

It seemed highly probable to Ashley that the Vigilante Virginian had moved to California where he continued his "mission of justice," as Rhonda called it. However, there were two more vigilante knife deaths in the eighties, including a man who was believed to have contracted HIV from a prostitute and who himself was later arrested for purposefully infecting other prostitutes with the deadly virus. He was murdered in 1984—also while awaiting trial.

That was the same year that Betsy Ingalls, the woman wanted for killing young mothers, had been murdered in the Blue Ridge Mountains. There were also four more vigilante knife deaths in California after 2003, when the killings started up again in Virginia.

If the same vigilante killed all of the victims Ashley had identified, he had to be traveling back and forth from Virginia to California. Maybe he was a businessman and had companies on both coasts? It was also possible that it really *was* two different killers like Lance suggested. She frowned, wondering how likely it was to have two killers with the exact same MO. She made a note to ask Ben.

Looking back over the dates of the murders, she realized there were no vigilante deaths in either state between 2015 and 2018—at least none that she could find. There had been a whopping seven in Virginia in 2019 but none in California that year. "Did the California vigilante move to Virginia—and now there are two in the Richmond area?" She shook her head. That was crazy. Still, she could find no vigilante knife deaths at all in California after 2014 and no indication that a knife-wielding vigilante went to jail. "Maybe he moved somewhere other than Virginia?" she said out loud. She wondered if she would find similar vigilante knife deaths in all 50 states. She knew she would have to look. Frustrated, she closed her computer and went to bed.

Chapter 77

Blue Ridge Mountains, August 2019
Dordi and Loc Tin

Loc Tin was back in the mountains. These days it was the only place he felt almost normal. He missed Lucy so much. He now understood why so many couples died within a few months of each other. He now believed it really was possible to die of a broken heart. Dordi was the only one who understood—he was just as miserable.

They sat in the rocking chairs on the porch, drinking whiskey and talking. Dordi said, "Linh would have liked this cabin. There's a big flat rock next to the water. I can just see her sitting there on a blanket, reading."

It was the third or fourth time he had told Loc Tin that, but he didn't mind—he was thinking about Lucy. "I promised her over and over I would take her back to Vietnam, but I never did." Then he told Dordi—for the third or fourth time—about spreading Lucy's ashes in the South China Sea.

Dordi rubbed the stubble on his chin, his mind elsewhere. Finally he said, "I would have liked to go back to Vietnam—see what it was like when it wasn't a war zone. But not Linh. She wanted to forget that part of her life." He took a deep breath, "She loved being an American." He paused, thinking about his wife, and then continued, "Remember that time she bleached her hair? Just between you and me," he paused and looked at Loc Tin, "Linh *did not* look good as a blonde." He laughed at the memory.

Loc Tin nodded his agreement, "I don't know what Lucy was thinking—letting her do that. I guess it was a slow day at the salon." The men laughed again, remembering happier times.

They fell silent for a long while. Then Loc Tin asked, "You really think it was the Agent Orange that caused Linh's breast cancer?"

He shrugged, "Jeremy thinks it's possible, though the VA says otherwise. Doesn't matter. Linh wasn't a veteran. But still, I would like to know if that's what killed her. Jeremy blames Agent Orange for Lily's heart condition and Lucas' autism." He shook his head, "I don't know."

Loc Tin knew without a doubt that Lucy had been exposed and was now convinced it was why she died. But he wasn't sure about Linh. He had read a great deal about the herbicide since his trip to Vietnam and now he told Dordi what he was thinking. "Linh was in Cam Ranh Bay most of her life. The Americans didn't spray there."

Dordi nodded, "I know. But what else explains the kids?"

"You. You were exposed."

Dordi had never considered that before. He leaned forward in his rocking chair and set his drink down. LT was right—he *had* been exposed. More than once. His second tour he had been stationed in DaNang. It was one of the most heavily sprayed parts of South Vietnam. And Linh was in Cam Ranh Bay. He looked at his friend. "Damn, LT. You may be right." He sighed and picked up his drink, still considering what Loc Tin had said. For once, Dordi was at a loss for words.

Chapter 78

Memoir: Killing Spree

I was in a bad place mentally. Some might call it post-traumatic stress disorder (PTSD), but the truth is I was just angry at the world. At God. In less than a month, I killed six people, including twin brothers in Philadelphia. They had kidnapped a woman hiking alone on the Appalachian Trail and kept her imprisoned in their basement for four months until she managed to escape. Although they were convicted of their crime, they were not eligible for the death penalty since the woman survived. But I managed to take them out just before their sentencing hearing. The others I killed were just as evil. They all deserved their fate, but the rage made me careless. I was angry but had no desire to go to prison for my crimes. When I heard on the news that the police had found hairs that did not belong to one of my victims, I knew I had to get myself under control. I asked myself, "Who are you really angry with?" After thinking about it, the answer was obvious. And I began to carefully plan my next assassination.

Chapter 79

San Francisco, California, late August 2021
Ashley and Friends

Emily and Tom's wedding was about a month away, but Ashley would see her friend on Friday. Emily, Vivian, and Dr. Jansen were attending a medical research conference that was being held in San Francisco. Although the meeting would not end until late Saturday morning, her friends would meet her for dinner and drinks Friday night. Then they would have Saturday afternoon and most of Sunday to explore San Francisco and catch up. Ashley knew Ben used to live in San Francisco and asked him to recommend a good restaurant. That discussion ultimately led to Ben going with her. Turned out, Heather, his old girlfriend, lived in the bay area, and he had been meaning to go pick up a couple of things from her apartment.

"You're sure you don't mind me tagging along?" Ben asked her for the tenth time.

"The more the merrier. You'll Like Em and Vivian," she had told him again and again. Even though it was last minute, he was still able to find a hotel room near the convention center, though he would not be in the main hotel with Ashley and her friends.

They left early on Friday afternoon, but traffic was awful and it was nearly 5:00 P.M. when they got to Heather's place. Ashley pulled into the parking lot of the apartment complex and parked. Ben jumped out and said, "I'll be right back." However, 20 minutes later he texted Ashley to tell her not to wait and he would catch up with them soon.

Ashley frowned at the text. Why did he need more than a minute to get something from his ex-girlfriend? But she responded with a thumbs up emoji and "Emily and Vivian. 6:00 P.M. Hotel bar. See you there?"

Ben texted, "You bet."

Ashley drove off, wondering. She and Ben weren't dating. But still, she thought there was *something*. Was she wrong? Maybe. She had spent a lot of time alone with Ben, but they never seemed to get past harmless flirting. She shook her head. He's picking something up that the old girlfriend has. No biggie. They're probably just talking—maybe even arguing. None of her business. Then why was she jealous?

"Whatever," she said aloud and tried to mean it. Friday night—he may have a hard time finding an Uber. "Ugh. That's HIS problem if he does," she angrily told the red light as she came to a stop.

By the time Ashley checked into her room, it was already nearly 6:00 P.M. There was no way Ben would be on time. "I guess he better hope we don't go somewhere else for dinner." She was wearing jeans—the clothes she had on at work—and had not really planned on changing, but now she did. She put on a casual dress that she thought showed off her modest curves and freshened her makeup. She walked into the bar at 6:15 P.M., still annoyed at Ben for no legitimate reason. She quickly found Emily and Vivian. They sat away from the bar in a seating area with couches and chairs around a small coffee table.

Vivian saw her before Emily did and jumped up first, embracing her friend. "Ashley! How are you? We have really missed you. Even Dr. J misses you."

"I seriously doubt that," Ashley replied.

Emily joined her friends and said, "No. It's true. She complains that no one's sequencing is as good as yours."

"Oh, well, that I do believe. I am the best, you know," She said feigning a pompousness that her friends knew she did not possess.

Emily looked around, "Where's Ben? I thought you were bringing your handsome army guy." She lowered her voice, "I promise I will find out if he likes you."

Ashley rolled her eyes as they took their seats. "We are not in high school, thank you very much. We are just friends. And, if you must know, he has been delayed by his ex-girlfriend." Vivian was about to respond when a tall, dark-haired man in a suit and tie came to their table with a bottle of wine and three glasses.

"You must be Ashley," he stuck out his hand and she shook it, clearly confused. He smiled, "I'm Jeremy, a colleague of Vivian's. She's helping me on part of my VA grant. I'll go grab another glass. Is Cabernet okay? Or would you like something else?"

Ashley, still confused just said, "Cab is awesome. Thank you."

As soon as he left, she asked, "Is that your VA friend? The one that got the info for my boss?"

Vivian nodded, "Yes. Jeremy is great. He's a physician but also does research. He just got a VA grant to look at burn pit exposures and reproductive diseases like endometriosis. He also works with Doctors Without Borders. His mother is Vietnamese, and he goes to Vietnam with them all the time."

Jeremy returned just as she said this, and he corrected her. "Twice. I have been to Vietnam twice. But I will go back. There is such a need." He sat down and Ashley poured a glass of wine for him.

"What do you do there? Treat women with endometriosis?" Ashley asked.

"Sometimes. They do have a high incidence of it in Vietnam, but mostly I just do general medicine. There are still not enough doctors in the rural areas, so whenever we go, people come from miles around to be seen. I also go by the orphanages and take care of anything that I can. Seeing the Agent Orange kids—that keeps me motivated," he told her.

"Motivated? What do you mean?" Ashley asked, sipping her wine.

He looked surprised, "You know, research is HARD. Sometimes I want to quit and just see patients." He took a sip of his wine. "As difficult as it is treating women with endometriosis—so many of them want to get pregnant and can't, and let's face it, there just aren't any good therapies to offer them. Anyway, as hard as that is, it's still easier than spending weeks putting together the perfect grant with my best ideas only to have it rejected because a reviewer didn't quite understand what I am trying to do or, worse, doesn't believe that manmade toxicants can cause disease in people. It's really frustrating and I sometimes think it isn't worth it." He stopped, thinking, "But then I see those kids," he shook his head, "and I realize I have to keep trying. We have to find a way to keep dioxin from destroying even more lives than it already has."

Ashley nodded. She knew exactly what he meant. The frustration he felt was the very reason she walked away from research, but she had also started feeling as though she had let down the victims of Agent Orange.

Jeremy continued his diatribe, "You know about the burn pits the military uses? It's Agent Orange all over again. In 20 years I suppose we'll be seeing Afghani children with the same damn birth defects."

"Or children of Iraq and Afghanistan veterans," Ashley added.

"Exactly," Jeremy agreed. Ashley and Jeremy continued talking about his research and how he ended up in reproductive medicine. She learned that his mother had been an orphan in Vietnam and lived on the streets for many years before meeting and marrying his father. "She died a couple of years ago. Breast cancer—some say linked to Agent Orange, but it isn't on the list the VA recognizes. My dad was exposed too, but he seems to be immune to its effects." He shook his head, "That man is invincible. Anyway, my sister—she was born right after they got married and died when she was just a baby because of a heart defect. My brother is mildly autistic but is amazing when it comes to computers. And then there's me—the baby they didn't mean to have."

"They told you that you were an accident?" Ashley asked, surprised.

"Not my mom. My dad told me later—after she died. She was afraid all of their children would have problems and so didn't want any more after Lily died. My dad convinced her to try again and they had Lucas. I wasn't planned, so I'm a lot younger than he is. I think that may be why I'm healthier."

Ashley was so absorbed in her conversation with Jeremy that she didn't notice when Ben walked in. Vivian asked her a question which made her look up. That's when she saw Ben, arm and arm with a very striking blonde woman. Even though she wore jeans and a simple white blouse, she still seemed glamorous to Ashley. She was glad she had changed clothes. Ben and the mystery woman walked over to the group, and he introduced himself and his friend. "I'm Ben, a friend of Ashley's, and this is Heather Sinclair...my...," he looked uncertainly at Heather.

She laughed and finished his sentence, "Friend. I am your friend," Heather said, shaking hands all around. "We used to date, but now we don't."

Ben looked apologetically at Ashley, "I meant to send a text, but I guess I got distracted. I hope you don't mind one extra."

Although the question was directed at Ashley, it was Vivian who answered. "No biggie. We were just discussing restaurant ideas for dinner." She looked at Heather, "Have you eaten?"

"No, and I am starving. But we may be better off staying here. The hotel restaurant is pretty good and everywhere else will have a long wait."

The group moved to the restaurant and were quickly seated. The discussions were lively and upbeat, and, much to her dismay, Ashley could not help but like Heather. She was funny and smart and, despite looking glamorous, seemed quite down to earth. She worked as a television journalist for one of the local stations, but of course, was hoping a bigger market was in her future.

"Being at a TV station in San Francisco sounds like a pretty good market to me," Ashley said.

"Certainly it is a step up from Topeka, Kansas—my first job—but I really want to go to LA or New York." She shrugged, "Just got to keep at it."

After dinner, Ashley begged off and told the group she would see them the next day. Ben was hanging on every word Heather uttered and didn't notice when Ashley left; however, Jeremy made a point of standing and saying, "It was really nice to meet you."

Chapter 80

Memoir: Broken Rules

I remember laying in the grass thinking I should be in a lot more pain since I had been shot at least twice. I thought I was dying and was largely okay with that. What I was not okay with was failing to achieve my mission. I made two mistakes. First, I broke my own rule: Never engage the target. Stupid. I wanted him to know why I was killing him. Why did he need to know? I knew he deserved to die. Why wasn't that enough? What did I expect? An apology? Remorse? The second mistake was even worse—never bring a knife to a gunfight. I didn't expect him to be armed. Stupid.

I had kept the man under surveillance for months and learned his routine. Every night between 10:00 and 10:30, he went out the back door of his condo for a smoke. He always sat on the right patio chair facing the park that was located adjacent to his building. He would stay out for about 20 minutes. Then he would go back inside and lock the door behind him. The man was divorced and lived alone. Not even a dog to keep him company. All the better for completing my mission.

In 1969, he had been one of the youngest admirals in the U.S. Navy and commanded a fleet of Swift Boats that patrolled the Vietnam shoreline. Long since retired, he now lived in Arlington, Virginia. It had taken me nearly a year to learn his name and then to find him. He was just one of many commanders that had been in Vietnam and decided which parts of the country would be subjected to the spraying of Agent Orange. Most were already dead—either by their own hand or simply due to advanced age. But a few were still around, and I had intended to kill them all one by one. This man's death was to be yet another "unintended consequence" of that wretched war.

My plan was the same as always. Come silently from behind, slit his throat, and leave him to die. The park's walking trail snaked by his back patio and was only a few yards away. I would do the deed and then act as though I were out for a late-night jog. Some might think it was stupid for a man my age to be out jogging late at night, but it certainly wasn't illegal. And if anyone did see me, how could they possibly expect that I was a killer? I could even act confused—as though I had dementia, if needed. Once this man was dead, my plan was to track down the others and kill every damn one of them. But I didn't stick to the plan. Stupid.

By 9:45 P.M., I was already in place. I was hidden in the bushes that separated his patio from the one belonging to his neighbor, patiently waiting. At 10:20 P.M., the man slid open the patio door and took his seat in the expected chair. He had just pulled out a cigar when I spoke. I did not intend to say anything, but the words tumbled out before I could stop them. "You killed people I care about. Now you will die."

The man—he had to be in his eighties—was remarkably quick. In an instant he was on his feet with a pistol pointed at me. He said simply, "I killed no one."

"Agent Orange. You gave the orders to spray it. You destroyed many lives with that order."

The man nodded but did not relax his grip on the gun. "Yes, I gave the orders in-country, but it was to protect my men. They told us the chemicals were harmless to people. I was lied to. We all were." He paused before adding, "I did what I had to do to protect my men."

I was still angry and wanted more from him. I took a step forward to ask him if he had been exposed, if he had suffered the painful rashes that so many developed after getting it on their skin. Or maybe he had developed one of the cancers caused by Agent Orange or perhaps he had a child that was disabled because of the chemicals. But I never got a chance to ask my questions. The moment I stepped forward, he shot me in the upper chest—probably aiming for my heart but missing it. Instinctively, I turned away from him, and the second shot hit me in the dead center of my back. I would later learn the shot severed my spine.

I collapsed to the ground and must have passed out. I awoke to a paramedic giving me oxygen. I could hear the policemen talking to each other. "The old man who lives in the condo nearest the walking trail said he heard arguing nearby when he went out for a smoke. He heard gunshots and called 911. We found this guy just off the trail. He's in bad shape, the paramedic doubts he'll make it. No wallet or watch. Looks like he was mugged. Poor old geezer. No need to shoot him."

An interesting turn of events, I thought. My intended victim shot me, dragged me to the trail, took my watch, and called 911. He didn't take my wallet because I didn't have it on me. He made it look like I was shot during a mugging. Why? Better for me this way. Was it also better for him? The policeman continued speaking, interrupting my thoughts, "If the dude manages to pull through, we'll interview him. See what he can tell us. But it doesn't look good."

I am to be interviewed. Yes, of course. They will want a statement from the "victim." And what will I tell them? My story should match the Admiral's story and solidify the theory the cop had already formulated. They are less likely to dig deeper if everything lines up neatly. I closed my eyes and feigned sleep, hoping to get additional details from those around me, but I was loaded onto the ambulance and learned no more.

Chapter 81

San Francisco, California, late August 2021
  Ashley and Friends

As promised, late Saturday morning as soon as the conference ended and they were able to get away, Vivian and Emily knocked on Ashley's hotel room door. They would have lunch at a nearby restaurant and then do some sightseeing. Although both Vivian and Ashley had been to San Francisco before, it was Emily's first visit to the city.

Ashley opened the door and motioned her friends inside. "I'll just be a minute—I want to straighten up a bit."

Emily and Vivian watched as their friend moved her suitcase to the closet and closed the door. She put away her makeup and hair dryer then rinsed her coffee cup and set it beside the sink. She wiped down the counter, threw away some trash, and put an empty water bottle in the recycle bin. Finally, she made up her hotel room bed.

"What are you doing?" Emily finally asked. "You know the hotel has maid service?"

"And you were always such a slob when you lived in San Diego. Honestly, watching you clean is freaking me out a bit," added Vivian.

"I know, I know. It's just that I have seen so many crime scene photos now. I keep imagining how terrible my apartment would look if I was ever murdered or something," Ashley responded as she continued to tidy the small room. "I don't want people judging me because of a messy apartment."

Emily and Vivian exchanged glances. Vivian said sarcastically, "Oh, sure.

That makes perfect sense."

When Ashley was satisfied that her hotel room was "crime scene photo ready," the three women left to try a famous, hole-in-the-wall sushi place. After lunch, Vivian and Ashley took Emily on a walking tour of the famous Haight-Ashbury neighborhood where Jim Morrison and the Doors got their start back in the sixties. Next they rode the trolley cars and took a stroll along the oceanfront.

Emily looked thoughtfully at the water and noted, "It's the same ocean that Sydney overlooks."

Finally, they ended the day at an upscale restaurant on Half-Moon Bay. They ordered a bottle of wine and the calamari appetizer.

"This has been an amazing day! Thank you for showing me around," Emily said, enjoying the view from their table overlooking the Pacific Ocean.

Ashley and Vivian expressed the same thought, "Thanks for the excuse to relax a bit."

"I wish we had time to visit Napa Valley," Emily said, wistfully.

"Next time. But tonight we can still enjoy the fruits of Napa," Ashley said, topping off everyone's wine glass.

"So what's the deal with Ben?" Emily asked, looking at Ashley. "I thought you and he were becoming a thing."

"That makes two of us, but clearly he is not over Heather. Honestly, if I weren't thoroughly heterosexual, I would be in love with her too. She's amazing. No point in trying to compete," Ashley said, sipping her wine.

"Don't say that! You're just as amazing." Vivian tried to be supportive of her friend.

"Sure, just in shorter, plainer packaging," Ashley agreed.

"Some guys don't like flashy packaging," Vivian insisted, making both Ashley and Emily laugh. "I'm not joking! Not all guys are into blondes with big boobs." The comment garnered more laughter from the other two women, so Vivian changed tactics. "Well, what about Jeremy? He seemed into you."

"Yes, yes—he might have been. At least till Heather showed up," Ashley said. Though, truthfully, she didn't think Heather was his type. "I definitely wouldn't mind getting to know him better. I would also love to go to Vietnam. Do you think that you have to be a doctor to join Doctors Without Borders?" Ashley wondered out loud.

"No idea, but Jeremy will know. Maybe we can try to find him later."

"The meeting ended today. Won't he be headed home?" Ashley asked.

Vivian shook her head, "He lives here, remember? He is at UCSF."

"Oh, right. I forgot," Ashley responded.

They returned to the hotel late on Saturday evening. Ashley was ready to turn in, but Vivian and Emily went to the bar for a nightcap. They promised to meet Ashley in the hotel restaurant for breakfast Sunday at 7:00.

The next morning, Ashley arrived first and was drinking coffee and playing Scrabble on her phone. She looked up when she realized someone was speaking to her. "Jeremy! Hey. What are you doing here?" she said, surprised. "I thought you would have gone home yesterday after the meeting ended."

"I had a meeting with colleagues from the Netherlands. An extra night in the hotel is a small price to pay for being able to talk face to face. I am heading out soon but wanted to enjoy the hotel's overpriced breakfast buffet one more time," he said, jokingly.

Ashley smiled, noticing that Jeremy was more attractive in casual clothes. She also realized he was quite a bit younger than she had thought on Friday night. "Do you want to join me? I'm waiting on Em and Viv, but they are late. Otherwise, I have only my phone to keep me company."

"Late night?" Jeremy asked, taking a seat.

"Not for me, but those two...probably so."

Ashley and Jeremy made their selections from the buffet and returned to the table.

"You said last night that you got out of research. What is it that you're doing now? You never really said. Something with criminal investigation?" Jeremy asked as they sat back down.

Ashley frowned, "Mostly I do PCR. All day, every day."

"Sounds...um...," he hesitated, not wanting to be insulting.

"Mind numbingly boring?" she finished for him. "Yes, it is. I thought I would be more involved in the actual crime solving, but that's Ben's job. He is teaching me some things, which is interesting, but that's not what they hired me to do. Lance, my boss, gave me a cold case to look at, but that's a mess. Now I am working with the forensics team trying to solve another case, but that's not going so great either."

"If you're unhappy, you can always go back to research."

"Maybe. But, honestly, I wasn't happy there either. Just a different kind of unhappy." She took a bite of toast.

"When are you happiest? And you can't say laying on a beach. I mean, what gives you satisfaction when you're at work?"

"Hmmm...," she thought for a moment. "I guess when I feel like I make a difference. I felt that way a lot when I was in the lab. I loved being part of the team that was really trying to answer questions that would help people. But I had no life. Dr. J was always trying to get me to go back to school, but I could see how all-consuming research can be and I didn't want that. I'd like to have a family someday. And if I do, I want to have time for them." She looked at Jeremy and felt her face flush. "I'm sorry. It must be even harder for you. You see patients *and* run a laboratory."

He shrugged, "Yes and no. My grants don't have to pay my salary. I make that from the hospital. I just need one grant, not two or three like some scientists do. Others have a big teaching load. I guess no one has it easy. But, like you said, the work is important. It really does make a difference."

She nodded, "Yes, especially if we can break the cycle and help the generation that isn't born yet." She paused before continuing, "At least that was the goal of my old lab. Maybe I *should* go back."

"Maybe you just haven't found your place yet," he replied.

"I have thought about doing advocacy, but I have no idea how to go about that. What about Doctors Without Borders? I guess you have to be a doctor?" Ashley asked.

"It's mostly medical professionals, but there are others as well. With your background, there might be an opportunity for you. I can give you the name of my contact there."

"Thanks. That would be great." Ashley hesitated and then said, "Emily mentioned that your mom was Vietnamese."

Jeremy nodded, "She was half Vietnamese. She never knew her parents, but knew her mom was Vietnamese. Based on when she was born, her father may have been French. Her skin was darker than most so he could have been of African descent. We really don't know."

"You should have your DNA tested," Ashley said. "You could find out what your mom was based on your results. Do you know about your dad's heritage? Or is he still alive?"

Jeremy looked at her blankly, "You're absolutely right. I don't know why I never thought to do that. Damn. I wish we had done that while she was alive. That would have fascinated her. My dad is just plain white as far as we know. But he's still alive. I can see if he wants to do it. But I definitely do." He pulled out his phone. "Which one should I get?"

After Jeremy ordered his kit, he and Ashley continued talking even after they had both finished breakfast. Finally, Vivian and Emily arrived, the latter wearing sunglasses.

"I need coffee," Vivian said, helping herself to the carafe on the table. "And aspirin."

Emily was also in bad shape. She put her head on the table as soon as she sat down.

"I take it y'all are not up for any more sightseeing?" Ashley asked, trying not to laugh at her friends, who were clearly hungover.

"I'll be better...someday," Vivian responded, head in her hands.

"What time is your flight?" Ashley asked, now more concerned than amused.

"6:00 P.M. Breakfast was a bad idea. I'm going back to bed," Emily said and Vivian agreed. The two women stood, and Emily looked at Ashley, "I'm sorry. I guess it's just you and Ben today."

"No problem. Just feel better." She stood and gave her friends a hug. "See you at the wedding." She watched them walk away and then sat back down.

"You and Ben have big plans?" Jeremy asked.

"Ben and Heather have big plans. He bailed on me as well." Ashley shrugged, "That's okay. I have GPS and a vague idea of where to go."

"You know, I have lived in San Francisco for a couple of years now but haven't had a chance to see much outside my apartment and the lab," Jeremy said.

Ashley smiled, "Want to join me then? Always more fun to explore when you have someone to do it with."

They finished their coffee and then headed out to see the city. They parted late in the day after exchanging phone numbers.

Chapter 82

Richmond, Virginia, June 2020
Kevin and Radhika

It was late—well past midnight—when the phone rang at the Vong home. The incessant ringing woke both Kevin and Radhika, but it was Radhika who spoke, "Who would be calling the landline at this time of night?"

Kevin shook his head but reached over to answer it. "Hello?" He listened a moment before getting out of bed and heading to the closet where he began pulling on jeans. He hung up the phone just as Radhika got out of bed.

"What is it? What's wrong?" she asked, concern evident on her face.

"It's Dad. He's been in an accident. They are taking him to St. Vincent." He pulled on a T-shirt and looked at his wife, tears filling his eyes. "They don't expect him to make it."

"What? What happened?" She embraced her husband, but he was too anxious to be comforted. He gently pushed her away.

"I have to go. I will call you when I know something." He knew she would want to go with him, but that would mean waking the kids.

"Are you okay to drive? I can call Wendy. She'll watch Timothy and Samantha." Wendy was their neighbor and friend.

Radhika followed Kevin as he hurried downstairs. He responded to her, "No. I'm fine. I need to go. I'll call you later." The front door closed behind him and Radhika stood in the foyer staring at it. She said aloud, "What kind of accident?" He had said he was going to the cabin for the weekend, and

Radhika had begged Kevin to talk him out of it. "He shouldn't be out there by himself," she had said. Kevin just reminded her that Dordi would be close by. "That's even worse," she had said, knowing how much they drank when they were together. But no one listened to her and now he was hurt. It was so predictable and preventable.

Loc Tin had always been stubborn, but now he was so much worse. He had not been the same since Lucy's death two years before. She thought he was becoming depressed. He spent more and more time at the cabin and even talked about living there full-time, like Dordi did. He said he liked to explore the woods, said it reminded him of Vietnam. However, she had been to the Blue Ridge Mountains and thought they looked nothing like the pictures of Vietnam that she had seen. At any rate, she worried about him. He seemed to forget he was not a young man anymore. Admittedly, he was in excellent health and he always came back from the cabin reenergized. But now she was worried. Had he fallen off a cliff or something? She shuddered. Her mind raced with a multitude of terrible possibilities. Would he survive whatever had happened to him tonight? And if he did, what would his life be like? Kevin would be devastated when his dad died, and she fervently hoped it would not be tonight. She could only wonder, worry, and wait. She looked at the clock. 2:30 A.M. She knew she wouldn't sleep anymore tonight and decided now was as good a time as any to reorganize the pantry.

Chapter 83

As always when he was working at the store, Billy had the TV on. The phone rang and he cussed because he didn't want to miss it when the cops arrested the guy they had been chasing for the last half hour.

"Hello. Feed Mill," he said gruffly into the receiver.

"Billy?"

"Yeah."

"This is Dennis Dordi."

"Who?"

"Dennis Dordi. I bought a cabin from Joe, or actually, my son did. The one nearest the lake. Couple of years ago."

"Oh, right," Billy said, remembering. "You and that Vietnamese guy throw knives."

"Yes. We have been known to do that," Dordi said, smiling.

"What can I do ya' for?"

"Well, my son Lucas and his wife, Eden—they need me to help them with my grandkids. I don't know if you know, but they are both very introverted. They thought it would be good for the kids to spend some time with me." Dordi sighed, wishing again that Linh was still alive. She was much better with the kids than he ever was. But then he turned his attention back to Billy. "Anyway, I am going to be staying with them for a while. I was hoping you could keep an eye on the cabin for me. It shouldn't need anything, but, you know, just notice if a tree falls on it or anyone looks like they are living there before I can get back."

"Oh, sure. I can do that. I'm always around. You want to leave me your number?"

Dordi gave Billy his number, as well as the ones for Eden and Lucas. He was hoping that he wouldn't need to stay with them long, but he agreed with them that the kids needed someone around that was comfortable at baseball games and swim meets. In truth, he was looking forward to it. It had been a long time since he and Linh were raising kids. He thought he might really enjoy it.

"Okay. Thanks Billy. I'll see you around before too long," Dordi said, sounding a bit more optimistic than he really was.

"No problem," Billy said and hung up. He sat back on his stool and looked at the TV. The credits were rolling and he had missed the ending. "Damn," he said again.

Chapter 84

It was 10:15 P.M and the Admiral was sitting on his back patio smoking, as usual. However, he had altered his routine slightly after the man with the knife set out to kill him. He had adjusted his chair so that his back was to the wall of his condo. He could now see reasonably well in either direction. He kept a watchful eye out, but he was not afraid. The pistol he had used to defend himself was at the ready, just in case. But that man would not be back.

The Admiral took a long drag on the cigar and contemplated recent events. Who was the old man with the knife? What was his story? Obviously, he had been there. Vietnam. And he lost someone. Maybe more than one. The Admiral could certainly sympathize. The war had taken everything from him. His son, Mark, had been drafted into the Air Force in 1970 and died only a few months after arriving in Vietnam. Shortly after their only child had died, his wife had left him for another man. Whenever he thought about it, his mind would hear Aretha Franklin singing "Chain of Fools" which had been playing on the radio when he picked up his mail that day. Thanks to government inefficiency, his "Dear John" letter came only two days after he learned of his son's death. Mark had never married, so the Admiral had no grandchildren.

Just as well, he thought. Mark had been stationed in DaNang, at one of the air bases that was part of Operation Ranch Hand. Mark loaded planes

259

with the deadly Agent Orange to be sprayed over Vietnam. There was no doubt in the Admiral's mind that any children Mark would have had would have suffered because of his son's exposure. Certainly, the same chemicals had taken a toll on his own health. Although the VA assured him that his cancer was not related to his Agent Orange exposure, he didn't believe them. No matter. He would not survive the year and had decided it wasn't worth spending his last days arguing with government bureaucrats for what would no doubt be meager compensation. At any rate, government money would not change his outcome, and his ex-wife—the closest thing he had to a living relative—deserved nothing.

He had lied to the police for the same reason. He did not want to spend his last days caught up in a courtroom battle. The Admiral had expected the man to die, and he would have been held responsible. Although he might eventually be cleared because he acted in self-defense, the investigation would take up time that he was unwilling to give. After the Admiral shot the man, he dragged him to the walking trail. He took his watch and would have taken cash from his wallet to further the impression of a robbery, but the man did not have it on him. Just as well. The police would assume the attacker had taken it. The Admiral had gone back to his condo and looked for any telltale evidence of the events. No blood, thanks to the small caliber weapon he had used. He found the man's knife—it was hefty, about 9 inches long with a curved blade—and placed it inside his gun safe, along with the pistol he had used. Then he called 911 and waited.

Unexpectedly, the man had survived. And, according to the news, he described his attacker as a "young, white punk." The description was very vague, and the police said the victim was uncertain as to what had been taken from him. The Admiral wondered if the man had feigned confusion or loss of memory. He had certainly appeared to be of sound mind on his patio that night. Probably the man was smart enough to let the police tell him their theory first and then his attacker just added enough detail to make the police theory plausible. Better for both of them if the police thought the old man was the victim. The Admiral was not without sympathy for the man. Who had he lost to the chemicals that would soon take his own life?

Chapter 85

Richmond, Virginia, October 2020
Kevin and Radhika

Kevin parked the car in his parents' driveway. After much discussion and angst, the decision had been made to rent the house, at least for now. At some point it would have to be sold but not yet. He had argued that it was a tough market and hanging onto it for a while made financial sense. In truth, he couldn't bear the thought of selling his childhood home. Once the decision to rent was made, Radhika had suggested they offer it as fully furnished. He knew she had suggested it to make the task at hand less daunting for him, but it was still a good idea and they found a tenant much quicker than anticipated.

Charles Walker had been transferred to Richmond from the West Coast and would be on his own for a few months until the school year ended and his wife and family could join him. He had signed a six-month lease and wanted to move in on the 1st of December. For this reason, the unhappy chore of cleaning out his parents' home could not be put off any longer. Today Kevin and Radhika would begin to remove his parents' personal effects from the home they had lived in for 30 years.

They sat in the car a moment as Kevin looked at the house. It was not a big—but big enough for Kevin and his parents. He was an only child. Kevin knew his parents had wanted more, but a big family was not in the cards for them. His mother had doted on him from the moment he was born until the day she died. Even when she was sick, she always thought of Kevin first. His father had been far more strict but was always kind and fair in his discipline and expectations. Kevin felt his had been the best childhood and hoped his children would someday look back just as fondly on their own youth.

"We need to get started," Radhika said, gently touching his knee as they sat in the car. She unbuckled her seatbelt and opened her door. She looked at him, patiently waiting. Finally Kevin sighed heavily and climbed out of the driver's seat. She took his hand as they walked up the front steps. He selected the familiar key from his key ring and opened the door. Radhika watched her husband as he looked around the living room. Her patience was growing thin. She knew this was hard, but they needed to make a lot of progress today. "Maybe we should start in the bedroom? Maybe go through your dad's clothes?" Kevin looked at her. His expression seemed to be one of confusion. As though he had forgotten why they were there. But then his face cleared, he rubbed his chin, and sighed again. Finally, he nodded. She grabbed a box and they headed for the master bedroom.

Radhika opened the sliding door to the closet. Thankfully, a year after her mother-in-law died, Loc Tin had asked her to help him sort through his wife's clothes. He wanted Radhika to donate them to a woman's shelter or find someone else in need who could use them. She was happy to help, but it had taken far longer to go through her things than it should have. As they went through the closet, Loc Tin felt compelled to tell her stories about Lucy. She had pulled out a lovely yellow and white silk tunic that she had never seen before and made the mistake of asking Loc Tin about it. He had smiled and told her that was part of the *Ao Dai* that she had made herself after they had immigrated to the United States. She had worn it the day they had signed the papers to buy their house. Although she embraced life in America, she had not forgotten her heritage and making the *Ao Dai* was a way to honor and remember her past. And so it went. Every piece of the woman's clothing seemed to be tied to some important event. It had taken three days to finally get through everything. Radhika had been grateful that Lucy had been frugal and had a fairly modest collection of clothes and shoes.

As Radhika began the task of sorting through Loc Tin's clothing, Kevin's eyes fell to the old army rucksack that sat on the highest shelf in the closet. He stood on a chair so that he could reach it, pulled it down, and knelt on the floor. He knew it held his father's "past life," as Loc Tin always told him. He had never been allowed to touch it and had always respected his father's wishes. But things were different now, and he only felt a slight pang of guilt as he worked the old buckles that held the flap in place. The bag and its contents had a dusty and dank smell. Radhika watched him as he carefully removed items and studied them. She sighed. It would be a long day, and she doubted they would make much progress.

In the rucksack, Kevin found some papers from his father's army days in Vietnam. It was obvious the papers had gotten wet at some point because they were wrinkled and fragile. Kevin handled them carefully. The writing was still legible although faded. Kevin had been taught to speak Vietnamese, but the written words were meaningless to him. Next he pulled out a cloth doll that had obviously once been white but was now yellowed. He looked at it a moment before handing it to Radhika.

"It looks handmade," she said, holding it carefully and stroking the yarn that formed the doll's hair. "I wonder if your dad's first wife made it?"

Kevin gave a sad shrug and then returned his attention to the bag. He found his father's ARVN uniform and looked at the patches sewn to it. Kevin had no idea what any of them represented, save for the yellow flag with three horizontal red stripes across the center—the flag of South Vietnam. He held up the uniform to his wife silently asking her the significance of any of the patches.

Radhika walked over to him and took the uniform. She pointed to a green patch with a tiger, three lightning bolts, and parachute embroidered on it. "This is the patch of the Special Forces," she said, clearly impressed. She looked at him and asked, "Your dad was Special Forces?" But she knew that Loc Tin refused to speak of his past and doubted Kevin knew any more than she did.

"I don't know. I know he was in the army for a long time. And that he conducted a lot of operations with the Americans. That's how he met Dordi.

But he never talked to me about all that. What little I know, I got from my mother."

Radhika nodded and started looking through the bag herself. She found a photograph, dated 1972. In the photo, Loc Tin held the hand of a small boy and stood next to a woman holding a little girl. She held it out for Kevin. He stood up from where he had been kneeling, took the photo, and sat on his parents' bed. "My dad and his first family. He never spoke of them when I was growing up. My mother told me about them when I was younger and made me promise not to ask him questions. But when we went to Vietnam, he couldn't stop talking about them. That's when I realized he had worried about them his whole life. But I guess he didn't want me and mom to know." Radhika just nodded. Loc Tin had kept so much inside that they never knew.

Although the first day Radhika and Kevin had spent trying to ready Loc Tin's home for Mr. Walker had not been terribly productive, the next few weeks had been better. Finally, just before December 1st when Mr. Walker would move in, the house was ready.

Chapter 86

September 2021
The Old Man

The knock at the door announced the arrival of his dinner. Without moving from his perch at his desk, the old man responded, "Door's open!"

An orderly the old man had not met before brought in a tray and set it in front of him. Tasteless chicken with overcooked green beans and mashed potatoes. The old man sighed. What he would give for a ribeye and glass of red wine. But apparently those days were over. As the orderly turned to leave, the old man, in the most pleasant voice he could muster, asked, "Will you turn on the news for me?"

Without a word, the orderly picked up the remote and clicked on the TV. The local news was just starting, and the old man picked up his fork and watched as he ate. After a few stories from around the nation, the newscaster turned to local news. Maria Barlow, the lead anchor, said solemnly, "Admiral James 'Jimbo' Higgins has died after an 18-month battle with pancreatic cancer. The Admiral served for more than 30 years with the U.S. Navy and commanded a fleet of Swift Boats during the Vietnam War. He was 85 years old."

The news saddened the old man for some reason. Despite having tried to kill the Admiral himself and despite him being the reason he was now in a wheelchair, he had a lot of respect for him. He wheeled his chair over to the corner of his apartment that served as a kitchen and found the bottle of bourbon his son had given him for his birthday a few months back. He opened the bottle and poured a generous glass. He lifted it into the air and toasted the Admiral's ghost, "Godspeed, you unlucky bastard."

Chapter 87

Sacramento, California, September 2021
  Ashley and Ben

Ashley was at her computer analyzing PCR data when someone knocked on the bookcase above her desk in the lab. She looked up to see Ben, who she had not spoken to since he ditched her in San Francisco.

She tried to act nonchalant. "Hey, Ben. What's up?"

"Do you have time for Rita's after work?"

She looked at him for a minute and debated how to respond. She was pretty sure he was still into his ex and, if she were truthful with herself, nothing had happened between them. She really had no reason to be mad. She also liked working with him and didn't want things to be awkward between them. Finally, she went with the advice her mother always gave her, "When in doubt, speak the truth." So she said, "I would love to, but I'm probably going to be late leaving. I have a lot to finish up before taking off for Emily's wedding."

"Oh, okay. Well, uhm...I just wanted to apologize for San Francisco. That wasn't cool. I...I just didn't expect...anyway. Just so you know, Heather and I broke up last year when I took the job here. Neither of us wanted to do the long-distance thing. But I guess now we both have decided to give it a try. Anyway, I...uh...I just wanted to tell you that."

Interesting, Ashley thought. It wasn't just my imagination. He noticed the spark between them too. But she appreciated his honesty, and she really liked Heather. She said sincerely, "Long-distance is hard, but it can work.

Look at Emily and Tom."

Ben looked relieved that she wasn't angry or upset. "That's true. Heather and I are practically neighbors compared to them." She just nodded and picked up her pen, signaling she needed to get back to work.

"Catch up after the wedding?" he asked.

She nodded, "I would like that." He turned and walked away, and she realized she wasn't all that disappointed that the romance ended before it even started.

Chapter 88

Richmond, Virginia, September 2021
Kevin and Radhika

It had been a year since Loc Tin's accident, and life for Kevin had never been the same. Radhika had tried a number of things to take his mind off his parents and the loss he was feeling. Nothing had worked. Now she had a new tactic. A friend of Radhika's, also from India, had her DNA analyzed and unexpectedly found out she was part Irish.

"Irish! Can you imagine? It was only about 6 percent, but still. How fun is that? We grow up thinking we are just one thing—white, Black, Asian—only to find out we are more than that. She has started tracing her family tree to try and see where the Irish part came from. She said it's really interesting," Radhika told him one Saturday morning. "Our heritages are so different, I thought it would be fun to see what mix Timothy and Samantha are." When she didn't get much of a response, she added, "I was thinking it might also be a way to honor your parents. You can see what you got from each of them and what they passed on to their grandchildren. Maybe we could even trace their lineages."

This got Kevin's attention, and he looked at her thoughtfully. "Yeah. Maybe we could do that." Once everyone had finished breakfast, with more fanfare than it probably deserved, Radhika brought out four *DNAStory* kits and made sure everyone collected their sample appropriately. As Kevin put the samples in their respective return boxes, Radhika signed her family up on the website, which would be how they received their results. However, before anyone in her family checked the "agree all" box, Radhika, a paralegal, carefully read over all of the fine print.

"This is interesting," she said to Kevin without looking away from the screen.

"What?" he responded as he sealed up the fourth box.

"It asks if we want to opt-in to having our DNA used by law enforcement." She looked at him and asked, "What do you think? Are you planning on committing any crimes?"

He smiled, "Maybe I already have." But then more seriously, "I don't have a problem with it. My dad spent most of his life getting criminals off the street. If my DNA helps them do that, what do I care?"

She nodded, checked the box and moved to the next issue she thought he would want to consider. "The *DNAstory* website also says most of its members are located in the U.S. If we are looking for connections outside this country, we should consider uploading our results into available international databases."

"Well, we definitely want to do that," Kevin surmised.

Radhika agreed. "Okay. That will have to wait until we get our results, but I can look into it in the meantime." She looked back at the screen. "Last question. Do you want your DNA to be discoverable by other *DNAstory* members? I marked 'yes' for me. What about you?"

"Yeah, sure. What about Sam and Tim?"

"Well, if our DNA is discoverable, not much point in hiding theirs." He nodded and she marked the appropriate boxes on the online forms. She closed the laptop and picked up the small boxes containing their samples. "I will mail these tomorrow." Then she marked both two weeks and six weeks on the calendar she kept on the refrigerator—the time frame in which results would be expected.

Chapter 89

San Francisco, California, September 2021
Jeremy and Ashley

Ashley heard her phone buzz just as she was walking out of her lab. She pulled it from her pocket and smiled when she saw it was Jeremy, "Hey. What's up?" They had spoken multiple times since her trip to San Francisco two weeks before.

"I got my DNA results back. I wanted to call you first since it was your idea," Jeremy replied.

"That was fast!"

"Fifteen days exactly—not that I have been watching my inbox or anything."

Ashley laughed. "So spill it. What are you made of?"

Jeremy said, "Well…it's a crazy mixture. Biggest contributions are from Vietnam and Northern Europe. But also a hefty chunk of Chinese and French and a small amount of Irish and Melanesian."

"Wow! Throw in some dog DNA and you could be the bloody glove," she said without thinking. She was not at liberty to discuss details of her cold case because Jeremy was not part of the investigative team.

"What?" he asked.

"It was an inside joke, sorry. What is mela…melaninin?"

"Melanesian. I didn't know either and had to look it up. It refers to someone from Melanesia," he replied.

"Well, that clears things up."

271

He laughed, "It's a group of islands off the coast of Australia. I think that must be from my mother's side because they are a darker-skinned people."

"Ooh—really wish we could analyze her. She would be so interesting," Ashley said, genuinely curious. "What about your dad? Did you ask him?"

"I asked him. He said he would think about it, which when I was growing up was another way of saying 'no, but I don't have a legitimate reason to say no,' or at least that's what it seemed to me. I sent him a kit anyway, but I'm not optimistic."

"Call him with your data. It may make him curious," she suggested.

"Maybe," he responded and then changed subjects, "When do you leave for Sydney?"

"Saturday around 7:00 P.M. I'm hoping I can sleep on the plane."

"You flying out of Sacramento?"

"No. The flight out of San Francisco was much cheaper—so worth having to drive over."

"That's great," he said. "Maybe we could get together before you leave?"

"Um, I would love to but not sure how much time we would have. My flight is at 7:00 P.M., but I have to be there at 4:00 P.M because it's an international flight. I guess I could drive over early and maybe we could have lunch."

"If you wanted to, you could come Friday after work and stay at my place. You could leave your car here and I could take you to the airport."

"Um…," Ashley wasn't sure how to respond. They had only *just* met.

"Sorry. I guess that sounded pretty forward. But I have a two-bedroom condo, and you'd have a private bathroom. I just thought it would be more relaxing for you than trying to squeeze in a lunch date the day you fly. I could make dinner Friday night and you could sleep in on Saturday if you wanted."

"Oh, um. Can I think about it and get back to you?" Ashley was very unsure but didn't want to hurt Jeremy's feelings.

"Sure—sure. Just let me know what you want to do," Jeremy replied.

Ashley told him she would call him later. They said goodbye and hung up. She immediately called Vivian.

Vivian picked up after several rings. "Hey, Ash! What's up? I was just finishing up with Dr. Jansen."

Ashley quickly filled her in on her conversation with Jeremy.

"Jeremy is a great guy. Definitely have lunch with him. I agree with him that it would be easier to already be in San Francisco. He's just trying to be helpful, but it won't hurt his feelings if it makes you uncomfortable," Vivian reassured her.

Ultimately, Ashley decided it was best to drive up on Saturday. They enjoyed lunch and she accepted his offer to leave her car at his place.

In the car on the way to the airport she said, "I'll be back late afternoon on the 29th. Just call me if anything comes up and you can't meet me. I can always grab an Uber."

"I don't expect there will be a problem, but I will text if there is. Not sure I can afford to call Australia."

She looked at him, her brow wrinkled, "We can video call for free."

"Really?"

"Really. Emily and Tom do it all the time."

"Huh. I had no idea."

She laughed and shook her head. "Welcome to 2021."

He dropped her off at the airport just before 4:00 P.M. He gave her a friendly hug and promised to pick her up two weeks later.

Chapter 90

Sydney, Australia, September 13-18, 2021
Ashley and Friends

Ashley landed at the Sydney International Airport late in the morning on September 13th having lost one day to travel and another 16 hours due to the time change. She had not gotten much sleep on the plane and was exhausted. She managed to find her way to baggage claim and retrieved her two large suitcases from the revolving belt.

"Blimey, mate! How long are you staying?" Ashley turned to see Tom, whom she had only met via video chat, eyeing her luggage.

"Tom!" Ashley said, relieved to see a friendly face. He grabbed the large wheeled bag and her carry-on, while she managed the slightly smaller wheeled bag.

"Which is more pressing, food or sleep?" Tom asked as he directed her to the exit.

"I don't know. Both are pretty high on my list."

"Well, you're staying at Em's parents' house. They have plenty of food so you can eat if you want or just go straight to bed. It's really up to you, just whatever you feel like. But try to recover soon because Emily can't wait to put you to work."

Exhaustion won out and Ashley collapsed on her bed without taking her clothes off. Twelve hours later, she began to feel human again. She wandered downstairs only to realize it was the middle of the night and the rest of the house was asleep. As quietly as she could, she tried to find something to eat.

"Ashley! I thought I heard a mouse," Emily squealed, delighted to see her.

"Did I wake you? I'm sorry. I just woke up and am sooo hungry."

"I know. That flight is awful. I have done it multiple times and it never gets easier," Emily said empathetically.

Ashley would spend the next ten days helping Emily with final wedding preparations. She was also excited that at long last she would meet Kristy, Emily's sister. Emily was very close with her younger sister and ultimately chose to do a fellowship with Dr. Jansen studying endometriosis because of her. Kristy had been diagnosed with the disease several years prior and had surgery in January in an attempt to treat it.

"How are you? Emily said the surgery went well," Ashley asked Kristy one evening when they finally had a moment to relax.

"Yes—I think it did. The pain is more tolerable now. Some days I don't have any pain at all, which is amazing."

Ashley thought that sounded awful—to be excited about "some" pain-free days. She didn't know what to say. "Emily is convinced your disease was caused by dioxin, because of the Agent Orange your grandmother was exposed to. Does your doctor agree?"

Kristy snorted, "No. He is the best doctor I have ever had, but, honestly, I think he thinks I am crazy when I say that. Em sent me a bunch of scientific papers to give him—and I did, but I don't think he even looked at them."

Once again, Ashley was at a loss for something to say. But Kristy changed the subject, "When does Vivian get in?"

"She leaves on Saturday—well, Saturday San Diego time. So she will be here on Monday," Ashley answered. "Dr. Jansen wasn't happy about Emily being gone a month, to say the least. Vivian was trying to be gone as little as possible."

Kristy nodded, "That's okay, we can handle it. My cousin Lisa will be here to help starting tomorrow."

The next day, Emily put Lisa, Kristy, and Ashley at a table and placed a box containing white mesh fabric, ribbon, and a huge bag of birdseed in the center.

"What's all this?" Ashley asked, but it was Kristy that answered.

"She wants us to make little bags of birdseed to throw after the wedding."

"Oh, instead of rice," Ashley nodded. "Okay. How many?"

"One hundred-fifty," responded Emily. She made sure they all had scissors and then left for her final dress fitting.

The three women sat at the table and got to work. Before long they each found a rhythm, and the completed bags started piling up.

Lisa made small talk. "Emily tells me you're a scientist like she is."

Ashley smiled, "Not exactly. She does research at UCSD, but I left academia." The confused look on her face made her continue. "Emily has her PhD and is trying to understand why some women have endometriosis when most don't. She is trying to understand what's different about them."

"Like Agent Orange exposure," Kristy added.

"Exactly. Environmental exposures or maybe genetic factors. Anyway, if you can understand what makes a person more at risk of a particular disease, you have a better chance of preventing it or treating it. That's what Emily does."

"Okay," Lisa said. "What is it you do then?"

"Well, I now work for the California Bureau of Forensics. It's a division of the California Bureau of Investigation. Basically I sequence DNA for use in criminal investigations."

"Oooh, like that TV show? *CSI*, I think?" Lisa looked genuinely impressed.

"Well, in theory, but the reality is a lot less exciting. But sometimes we help law enforcement get a conviction or clear someone that has been accused of a crime." Ashley really wanted to tell them all about the Vigilante Virginian, but she wasn't allowed to talk about it to anyone outside the CBF. Instead, she focused on tying a tiny ribbon to her latest bag of birdseed. "Em says you're a lawyer?"

She nodded. "I specialize in international adoptions, especially Vietnam."

Now Ashley was impressed. "That's really awesome. Do you speak Vietnamese?"

"Yes. Read and write as well. Other than me, my whole family was born in Vietnam. My brother, Tony, was five or six when they came to Australia. Anyway, I grew up speaking both English and Vietnamese. I am really glad too. It makes me far more valuable to my law firm and a better lawyer for my clients."

The women continued to talk and make birdseed bags. Ashley asked Lisa numerous questions about Vietnam and her advocacy work. "I would love to do something like that. You are really changing lives by helping the kids who have no one else."

"Not no one. The people who run the orphanages are amazing. They give so much love and support to these kids. It's the only reason any of them have a chance at a decent life. But they need a lot of donations to keep the doors open, so I do what I can to raise awareness and that helps."

"And the adoptions—you facilitate those?" Ashley persisted.

"Yes, of course. I wish we could find homes for them all, but the orphans never stop coming. Most are never adopted and age out of the orphanages when they are 15 or 16."

"That's so young! What happens to them?" Ashley asked, concern evident on her face.

She shrugged. "I guess the same thing that happens anywhere—they do the best they can. Some find success; others don't." Lisa tossed the bag she had just finished onto the growing pile.

Ashley just nodded. She had never before considered what happened to older orphans who were never adopted. She was about to ask Lisa if there were any opportunities to help, but just then Emily walked in. She was happy and smiling. "Wow! You have done so many birdseed bags. Should we count and see if there's enough?"

All three of the women responded, "Yes, please."

"We may be out of birdseed anyway," Ashley added as she dropped her jacket on top of the not-so-empty bag.

Chapter 91

Ashley and the other bridesmaids were watching Emily as she had finishing touches added to her hair and makeup. The wedding would start in a couple of hours.

Ashley's phone was on the table next to her and announced an incoming video call from Jeremy. She smiled when she answered, "Hey, Jeremy! What's going on?"

"Oh," he sounded surprised. "You look great. You're all dressed up."

"Emily and Tom's wedding—it starts soon."

"Really?" he asked. "I thought that was tomorrow."

Ashley laughed. "I'm in Australia. It *is* tomorrow."

"Oh, right. I forgot. I'm sorry to bother you then. I can call you later."

"No, now is fine. I have a few minutes. What's going on?" she assured him as she walked into a different, currently unoccupied room.

"Oh, well, if you're sure. Um...you remember I got my DNA results?" he asked, sounding uncharacteristically uncertain.

"Yes, of course."

"Well, it turns out I have a sibling. Well, a half-sibling. Mix of Vietnamese and European. I had no idea."

"Wow! That's amazing news! Are you excited? Do you think you'll try to meet them?"

"I don't know. I just now got the email. I haven't responded. I'm still just trying to comprehend it."

She sensed he was holding something back, "What's wrong? You sound worried."

"Not worried. Well, maybe worried. Um...it's just my dad. He talked a lot about the orphans in Vietnam. It really pissed him off that so many soldiers were careless and fathered children with Vietnamese women and then abandoned them. That's how so many ended up on the street. Just like my mom. I think he would be really devastated to know he left a child behind like that. So I'm not sure what I'm going to do."

"Oh, yeah. I guess I can understand that would be a really awkward position to be in. I am so sorry, Jeremy. That really is a tough situation. I don't know what to say," she replied.

"Hey, look, I know you're busy. I just needed to tell someone. I don't expect you to have all the answers," he said, trying to sound upbeat. "I'll let you go. I'll see you at the airport in a few days."

"Hey, I'll buy you dinner when I get in and we can talk. Okay?"

"That'd be great. Thanks, Ash."

Ashley hung up the phone, thinking about what he had said. She felt bad for Jeremy—and even worse for being the one who suggested he get his DNA tested. She genuinely hoped she could think of something reassuring to say before she landed in San Francisco the following week.

Chapter 92

Sydney, Australia, September 25, 2021
  Tony and Rebecca

Emily and Tom had just been pronounced "husband and wife" when Tony's phone announced a new email. Rebecca glared at him. His phone was supposed to be on silent. As the newlyweds walked down the aisle as a couple, Tony pulled out his phone to turn off the sound. But he couldn't help but read the message on the lockscreen. GEDMatch had found a relative. He immediately opened the message and read, "Congratulations! GEDMatch has identified an individual with whom you share significant DNA. Based on our algorithm, the relative may be a half-sibling, your grandparent, or your grandchild. Click the link for detailed information and to connect with your relative!"

Tony's heart leapt to his throat. A relative! A *real* blood relative. He knew it had to be a half-sibling, and he could not hide his excitement. By now, the wedding party had left the church, and those in attendance were drifting out as well. He touched his wife's arm. When she turned to him, he held out the phone with the email open. She read it and smiled broadly. She was nearly as excited as he was.

"This is so amazing! This means your dad is alive!" She realized she was being too loud and lowered her voice, "Or at least survived the war."

She and Tony sat back down and read the full email which contained important details about his relative. They whispered excitedly for a few moments, but then Rebecca told him, "We should probably keep this between us—just until after the reception. We don't want to upstage Tom and Emily on their big day."

He nodded in agreement, but he could not keep his elation hidden. Fortunately, everyone's mood was light, and no one noticed that he was especially happy.

Chapter 93

Sydney, Australia, September 25, 2021
Emily and Tom's Wedding Reception

After the wedding service, the guests made their way to a nearby event space for the reception. The bridal party was seated at a long table set up at the head of the room. A small dance floor took up a third of the room and large round tables with white tablecloths filled the rest of the floor space. While the guests ate, Emily and Tom made their way around the room speaking to each and every one.

Eventually, the meal was over, toasts had been made, and the cake had been cut. Older guests began to leave, and the younger guests took to the dance floor. Ashley was on her second—or maybe it was her third—glass of wine. She wasn't sure she could remember, but she was certain she didn't care. She was having a wonderful time even if she was the only single woman in the room—she wasn't of course, but she felt as though she was. She was sitting at the head table watching the couples dance when someone sat beside her. She glanced over to see Tony, Emily's cousin. Or was he her uncle? Really, Ashley, she asked herself, how much wine have you had? She looked at Tony who clearly had something to tell her. "What's up?"

"I did a DNA test," he said, excitedly.

"Okay. Good for you," Ashley responded, completely unsure why he thought she would care, but she tried to act interested. "Did you learn anything?"

"I have a brother!" he whispered.

Now it started coming back to Ashley. Tony was orphaned in Vietnam, and Anh, Emily's great Aunt, had adopted him. He knew his mother and sister were dead but had no information on his father. Ashley put the information she knew together. "That means your biological father survived the war."

"Exactly! And according to this email—he held up his phone—I have a half brother. He lives in the U.S." Then Tony caught sight of his wife looking at him pointedly and hastily added, "But don't tell anyone. Don't want to upstage Emily on her big day. I just wanted you to know because it was your idea."

As Tony hurried away, she wondered what he meant by it being her idea. The only thing she could think of was how she had bought Emily's kit last year and made her send her sample back. That led to Anh finding her long-lost daughter, and, she theorized, it led Tony to try and find his dad. "Okay, I don't mind taking credit for happy endings," she said to herself and decided she deserved another glass of wine for her good deed. But when she stood, she nearly lost her balance and had to grab the table for support. She decided maybe it was time to switch to coffee.

A few days later, Ashley and Vivian were on a flight headed home. Emily would return after she and Tom honeymooned for a week at a mountain lodge in Tasmania. They had been saving for the trip since announcing their engagement nearly a year before. Ashley hoped it was everything that they were anticipating. Emily still had over a year left on her commitment with Dr. Jansen, and although they had tried to find Tom a visiting professorship at UCSD, so far they had not been successful. It was looking like they would spend the first year or so of their married life on different continents. So Ashley thought splurging on the honeymoon was probably worth it.

They settled in for the long flight. They would land in San Diego—hours and hours later—and Vivian would go home while she had to catch a connecting flight to San Francisco. She was regretting the cheaper flight. She could have flown all the way to Sacramento, but then she smiled remembering that Jeremy would pick her up. It would be good to see him. Soon the melatonin that Emily had given her kicked in, and Ashley dozed off.

Chapter 94

Sacramento, California, October 2021
Vigilante Investigative Team

Lance had called a meeting to discuss the vigilante case. "The Virginia DA's office called. They are getting really anxious and want an update. Where are we?"

Ben said, "Ashley has spent a lot of time looking for other vigilante murders, but I don't know what she has found." He looked at her, "Can you fill us in?"

Although she was a little nervous being put in the spotlight, she was careful not to show it. She just stood, walked to the white board, and picked up a marker. "We have identified a total of 15 cases in the Virginia area that we are reasonably certain are our guy. Most of the murders occurred in the Richmond area, but a few were farther out. I found four in surrounding states." She wrote the names of the victims and corresponding date as she spoke, occasionally referring to her notes. "All of these men and one woman were killed by a knife, their throats slit—most likely from behind." She pointed to the board. "You can see there are two big time gaps among the killings in the Virginia area—1993-2004 and again between 2015 and 2018."

"Maybe he used a different method for a while?" Rhonda suggested.

Ben shook his head, "Unlikely." He thought for a moment, "But maybe he was convicted for another crime. Could he have been in jail then?"

"Maybe," Ashley said. "However, I personally think the Jacobs murder

285

here in California was also committed by the Vigilante." She added Jacobs to the list but with a question mark next to it since she could not be certain. "Because my gut tells me Jacobs belongs on the list, I started looking for other vigilante-type knife deaths in California around the same time. I found three others." She added the names and dates to the list—again with a question mark beside each one.

Ben drummed his fingers on the table and looked at the white board. "If Ash is right about the Vigilante Virginian offing Jacobs, could he have moved to California during the time gaps?"

Ashley went back to the board. "That's what I was thinking too. But there are also vigilante deaths with the same MO in California when the killer was active in the Virginia area." She added the other names and dates to the list. She then went back over the entire list and added, "VA" or "CA" beside the date. "You can see there were several murders in California during the big time gap in Virginia, but the Cali deaths continue even after the break in Virginia is over."

"Yeah. I see what you mean." He frowned, looking at the board. "What do you think?"

Ashley realized the question was directed at her. She took a deep breath and began to tell them her theory. "Well, it seems to me we either have one killer who travels a lot, or we have two killers with identical MOs."

Ben frowned, "Both theories seem unlikely."

Ashley nodded and continued. "But one has to be true. Right? So I got to thinking—if there is more than one vigilante—why not three or four with the same MO?"

Ben shook his head. "No, no. That would be really unlikely."

Ashley was getting annoyed. She wished he would just shut up and let her finish, but she kept her cool and continued as though he hadn't spoken. "To help rule in or rule out the possibility of multiple killers, I decided to pick a couple of random states and see if any deaths fit the profile. First, I looked at Mississippi. Lots of hunters there with excellent knife skills. A lot of veterans. And, at least in the recent past, most of the men tend to not be tolerant of other men who hurt women and children."

She had Lance's attention now. "That's a pretty good rationale. Did you find anything?"

"No, not a single death that perfectly fits our MO," Ashley said, definitively. "Next I looked at Oregon. Population demographics and attitudes similar to California. Nothing again." She looked at her colleagues. "It seems to me we are looking at one person. He must have strong ties to both Virginia and California."

The room was quiet for a moment. Everyone studied the board and thought about Ashley's conclusion. No one agreed with her—at least not out loud—but she noticed no one publicly disagreed with her either. She had nothing else to say and took her seat at the table.

Finally Lance spoke. "Where are we with DNA? That will tell us for sure if we have one killer or two."

Ashley shook her head. "Not good. We have high-quality DNA from the Jamison case, though we can't be certain it is from the killer. Even if it is, there are absolutely no matches in any database that Rhonda has access to. Then there is the bloody glove from Jacobs, which, again, multiple profiles because it was handled by everyone *and* their dog."

"Not to mention the glove may not have anything to do with the crime even if Ashley is right and it was committed by the Vigilante," Lance reminded them unnecessarily. "I still say the genealogy is our best chance of catching him," Lance continued. He looked at Rhonda.

She held up her hands in frustration. "Then find me a good sample! You heard Ashley. Mystery DNA and contaminated DNA. I can't work with that. I am not a magician."

Lance frowned. "In other words, we are nowhere." He looked around the table. No one disagreed.

Chapter 95

Trans-Pacific Flight, November 8, 2021
Tony and Rebecca

Tony was finally on a plane to the U.S. It was the same flight he had taken nearly a year ago to meet Mikayla.

After more than a month of emails, planning, and phone calls, Tony was going to meet his other family—the family with whom he shared DNA. He was so grateful to Anh for taking him in when he was a child and giving him an amazing life, but he was overwhelmed to know he had more family. He had wanted Rebecca to come with him, but the flight was expensive and they had decided it was best if he came alone. However, at the last minute Anh and Lanh had surprised them by buying a ticket for Rebecca. Their flight left Sydney at 11:20 A.M. and would arrive in Richmond after layovers in Los Angeles and Atlanta. Altogether, they would be in the air nearly 24 hrs.

"My brother, Kevin, will meet us at the airport," Tony told Rebecca as the pilot announced their approach to Richmond.

She smiled at her husband. He was as excited as a kid at Christmas. They had offered to stay at a hotel, but Kevin and his wife insisted they stay with them. Radhika said they had room and thought the men would stay up late every night—best if we were all together. Rebecca suppressed a yawn. She hoped it wouldn't be rude to go to bed as soon as they got to Kevin and Radhika's.

Chapter 96

About a month after their last meeting, Ashley called everyone together to discuss the Vigilante Virginian case.

"I may have had a breakthrough," she spoke as soon as everyone was seated at the table. "Actually, I do have good news. I'm just not sure how helpful it will be."

"Well, don't keep us in suspense. Out with it," Lance said, anxiously.

Ashley nodded, "Remember the bloody glove from the Jacobs case?"

"Yes," Rhonda said. "The contaminated sample?"

"Yes. Only now I have been able to match one of the profiles from the glove to the DNA from the gray hairs at the scene of Jamison murder."

"You can tweeze out individual profiles from a mixture?" Rhonda asked, surprised.

"No. I don't think so, but that's not what I did. Previously I cut out the largest blood sample from the glove, extracted the DNA, and analyzed it. It was on the outside of the glove—the middle finger. I didn't know it at the time, but multiple people had handled it before someone finally bagged it. Anyway, I identified six people and a dog. But then I got to thinking, anyone that handled the glove after the killer would have only contaminated the outside, but the killer's DNA should also be on the inside, assuming he had worn it at some point." Ashley looked at her audience. They stared at her expectantly. "I turned the glove inside out and although didn't see any

289

blood, I swabbed it pretty thoroughly hoping to pick up skin cells. Luckily, I was able to get a decent amount of DNA, and that one profile matched the gray hair DNA from the Jamison case. I think this means we can be certain that the Vigilante Virginian killed Jacobs."

"And it also means the gray hairs from the Jamison case belong to the killer!" Lance slammed his hand on the table, clearly excited.

"And that we are looking for one vigilante—not two," Ben added. He looked at Ashley, "This is really good news."

Rhonda was more reserved. "Sure, this is great, but if I can't find a relative, we are still nowhere." Then she stood, picked up her notebook, and left the room.

"So this really isn't helpful?" Ashley asked, disappointed.

"No, it's very helpful," said Lance, patting her on the shoulder. "We now know we have one man guilty of at least"—he looked at the board, which still held the victim list that Ashley had made at their last meeting and counted "26 murders. Damn." He looked back at Ashley. "We will get this guy. We just have to keep digging," he said as he walked out.

Ashley looked at Ben, the only other person in the room. "What do you think?"

"Knowing for sure that we are just looking for one killer is huge. Now we just need someone we can match the Jamison/Jacobs DNA to and we will find him." Ben got up from the table and walked out, leaving Ashley alone with her thoughts.

Ashley sat at the table by herself, thinking. Her job had been incredibly boring when she was just sequencing DNA, but she realized searching for a killer was incredibly stressful. She rubbed her temples and thought about the question Jeremy had asked, "When are you happiest?" Well, she thought, I don't think it's hunting serial killers. She sighed heavily and said to herself, "You really need to figure out what you want to do with your life." Finally she gathered her things and left the room.

Chapter 97

November 12, 2021
The Old Man

The old man put the pen down and closed the last notebook. Once he started writing, he couldn't stop. He asked his son to bring him more notebooks, and he had. The old man had filled a dozen of them. His son begged him to let him read what he had written, but he refused. The old man told his youngest son, "I'll be dead someday, then you can have them and do with them as you see fit."

He put the notebook in the box with the others. He closed the box, placed it on his lap, then wheeled over to the closet. Because of the wheelchair, it was a bit awkward wrestling the box into the corner of the closet, but over the months since his accident he had gotten better using the chair, and before too long the box was where he wanted it. It was out of the way but would be readily found when the time came.

The old man looked at the box and smiled. For the first time in a long time, he was glad he wasn't dead. His past was locked away, though not forgotten. There was a knock on his door and the old man cheerfully responded, "Debbie? Is that you? Come on in!"

Debbie had volunteered to take him outside this morning to meet a special visitor. She walked into his apartment as he wheeled into his living room. She smiled and said, "Mr. Vong, are you ready?"

He smiled back at her. "Yes. Let's go see my first-born son. Kim and I named him Lam, but I hear he goes by Tony now."

Chapter 98

November 12, 2021
Loc Tin and Tony

Tony and Rebecca had spent the last few days with Kevin and Radhika. It had been amazing getting to know them, and he and Tony had both been surprised to find that they had much in common. Foods, habits, even the sports and movies they enjoyed were all very similar. They even took their coffee the same way—no cream but lots of sugar. But today would be even better. Today Tony would meet his father. Kevin had explained about the accident and that he had lived with him and Radhika for a while, but that the assisted-living community seemed to be better for him. Tony understood. He loved his parents but wasn't sure he could live with them now.

Kevin pulled into the parking lot and parked near a green space with a wide, paved path. Coming up the path was a pretty, young woman pushing a wheelchair.

"That's Dad and his friend, Debbie," Kevin said, pointing.

Suddenly Tony was very nervous, and his hands felt sweaty. He wiped them on his jeans before he got out of the car. He saw Loc Tin and waved. The older man took control of the wheelchair and quickly rolled over to Kevin and Tony, who were walking toward him. Debbie had to hustle to keep up.

"Lam?" Loc Tin said, then corrected himself, "I...I mean, Tony. Your mother and I named you Lam," he said, tears in his eyes.

Tony knelt beside the old man. "It's good to finally meet you."

Loc Tin wrapped his arms around his son for a long moment. Then Tony took charge of the wheelchair and took his father to a small patio just off the trail where they could talk. Tony sat on the bench and the two men were able to talk face to face. Debbie and Kevin hung back, giving them privacy.

"Wow. It's just so amazing that they found each other after all this time," Debbie said. Kevin just nodded, watching his newfound brother with his father. Clearly a tremendous weight had been lifted from the man—a weight Kevin never even realized was there. "Mr. Vong told me lots of stories from when he was a kid. He even told me stories about you and your kids. But he never once mentioned he had a family before you and Lucy."

"He never talked about them. I think he didn't want me or my mom to feel—I don't know—second class or something."

Debbie tried to think of something to say, but nothing seemed appropriate. Just then Loc Tin, with a big smile on his face, wheeled over toward them, Tony right behind him.

Loc Tin held up a small photo album. He said to Kevin and Debbie, "Look at my other grandchildren. Twin boys!" Then he looked at Tony and asked, "Which one is which again?"

Tony gently took the album from him and flipped it to the last page. "Rebecca wrote on this one for you. Joseph on the right and Jonathan on the left." He pointed to something else, "And that's their birth date."

Loc Tin nodded a thank you and flipped through the book again. Rebecca had filled it with pictures from throughout Jonathan and Joseph's 17 years.

Suddenly Loc Tin closed the book and said, "I think I would like to take my sons to lunch." He looked at Debbie, "Would you like to join us?"

"Oh, no. Thank you. This is your time with family. I will see you again next week." She said goodbye to Kevin and Tony and then quickly left.

"She seems really nice, Dad," Kevin said as he watched her leave. "I think she has been good for you."

"Yes. Yes, she has. She's a good kid. Don't know why she puts up with me but glad she does." He wheeled himself over to Kevin's car. "Now, how about that lunch?"

Chapter 99

Ashley's phone buzzed in her pocket as she was loading her samples into a 96-well PCR plate. She ignored it and carefully kept her hands steady knowing she only had enough DNA for one run. "No mistakes," she thought to herself. In the ten minutes it took for Ashley to finish her work, her phone rang three more times, alerted her to two text messages and a missed video chat. The sounds were distracting, and she was becoming concerned that something was wrong

When Ashley was finally able to look at her phone, she saw that both calls and one text were from Emily asking her to call ASAP. The second text was a number she didn't recognize. The text just said, "THANK YOU!!" followed by a heart emoji. The video chat was from Anh in Australia. Confused, she dialed Emily who picked up instantly.

"Ashley!" Emily said so loudly Ashley had to hold the phone away from her ear.

"What is going on?" Ashley asked, still confused.

"Tony met his father! Well, his biological father."

"Really?" Ashley asked, genuinely excited. "That's amazing! He told me at the wedding that his father had survived the war, but he didn't know if he was still alive."

"He is! He lives in Virginia. Tony is so happy! And It's all because of you!"

"Because of me?" Ashley asked, but then remembered that Tony had said the same thing. "I don't understand. I didn't do anything."

"Yes, you did!" Emily squealed. "My Aunt Anh found Mikayla because you practically forced me to take that DNA test. Finding Mikayla was what prompted Tony to try to find his dad!"

"Speaking of which, you still owe me $50 for that *DNAstory* kit," Ashley teased. She walked to her desk and sat down before continuing, "But seriously—you would have done the DNA test even if I hadn't bought it for you."

"That's the thing, Ashley," Emily's voice grew quiet. "I'm not sure I would have. I mean, I know I promised my Aunt Anh, but I really didn't think we would find Mikayla. The odds just seemed against it. I only did it because of you. Without you, none of this would have happened."

"Oh," Ashley said, at a loss for words.

"When I was in Australia before the wedding, I apologized to Aunt Anh. I told her that I thought doing the DNA test was pointless and, honestly, the thought of having my genetic information made public made me uncomfortable. I told her I only did it because of you. Anh was very understanding, but also extremely grateful to you. *You're* the reason she found Mikayla. And now Tony has found his dad. I can't even begin to tell you how huge this is, Ashley."

Ashley felt her face flush. She wasn't used to people making such a fuss over her. She responded, "Well, in that case, I'm glad I was so pushy." Then Ashley quickly changed the subject, "Tell me more about Tony and his dad. When did they meet?"

"Tony is here now—in the States!" Emily said, excitedly. "His family lives in Richmond so he and his wife are staying with his brother. Did I tell you he has a brother?" She asked but continued talking before Ashley could respond, "They are having a big Thanksgiving dinner and they really want you to come! They are going to call you and invite you—please try to go."

Ashley's phone buzzed again. She looked at it and saw it was another text from the same unknown number as before. It said, "PLEASE CALL!" with another heart emoji. She turned her attention back to Emily, "They want me to come to Richmond?"

"Yes! Tony has wondered about his dad his whole life but never would have thought to look for him if Anh hadn't found Mikayla. They know you are the one that made me keep my promise to Anh and take the DNA test. And Tony's dad—he never knew whether or not his children survived the war. Can you imagine worrying for 50 years not knowing what happened to your family? Now he does! And he got to meet his son! They are just so happy and they want to thank you personally."

"I would love to see Tony again and I would really like to meet his dad, but I'm not family. It might be a little weird. Are you going to be there?"

"Yes. I'll fly out Wednesday late and stay through the weekend. I have a hotel room. You can stay with me. Please try to come! It would mean so much to everyone."

Ashley promised she would consider going to Richmond. She wasn't going home to Mississippi this year and had planned to take Rhonda up on her invitation to spend Thanksgiving with her and her extended family. Ashley knew Rhonda would understand if she changed her mind.

After she and Emily hung up, Ashley called the number that had left her the text messages. Apparently, Tony's entire American family was gathered around the phone and all wanted to say thank you to her. Just as Emily had said, they invited her to come for Thanksgiving. Ashley thanked them and promised she would try to make the trip. Shortly after she hung up from speaking to Tony and his new family, Anh, Tony's adoptive mother, reached out again.

Ashley accepted the video call and a smiling Anh greeted her. "Ashley! It is so good to see you again. Tony is so happy! And I was able to talk to his father and tell him all about his childhood. It was just like when I met Mikayla's mother and she told me all about when she was growing up." The woman dabbed her eyes before continuing. "We all just want you to know how grateful we are to you. None of this would have happened without you!"

Ashley was embarrassed by all the attention and praise, but she also felt really good. After she and Anh said goodbye, Ashley remained at her desk thinking about Emily and her family. It hadn't seemed like a big deal when she ordered the kit for her. Ashley had just always found DNA interesting and loved seeing people's results. Maybe that's what she should do, she thought. Family genealogy instead of forensics. Helping people find lost relatives sounded a lot more fulfilling than hunting down serial killers. The idea made her smile as she stood and turned her attention back to her work. She was still smiling an hour later as she gathered her things and headed home for the night.

Chapter 100

Sacramento, California, November 16, 2021
 Vigilante Team

Less than a week after their last meeting, Rhonda called the group back.
"We have a match! A really close match! A first-degree relative. Parent,
child, or sibling of the killer!"

"So now you can do the genealogy?" Ashley asked.

"Yes. Now that we have a name, we just scour the public records and find
out who he is related to! One of them will be the Vigilante!" Rhonda was
positively giddy.

Chapter 101

Ashley was leaving for the day when she noticed Rhonda was still in her lab. "Shouldn't you be on your way home?"

Rhonda looked up. "Thanksgiving break. The kids are with their grandparents so I don't have to rush to pick them up today."

Ashley nodded, "Have you found anything—any leads?" She didn't have to explain what she meant. They were all anxious for progress on the Vigilante case.

"Yes, actually. I now have two first-degree matches to our Vigilante. TWO! I was going to do a little more research to confirm, but everything fits so far."

"What fits?" Ben had just walked into the lab and overheard Rhonda.

"I am almost certain I know who the Vigilante is," Rhonda said, not even trying to hide her excitement.

"Seriously?" Ben said, incredulous.

"I thought you said he was a hero and we shouldn't try to catch him," Ashley chided.

"I do think he is a hero, but my job is to find him. And I am certain that I have."

"Where's Lance?" Ben asked. "He should hear this."

"Oh, he had to leave early—something with his sister," Ashley replied.

"Okay. I guess we can fill him in later," Ben said. He turned to Rhonda,

"What have you found?"

Rhonda finally looked away from her computer. She stood and walked over to the white board. "We now have two—yes, two—*first*-degree relatives of the gray hair guy, both sons—half brothers. One son also has two children and they share the right amount of DNA to be the grandchildren of our suspect."

"Two sons? I thought there was only one," asked Ashley.

"Well, I got the notification on Friday that we had another hit, so I started working on his family tree. Guy named Kevin Vong. Not much there, but enough. His wife is Indian. India Indian. The children are theirs. Kevin's parents were Vietnamese refugees. Got to the States in '76. Spent a few months at a refugee camp in Arkansas before being sponsored by a church in Richmond. As far as I can tell, they've been there ever since. Bought a house in 1990. The family still owns it, but it's a rental now. Interestingly, Vong also owns a cabin in the Blue Ridge Mountains. The same cabin where that woman"—she looked at her notes—"Betsy Ingalls was killed in 1984."

Ashley was excited now, "You're right. Everything fits for the Virginia killings. The location, the ethnicity, and the timeline. This Vong guy could even have killed the guy at the convenience store—the broken neck guy. That was in '78, I think?"

"Right."

Ashley frowned, "But what about California? Any ties to that state?"

Rhonda shook her head, "Nothing concrete. Took a couple of trips out there a few years ago, but it's hard to search records farther back. It's definitely conceivable that he's responsible for the vigilante knife deaths in this state, but no way to be sure. I did find an interesting tidbit, though." She looked at Ashley to make sure she was listening. "When Vong and his wife were pulled out of the South China Sea by the Navy, the records state that their boat which had sunk in a storm was named"—she paused for dramatic effect—"*The California Dreamin'*!"

"No way!" Ashley said, excited.

But Ben was not impressed. "It's an interesting detail, but it would not even be considered circumstantial evidence in a trial. What else do you have?"

Rhonda was annoyed and exchanged a glance with Ashley. Clearly, she thought the boat's name meant something as well. Rhonda looked back at Ben and said, "Well, it doesn't really matter if we understand the guy's connection to California or not. Thanks to Ashley, I definitely have him for both Jacobs and Jamison. His killing days are done." She nodded to Ashley.

"Yeah," Ben agreed. "Without your ingenuity with the glove, we would still be nowhere."

Rhonda continued, "Interestingly, Vong is ex-military *and* became a cop. He was with the Richmond police for years. He would know all about fingerprints and DNA. That's how he eluded getting caught for so long. But we have him now," Rhonda said, thumping her hand with the marker. Then, thoroughly enjoying herself, she continued. "I found Tony first. He's the other son. His profile linked to the Jamison DNA more than a week ago. But it didn't help because he was adopted. I am guessing he did the DNA analysis hoping to find his dad. Lucky for him and us that his half brother Kevin also did DNA testing. Probably because both their families include so many immigrants, they opted to add their profiles to GEDMatch. I got the notification about him on Friday." She then turned to face the white board and started writing:

Kevin Vong, age 41. Lives in Richmond, Virginia.

Parents: Loc Tin Vong (living) and Lucy Vong (deceased, 2018)

Tony Pham, age 51. Lives in Sydney, Australia.

Parents: Loc Tin Vong (living) and ??? (presumed dead)

Adoptive Parents: Anh Pham and Lanh Cam

"Australia? No kidding?" Ben said.

"Once I got the notification that Kevin's DNA also linked to the DNA we submitted—well, everything was easy after that. We can be reasonably certain that Loc Tin Vong is the Vigilante Virginian!"

Rhonda and Ben high-fived each other, but Ashley had turned very pale and was leaning against the wall.

"Ashley, are you okay?" Ben asked, very concerned.

"No, No, No...," Ashley said, shaking her head. She stared at the name

Rhonda had written on the board. Tony Pham. Emily's cousin. His father was the Vigilante Virginian. And she had been instrumental in uncovering that horrible truth.

"What is it? What's wrong?" Ben asked.

"Do you need to sit down?" Rhonda now stood next to Ashley, pulling her over to a chair.

Ashley looked at Rhonda and Ben, who were staring at her—obviously very concerned. She tried to explain, though it took her several tries before she could put together a cohesive sentence. She explained that they were talking about Emily's family—one of her closest friends. Tony had finally found his father—Loc Tin Vong. "They only just met... and now he will be sent to prison." Ashley put her head in her hands. "It's all my fault...it's all my fault. Oh...," she started to cry.

"This is NOT your fault. You didn't kill anyone," Rhonda tried to comfort her.

"I think I'm going to be sick...," Ashley left the room and hurried to the bathroom down the hall.

"What should we do?" Rhonda looked at Ben, hoping he could fix this, but he was just as at a loss as she was.

When Ashley returned, Ben suggested they go to Rita's and consider options.

"What options? There are no options," Ashley said, but allowed herself to be led to Rita's.

A couple of drinks later Ben said, "Only the three of us know. We could sit on the information. You said he is in a wheelchair now. His killing days are done anyway."

Ashley shook her head. "I can't ask y'all to do that. This is serious. He killed so many people. Even if we agree that they deserved it, he had no right to kill them. I just...," Her eyes filled with tears. "I just keep seeing him being arrested with his family right there. To see your dad hauled away in handcuffs...I know if he is the Vigilante, he has to face the consequences, but Emily's family...they only just found him. You should have seen Tony at the wedding when he found out he had a brother. And then that his father was still alive! He was so happy. They're planning a big Thanksgiving thing. Do you know they invited me to fly out to Virginia for the holiday? Loc Tin and Kevin want to meet me because they think I am responsible for their finding Tony. And now this." Tears streamed down Ashley's face, and she put her head on the table.

Rhonda looked at Ben, "Well, we still have to have DNA from the suspect to confirm. They won't arrest him just on what we have. That will take time." She thought for a minute, "and maybe I've been busy and don't connect all the dots until after the holidays. That would at least give them Thanksgiving together as a family."

Ashley looked up, "Can you do that?"

Ben shrugged, "Only the three of us know."

"We all agree then? We'll have a meeting with Lance on Monday, and I'll go over all this again. Can you act like it's the first time you have heard it?" Rhonda asked and both Ben and Ashley nodded.

"Ashley?" Ben said, and she looked at him, "Best if you don't go to Virginia."

"I know," she said, her eyes still red, but calmer than she had been earlier. She looked at both of them. "Thank you. I really appreciate it."

Two days later, the day before Thanksgiving, Ben had another idea to run by them and asked them to meet him at Rita's after work. When they were all seated at a corner booth, he asked, "What if we could warn him? Give him a chance to be prepared? I don't think he would make a run for it, but it would give him time to make peace with his family."

Ashley bit her lip, "Can we do that?"

"More importantly, how would we do that?" Rhonda asked.

But Ben had already given the idea some thought. He asked Ashley, "Do you know if he watches the news?"

Ashley looked at him, confused, "What?"

"Does Mr. Vong watch the news?" Ben asked again.

Ashley shrugged, "I have no idea, but he's in his seventies—isn't that what they all do?"

Ben nodded. "I was thinking that I could call Heather—see if she knows anyone at a local station in Richmond."

Rhonda chimed in, "I see what you're thinking. But I don't think it has to be a local story. When we caught the Green River Killer, that made national headlines. If we 'leaked' that we were closing in on the Vigilante Virginian using the same techniques…"

"It would make the national news! He would have to see it!" Ashley interrupted and finished the thought.

Ben nodded. "It should work—just to give him some time before he is arrested. Get his affairs in order."

"But there will be hell to pay if anyone finds out who her source is." Ashley grew concerned. "I don't want anyone to get in trouble doing a favor for me."

Rhonda shook her head. "It isn't a favor to you. At least half of the country thinks the Vigilante Virginian is a hero—including me."

"That won't matter to Lance or anyone else at the CBF or CBI," Ashley responded.

"No," Ben said, "But the list of people that could leak the story will be reasonably long once we file our report. It would be difficult to trace it back to us."

"But Heather is your girlfriend. Won't it be obvious?" Ashley was grateful for the plan but was still concerned.

"Maybe to Lance, but no one else. And unless one of you give me up, it would be difficult to prove." Ben said.

"And not worth the effort. Again, many people—even in law enforcement—think he's a hero," added Rhonda.

The three of them sat there for a moment without speaking. Then Ben repeated the plan so that they were all on the same page. "Monday Rhonda will call a meeting. She'll walk us through the data with Lance this time. He'll file the report. By Tuesday enough people will know that we can give Heather the go-ahead. We won't give her the name just that we believe we know who he is."

"And how much time will that give him—before the police knock on his door?" Ashley asked.

"Not long. They will need an arrest warrant, but that could be pretty quick since the DA is anxious to get this guy. Maybe a few days, a week at most," Ben guessed. "I would expect they would bring him in for questioning within a few days of the report being filed."

"And to get a DNA sample for confirmation," Rhonda added.

"Still, he should have a couple of days at least after Heather breaks the story. It will be up to him what to do with that time," Ben concluded.

Ashley nodded. It wasn't a great plan, but it was something. She started to go when Ben stopped her. "You can't tell Emily. You know that; right?" She nodded, annoyed that he felt the need to tell her that but also annoyed that she probably needed to hear it.

As planned, November 29th, the Monday after the Thanksgiving holiday, the Vigilante team, complete with Lance, met again. Rhonda seemed just as genuinely excited and pleased with herself as she had the previous week. Lance was so blown away by what she had discovered he failed to notice that Ashley and Ben were uncharacteristically reserved.

Tuesday morning Lance filed his report. A few hours later, Ben gave Heather the go ahead.

Just after noon, Heather called to tell him everything was set. "I'll break the story on the 5:00 P.M. national news. The same story will be repeated on the local news out of Richmond at 6:00 P.M."

Ben nodded. "So it won't matter if he watches the local news or the national—he'll see the story either way." He thanked Heather, hung up, and went to find Ashley and Rhonda.

The plan was in full swing.

Chapter 102

November 30, 2021
The Old Man

"Good night, Mr. Vong! I'll be back on Thursday. The weather should be nice and we can go outside again," Debbie said as she wheeled him over to his table. The orderly would be bringing his dinner soon.

"Thank you, Debbie. I look forward to your return." He smiled at her and then asked, "Would you mind turning on the TV for me? The news should be on soon."

"Certainly," the young woman replied. She picked up the remote and pushed a button.

As she handed the remote to Loc Tin, the female announcer teased an upcoming story. "Tonight we bring you breaking news on the hunt for the Vigilante Virginian. The man who has terrorized the city of Richmond for more than 40 years may soon be in custody. The full story after the break." Suddenly a large man in a suit and tie was asking if you had been injured because of a drug you had taken—his law firm would take on the case.

"Oh," Debbie said, responding to the news teaser. "I would really like to see that story. Would you mind if I stayed for a few minutes?"

Loc Tin was still looking at the TV, and Debbie wasn't sure he had heard her. "Mr. Vong?"

He rubbed his face and looked at Debbie. "Of course, my dear. Stay as long as you like."

Debbie smiled and pulled up a chair next to his wheelchair.

The news program resumed, and, as promised, the Vigilante Virginian was the lead story. Maria, the local newscaster, introduced Heather Sinclair with the NBC affiliate in San Francisco.

"Thanks, Maria," Heather began. A sign announced to the audience that she was standing in front of the California Bureau of Investigation. "An anonymous source working with the CBI has stated that they believe they now know the identity of the Vigilante Virginian. As most viewers are aware, the man known as the Vigilante Virginian is believed to have murdered at least 26 people in multiple states. Now DNA evidence left at two of those crime scenes—the Jacobs murder in California and the Jamison murder in Virginia—have allowed the CBI to identify him."

"But isn't it true that all of the victims had been accused of heinous crimes?" Maria asked.

"Yes—hence the nickname Vigilante Virginian. However, the recently elected District Attorney of Virginia vowed to put a stop to vigilante justice and asked the CBI for assistance. Using the same, somewhat controversial technique known as forensic genealogy that was used to bring the Green River Killer to justice, they are confident that they have now identified the Vigilante Virginian. However, they will not release the name until he is in custody."

"Heather, does the CBI have any idea how quickly this person will be publicly identified and arrested?"

"My source is confident that his name will be released within the next week, so I would expect an arrest would be imminent."

"Thank you, Heather." Maria filled the screen and continued, "In other news, traffic on I-95 was delayed for several hours after an 18-wheeler all the way from Atkins, Arkansas, ran off the road and overturned, spilling nearly 5,000 jars of dill pickles. The driver escaped with only minor injuries, but the pickles could not be saved."

Loc Tin stared at the TV for a moment but then said to his friend, "Turn it off, Debbie. I'm suddenly very tired. I hope you don't mind..."

Debbie jumped up. "Of course not, Mr. Vong. I just have a real interest in the Vigilante guy."

"Oh, really? Why?" Loc Tin asked, genuinely curious.

She sat back down again, "Do you remember the Jamison case?"

Loc Tin pretended to think for a moment. "Was he the man who killed students at a middle school?"

"Yes! He killed his ex-wife and then students at a school. He also killed a student teacher. Jennifer Foster." Debbie's eyes filled with tears. "Jen was a friend of mine from high school. She was only 21."

Loc Tin took her hand. "I am so sorry, Debbie. I didn't know."

Debbie wiped her eyes with her sleeve and shook her head. "You couldn't know. I don't talk about it. I still see her mom sometimes. She will never be okay." Suddenly her voice hardened, "I hope Jamison burns in hell and that the Vigilante Virginian is *never* caught."

Loc Tin was taken completely by surprise at Debbie's outburst. He had only known her to be happy and bubbly. Maybe she was not as naive and overprotected as he thought.

"Debbie, I believe I would like a bourbon. I don't suppose you drink? I'd be happy for you to stay and have one with me."

"Why, yes, Mr. Vong, I would like that very much." Debbie paused. Then she added, "I might need to mix it with a little water—or Coke if you have it."

"I think my son left a can of Coke the last time he was here. And I think it's time for you to call me Loc Tin—or LT. My friends call me LT. If we are going to drink together, we shouldn't be so formal." He told Debbie where to find the bourbon and Coke, and he watched her prepare the drinks. Clearly, she had done this before.

Debbie set the drinks on the table and held up her glass and said, "To the Vigilante Virginian, wherever you are!" They clinked glasses, and then Debbie added, "I hope he saw that broadcast. If he's smart, he'll get the hell out of Dodge."

Loc Tin smiled and sipped his bourbon.

After Debbie left, Loc Tin called Kevin, who was surprised to hear from him since he and Tony had seen him earlier in the day.

"Dad. Hi. Are you okay? Is something wrong?" Kevin asked, anxiously.

"I'm fine, Son. But I need a favor."

"Sure, Dad. Anything."

"I know you and Radhika cleaned out our house, but I was wondering if you had my old ARVN rucksack. It was on the top shelf in mine and your mother's closet. Did you find it?"

"Yes, I have it here. It's in the basement. I knew it had your personal things from...from..."

"It's okay, Son. It's from my life before you and your mom. Can you get it and bring it to me tomorrow?"

"Uh...yeah, sure. I can bring it with me after I take Tony and Rebecca to the airport. Is that okay?"

"That will be fine. I just need to get something that's in it."

"Yes, sir. I will get it now and put it in the car. I'll be by around 6:00 P.M. Hey, maybe I could pick up dinner and we could eat together."

The old man smiled, "I would like that very much."

Chapter 103

December 2, 2021
The Old Man

Debbie pushed Mr. Vong's wheelchair along the path that wound its way through the lush grounds of the assisted-living facility. It had taken a while, but he had eventually come to appreciate being here. It was a nice place with a mostly friendly staff. The food could be better, but it could be worse, he supposed. He hoped the rent from his and Lucy's house was enough to pay for his being here. No matter now, he thought.

Although he wasn't tired in the least, he pretended to nod off now and again. So much so that Debbie finally asked, "Mr. Vong, are you okay?"

"I'm fine, Debbie. Just tired. I think I need to go back to my room—maybe lay down for a bit. I think all the excitement of the last few days has been harder on the old body than I thought."

"Okay, Mr. Vong. I'll be back on Saturday and we can try again."

Loc Tin smiled but said nothing. Back in his room, she asked if there was anything he needed before she left.

"No. Thank you." Debbie started to leave, but Loc Tin spoke again, "I hope you know how much I appreciate your friendship."

Debbie smiled, walked back to him and knelt so they were eye level. "Thank you, Mr. Vong. You mean a lot to me too."

"Didn't I tell you to call me LT?"

She laughed as she stood. "Yes, but that will take some getting used to. I promise I'll try." She opened the door and turned back to him, "Good night

Mr...uh...LT." She smiled at him.

He smiled back and said, "Goodbye, Debbie."

After she left, he wheeled over to the counter and picked up the old rucksack. He rubbed his hand over the faded cloth and then worked the familiar buckles. He pulled out his ARVN uniform with the Special Forces patch. He remembered the day it was given to him, and he swelled with pride. Dordi had asked to be the official bearer of the news that he had succeeded in becoming the Vietnamese version of the Green Berets. He had given him the patch, shook his hand, and then stepped back to salute him. Dordi had made a big production of it all, knowing how hard he had worked to earn it. Later Kim had sewn the colorful patch onto his uniform.

Loc Tin smiled, remembering that day so long ago. Then he thought about the day that he and Dordi had first met. They had quickly become as close as two men could. Nevertheless, it had been a long time before Loc Tin had let him visit him in the nursing home. Loc Tin was embarrassed and didn't want Dordi to see him so weak. He couldn't bear the thought of the man pitying him. But Dordi had been the same as always. He'd brought whiskey and cigars, and they had smoked in his non-smoking room. They got drunk and laughed uncontrollably. They told the same stories to each other yet again. As always, thinking of Dordi made him smile. But this time thinking of Dordi—his brother-in-arms—made him think of Bao. Over the many years of his life, he had held onto the belief that his brother had survived the war and that one day their paths would cross again. Loc Tin sighed heavily. He knew now he would never see Bao again.

He turned back to the rucksack searching for what he needed. Instead, he found the only photo he had of Kim and their children. He had to fight back tears remembering Suong and her too short life. He caressed her image for a moment and then turned to his son, Lam. He knew his name was Tony now, but in this moment, he was Lam. He was grateful that he had survived the war and had done well, but he was also saddened at the life that might have been if his first family had survived. A useless emotion, he knew. Loc Tin wheeled over to his desk and set the photo down. He wrote out a note asking Kevin to send it to his brother. Although it was irrational, he could not bring himself to write the name Tony.

Finally, he returned his attention to his army bag. Buried in the bottom he found what he needed. It was a small metal box with the "U.S. Army" logo stamped on its lid. His fingers traced the letters, and he let his mind drift back to Vietnam and the many missions he and Dordi had undertaken. They thought so much alike. When it was just the two of them in the field, it was like they were the left and right hand of the same person. They knew exactly what the other man would do and that made them lethal to the enemy.

He shook his head and once again forced his mind back to the box and the task at hand. The box was rusted shut and his hands were misshapen by arthritis, but finally he succeeded in opening it. Inside wrapped in a piece of faded green cloth was the capsule he had been given before he and Dordi set off for Cambodia to rescue Blizzard—just in case they had failed and were captured. He had almost refused to take it. He had been so young, and he was convinced he and Dordi were invincible. Now he was glad he had it and wondered if the cyanide would still be effective. He would soon find out. He looked around at the small, tidy apartment. He had known from the beginning that he would die here, and now the time had come. His eyes fell to his grandchildren's artwork, and he regretted not asking Kevin to bring them to see him the night before. Too late now.

He wheeled over to his bed and was grateful, once again, that he could still manage getting in and out of his wheelchair on his own. He had lied to Debbie when he told her he was tired, but suddenly he really was. He lay in bed and briefly thought again of his families. He thought of his first wife—a good woman whom his parents had chosen for him. She did not deserve her fate. He thought of the children they had had— his precious daughter Suong, yet another victim of the war, and his son Lam, now Tony. Loc Tin hoped he would not come to regret having found him. He thought of Lucy—the love of his life—and his son Kevin, who, more than anyone else would have to live with the burden of his father's sins.

He rolled the small capsule between his fingers. With luck, there would be no autopsy. Debbie would tell whoever found him that he had not been feeling well and had turned in early. He hoped they would assume he simply died in his sleep of old age. He preferred that his son—no—his *sons* not know he took his own life, but perhaps it didn't matter. The truth would come out either way, but at least he could save them the pain of a trial. He was guilty and it was time to accept the consequences of his actions. He put the capsule in his mouth, closed his eyes, and bit down. In less than three minutes the Vigilante Virginian was dead.

Chapter 104

December 3, 2021
Emily and Ashley

Emily was crying, "He's dead, Ashley! He's dead!"

"Who's dead?" Ashley's mind raced through all the people they knew in common. "Tom? Is Tom okay?"

She heard Emily take a ragged breath. "He's fine. It's Loc Tin. Tony's dad. He's dead. The orderly found him this morning when he brought him breakfast."

"Mr. Vong is *dead?*" Ashley said, bile rising in her throat. "What happened?" She nearly choked on the question.

"I don't know. He died in his sleep maybe. He was in bed—dead. Somebody—I don't remember who—said he had been dead for a long time. Oh, Ashley, it's so awful!! Tony doesn't even know yet. His flight left last night. We won't be able to tell him for hours." She had begun to cry again.

"Where are you? Are you by yourself?" Ashley knew things were only going to get worse once he was revealed as the Vigilante.

"I'm back in San Diego. Vivian's here," Emily hiccupped.

Ashley debated whether or not to tell Vivian what was coming. She knew her relationship with Emily was likely to be damaged beyond repair very soon. She hoped she wouldn't lose Vivian as well. In the end, she just asked her to stay close to Emily and to call if she could do anything. Ashley said goodbye after Vivian promised to keep in touch. Ashley sighed, wondering how soon before everyone knew the full story.

Chapter 105

December 6, 2021
  7:00 A.M., EST

The coroner had ordered an autopsy of Mr. Vong because his body smelled vaguely of almonds, suggesting cyanide poisoning. Suicide or murder? The coroner first thought the old man had been murdered, but he had not been a wealthy man and the additional information provided by the police made suicide far more likely. When the medical examiner completed the autopsy and filed his report, the cause of death was listed as "suicide."

Chapter 106

December 8, 2021
3:00 P.M., EST

"Hey, Heather," Ben answered the phone as soon as it rang.

Heather could hear how anxious he was. "The story will break on the 5:00 P.M. national news. It will be the lead story. Maria Barlow from the Richmond affiliate will be a guest anchor. She will reveal his identity."

Ben thanked her. He hung up and went to find Ashley and the rest of the Vigilante team.

5:00 P.M., EST

A few minutes before 2:00 P.M. their time, Ashley, Ben, Rhonda, and Lance gathered in the breakroom to watch the national news broadcast from New York City. By now Loc Tin's family knew that he was the Vigilante. The police had already been in contact with them and explained about the man's secret life. They had been devastated all over again. The jury was still out on whether Ashley and Emily's friendship would survive, but Emily's Aunt Anh had already called her. "It isn't your fault, Ashley," she had said. "Loc Tin knew what he was doing and had to know he would get caught someday. Tony is still happy to know who he is and to have met him. And he still has Kevin." Her words had made Ashley feel better, but Emily still hadn't returned her phone calls.

She had talked to Vivian who had told her, "Emily is just really upset that

316

you didn't tell her. I think she knows deep down that you couldn't, but right now she is just really hurting. I think she just needs someone to blame and, unfortunately, that's you."

Ashley heard the intro music that signaled the news was about to start and turned her attention to the TV.

Maria Barlow filled the screen, looking even more serious than usual. She said, "Coming up tonight, we now know the name of the Vigilante Virginian—and he has struck again. Details on the next edition of America's Nightly News."

Ashley and her team didn't move—just silently watched and waited. After what seemed like a dozen commercials, the national news broadcast finally began.

"Good evening, America. I'm Maria Barlow, guest anchoring America's Nightly News. Tonight we have breaking news from Richmond, Virginia." The camera changed angles, Ms. Barlow turned her head to face it, and then continued, "The Vigilante Virginian has struck one last time, this time taking his own life using a cyanide capsule, also known as a suicide pill. His name was Loc Tin Vong, and he was a decorated veteran of the Army of the Republic of Vietnam. It is believed that Mr. Vong may have had the suicide pill since the late 1960s when he was hand selected for the Vietnamese Special Forces.

"It was well-known that Mr. Vong had participated in a number of covert assignments alongside the U.S. Special Forces. He and his wife, who died of cancer in 2018, immigrated to the U.S. in 1976, eventually settling in Richmond. Mr. Vong served for nearly 30 years with the Richmond Police Department, rising from a beat cop all the way up to detective. He was well respected by his colleagues, who were saddened by his death and shocked to learn of the man's secret life.

"The family of Mr. Vong has asked for privacy in this difficult time as they too were unaware of Mr. Vong's vigilante activities. The family has also expressed their appreciation to the citizens of Richmond who have largely shown the family kindness and sympathy since the identification of Mr. Vong as the Vigilante Virginian. Unconfirmed sources say that Mr.

Vong left a lengthy memoir, detailing 16 vigilante deaths—including several outside the state of Virginia. We will bring you more of this story as it becomes available."

Ashley looked at Ben, "Sixteen?" Ben stared at the TV, frowning.

5:10 P.M., EST

One hundred miles from Richmond in his cabin in the Blue Ridge Mountains, Dennis Dordi stood and turned off the TV. He walked over to the cabinet and pulled out an unopened bottle of Pappy Van Winkle. He poured himself a glass of the expensive bourbon and held it up, "Godspeed, LT. Godspeed."

End Notes

Lives Intertwined was not a solo endeavor. There are many people who deserve recognition for their help in making this book a reality.

I would like to specifically thank and acknowledge Mr. Robert Long-hauser, SP4, US Army. He served in Vietnam in 1968 with the 1st Infantry Division, stationed at DiAn. He was in charge of the High Awards Divisional Department (Medal of Honors and Silver Stars) and was himself awarded the Bronze Star and Army Commendation for Service medals during the Tet offensive. He was honorably discharged in 1970 from Fort Bliss, TX. Bob was kind enough to share with me his written, as yet unpublished, memoir of his time in Vietnam. I drew heavily on his experiences to craft several chapters set during the war within *Lives Intertwined* and I offer my sincere gratitude to him. Additionally, since I am not a soldier and have not served my country during wartime, he graciously read the book prior to publication and provided insight and suggestions to help ensure parts of the story were realistic.

David England, my friend and brother-in-law, is an avid hunter and was essential to helping me understand both weaponry and technical skills that Loc Tin needed to survive the war. Even more important, David read the "final" version of *Lives Intertwined* and made a significant suggestion that added both depth to the story and led to the plot twist at the end.

I would also like to express my gratitude to my sister, Leana Bruner England, who, just as she did for the first book, read multiple drafts of *Lives Intertwined*. She was instrumental in reading behind me to ensure the story and storylines remained consistent. Her suggestions and reactions to various parts of the novel were essential as the story unfolded and in the crafting of the final version.

Kevin Osteen, PhD, my friend and scientific partner, read many, many individual chapters over the course of the book's development as well as responded to story ideas on the fly whenever they occurred to me. I am extremely grateful to him for these discussions.

My close friend, Christina Meza, read multiple chapters to ensure they were readable to a non-scientific audience and painstakingly proofread the final manuscript (except for this section which probably shows the reader how important she was to the rest of the book!). Importantly, after reading *Lives Intertwined*, Christina asked several questions that made me realize that certain, important details that were in my head had not made it on to page—details that the reader needed and I'm indebted to her for these observations.

Antoni Duleba, MD, a friend and colleague, read *Time Intertwined* about the same time as the war in Afghanistan came to its terrible conclusion. It was his brilliant idea to weave the tragedy of the Fall of Kabul into *Lives Intertwined* and I sincerely appreciate this recommendation. Paula Austin, a close friend and retired U.S. Marine, provided important insight into multiple concepts of the story and I am very grateful for her insight and suggestions. She was also the final beta reader before the book was published. My friend and neighbor, Danny Warren, a retired Nashville Metro police officer, answered numerous questions about law enforcement that helped keep the story realistic. Finally, numerous publicly available books and websites were useful to me as I wrote *Lives Intertwined*. These are listed within the appendix.

Author photo credits: Erin O. Smith (inside) and Audrey Noe (back cover)

Darkness and Light Intertwined

Excerpt from *Book 3 of the Agent Orange Trilogy*

San Francisco, California, September 2021
Ashley and Jeremy

Ashley kept her eyes on the "fasten seat belt" light and released the restraint the instant the captain turned it off. She stood and stretched, glad to finally be home. Well, almost. She lived in Sacramento but had left from San Francisco because the flight was cheaper. Her friend Jeremy would pick her up—she had promised to take him to dinner tonight. She was grateful Emily, whose wedding she had just attended, had given her melatonin for the flight back. She had actually slept and felt far better now than when she had arrived in Sydney two weeks before. Eighteen hours on a plane was not her idea of a good time.

She grabbed her carry-on and waited impatiently for her turn to deplane. Finally, she was in the terminal and made her way to baggage claim. She quickly found the carousel that promised to bring her luggage and saw that Jeremy was already there. He smiled broadly when he saw her, and she was suddenly aware that she must look wretched. She also needed to brush her teeth. She gave Jeremy a brief hug and thanked him for coming.

"No problem at all." He helped her get her bags, and they made their way to his car. As they left the airport, Jeremy said, "Do you still feel up to going out to eat? I know you must be exhausted."

Ashley knew Jeremy was anxious to discuss his DNA results—he had recently learned that he had a half-sibling. He had been unsure of what he wanted to do because he didn't want to upset his father. She suppressed a yawn and said, "I'm okay. More hungry than tired, so dinner would be nice. As long as you are still up for it?"

Jeremy drove to a family-owned place not too far from his apartment. It was the middle of the week, and the place wasn't crowded despite being dinnertime. They were seated quickly and within 30 minutes of arriving were enjoying wine and an appetizer of fried calamari.

"Tell me about your half-sibling. What do you know?" she asked as she dipped a piece of fried squid into the spicy tomato sauce that came with it and popped it into her mouth.

He shook his head, "I know nothing, really. I printed out the file but haven't looked at it. I'm not sure I want to." He hesitated, "Dad will just be so angry with himself. He and my Mom were married for — what? — 40 years? He rescued her from living on the streets in Vietnam and knew how hard her life had been growing up that way. It would devastate him to learn he fathered a child in Vietnam. I'm not sure it is worth it."

She nodded, "I get it. The mixed-race orphans were treated so badly. He would probably beat himself up knowing he had abandoned one to that life. You don't have to tell him, you know. But it is still worth knowing he or she is out there. At least look at the information first. Then you can decide what to do."

"I suppose," he said, handing her the pages he had printed. "You look at it. Tell me what it says."

She took the papers from him and looked them over carefully. Something she read clearly startled her, and he asked anxiously, "What...what is it? What do you see?"

She sat the papers down and picked up her wine glass to give herself time to think. She had no idea how to tell him what she now knew.

"Just tell me. Whatever it is. It can't be any worse than what I already know."

Oh, yes, it can, Ashley thought. She sat her glass down without drinking and looked at him. As gently as she could she said, "Your half-sibling is not your father's child. She is your mother's child."

This fact had been obvious to Ashley because she had previously seen

Jeremy's DNA results. Jeremy had told her that his mother had no idea who her parents were but that her skin was darker than most Vietnamese and certainly darker than his blue-eyed father. He had wondered if she had some African ancestry. Jeremy's DNA revealed an eclectic mix of Northern European, French, Vietnamese, Chinese, and Melanesian—a dark-skinned people who originated off the coast of Australia. It wasn't hard to guess who he had gotten that from.

Jeremy shook his head, "That's not possible. My mom was only 19 when they got married. When would she have had a baby?"

"I don't know," she said as she took his hand. "But your half-sibling is also part Melanesian. She has to be your mother's child."

He took the papers from her and read it for himself. His sister was 8 percent Melanesian. He was 6 percent. The percentages of Chinese and Vietnamese were identical. He was a bit more French than his sister. However, the remaining European ancestries were very different between them. Jeremy had small amounts of Irish and Italian but his sister did not. She was nearly 20 percent German; Jeremy had none. Ashley was right. The half-sibling was from his mother. She was born three years before Lily—meaning his mother had had a baby before she and his father married. "I...I...don't understand...," Jeremy looked at Ashley.

"Maybe you should talk to your dad," Ashley said gently.

He looked up at her, clearly confused. "She would have been only 16 when this woman was born. That was three years before my parents were married. I just never thought...never thought..." His voice trailed off, and he contemplated the meaning of this new information.

Jeremy knew from his travels to Vietnam that most of the homeless children, both boys and girls, turned to prostitution to survive. However, he somehow thought his mother had escaped that life. Now he wondered. Is that how his parents met? Was his dad a client? The thought made him sick to his stomach.

Their food came, and Jeremy tried to eat. He knew Ashley was famished and didn't want to make her uncomfortable by not eating, but his stomach churned and he could only pick at his food.

Ashley watched Jeremy struggling with what he just learned and tried to think of something to say that would make him feel better. She said again, "Talk to your dad."

"Do you think he knows?"

She shrugged but then thought about it. "They were married a long time. I think she would have told him."

Jeremy nodded, "Mom hated her past—hated her life in Vietnam. She never talked about it. Maybe this is why." He picked up the papers again. He read aloud the little bit of information that *DNAStory* had provided about his relative. "Her name is Melinda Barker. She is 49 years old and lives in Jackson, Mississippi."

Ashley nodded. She had read that info as well. "You know my parents live about 30 miles outside of Jackson—in Crystal Springs. If you want to try and meet her, I'll go with you and we can stay with them."

Jeremy looked at her blankly. "Meet her?"

"Why not? Meeting her won't change the past. It won't change whatever happened to your mom. But Melinda is your sister. Your *sister*. Right this very minute she's probably wondering about you. That may be why she did the DNA thing. She probably wants to know more about where she came from. Your mom grew up on the street. She must have taken Melinda to an orphanage so she would have a chance at a better life than the one she could give her." Ashley leaned forward and took Jeremy's hand again. "She did the right thing by her child. She saved her from a life on the street. And Melinda must have been adopted, otherwise she wouldn't be in the States."

Jeremy looked at her, uncertain. "I...I'm not sure. I...I don't know if I want to meet her or not. My dad...I just don't know."

"What would your mom want?"

Jeremy looked at her uncertainly, "What do you mean?"

"If your mom was here at this table and she saw this information about her daughter—her first child—what would she do?"

Jeremy responded without hesitation, "She would be on the first plane to Mississippi." He leaned back in his seat and sighed heavily.

Ashley said gently, "I don't think the circumstances of how that child came to be would matter. Your mother loved her enough to give her up. But I imagine she would have spent her life wondering and worrying about her."

Jeremy nodded, "She would want to know that she was okay."

Ashley agreed. "I think so."

Appendix

The following books and websites were valuable to me as I wrote *Lives Intertwined.*

Agent Orange and Burn Pits
Websites and online articles:
Websites and online articles:
https://burnpits360.org/about-us/
https://look.substack.com/p/when-the-full-truth-emerged-it-was
https://www.u-s-history.com/pages/h1860.html
https://www.vietnamfulldisclosure.org/children-agent-orange/
https://www.va.gov/disability/dependency-indemnity-compensation/
https://grist.org/article/veteran-wins-groundbreaking-claim-for-agent-orange-exposure-at-georgia-mili/
https://myfox47.com/2021/05/31/owatonna-veteran-who-won-famous-agent-orange-case-remembered/
https://theconversation.com/agent-orange-exposed-how-u-s-chemical-warfare-in-vietnam-unleashed-a-slow-moving-disaster-84572
https://www.militarytimes.com/news/your-military/2019/07/12/why-dod-is-still-using-burn-pits-even-while-now-acknowledging-their-danger/
https://embryo.asu.edu/pages/re-agent-orange-product-liability-litigation-1979-1984
https://www.acq.osd.mil/eie/Downloads/Congress/Open%20Burn%20Pit%20Report-2019.pdf

Scientific Publication:

Matthew Meselson, One Hundred Years of Chemical Warfare: Research, Deployment, Consequences (2017). In:From Charles and Francis Darwin to Richard Nixon: The Origin and Termination of Anti-plant Chemical Warfare in Vietnam (editors: Bretislav Friedrich, Dieter Hoffmann, Jürgen Renn, Florian Schmaltz, Martin Wolf) pp 335-348 SpringerOpen

Forensic Genealogy:

Websites and online articles:

https://www.forensicgenealogists.org/

https://images.squarespace-cdn.com/content/v1/55d49893e4b0caee6f7
7186f/1515730408650-PA36RA6AZ8IODZYV7839/ke17ZwdGBToddI8
pDm48kBYk1nwJ0umbKYXpeRrJYfh7gQa3H78H3Y0txjaiv_0fDoOvxcd
MmMKkDsyUqMSsMWxHk725yiiHCCLfrh8O1z5QPOohDIaIeljMHgD
F5CVlOqpeNLcJ80NK65_fV7S1USd1pG7FQBdKOH-jh_H5SUaIMW4p
ZZBB8Q3oyahgMYWPDk-aW0WIdZ70CxZYZblwSA/Relationship_Cha
rt_FINAL_August_2017-2.jpg (discusses the relationship between people based on shared centimorgans of DNA)

https://www.independent.co.uk/news/long_reads/golden-state-killer-women-dna-genes-crime-cold-cases-a8894521.html

Scientific publications:

Andreas Tillmar, Siri Aili Fagerholm, Jan Staaf, Peter Sjölund, Ricky Ansell (2021) Getting the conclusive lead with investigative genetic genealogy - A successful case study of a 16 year old double murder in Sweden Forensic Sci Int Genet 53:102525. doi: 10.1016/j.fsigen.2021.102525.

Guerrini CJ, Wickenheiser RA, Bettinger B, McGuire AL, Fullerton SM (2021) Four misconceptions about investigative genetic genealogy. J Law Biosci. 2021 Apr 13;8(1):lsab001. doi: 10.1093/jlb/lsab001. eCollection 2021 Jan-Jun. PMID: 33880184

Green Berets:

Websites and online articles:

https://www.historynet.com/studies-and-observations-group-vietnam.htm

https://donmooreswartales.com/2010/03/17/sgt-chuck-walsh/

Personal Stories from the Vietnam War

Websites and online articles:

https://www.wearethemighty.com/mighty-history/australian-army-vietnam-war-feared/

https://www.bbc.com/news/in-pictures-33408096 (stories from the North Vietnamese soldiers)

https://aph.org.au/2021/04/aftermath-vietnam-veterans-and-their-historians/

https://www.soaringproductions.com.au/

http://archive.vva.org/archive/TheVeteran/1996_06/featureHarryHueTran.htm

http://boatpeoplememorial.com/mississauga/life-story-of-a-former-vietnamese-boat-people-refugee/

Books:

ARVN: Life and Death in the Vietnamese Army, by Robert K. Brigham

SNAFU: My Vietnam Vacation of 1969, by Tom Haines

I Did Not Miss the Boat, by Lea Tran

Vietnam's Orphans:

Websites and online articles:

https://soworldwide.org/vietnam-center-of-hope/

https://www.dailymail.co.uk/news/article-2579939/Children-suffer-horrific-effects-Americas-use-chemical-weapons-Vietnam-War.html (WARNING: Graphic Content)

Book:

War Cradle: The Untold Story of Operation Babylift, by Shirley Peck-Barnes

Vietnam War history

Websites and online articles:

https://www.britannica.com/topic/Viet-Minh

Vietnamese women and nail salons

Websites and online articles:

http://www.takepart.com/article/2015/05/05/tippi-hedren-vietname
se-refugees-nail-industry

About the Author

Kaylon Bruner Tran, PhD, is an active medical research scientist at Vanderbilt University Medical Center in Nashville, TN. She is best known for her medical research examining endometriosis and the generational effects of environmental toxicant exposure. Much of her research is focused on dioxin, the chemical contaminant in Agent Orange, that has been linked to numerous adverse health effects in veterans, their children, and multiple generations of Vietnamese citizens. Throughout her career, Kaylon has always felt a strong desire to connect the lay public with the research community. For this reason, she always includes a bit of science in her novels. She currently lives in Nolensville, TN USA but will eventually return to her home state of Mississippi.

You can connect with me on:

🌐 https://kaylonbrunertran.com

f https://www.facebook.com/KaylonBrunerTran

🖉 https://www.instagram.com/kaylon_bruner_tran

Also by Kaylon Tran

Time Intertwined: Book 1 of the Agent Orange Trilogy
Time Intertwined weaves neglected aspects of the Vietnam War into solving a modern-day genealogical mystery.

Darkness and Light Intertwined: Book 3 of the Agent Orange Trilogy
Linh was abandoned as an infant and grew up an orphan on the streets of Vietnam. *Darkness and Light Intertwined* is the story of not just secrets and survival but of finding light after the darkest of times.